Totally Bound Publishing books by Pamela L Todd:

Escaping Normal

What's her Secret?
Now You See Me

What's her Secret?

NOW YOU SEE ME

PAMELA L. TODD

Now You See Me
ISBN # 978-1-78430-316-7
©Copyright Pamela L. Todd 2014
Cover Art by Posh Gosh ©Copyright October 2014
Interior text design by Claire Siemaszkiewicz
Totally Bound Publishing

Published in 2014 by Totally Bound Publishing, Newland House, The Point, Weaver Road, Lincoln, LN6 3QN, United Kingdom.

NOW YOU SEE ME

Dedication

For Matthew, for giving your unconditional support
And for Hayley, who gets it.

Author Acknowledgment

First on my list of thanks has to be my awesome little family unit. Huge thank you to my husband for giving me your unconditional support and understanding when I disappear into my head. Even if you don't like make-believe.

Hayley, my first ever reader. Thank you for your spectacular cheerleading during my writing career. I never thought I would be writing an acknowledgements page, but you always said it would happen. I should never doubt your wisdom!

Meg, my most inappropriate friend, thank you for being you. You never fail to cheer or make me laugh so hard it hurts. And thank you for the pictures of your cats.

Stephanie, aka best boss on the planet. You were the first person to know this book would come to life. Thank you for being my sounding board when my characters were stroppy and refused to cooperate, and for doing a happy dance with me when the book was accepted.

Ginormous thanks must be given to Totally Bound for giving my book a home, and more specifically, Sarah Smeaton, editor extraordinaire! Your support and guidance throughout this process has been invaluable and I cannot thank you enough. The fact that you totally get these characters means the world to me. My book couldn't have been in better hands. Thank you just doesn't seem strong enough.

And last, but by no means least, thank you, dear reader. I hope you felt stuff.

Chapter One

"Same again?" The waitress reached for my empty coffee mug, her quick movements startling me from my concentration. "Large Americano?"

I flashed her a distracted smile. "Yes, thanks."

In the few minutes it took for her to make my deliciously strong coffee, I circled another couple of potential housing solutions. The newspaper was beginning to resemble a bleeding word search puzzle.

She placed the full-to-the-brim mug down on the tiny sliver of free space. "Looking for a new place?"

Ah. She was a chatter. *Note to self — little out-of-the-way cafes in New Town aren't prime solitude spots.* I gave a non-committal shrug and avoided eye contact.

Her neon green painted nail pointed like a dart to an ad I hadn't circled. "That one looks mint. Why haven't you circled it? Looks fab, that does."

With an inward sigh I slumped against the hard plastic backing of the chair. "It's a typo."

"You think?"

"Definitely," I mumbled. "At least one digit is missing."

"Maybe not."

"That area, it's more likely to be *two* missing digits."

She grinned. "Or maybe it's a hot rich guy looking for company. Or someone ballsy enough to call their bluff. You never know."

A surprised laugh bubbled in my throat.

Her smile widened. "Go on, give it a ring. You look like the kind of person about to stumble on some great luck."

I stared at the four short printed sentences a beat longer. It was only one phone call, after all. One phone call in which someone would answer, annoyed at having to field useless callers over a misprint.

"Let me know what they say. Enjoy your drink." With a flounce of her black tutu skirt, the waitress disappeared back behind the counter.

I let out a breath I hadn't been aware I was holding. It was the closest thing I could call to a social conversation I'd had in a very long time.

The ad glared at me, almost daring me to pick up the phone. *Fuck it.* I typed the number into my phone, waited as it rang and rang and rang.

Just as I was about to hang up, a low, gravelly voice answered. "Nate Harding."

Surprised anyone had answered at all, I was too shocked to speak.

He sighed. "Hello?"

I cleared my throat. "Hello? I'm ringing about the room for rent. I saw the ad in this morning's paper and—"

He rattled off the street address. "I have a meeting in an hour. Can you be here before then?"

"Um…" I ran a quick travel calculation in my head and aired on the side of caution. "I can be there within twenty minutes?"

"Make it fifteen."
"Okay. But I just want to check—"
He hung up.

* * * *

Ainslie Place turned out to only be a ten minute walk from where I was, but I stared in confusion and disbelief at the wide black door with roman numerals for probably the same amount of time. There was no chance…nowhere near the realm of possibility that this was the place—or that it was for the amount stated in the paper.

In the end it was only politeness that made me walk up the smooth steps and ring the bell. Something told me the man who answered the phone would not tolerate being stood up. The corner town house loomed tall and foreboding above me as I waited. Stormy gray sky reflected in its windows, all four stories of them, and I imagined matching cold interiors, as though the chill permeated the veins of the house.

The door swung open, and I jolted back a step, gripping the wrought iron railing for support.

"You're late."

I squeezed the railing harder as I took in the man who owned the voice from our conversation earlier. It was a word that was given new definition. *Own*. He owned the air, the space he occupied, the floor beneath his feet. His presence was large and controlled as though he took up more room than the average person.

The first thing that hit me was his build—tall, broad shoulders, narrow waist. The long sleeves of his T-shirt were pushed up to below his elbows, revealing thick, muscled forearms. The well-fitting jeans wrapped around strong thighs and I could only imagine how well they would mold to his ass.

And black Chuck Taylors on his feet. He was nothing like I'd expected, in every way.

But it was his face that made my breath catch, my knees buckle and my stomach clench. Dark, poker straight chocolate hair, short and stylish. Warm whiskey-brown eyes topped with two drawn together eyebrows, a frown creasing his forehead.

"Do you want to see inside, or is the hall enough for you?"

That voice did lethal things to my insides—a deep, low Scottish brogue, perfectly articulated but with an almost animalistic undercurrent that seemed hardwired to my sex drive. I took a breath, considerably deeper than needed to hopefully jump start my brain. "I'm sorry. Yes, I would like to see inside. Thank you."

He stood aside and gestured for me to enter. As I moved past him, I realized the top of my head barely cleared his shoulders and the sharp, masculine scent of him hit me everywhere it counted. Shutting the front door, he walked brusquely past me.

The sound from our shoes echoed on the smooth, shiny oak flooring of the vast entrance hall. He led me to the rear of the house and up bouncy, carpeted stairs.

"There are two bedrooms on this floor. You can have either, though I recommend this one." He pushed open a closed door and I was hit with a sensory overload. The smell of fresh paint hit me first, the pale green walls too perfect to be anything other than freshly finished. A large walnut sleigh bed dominated the space and four tall sash windows had views of the street I'd stood on just minutes before.

I couldn't help but smile as I moved farther into the room. Everything from the plush rug to the bronze and dark umber Georgian chandelier screamed wealth and luxury. It was a place so far removed from me that I felt as though I'd momentarily stepped into another world.

"This one has the en suite. Only a bath, but there is a shower room on the half landing if you prefer." He grasped the door handle and stepped back.

I took his hint to leave the room. Across the landing he opened another door and let me briefly glance inside. "Sitting room, TV, whatever. Downstairs has the bigger lounge. The top two floors are mine." He was already halfway down the stairs before I realized, and rushed to catch him up.

I followed him into an impressive kitchen complete with open fireplace and an enormous piece of artwork, which looked as though nothing supported it bar the mantelpiece. It blurred the lines between modern and traditional, all the latest appliances polished and sparkling, but the flooring continuing from the hall and the wooden cabinets warmed the room.

He gestured to a stool at the large island and I perched perilously on the edge, watching his graceful, confident movements as he worked a coffee maker that I never in a million years would be able to fathom.

"There's a small study down here. Poky patio area outside. Rent includes all utilities, so don't worry about working out phone calls or hot water." Already done at the coffee maker, he placed a wide, round cup in front of me. "Sugar?"

I shook my head, already knowing it was delicious, just by the aroma.

"Do you want the room?"

His question was so abrupt it took me a moment to formulate my answer. I let out a breath, sure that at any moment I would be unceremoniously kicked out of his house. "I'm truly sorry, but I think I've wasted your time."

The frown deepened between his eyebrows. "You didn't like it? I told you there was another room."

"No, it has nothing to do with the room. The room was beautiful, really, I've never seen..." A lump hardened in my throat. The sudden wave of emotion took me by surprise and I squashed it down before it was written all over my face. "The room was gorgeous. I'm afraid I just can't afford it."

"Didn't you read the rent price before you called?"

"Yes, but I thought it was a mistake. And after seeing the room, I definitely know it was a mistake."

"What paper did you see it in?"

I pulled the battered newspaper from my bag and slid it across the island to him.

He turned quickly to the housing pages, scanning the ads until he found his. For a minute he was still and quiet. Then he folded the newspaper and tossed it in the recycling bin. "Do you want the room or not?"

"But, it was a mistake, wasn't it?"

"You came to see a room advertised at that price. You've seen it. Now for the last time, do you want it or not?"

This could not be happening. No way did this kind of thing happen to someone like me. "What about credit checks? References? Employment history?"

He huffed out a breath. "You do remember me telling you I had a meeting?"

"I'm sorry, it's just…you don't even know my name. Why would you offer me that room without knowing a single thing about me?"

"So tell me about yourself." His eyes flickered to the clock. "Quickly."

"Oh, um, my name is Jo. Jo Carpenter. I'm twenty-six, I've lived in Edinburgh for a few months. I work the night shifts in a bistro bar in Grassmarket so I'm out late most nights. I'm clean, tidy. No pets. No boyfriend."

He raised his eyebrows. "Why would I care if you have a boyfriend?"

My cheeks warmed. "The last place I looked at the landlord said I couldn't have it if I had a boyfriend."

He snorted a laugh. "Slimy pervs. Bring men back or don't, I really don't care. I only have one rule—treat my house with respect or leave. Simple as that."

I took a gulp of coffee, wincing as it burned my throat. "You can't be serious. Isn't there another applicant better suited to your…lifestyle?"

"Every person that has come to view the room has been so far up themselves I don't know how they walk. Either divorcees looking for a pad similar to what they've been kicked out of or posh brats sponging off Daddy." He rose and set his cup in the sink. "You need a place to live. I want a tenant. I travel for work, so it would be nice to have someone here for security."

"But you'd lose so much rent money."

He shrugged. "I don't really care—or need it. So. Very last time. Do you want it?"

It was on the tip of my tongue to say no. Thanks, but it's not for me. I didn't need the sort of distraction a man like Nate Harding would be. But my mind drifted to the beautiful bedroom above us. I saw myself sleeping in the big sleigh bed, relaxing in the bath…chilling out in the living room after work.

I could squash my attraction for him. To stay here, I would have to. Unable to speak, I gave a soft nod.

Reaching into his pocket, he tossed a set of keys across the island. "Move in when you like."

The keys were warm from his body and I closed my fist around them, as though afraid they would disappear. "Thank you, Mr Harding."

For the first time since arriving, his face softened, though almost imperceptibly. "Call me Nate."

Chapter Two

It took all of five minutes for me to pack. Barely any personal possessions to speak of, all I owned were the clothes I needed plus a few necessities. I settled the bill with the woman who owned the cozy Bed and Breakfast I'd been calling home for the last week. On my way to view the room earlier, I'd noticed a few express supermarkets and decided to call into one before unpacking. Better to arrive with my own food than forget and need to pilfer something from my new landlord. His luxurious house suggested he probably snacked on caviar and Bollinger, though he looked more like a rare steak man.

God. That was going to take some getting used to. I couldn't even comprehend how much a house like that cost. And my rent probably covered his parking permit. He more than likely ate out every night, just because he could, and had a cleaner come round every day and a never ending line of beautiful, thin, long-legged, coiffed beauties to share his bed.

An image of him on top of some faceless woman burned in my mind, my body responding in a way that was long lost to me. Quickening my pace, I hurried into the supermarket and began throwing things into the basket. Bread. Lemon juice. Floss. Garlic clove. Jam. Squash. Batteries.

Loaded down with my holdall on wheels and a few heavy carrier bags, the heavens took that moment to rumble and unleash torrential rain. With a startled shriek, I broke into a run and hoped I was going in the right direction. After a few wrong turns, the wide stone steps and black front door eventually loomed ahead. Hauling my bags behind me, I tried to juggle everything and find my new set of keys.

The keys and the door cooperated after a few choice words and opened for me, the security unit my next obstacle. Dripping wet and probably ruining the hardwood flooring, I punched in the code, heart beating double time when the display flashed red and asked me to try again.

"Shit, shit, shit," I hissed, digging in my pockets for the piece of paper Nate had written the code on. The alarm beeped louder and I entered the numbers again. A second later an eardrum bursting wail sounded and I nearly had a stroke.

"*Fuck, fuck, fuck.*" Over the relentless wailing, I dimly heard a phone ringing. Darting in its direction, I found a handset on a counter in the kitchen.

"Hello? Hello?" *Please be the alarm company. Please be the alarm company and they can turn it off. Please be the alarm company and they believe me that I live here and they won't phone the police.* A night in the cells was not on my agenda.

"Is this Jo—or are you trying to break into my house?"

Fuck, fuck, fuck. Not the alarm company. My landlord. "Nate? Yeah, it's Jo. I put the code in but the stupid thing just keeps *screeching* at me."

"Hold on, Jo. Yes, this is Nathaniel Harding. No one is attempting a break in, it's my new tenant. Yes, deactivate it. Thanks."

Abruptly the wailing stopped, yet my ears kept ringing. Pressing my hand to my forehead, I slumped over the counter.

"Jo?"

"Here," I said, meekly, feeling for all the world like I was about to have a severe telling off.

"It's star number star. Okay?"

Fuck. Fucking star. Of course I forgot the fucking star. "Okay. Star number star, got it."

The line disconnected.

* * * *

A quick inspection of the kitchen cupboards confirmed my guess — Nate Harding had wicked expensive taste in food. Only the best graced his shelves. Crisp, fresh vegetables in the fridge, as well as the surprising casserole dish with what looked like homemade cottage pie. I found an area in the pantry to stash my meager purchases, hoping they were far enough from view it wouldn't embarrass Nate if company saw it, but reassuring to him I wasn't just chowing down on his food. He might be renting me a room so cheap I was practically robbing him, but I would never be accused of being a mooch.

I carried my bag upstairs, too scared to pull it behind me in case it snagged the carpet. And I was in the room. My room. *Christ, is this really mine?* It still felt surreal just standing in it. Leaving the bag in the middle of the room, I stood in front of one of the large windows. The street was virtually deserted, save the occasional person rushing past whilst wrestling with an umbrella. Rain pinged off the window, blurring the view.

My assumptions about the interior couldn't have been more wrong. I had thought the inside of this house would be cold and clinical, so modern and minimalist there would scarce be any furniture. But really, it was surprisingly warm. The house itself was a renovated Georgian town house and whoever was in charge of the interior had kept it true to its roots. Delicate cornicing and fine period details brought the house back to its original elegance, with the wealthy touch of modern luxury.

I kicked off my soaked ballet flats, unable to contain the soft sigh upon my toes meeting the plush carpet. Opposite a beautiful armoire was a door slightly ajar. Pushing it open, I realized this was the en suite Nate had mentioned. And seriously? I had never seen such an enormous bathroom.

A long, cream cabinet with a solid marble counter top ran along one wall. Complete with bulbed mirror, sink, dozens of drawers and cupboard doors, I had to wonder what kind of woman was able to fill all the space. But what grabbed my attention and held it was the bath.

Situated in front of the window, the claw-footed freestanding bath was absolutely gorgeous. The taps sparkled and I imagined myself surrounded by soft bubbles and hot water. First thing tomorrow I was splurging and buying bubble bath.

Unpacking took all of a few minutes. Everything I owned fitted easily in the armoire, with no need to put anything in the matching chest of drawers. With Nate not here, it was the perfect time to arrange my things, just the way I liked it. Backpack under the bed, out of sight but within easy reach, baseball bat under the pillows. Ballet flats near the door.

Once satisfied, the bath beckoned.

* * * *

It was my night off, so after soaking in the bath until I resembled a prune, I dressed in cotton shorts and loose T-shirt then set off to investigate the rest of the house. The sitting room across from my room was soft and welcoming. Huge squishy couches and arm chairs surrounded another fireplace, this time with a flat screen TV mounted above it instead of what would probably be priceless artwork. One wall was made up of shelves, filled to the brim with books. I could easily see myself spending a lot of time in there.

I spared a glance at the stairs leading up, wishing I was either less curious or more brave when I wondered what it was like up there. After meeting Nate and seeing his house, he was awash of contradictions. His clothes were casual yet no doubt expensive and a lot of his home was traditional. Granted, it was expensive traditional. I could picture him in an enormous penthouse apartment with stark walls and sharp lines. Perhaps there were many things I had yet to discover about Nate Harding.

The sitting room downstairs was pretty much a show room, with uncomfy couches and a coffee table bearing books I doubted had ever been read. And there was no TV. I bet Nate and his friends retreated into this room after eating a delicious five-course catered dinner party, sipping brandy and talking about stocks and investments.

Off the entrance hall was the predicted dining room and sturdy walnut table, big enough to comfortably sit twelve people. There was a utility room just off the kitchen and the study Nate had mentioned was more like a study cubicle in a library. Solid wooden desk with sleek iMac and portable phone. I couldn't even remember the last time I had been on a computer.

The rain had dried up and the sun had decided to make an appearance. I sat at the island, the heat of the rays warming the room, despite it being almost eight in the evening. There was still no sign of Nate, though I was grateful to have the time to adjust without the added pressure of acclimatizing to him also.

I made toast and jam for dinner with a sugary cup of tea. There was no evidence I'd ever been there when I cleared my things away, like I was ghost rather than a tenant. I left an envelope propped up against the coffee maker, sure that would be the most obvious place for Nate to see it, with a check for a few months' rent.

When I slid between the cool sheets a few hours later and there was yet no appearance from my landlord, I had to wonder just how long my luck would last.

This was the kind of house people dreamed of living in — the kind they kept their noses clean for and didn't put a toe out of line, in case it jeopardized their place in it. For a girl used to bedsits and B & Bs, Nate's house was a paradise, a mirage in the desert. Chances were I would see him again soon enough and if he somehow found out more about me, I would be out, looking again for a temporary place to lay my head.

Which was a shame. Because for a moment, a tiny heartbeat, I imagined myself standing still here. Pausing to catch my breath.

Only time would tell.

Chapter Three

A full five days passed before I saw Nate in the flesh again. I was sitting at the bottom of the stairs lacing my red sneakers when I heard the front door slam shut. His keys chinked in the dish on the console table and when he rounded the corner and came into view, he was tugging at the collar of his T-shirt.

He stopped short and blinked, as though for a moment he had forgotten I lived in his house. "Going out?"

I nodded. "Work."

Nate frowned. "Late, isn't it?"

"Eight till two. I usually do the night shifts." I finished tying the laces and stood up. He was still taller than me, despite me standing on the stairs.

"Right. Bar." He shook his head. "Sorry, I forgot. Grassmarket, wasn't it?"

"Yeah."

"Do you want a lift?"

My eyes widened at his offer. "Oh, no, really it's fine. It's not far and it's a nice night."

His frown deepened. "You shouldn't really be walking around at night alone."

"I'll be fine. I can look after myself."

Nate folded his arms across his chest. "I bet you don't even have any form of protection on you."

"I do, actually. Lemon juice."

His lips twitched. "Lemon juice?"

"Yeah." I reached into my bag and pulled out the small lemon-shaped bottle. "Squirt this in someone's eye and it hurts like a fecker. Safer than a spray with no lasting damage. Gives ample time and opportunity to run away, though."

"You've thought this through."

I looked down, avoiding his eyes. "It's better to be prepared."

"Yes, it is."

With an unconvincing smile I darted around him and out of the front door before he could offer to drive me again.

* * * *

The summer months were always busy, no matter what city. Next month would be crazy and the tips incredible. August in Edinburgh was tourist mad with the Fringe. July was the calm before the storm and I savored that calm. Who knew? I might actually be around for August. At least it would bump up the cash hidden at the bottom of my backpack.

Slowly but surely I was growing used to Nate's house. I still jumped at every noise, every creak and groan of the building. That was something that would never go away, no matter how long I was there for. Nate and I were like ships passing in the night, never seeing each other for more than a few minutes at a time.

Even more slowly, I was discovering the area I now lived in. Ainslie Place in New Town felt historic with its elegant curved streets and yet was only a stone's throw from the bustle of Princes Street. I adored Stockbridge and often jogged along the Water of Leith walkway.

I returned to the house one evening after a run and said a silent prayer when the alarm didn't beep at me. Nate was home, somewhere, which made my heart thump even more erratically in my chest. I was drenched in sweat and could think of nothing but water, a cool shower and clean, dry clothes.

For a moment I stood in front of the open fridge, breathing in the cold air, goosebumps breaking out over my feverish skin. Half the bottle of water was gone before it registered that there was someone else in the room with me.

Perched on a stool at the island was a tall, slim woman. Her smile widened when I met her large hazel eyes, making her beautiful face even more beautiful. Her hair fell in loose, rich chocolate curls and it looked like she barely wore any makeup, one of those naturally good-looking people. Typical.

She was everything I pictured Nate being attracted to. The printed dress she wore clung to her curves, its expensive cut flattering her more than anything I had ever worn.

I hated her on sight.

"Hi, I'm Suze." She held out her hand for me to shake. And she was nice. Of course she was nice.

I looked down at myself, realizing even my arms were sweaty. How could this woman want me and my sweat anywhere near her? I was saved from answering by Nate striding into the room. His presence was the first thing I was aware of — the hot flash that went through me when I realized that yes, he was just as handsome as I remembered, if not more so — the child on his hip second.

Rebellious dark brown hair fell every which way and she smiled around the set of keys she seemed to be chewing on. Her eyes reminded me of an animated character's — big and round, full of wonder, not yet affected by the harsh realities of life. And, most noticeably, the color of warm amber whiskey.

"I expect full reimbursement for what your daughter just did all over my towel." Nate stopped when he saw me standing like an idiot in front of the fridge.

"I'm sorry, I was just getting a drink. I didn't realize you had company."

Suze rose and swatted Nate on his biceps before taking the small girl. "What the hell have you been doing to get her petrified like that?" She turned to look at me. "He's the most unsocial grouch you'll ever meet. Don't take it personally."

Both stared at me and it became painfully clear the most unsocial person in the room was me. "Um, he's not... I don't... I'm not." I closed my eyes and took a breath. "Sorry, I think that run scrambled my brain. I'll get out of your way."

"Come back down once you're changed. I want to get to know you!" Suze called to my retreating back.

Fantastic. Great. Awesome.

* * * *

I spent longer in the shower than was necessary. Maybe it was wishful thinking that if I took a super long time, they'd go about their evening and forget about me. All I could think about as the water washed away the evidence of my run was that Nate was apparently nothing like I thought he was. He had a daughter? And what was the situation between him and the mother? There was definite affection. But I had seen no evidence of a child anywhere in the house. Maybe it was upstairs. But why didn't Suze and the girl live here, with him? Was it a friends with benefits thing that had ended up with them getting more than they bargained for?

If that was the case, were they still sleeping together?

And if they were—of which it was none of my business—why did that make me want to mess up Suze's pretty face and show Nate exactly what he would be missing with me?

God, I needed help.

I dressed in black leggings, a long green vest and black slouchy cardigan. My shoulder length so-dark-brown-it-was-practically-black hair fell in choppy waves and after arguing with myself, I applied a light coat of mascara. Anything more would be obvious I was trying to make an impression.

Nate and Suze's voices floated into the hall from the kitchen, so there was no other option but to join them. There was an open bottle of red wine between them at the island, an extra glass in front of an empty stool.

Suze smiled when she spotted me lurking in the doorway and patted the stool beside her. "About time. Get over here and have a drink."

I took my seat beside her, glancing at the small child in a high chair at the end beside both of them. Okay, so my heart melted a little at the sight of her. And I was not a kid person—at all. The last interaction I'd had with one was when I *was* one. But she was squidgy and cheerful, her chubby hands grabbing at a mess of Cheerios on the counter.

"So," Suze said, swiveling to face me. "You're Jo?"

"That's me."

"Nate hasn't told me a thing about you. Though that doesn't surprise me."

Nor me. Who in their right mind would tell an ex, or current whatever-she-may-be, about a young, female roommate?

I glanced at Nate, my insides lurching when he met my eye. He poured me a large glass of wine with an unreadable expression.

"Come on then, Jo. Life story. While we're young." She winked at me.

Nate sighed. "Christ, leave her alone, Suze."

"I'm hardly going to get the story from you, am I?" She shot at him. Suze patted my hand. "Are you from the city?"

I shook my head. "Newish arrival."

"Where are you working?"

"Red Bar, the bistro in Grassmarket."

The room went quiet with the telltale sound of a dirty nappy, followed by a delighted giggle. Suze batted her eyes at Nate.

"Fine. Don't moan at me when you get the bill if she ruins another towel." Nate lifted her from the high chair and left the kitchen.

Suze topped up our wine glasses. "Perfect timing. Now you can really give me the goss. How has it been living here? Nate can be...well, a bit Nate. But he means well. He's got a heart of gold, really. Though it is a bit tarnished nowadays."

"Um, there isn't a lot to say, really." I stroked the stem of the glass, avoiding her eyes.

"Don't feel embarrassed. There's nothing about him that could shock me. Not after all these years, anyway."

What was she hinting? Did she honestly expect me to tell if there was something going on between me and Nate?

"His ex used to gripe and moan at me about stuff that was so stupid I felt like shaking her. But, well, look how that turned out."

I narrowed my eyes. "He talks about girlfriends and stuff to you?"

"Yeah, why?" She shrugged. "It's a bit weird, I suppose. But we've always been close like that."

"So it seems."

"You could do worse, you know. I mean, sure, you live with him and there's all the issues he still has, but you won't find anyone else like my brother. And I can tell he likes you."

I had just gulped a mouthful of wine when she dropped that bombshell. *God, wine coming out of my nose has to be the least attractive sight ever.*

"Shit, sorry. Are you okay?" Suze asked, shoving a handful of napkins at my face.

"You're his sister? Nate's your brother? You're siblings? Like, biological ones?"

Suze frowned. "Yeah, why?" Then it hit her and the grin spread across her face. "Christ, did you really think we were involved?" She laughed, a cackling noise. "No wonder you kept giving me weird looks! Brilliant. Wait till I tell him."

"Oh, God, please don't." I clutched her hand. "I'm humiliated."

Her face softened. "Don't be. So, now that's all out there and the record is straight—how are you finding it here?"

"It's different," I said eventually. "The place is gorgeous and huge. I barely see Nate, so it's almost like living alone."

"What do you mean, you barely see him?"

"Just what I said—I barely see him. I work a lot of nights. Most of the time he isn't home when I leave and I'm not up before he leaves in the morning."

Suze cursed under her breath. "He's turned into such a workaholic since Kate. It's not good for him."

"Who's Kate?" I asked, going for nonchalance and failing miserably.

Suze's lip curled as though she smelled something rotten. "The ex. She broke his heart and now he pours everything into the business, like if he's focused on that he doesn't have to think about what happened."

I didn't want to ask. Really didn't want to. But curiosity and all that. "What happened?"

Suze never answered, with Nate re-entering the kitchen.

"I dread to think what she's been saying," Nate said, flashing me a quick smile as he put the child back in the high chair.

Suze huffed. "You think so little of me."

"I know you. There's a difference."

I smiled into my wine glass, surprised it was almost empty. Nate made to refill it, but I held my hand up to stop him. "No, thanks. I don't like to drink too much."

Suze nudged me. "And here I was thinking we were going to be such good friends." She turned to her daughter. "Well, Tilly, what do you say we hit the road and leave these two to their evening?"

"I thought you were staying for dinner. You did bring it, after all."

Suze lifted Tilly from the high chair. "I promised Mum and Dad I'd call in and eat with them. They've not seen us for a few days. You know what they're like."

"More for me, then."

"More to share, you mean." She nodded her head in my direction.

My cheeks burned. *Oh, God, not a pity dinner invite, please.*

Nate's eyes darted from his sister to me then back again, the look turning murderous.

"You're not a veggie, are you, Jo?" Suze asked, her eyebrows lowering as though daring me to contradict her.

I shook my head.

"Good. I made a curry. Hope you enjoy it!" She kissed my cheek, then Nate's, lingering for a few moments and I knew she was whispering something. Whatever it was turned his face even more thundery.

Nate rose to see her out. I waited a beat before hoping to escape unnoticed upstairs to save Nate from feeling like he had to feed me.

"Hey, get your arse back in that kitchen. I don't appreciate my food going to waste," Suze called from the front door. God, that woman had Superman sight. "Oh, and, Jo?"

I peeked around the corner to her. Tilly was now in a pushchair, blowing raspberries at us all.

"Are you free tomorrow?"

I nodded.

Suze grinned. "I'll call round for you in the morning. We'll go for a walk, have a coffee or something."

Nate ushered her out of the door, hissing something under his breath that only made her laugh. He kept his back to me for a second, his face softened by the time he turned. "Come on. She'll throw a fit if you don't eat with me."

"Oh, it's okay. I really don't want to trouble you."

Nate paused beside me in the doorway. Everything about him overwhelming. My spine flattened against the frame and for a split second I could have sworn he considered trapping me there and kissing the life right out of me. "It's no trouble, Jo."

Chapter Four

For a horrifying moment I thought Nate would expect us to eat in the dining room and it would be stiff and formal with forced conversation. Instead he motioned for me to take up my vacated stool whilst he went to work.

"Can I do anything?" I asked, watching him move around the kitchen.

He flashed me a smile over his shoulder. "If there's one thing I've got down pat, it's reheating Suze's culinary delights. Ten minutes okay?"

I smiled. "Ten minutes is perfect, thank you."

Nate hit a few buttons on the microwave and it whirred to life, the smell permeating the air a few moments later. He heated up some easy cook rice and transferred a couple of naan breads from their wrapping to the oven to warm up.

"This is one of the few things she trusts me to prepare in the kitchen without burning the entire house down."

"She does this a lot? Brings over food for you?"

Nate nodded. "A few nights a week. Pretty pathetic, isn't it? A man having his younger sister, who is a single mother, cook for him."

I let his words sink in before considering my answer. "I think it's nice she wants to take care of you. You clearly have a very close relationship."

Nate smirked. "Yeah, she's harder to get rid of than a rash." He shrugged. "Her heart's in the right place."

"So she's a single mother?"

His shoulders tensed. "Her charming boyfriend ran a mile when she missed her period. Man of the year, right?"

"It wasn't a planned pregnancy then?"

"Not that she's told me." Nate stirred the rice. "She says she doesn't care, that she's happier just her and Tilly. But you see it in her eyes when she sees happy families and knows it will never be like that for her."

"Never say never."

He stilled. "That's what I keep telling her."

Our eyes locked and held. Something unsaid flitted between us and like a coward, I broke the contact. "Tilly seems a really good baby. How old is she?"

"Nineteen months, but she's a little on the small side. Cute as a button and bright as a spark, speaking a fair bit already and learning more words every day, usually from Suze's colorful vocabulary. We've all had to learn to watch our mouths. She's going to be running rings around all of us pretty soon." His whole face relaxed when he talked about his niece.

I'd never thought I'd be one of those women who got turned on by a family oriented man.

"Do they live around here?"

Nate nodded. "In a flat on Clarence Street."

"Must be nice having them both so close."

His lips twitched. "Sometimes it's too convenient. Suze feels like she needs to check in on me. She'll do it to you too, now."

Something about that sentence made my stomach clench and not in a good way. It had been a long time since anyone had cared enough to check on me. I didn't like to encourage affection and really didn't want to have anyone notice if I disappeared.

"Water or wine with dinner?"

I closed my eyes for a second, swallowing down the panic. "Water, please."

"Give it a few weeks. Suze will turn you into a raging alcoholic." Nate poured me a glass of water and ice from the fridge then started dishing up dinner. "Has the bar been busy?"

"Yeah," I said, accepting the heaped plate he handed me. "And getting busier every day."

"Just wait till next month."

"That's what they tell me. I'll probably do extra day shifts to help out." Digging into my dinner, I couldn't help the moan that came out.

Nate paused with his fork midway to his mouth and I clamped a hand over mine.

"God, sorry."

He smiled into his dinner. "Don't be. Though I'm not sure Suze would appreciate the reaction as much as I did."

My whole body warmed. The look in his eyes when I finally met them was charged and electric. A part of me wanted to shove dinner aside and pull him to the floor with me.

I cleared my throat and ignored the ache between my thighs. "What about you? Suze mentioned you're at work a lot. And I think you mentioned that you have to travel for work sometimes?"

The smile fell from his face. "I'm kept going. And I'm leaving in the morning for a trip — I'll be gone for ten days."

Leaving me to rattle around alone in this big house. "What do you do?"

"I own a web development firm."

Wow. "Oh...well, that's, great?"

Nate's lips twitched. "What? You didn't think I had a serious job?"

My cheeks warmed. "No, you're just so young. I mean, you can't be more than thirty?"

"Thirty-two."

Wow. "Huh. Congrats, then. You know, on the firm and the...thirty-two."

"Thanks."

"You're welcome."

Shoot me.

* * * *

The bell started ringing about half-past eight. After dinner the night before I'd retreated to my room and hadn't come out for the rest of the night. I'd heard Nate tread softly past my door, my heart pounding when he'd paused before continuing up his stairs. At six the next morning I'd woken up on full alert when he'd bounded back down and I hadn't relaxed until I'd heard the front door close and the sound of his car starting.

The monitor on the wall by the front door showed Suze hopping impatiently on the balls of her feet, grinning manically at the camera lens. Opening the door a crack, I saw her with Tilly comfortably sitting in her pram.

"Morning! Are you ready, or do you need a bit more time?"

Ready? It was eight-thirty in the morning. I didn't start work until seven that night. Why the hell would I be ready at this time of day?

"Did you forget I was coming?" Suze asked, her smile threatening to fall.

And dammit if my heart didn't give a squeeze of guilt. "Sorry, give me five minutes?"

"Wait, do you fancy going for a swim then a coffee? Tilly loves the pool and she'll be knackered afterwards, giving us time to chat."

I forced a smile. "Make it ten."

Suze's smile was back in full force when I returned. The three of us walked the short distance to the nearby leisure center, Suze chatting as though we'd known each other for years instead of hours. I dodged the usual questions, resorted to my old distraction techniques when they got too personal and mostly used Tilly as a buffer. Seemed cooing over a baby *always* charmed the pants off parents. And with Tilly, it wasn't hard to coo. I even caught myself doing it a few times unintentionally.

As leisure centers went, this one was big and well equipped. There was a state of the art gym and personal trainers, classes, four pools and a sauna. The changing and shower areas were communal and after having a near heart attack when I saw a hairy older gent wandering around in swimming shorts that bordered on indecent, Suze grabbed my arm and pulled me into a family unit. Basically a changing room big enough for a bunch of people to be in at once.

"I bet people have sex in here," I commented, pulling my swimming costume from my bag.

Suze paused with Tilly in the air, about to put her down on the changing table. "Shit. Grab the changing mat, would you? I feel like I can see sperm everywhere, now."

Suze and Tilly were happy splashing around in the toddler pool which was considerably warmer than the one I had been swimming lengths in. Once my muscles began protesting from overwork, I joined them, feeling like I was slipping into a warm bath.

"Nice swim?"

"Yeah. Knackered now."

Suze smiled. "You have a healthy glow about you, at least. You should get the sun a bit more. Do you the world of good."

"God, you mother everyone, don't you?" I nudged her with my elbow.

She sighed. "I wish I could say it was Tilly who brought it out in me, but no. I've always been like that. Sorry."

"Don't apologize. There's nothing wrong with wanting to take care of people. Dinner last night was incredible, by the way. Best meal I've had in a long time."

"Aw, thanks." She shrugged. "It's no hardship. I love cooking and Nate is so completely useless. It makes me feel better that he's eating a proper meal a few times a week."

"He's not a domestic goddess then?"

Suze snorted. "You have met him, right? Nah, he's all right, really. Just not one for looking after himself."

I focused on a freckle on my arm. "Did Kate do all the cooking?"

She let out her cackle laugh. "Kate? Cook? When she could pay someone else to do it for her? Yeah, right."

"Oh, one of those, then?"

Suze nodded, bouncing Tilly in and out of the water to her delight. "The biggest one of those. I honestly don't know how Nate has any money left. I'm surprised she didn't piss it all down the drain."

"So, he was more money sensible?"

"He had to be! She wouldn't lift a finger to anything that she could pay someone to do instead. Catered dinner parties, cleaners, restaurants, spas, personal shoppers. Laziest, most spoiled cow I ever had the misfortune of meeting."

"What did he see in her?" I wondered aloud.

"They met at university and were on and off for a few years. I think in the end he just resigned himself to his fate and forgot how relationships are supposed to be—mutual trust and respect. Considerate. Gentle. *Faithful.*"

My eyes snapped to hers, and Suze looked away. "Faithful? She cheated on him? Who the fuck would cheat on Nate?"

Her eyes widened and I cringed.

"Sorry. Sorry, Tilly."

"Yeah, she cheated on Nate. But, seriously, don't let on you know all this. He'd go mad."

"I won't say anything." I leaned against the pool wall. "I can't believe it."

"Believe it. With his best friend and business partner, of all people."

"*Jesus.*"

Suze nodded. "I think he took that harder than the actual cheating. It's why he works so hard now. That business is all he has, so he nurtures it like a child. Protects it. Cares for it. Our dad is—was—a programmer. Set up one of the first firms here in the eighties. Nate went to work for him straight out of uni and since he's Nate and, like…a protégée or whatever,

Dad made him partner really early on and so it was Harding and Son. Then when Dad retired, Nate brought Derek on as partner, so it became Harding and Quinn. Now it's Nathaniel Harding. He took it way further than Dad ever did—it took years but it's really profitable now. He has loads of clients in America and travels there all the time."

My heart pinched. No wonder he took care of it.

"Seriously, I didn't tell you any of this." Suze's eyes went solemn. "And don't treat him any differently. Like I said last night, he's got a heart of gold. But I think it's still a little broken."

After that, Suze launched into a rant about the other mothers at her parent and child group. My head was swimming with everything she had told me about Nate, so it was good she didn't really need me to participate in the conversation. To help her blow off steam, I volunteered to have Tilly while she went for a grown-up swim.

I've never seen someone hand over a child so bloody fast.

So Tilly and I bonded and my heart melted a little bit more. We floated around the little warm pool, me bobbing her up and down as she squealed with laughter and clapped her hands. The logical part of my brain warned it wasn't a good idea to get any closer to this family. But at that moment, I simply didn't care.

After swimming, Suze led the way to a small café with mismatched furniture and signs that boasted the best coffee in the country. We settled on couches that felt like being enveloped by a marshmallow whilst Tilly, as predicted, snoozed oblivious in her pram.

Suze ordered us coffee and scones, and before I knew it, Tilly was waking up and demanding lunch and we were back at Nate's with Suze raiding his pantry. We ate lunch on the patio while Tilly walked unsteadily across the uneven stone and unearthed the few wilting flowers in pots.

The entire day passed in a blink and Suze was kissing my cheek with promises to see me again in a few days. There was a smile on my face and a glow inside my chest as I lay down to take a pre-work nap.

Is this what it feels like to have a friend?

Chapter Five

Suze had told me not to act any differently around Nate now I knew all about his torrid break-up with Kate. But how could I not? A lot of questions I had about him suddenly had answers. Like why he gave me a run for my money in the distance department. Why he threw his entire self into work. I felt for the man. That was all. No one deserved to be betrayed. And it did nothing to quell the fire in me whenever I thought about him, remembered his strong arms and protective height.

Just like before Suze's revelation, it was rare we were in the same room at the same time. But once he was home from his trip, Nate's past felt like a living, breathing presence in the house with us. I knew he at least suspected Suze to have told me *something*. He knew his sister entirely too well to think differently. But so far he hadn't brought it up — and neither had I.

But then one night, he did.

Depending what way you looked at it, it was either very late or very early. I had finished work for the night and came home, expecting to be greeted by still silence, just like usual. Instead, the low murmur of music and lamplight spilled out into the hall from the sitting room.

Poking my head into the room, I was not prepared for what I saw.

Nate was sprawled on one of the uncomfortable couches, arm thrown over his face, gripping a bottle of whiskey in the other hand. A floorboard creaked under my foot and he lifted his arm to peer up at me.

"The wanderer returns," he mumbled, slumping back down.

I took a breath and made myself venture farther into the room. I perched on the edge of the coffee table in front of him. "Are you okay?"

"Just super."

"Yeah, you look it."

With a groan, Nate heaved himself up into a sitting position. He rested his elbows on his knees and hung his head. At this proximity, his scent slammed into me—strong and masculine with the smoky smell of whiskey creeping in around the edges.

"Do you want to talk about it?" This was the first time I had even remotely pushed to get someone to open up to me. But I couldn't leave Nate alone in this, when whatever had happened was clearly upsetting him.

Nate sighed and reached for me. More accurately, behind me. His face was inches from mine and my breath caught in my throat. His blood-shot eyes flickered to mine and he dropped a package on my lap.

Inside was a black velvet jewelry box, the size too perfect to be anything other than a ring.

"She couriered it over this afternoon. Considerate bitch, isn't she?"

"I'm sorry," I said, my voice softening.

Nate shrugged and took a swill from the bottle. "When did my darling sister tell you, then?"

"She just mentioned you were in a serious relationship and it didn't end well."

He narrowed his eyes at me. "I'm too drunk to argue with you. But thanks for trying to spare my pride."

"How long has it been since…?"

Another shrug and swill. "Few months."

"Do you miss her?"

Nate froze. "No one has asked me that before."

"Why not? It's a legitimate question."

Nate barked a humorless laugh. "Because Kate was a money-hungry, narcissistic cow. No one in their right mind would miss her. Or think that I would."

"So why were you with her in the first place if that was how you felt?"

Nate blew out a breath. "Shit, Jo, stop questioning me, would you? Sometimes you're with someone for so long you forget the reasons why you're together. I didn't always think she was just out for my money. And I don't miss *her*."

"It's okay to miss her companionship. It's okay to be lonely."

He pinned me with his gaze. Shifting forward until he was right in my space, his open legs encasing my squeezed closed ones, he grazed my thighs with his hands, gently enough to be brushed off as unintentional. But that touch, his very proximity, had my blood roaring.

"You think I'm lonely? You think I have a shortage of women waiting, willing, *begging*, to fill my empty bed?"

I closed my eyes. "Meaningless sex isn't companionship."

"Sex with me is never meaningless. Even if it's only once, it's not like the woman doesn't get anything out of it. And you know what? They're grateful for it."

On anyone else the blatant cockiness would have been an instant turn off. But on Nate...I had a feeling he was simply telling the truth.

I took an unsteady breath, terrified to meet his eyes and what I would find there. *God help me...I would be grateful.*

"Are you afraid of me, Jo?"

"No," I whispered.

He leaned closer until his lips brushed my ear. "I would devour you whole, little girl. Maybe you should be afraid."

I jumped to my feet, and he stumbled back onto the couch. A second longer in that position and I would be right smack in the begging category. Nate rubbed a hand over his eyes.

"Shit, I'm sorry, Jo. I'm a fucking mess."

"Yeah, well, you're an endearing mess." I glanced at the mantle clock. "It's late. Go to bed. If you don't have a hangover, things will look better in the morning."

He nodded and rose unsteadily to his feet.

My hand shook as I offered it to him. "Come on. I'll help you."

His eyebrows drew together as he perused my extended hand. Like he couldn't remember how to accept help when it was offered. But then he slipped his hand into mine and grasped as though I would take back my offer as quickly as it had been made.

At the foot of the stairs he groaned. "I knew I should have built a fucking elevator."

A laugh bubbled in my throat. "There's not that many."

"Not for *you*."

I pulled him along behind me as he sighed. We were two steps from my landing when he stopped. My arm jerked back and I stumbled. Despite his compromised motor skills, his free arm came around me lightning quick, banding under my breasts and steadying me firm against his chest.

He moved his hips and I felt the hard length of his cock at my back. I gasped and had no control over myself when I pressed more firmly into him. Nate's breath stirred my hair as he groaned, his forearm corded with restrained muscles. I moved my hips, almost imperceptibly but enough for him to make another agonizing noise. Nate stroked his thumb and brushed the underside of my full, heavy breasts. My nipples strained painfully against the constraints of my bra.

Nate squeezed me a fraction tighter and a low, tortured moan slipped from my mouth. I felt his breath on my neck and for a brief second, his tongue traced a line over my racing pulse, tasting me.

He let me go just as abruptly. "Fuck," he groaned, forcibly moving me away from him. "Go to bed, Jo, for both our sakes."

My cheeks burned in shame as I bolted into the sanctuary of my room. Had that all been one-sided? I trembled in the middle of the room, my body a live wire of energy. For a hopeful second I imagined him bursting into the room and claiming me. Fuck that it was inappropriate and he was in a position of power over me.

But his slow, weary footsteps continued to his floors. A single, traitorous tear slid down my cheek. Rubbing it away furiously, I squashed all the heightened emotions down far inside me. He had rejected me.

Lust no longer clouded my every thought, and I knew it would have been a bad idea. He was drunk. He was my landlord. Either way, someone would be taking advantage of the other. It just wouldn't be clear who.

* * * *

I woke late the next morning, irritable and frustrated. Having spent most of the night tossing and turning, painfully turned on, safe to say I wasn't a happy camper come late morning. After showering and dressing in skinny jeans and loose vest I trudged downstairs for a strong hit of caffeine, thanking the gods that Nate was such a workaholic and guaranteed to have long left the house.

Instead he sat at the island, nursing a cup of coffee.

Usually Nate was clean-shaven and rocking designer jeans. This morning his face had the shadow of stubble and he wore jeans that looked broken in by years of use and a faded T-shirt. It was like seeing a totally different man. His eyes snapped up to mine when I entered the room, a tiny smile pulling at one corner of his mouth.

"Morning," I said, reaching for a cup.

"Morning," he said, his voice a tone lower than normal that sent shivers down my spine. "Sorry about the coffee this morning. It's on the strong side."

I smiled. "Suffering?"

"Nothing a full breakfast won't cure, which I'm treating us both to since I was an absolute tosser last night."

Taking my coffee to the island, I sat opposite him. "You didn't do anything wrong, Nate. People get pissed all the time."

"I crossed a line with you and I shouldn't have."

Forcing my smile to stay in place, I shrugged. "It's forgotten. Don't worry about it."

He nodded and traced the rim of his cup. "Do you have anything on today?"

"Nope, rare day and night off. You?"

"Perks of being the boss—no need to work a Saturday if I don't want to."

"Lucky sod."

His smile widened. "That's me."

Nate took us to a tiny greasy spoon cafe and ordered two full English breakfasts. Our plates arrived, heaped to the heavens and smelling divine. Nate attacked his with vigor, finishing well before I did. We stayed for another coffee before leaving to take a walk around the botanical gardens to help with digestion.

I groaned and clutched my tummy. "I think that food has melted my intestines."

He smiled. "How long has it been since you ate that much in one sitting?"

"That was the *only* time I've eaten that much in one sitting."

"You're missing out, seriously."

"See, that's what's so unfair. Men can eat what they like and stay looking amazing. Girls? Forget it. I'm going to be doing laps every day for a month to work that meal off."

Nate snorted a laugh.

"So," I said, trailing my fingers over the plants lining the path. "Do you want to talk about what happened yesterday?"

"I thought we already did."

"No, I mean the part that made you get trolleyed."

Nate's jaw clenched. "Oh. No, not really."

"It might help."

He sighed. "You're worse than my sister. You know that?"

I shrugged. "Just trying to lend an impartial, friendly ear. Forget it."

With a heavy breath, Nate dropped onto a nearby bench. "I told you she couriered it over? Well, she's been playing this game for fucking ages, now. I ended the relationship eight months ago, after I caught her and my business partner in our bed. She cried, begged, pleaded for a second chance. You don't get chances after that. It's done."

I nodded, in total agreement.

"So once she realizes she's had it, she launches herself into a very public relationship with the bloke she cheated on me with. Then comes the apologies and the visits for 'closure'. I've been telling her to return the ring pretty much since the day I kicked her out. For ages she kept saying she wasn't ready. It felt too final." Nate shrugged. "I suppose it's been going on for such a long time it was a shock when she finally did it."

His words hung in the air around us, heavy and melancholic.

"Well," I said after a few beats. "I think you had a lucky escape. Nate and Kate? Sounds like a warped TV show."

Nate hung his head back and bellowing laughter poured out of him. He rubbed his eyes and gave me the most beautiful smile I've ever seen. "Thank you."

I shrugged. "I call it like I see it."

He stretched his long legs out in front of him and rested his elbows on the back of the bench, the most relaxed I'd ever seen him. "You've been a lot cooler about all this than I had any right to expect. And I am sorry about last night. I shouldn't have said those things to you. It's no excuse, but I was pissed beyond belief and you were there—young and beautiful. To be honest, I'm surprised I haven't tried to seduce you before."

You wouldn't have to try very hard.

"Come on," Nate said, taking my hand and standing up. "I need to keep walking or I'll fall into a food coma on this bench."

We wandered for an hour or so around the gardens, the conversation considerably lighter. When we looped back to the house, Nate didn't come in with me, saying he was going to drop in on Suze for a bit. He gave me a wink and reminded me it was star, number, star.

Chapter Six

The next week flew by with both Nate and Suze being around more frequently. I ate dinner with them twice and met Suze for coffee a couple of mornings. Work was considerably busier and the tips were better.

It was my first August Saturday night in the bar and there hadn't been a break in customers for hours. By midnight I was both buzzing from the frantic energy and exhausted. Carly, the other girl I was working with, signaled to me that I was due my break. I smiled my thanks and pushed my way through the crowd to get outside.

The night was humid and airless but felt like ice water after being inside for so long. I leaned against the cool glass of the front windows, not caring that my lungs were filling with cigarette smoke.

"Jo?"

I cracked open one eye and saw Nate headed straight for me. On his arm was the skinny, tall-legged beauty I'd predicted and there was another couple trailing behind them.

"Hey."

"Kept busy, I see?" He smiled. The woman on his arm scowled.

I glanced at her then back to Nate, who was far, far, friendlier. "Seems that way."

"When are you on till?"

"Closing." I folded my arms beneath my breasts, a thrill going through me when Nate's gaze dropped for a long second.

Nate nodded. "See you later then?"

"More than likely."

He frowned at my tone but gave me a short nod by way of parting, and let his companion pull him away. Customers didn't get the friendliest Jo for the rest of my shift. Seeing Nate had thrown me, and if I were being honest with myself, it was because I had been reminded just how far out of my reach he truly was. A guy like Nate Harding didn't look twice at a girl like me.

* * * *

A little after four in the morning and my mood was no better than it had been after I'd seen Nate. My thoughts still tumbled around in my head as I turned my key in the lock and closed the door behind me with a quiet click.

"Nate." His name, spoken in a breathy whisper, floated from the living room.

A purely male sound answered, low and deep.

Before I could even question my motives, I moved closer to them. And there, in front of the lit fireplace even though it was August, they were—naked and slick with sweat. Nate pushed into her, her long legs wrapped around his lower back as she whispered for him to fuck her harder, faster. He grunted and obliged.

My body tightened, pulsed. I couldn't move. Couldn't look away.

The veins in Nate's neck corded and he pounded into her again, again, again. My breath left me in a gasp and even though she was moaning in his ear, he heard me.

Nate's head whipped around to where I stood, open-mouthed, flushed and so, so painfully aroused. He held my eyes and didn't let me go. His woman grasped his broad shoulders, nails digging in as she voiced her orgasm.

I moistened my lips and Nate's eyes zeroed in on the spot. His teeth clenched and he slammed into her one last, powerful time. She grabbed his chin and forced him to kiss her. Our connection broken, I rushed from the spot and up the stairs. My heart pounded and I panted.

In the bathroom I filled the bath, grasping the porcelain edges as I tried to catch my breath. I tore the clothes from my body, skin goosebumping as it met the cooler air. Sinking into the warm water, I tried to put them out of my head. Tried not to think about how powerful and *male* he looked fucking her. Tried not to picture myself under him.

Biting my lip, I whimpered as my clit throbbed. My entire body felt on fire. I slipped a hand under the water, my stomach quivering as my fingertips grazed over-sensitive skin. My pussy ached, wet and desperately close to release. I dipped my fingers inside and I cried out, arching my back. Water ran in rivulets between my full breasts and I palmed one, rolling my hardened nipple. I pumped harder with my fingers, my sex muscles contracting and hovering over the precipice of orgasm. Pressing my thumb against my clit, I exploded around my hand, wishing it was Nate making me come for him.

* * * *

Suze and Tilly were on the kitchen floor, Tilly a one-girl-band as she hammered various pots and pans with her makeshift wooden spoon drumstick, whilst Suze shook an empty drinks bottle filled with rice.

"I'm so glad you two came round. I've never had a migraine this fun," I shouted over the noise of Suze chanting nonsense to the rhythm of her homemade maraca.

Suze stuck her tongue out at me but ceased the shaking. "Want to go shopping when you're done? I really need some new bras." She stood up and reached across the island to stick her finger in my mixing bowl. "Cor, this is lush. What are you making?"

"Yeah, if you like," I said, swatting her hand. "And I'm making muffins."

"I didn't know you could bake. Do you do it often?"

I shrugged. "Sometimes. Not really." Truth be told, it had been a long time since it was even a dim possibility. Ovens weren't a constant luxury.

"I'm shite at baking. Cooking, yes. Baking, no. Mum used to all the time when we were wee. You always knew when we got home from school that she'd made something. The whole house would smell amazing." Suze laughed. "And whenever her and Dad'd had an argument, she'd go mental with the baking."

"Hmm." I spooned the mixture into the muffin cases.

"So," Suze purred as she moved around to my side of the island. "Everything okay with you and Nate?"

Apart from the fact that I'd gotten myself off last night after seeing him pounding the hell out of another woman? Yes, we were fucking ace. "Fine."

She dipped her finger into the bowl again. "Sure, if you say so. You're tenser than a...really tense thing. Has he made a move yet?"

"*No.*"

Suze laughed. "But you want him to? Hence all the baking your feelings? Trust me, he'll make a move. I've seen him eating you up with his eyes."

I sighed. "Suze, if you promise to shut up *right this second,* I'll let you lick the spoon."

"Deal," she said, grabbing for it.

"Ah ah! Patience, heard of it?" I finished filling the last cases and put the tray into the oven. Instead of handing Suze the wooden spoon, I brandished it in front of her face. "I mean it, Suze. Please drop this. It's not happening, okay?"

She rolled her eyes. "Yeah, yeah, believe it when I see it."

I laughed. "You won't see anything. That's the point."

The front door opened and closed, Nate's tall frame filling the doorway a moment later. My cunt tightened as I imagined his back arching as he thrust into that woman, the sheen of sweat on his skin and the feral look in his eyes when he caught me watching them.

Nate's eyes flickered between me and Suze before settling on me, still brandishing the spoon. "Has she been naughty again? I keep telling her about this behavior but she pays no notice."

Suze rolled her eyes. "Ha ha. She was just about to give me that spoon, so bugger off."

Nate came farther into the room. "What is that smell? Are you baking?"

"Muffins."

He grinned. "I always knew my timing was perfect."

Suze huffed. "And so is someone else's. Come on, Tilly." She picked up her daughter and we got the lovely smell of her nappy as they walked out of the room. "And don't you dare touch that spoon!"

"What is it with you two and the spoon?" I asked, about to drop it back into the empty mixing bowl.

Nate caught my wrist and tugged me closer to him. My breath caught in my throat at the intensity in his eyes.

"Because licking the spoon is the best bit."

"Suze told you not to touch it," I said, my voice barely above a whisper.

His smile widened. "And I'm not going to." Nate dipped his head and took the spoon into his mouth, keeping his eyes on me the entire time. He pulled back and winked.

I was soaking wet. If I claimed his mouth right now, it would taste of chocolate. His tongue would sweep over mine and I would suck it harder into my mouth, devouring the taste of him.

Nate's thumb pressed the pulse in my wrist and I knew he felt it speed up. His eyes were hooded and he leaned an inch closer. I dropped my gaze and instantly my sight was drawn to thick outline of his erection, straining against his jeans.

I opened my mouth to say something, though I've no idea what. Maybe to remind him of Suze's proximity, but more likely to beg him to finally put me out of my misery.

He smiled and pressed his mouth to the shell of my ear. "Save that thought, okay?"

A shiver snaked up my spine and I wanted to sink into the warmth of his body.

Nate released his hold on my wrist and took a step back. "I'm going for a shower. Save me a muffin."

I still hadn't fully regained my senses when Suze brought a freshly changed Tilly back into the kitchen a few minutes later. Every day he was making me care less and less why this was a terrible idea.

* * * *

Suze cleared her throat behind me, making me jump and slam back down to earth. Turning to face her, she plucked the garment out of my hand. "You're skinny as a rake, sweets. Those boobies would never fit in this circus tent."

So I'd been examining a bra at least three cup sizes too big for me. I should really pay more attention.

"What's up with you today?" Suze asked, reaching for a lacy purple set.

"Nothing why?" I moved around the racks, trailing my fingers over a sheer black slip. *Nate would like this. It wouldn't last a minute without being ripped to shreds.* Yanking my hand back, I moved in front of T-shirt bras. Safe. Practical. Least sexy thing in the shop.

"Because you're so distracted I can barely get a word out of you. And you keep salivating over the sexy stuff. So. Tell me. Who do you want to look sexy for?"

"No one." My cheeks burned. No way she would believe me now.

"Liar."

I huffed and shifted a few feet away from her.

She just followed. "*And* you're crabbit as sin. You're sexually frustrated, aren't you?"

"God, Suze, I don't want to talk about this with you okay?"

She laughed. "Okay, so that was a yes, and also it was about Nate. Good to know. Does it have anything to do with the licked-clean spoon?"

"Seriously. Please shut up." I let out a breath. "Why are we in here, anyway? Have you got a hot date or something?"

Suze shrugged. "Maybe. I just like having nice underwear. Just in case. Sexy tits and ass counters the baby shock."

My bad mood softened. "Suze, any guy worth his salt would take one look at you and Tilly and know he's onto a good thing."

"Right back at you, Miss Frustrated."

* * * *

That afternoon at work I wore one of the new sets I'd bought with Suze. Cerise satin balcony bra with cutaway details. I felt sexier than ever and it added an extra bounce to my step, which was helpful. The dreaded back shift, three till eleven, stretched into oblivion.

I sat at the bar sipping an ice water, hating how quick my break was flying by. A woman took the empty stool beside me, smiling when I glanced at her.

"I suddenly don't feel quite so pathetic," she said.

"Excuse me?" I frowned.

"A woman drinking alone at a bar always looks sad and pathetic. We're going to change that. We are independent women, and damn it, we can drink if we want to."

Usually people who drank alone in bars were looking for a quiet place to organize their thoughts — or have the music drown them out. Maybe she wanted to appear independent, but here she was at the first hurdle, already begging for a partner in crime.

"I actually have a reason for being here," she said, leaning a little closer to me.

"Oh." I couldn't care less what the reason was. Suddenly time flying was a damn good thing.

"The woman sleeping with my fiancé has been seen here."

Oh, God, not another infidelity bust.

"Actually, she works here, from what I can tell."

If that was true, it could be any number of my co-workers. The few I sort of knew wouldn't think twice about sleeping with a man in a relationship. And we had dozens of other summer workers to help out over the Fringe.

"That's terrible." I unzipped my hoodie, revealing my tank top brandishing the bar's name then went back around the bar, stuffing my hoodie in a little hideaway. "Can I get you a drink while you wait for her?"

Her eyes widened for a fraction before slowly trailing over me, sizing me up, judging me and if she thought I was the one screwing around with her man. "Large white wine."

As I set the drink in front of her, my gaze flickered over her shoulder, at a man shouldering his way to the bar.

Nate.

His lips began to pull into a smile before it froze when he saw the woman at the bar. "What are you doing here?"

She turned and slapped on a coy smile. "The girls tell me you've been hanging around here. Or more accurately, a bar whore."

"The girls don't know their arse from their elbows. Since when have you listened to their gossip?"

She sighed. "Don't fight with me, Nathaniel. I have a right to know, don't you think?"

His eyes hardened. "Not in the least."

The woman rose, brushing her breasts against his chest. "Let's take this somewhere a little more private."

Nate flashed me a look but took her elbow and steered her to one of the booths that lined the far wall. I'll give her her dues. She pulled out all the stops—stroked the stem of her wine glass, put her cleavage on display. Took any excuse to touch him.

I wanted to rip out her fake hair by the extensions.

Nate leaned back and looked over at me. A slow, sure grin spread across his face. He turned to say something to her, before striding back across to me.

"Friend of yours?" I asked, arching an eyebrow.

He let out a heavy breath. "That, is Kate."

My eyes widened. "Shit, really?"

"Really."

"What does she want?"

"To find out who you are."

"*Me*?" A nervous laugh escaped me. "What the hell for?"

"Her friends have seen a beautiful woman coming and going from my house. And they saw that same beautiful woman here. Apparently you're the new girlfriend who is trying to steal me away from her."

I frowned. "Didn't she sort of give you up when she shagged your mate?"

He sighed. "Try telling her that. It's fine for her to be in a relationship. But me? Forget it. In her mind, I will *always* belong to her."

"Selfish cow."

Nate gave me a wicked smile. "Want to drive her bat shit crazy?"

"Why don't I like the sound of that?"

He reached across the bar for my hand. Drawing it to his mouth, he pressed a light kiss to my knuckles that I felt deep down inside me. "Don't make me beg," he said, voice gravelly.

"I finish in an hour."

Nate's smile turned cat-that-caught-the-canary and when he kissed my hand again, for a tiny moment his tongue flickered out. Was this part of the game or something real? Because whatever it was, he had me completely convinced.

The last hour of my shift dragged. I couldn't help but look over at their booth, pleased to see Nate lounging and relaxed whilst Kate could have shattered her glass her grip was so tight. Once finished, Carly served me two Coronas with lime and I made my way, somewhat begrudgingly, to where Nate and Kate sat.

Her eyes raked over me, and apparently I was found wanting. Nate, however, grinned his welcome, his hand finding my thigh the instant I slid into the booth beside him.

"Didn't you think to ask if I wanted anything?" Kate asked.

I shrugged and passed Nate his beer. "I couldn't really care less if you wanted something or not."

Nate snorted and pulled me closer to him, molding me to his side.

"Nathaniel has been telling me all about your relationship." Kate tapped her nails against her empty glass, the sound getting my back up. "It seems that for a new relationship, it's moving very fast. To some people that might seem suspicious."

"In what way?" Nate's thumb stroked my inner thigh, melting all my brain power. If this bitch wanted a throw down, I had to cut her off at the knees.

Kate leaned closer to me. "He is incredibly wealthy, which I'm sure hasn't escaped your notice."

I laughed. "Oh, you think I'm after his money? Listen...Kate, was it? Unlike some, I couldn't give a shit about what Nate may or may not be worth. There's one thing about him that I'm after. You may not remember, since you were so happy to jump on someone else's. It's his dick. That big, beautiful dick that he fucks me with so hard every night. Are you getting the picture, or do I need to paint you a visual?"

Blood stained her cheeks. "I think I'm getting it, yes."

"Glad to hear it."

Nate squeezed my leg and pressed a kiss to my shoulder, his lips curving into a smile.

Kate's phone let out a shrill bleat and she scrambled in her bag to find it. She gave us an apologetic smile before answering.

"You fucking floored me with that little speech," Nate whispered in my ear as Kate tittered into her phone.

A thrill went up my spine at the nearness of him and the tickle of his breath on my ear. "Glad you liked it," I said, turning my face closer to his.

His eyes locked on mine, our mouths a hair's breadth apart. "Suze tells me you went shopping today. Did you buy anything?"

"Yes."

"What? Would I like it?"

I all but squirmed in my seat. "I'm counting on it. And I'm wearing it now."

Kate laughed, the noise so shrill and fake it hurt my ears.

Nate's eyes flickered to her before landing back on me. "Do you know who she's talking to?" Nate leaned further into me, so much so that his lips touched the shell of my ear. "The woman you watched me fucking. It was her who told Kate about you."

My whole body shivered. How could him talking about fucking another woman turn me on so effortlessly? But it did. My knickers were drenched and if he asked me to right now, I would leave with him. Leave and make him forget about fucking anyone else except me.

"I had to have her another time after you walked away. I flipped her and started all over again."

I clenched my thighs together, desperately seeking some relief from the ache between my legs. Nate grasped my thigh harder and I almost cried out.

"Sorry about that," Kate said a little too loudly.

"It was no trouble," I said, taking a large gulp of my beer.

Nate drained the last of his and set the empty bottle back on the table. "We had better be going. I trust this is the end of all this now, Kate?"

She sighed. "We will always be in each other's lives, Nathaniel. Why don't you see that?"

I gave her a smile. "Because now he just sees me."

Nate threaded his fingers with mine as we scooted out of the booth and headed for the door. The night was alive when we stepped outside. The area was notoriously busy and the chatter and buzz was a familiar noise. I stopped at the main window of the bar. "Hey, wait a minute."

"What?" Nate asked, turning to me.

"Come here," I said, plucking on the material of his shirt. Slipping my hands around his neck, I pulled him down to meet my mouth. At first he was too shocked to respond. But then his arms came around me, holding me firm against him.

"What was that for?" he asked, voice husky.

"Had to go out with a bang, didn't we?"

His eyebrows drew together. "How can you even be sure she saw anything?"

"Trust me," I said, my own voice thick with need. "She's watching."

Nate lowered his head and his lips claimed mine. This time his kiss was forceful and demanding. And I gave him everything he wanted. He breathed in my cry when his tongue entered my mouth.

Someone whistled and I didn't care. I gripped him tighter, fear nudging through my arousal that this would end at any moment.

He tugged on my lower lip before pulling away.

I had no idea if that was for Kate's benefit or simply because he wanted to. Nate's hips then pressed into mine and I knew, even if that kiss was to make his ex jealous, I had still made him hard as fucking rock.

Chapter Seven

We walked home in relative silence. My body thrummed with energy and I was aware of every single thing Nate did. How his breathing sounded. The feel of his shirt sleeve as it brushed my arm. The glint of a streetlight off the face of his watch. His easy, confident walk. I chewed the inside of my cheek and wrapped my arms around my middle, sure if I didn't I would shove Nate into the nearest close and beg him to destroy my body.

It felt like an eternity before we reached the house, my body sensitive and on high-alert. Nate unlocked the door and in a heartbeat he pressed me into the wall, his hips on mine. He grasped my face, a feverish, desperate look in his eyes.

"Fuck, Jo," he whispered, grinding his pelvis harder into me, the thick, rigidness of his cock making me cry out. Nate slid his palm between us, cupping me. With a gasp I rocked my hips into his touch. He growled in my ear and unbuttoned my denim shorts.

This was happening. Right here, up against the wall in the entryway. Neither of us had the patience or mind to move upstairs. This had been building between us for too long to prolong anything. I needed him inside me, to feel the thickness of him stretching me. I would come in seconds.

Nate reached into the satin of my knickers, fingers gliding against my slick lips. I gripped his shoulders as he slowly entered one finger inside. With his other hand, Nate hooked behind my knee and guided it up onto his hip, his touch inching further up my leg before he squeezed my ass. I moaned and leaned into his touch and was rewarded with another finger.

Nate held my eyes as he moved them back and forth, my cunt tightening and so, so wet. He hit the sweet spot inside me and I shuddered, my body jerking.

"Fuck, Jo," Nate growled in my ear. "You feel so good."

I arched my back and grabbed his neck, knotting my fingers in his short hair. Nate groaned and increased his speed, fucking me faster with his fingers.

A cry from the sitting room had us both freezing. Our eyes locked, neither of us daring to move. It came again, this time both of us realizing who had made the sound. Suze groaned and shushed her daughter, the sound of her shifting on the couch drifting out to us in the hall.

Nate swore and ground the heel of his palm against my clit. My knees buckled and he held me up with the fingers deep inside me. He slammed his mouth on mine just as the orgasm burst from me, swallowing the noise with greedy pulls.

"Nate?" Suze's groggy voice called.

He kissed me, hard and deep one last time and I sucked on his tongue. Nate squeezed his eyes shut. "Yeah, Suze," he replied, his voice gloriously thick and rough. Nate pulled his hand from me and buttoned my shorts.

"Oh, hi, Jo," Suze said, appearing in the doorway, her face pulling into a wide yawn. "Were you two out together?"

"I was in the area as Jo's shift ended. We shared a taxi home," Nate answered smoothly.

I had no idea how he could formulate a sentence. My mind was still coming back down to earth, my body tingling, and, despite the best orgasm I've had in years, I still wanted, needed more from him.

"You're all heart." Suze scrubbed a hand over her eyes. "I hope you don't mind, I let myself in. Got into world war three of fights with Mum. Didn't want to go home after. You two fancy a glass of wine?"

"Sure thing. Go pick what you want," Nate said. "Where's Tilly?"

"She was asleep in her pram when we got here so I just left her in it. She's a bit like her uncle—can sleep anywhere."

"Ha."

Suze grinned and padded into the kitchen.

Nate touched my shoulder, urging me forward. I appreciated the help since my motor functions weren't fully back online yet.

A shiver crawled up my spine when I felt his lips at my ear.

"You're fucking beautiful when you come," he said, before moving past me into the kitchen.

I stared after him, heart pounding as his words imprinted themselves on my mind to be remembered forever. With a deep breath I followed him into the room and clutched the island for support for my wobbly legs.

Suze poured us all a generous glass of red wine. She sat beside me at the island, gulping down half her glass before I had even picked mine up. I clenched my thighs together, my pussy still tingling with aftershocks from Nate's hand.

"What was your argument with Mum about then?" Nate asked, leaning against the counter. His body resembled a jungle cat. Lean, powerful, strength packed into every part of him. At ease but fully alert, aware of everything in his surroundings.

Suze let out an exaggerated sigh. "The usual. I asked her to have Tilly tomorrow night because of this date I have. She tsked and said I should bring her along, just to give Mitch a proper shock and let him see we're a package deal."

Nate snorted a laugh. "Well, you want to make sure you like him first before introducing him to Tilly. Does he know about her?"

"That's what I said!" she cried. "Yeah, he knows. We met at a toddler group a few weeks ago when Mitch brought his nephew. But anyway, Mum's refusing to have her for me. And unless you have a break in your stressy work diary and no social outings planned, I'm buggered. I *really* don't want to cancel on this guy. He's bloody gorgeous."

Nate's forehead creased. "Shit, sorry, Suze. I'm going out to dinner with a potential client tomorrow night. If he goes with my firm, it'll be a huge project for us."

Suze gave him a smile though it wavered at its edges. "It's okay. Don't worry about it. I knew it would be a long shot."

"Um," I said before clearing my throat. "I have the night off tomorrow. If you wanted, I could watch Tilly for you."

Suze stared at me for a minute.

"I mean, I understand if you don't want me to. It's a big deal leaving your child with someone you barely know."

She clutched my arm. "Are you being serious?"

"Um, yes?" I felt a prickle of unease.

Suze grinned and threw her arms around me. "Thanks, Jo. Thank you *so* much!"

I couldn't help but smile in return as she let me out of her bear hug. "It's no problem. Can't be having you let down Mitch."

"You're a lifesaver, seriously! Is seven okay? Mitch is picking me up at eight and I want time to get myself ready without worrying about Tilly somehow getting jam all over the dress I'm wearing."

"Make it half six, just to be sure."

She squealed again and rattled off a very detailed, very excited description of the new dress she was wearing, just for the occasion.

I smiled into my wine glass, a warm glow blooming inside me. Glancing up, I saw Nate watching me. For a moment he was still, the look in his eyes somehow more intimate than a few minutes ago when he'd had his fingers buried inside me. But then the corner of one lip twitched before he smoothed his features blank.

My stomach clenched in anticipation.

* * * *

Nate insisted that Suze and Tilly take the other room on my floor, and as he was helping Suze bring all her stuff up, I stole into my room and closed the door with a soft click. To keep myself busy, I filled the bath, planning on soaking and relaxing for as long as it took. Nate didn't strike me as the kind of man okay with banging me senseless with his sister and niece very close by. Downstairs we hadn't had a choice. We'd both been past the point of no return. But I couldn't be certain he wouldn't come into my room and pick up right where we'd left off.

Despite my earlier desperation for him, I needed the space. Now that my lust had cooled and rational thinking had returned, I could once again think logically.

Slipping into the hot water, I hissed as it stung my skin for a blissful moment. The steam clouded the room, shrouding and concealing me. I let out a breath and sunk deeper into the water. The moment I closed my eyes, all I could see was Nate and the ferocious, hungry look in his eyes as he'd pinned me against the wall. It had been a long time since I'd wanted anyone even half as much as I wanted him. I wanted him to take my body and leave me ravished and spent.

Later, when I crawled into bed, I tried to tell myself I could resist him. That it would be no time at all before some beauty stole his attention and he forgot about the strange, broken girl living in his house. He deserved someone who could give him their entire self...not a shell of a woman with an empty heart.

If I was smart I would brush the whole night off and forget about it. Nate had gotten off lucky. Who in their right mind would want anything to do with me, if they knew the real me?

I rolled over in bed, groggy with sleep, soft and warm. Stretching my arms out, I came into contact with something. Someone. A sleepy smile spread across my face.

"I wondered how long it would be before you did this."

He shifted closer to me, swung a leg over until he straddled my hips. He bent and pressed a kiss to my throat, slowly making his way upward until he nipped at my earlobe with his teeth.

My fingernails raked down his back as I pressed my hips up to meet him. The hand caressing my throat grasped me, the hold tightening, and for a brief second I thought it was because he couldn't control himself. But when he whispered in my ear, I knew. This man knew exactly what he was doing.

"Found you." His hand squeezed until I couldn't breathe.

I tried to buck him off, clawed at his hands until I had the sense to reach under my pillow but came up empty.

He pulled back, his hands still crushing out the life in me. And in the dim morning light I finally saw his face. He grinned and lunged for me.

I lurched up, gasping for breath and trying to force myself fully into consciousness, the sheets like unbreakable binding around my legs. It felt like an eternity before I was freed, though I was up and clutching my bat before barely a second had passed. My eyes darted around the room, sure I would spot him any second, lurking in a shadow, watching me with that smile of his.

Slowly my heart calmed and I could suck in enough breath to stop gasping like a fish out of water. I tucked the bat back into its place and went into the bathroom to splash some cold water on my face. My hands shook and my entire body trembled.

* * * *

The light was gray and dim when I slipped outside, clutching my coffee mug. The sun was slowly burning off the haze and it would be another hot August day. But right now I was thankful for the chill that made my mind alert.

After a nightmare, I always craved the outdoors. For some people they felt safer inside, with their locked doors and windows, hiding under the bed covers, hoping the boogeyman didn't think to look under them. But the only place I ever felt truly safe was in an open area. Somewhere to run. Somewhere to flee to.

I pulled the oversized cardigan tighter around my shoulders and sipped the rich, strong coffee. Movement on the wall surrounding Nate's patio pulled my focus, and a skinny ginger cat jumped down, keeping close to the wall but not taking its eyes off me.

For a while we observed each other. The cat was wretched and pitiful, more than likely a stray. It was painfully skinny, though didn't appear flea ridden or diseased in any way.

I rolled my eyes. "Fine, here." I tossed a piece of the buttery toast I had been forcing myself to eat. The cat jumped at my voice but leaped on the toast, licking the melted butter before nibbling on the bread.

"You'll never get rid of that thing now."

This time it was me who jumped at hearing a voice. Coffee sloshed over the edge of the mug and burned my leg. I stood up, wiping at the spill and feeling my cheeks scorch hotter than my leg.

"Sorry, did I scare you?" Nate asked, sitting on the step a few higher than mine.

"Startled, that's all." I managed a wobbly smile and sat back down, my shoulders slumping when I saw the cat had disappeared.

"I think I startled your new friend away."

"Mmm."

Nate waited a moment before speaking again. "Everything okay? You seem out of sorts this morning."

I shrugged. "I didn't sleep very well."

He chuckled—the sound so low I felt it everywhere. "I know the feeling."

"Are Suze and Tilly awake yet?"

"You'd know about it if they were. Did Tilly keep you up?"

"No, I didn't hear a thing."

"You know, I'm a little disappointed." Nate leaned closer to me. "I thought you would sneak up to my room last night."

A laugh bubbled in my throat. For the first time that morning, my nightmare wasn't the foremost thought in my mind. I twisted around to look at him, smiling at the boyish grin on his face. "Like I was at a friend's house and her older brother was trying to corrupt my innocent ways?"

His grin widened. "There was nothing innocent about what we did in the hall last night. And it's *my* house."

I bit my lip, my insides fizzing. "I thought your floors were off limits."

"They are. To anyone but you. And just so we're clear, if the urge ever takes you, you would always be warmly welcomed if you decided to visit one night. Or morning."

His eyes mesmerized me. I drowned in them, in their warm chocolate gaze. Right now he was daring me with them. He had offered himself on a plate and I only had to accept.

A clattering sound in the kitchen broke the contact and I jumped again at the sudden noise.

"You really didn't sleep well, did you?" This time Nate's eyes were observant and calculating.

I felt naked and exposed in front of him, as though my secrets were only a tiny scratch beneath the surface away and any second he would see them.

"Right, who's having breakfast?" Suze called from the kitchen.

Nate stood and held out a hand for me. I closed my eyes for a moment before sliding my hand into his. He pulled me up and didn't let his hold on me go. At the door to the kitchen he squeezed my hand and dipped to press a kiss to my temple.

* * * *

Tilly and I were on the floor of the posh living room, a mountain of toys between us. Tilly crawled around, putting her doll in the pram, taking it out again then swapping it with a teddy with no eyes.

I was playing with a baby's first tablet.

"Okay, are you absolutely, positively, totally and completely sure you want to do this?" Suze asked, biting her fingernail and looking at me with eyes like saucers.

"Yes, for chrissakes, Suze. Will you stop asking? You're freaking me out. What if something happens? What if there's a fire? What if there's a fire and we can't get out?"

"Oh, fuck," Suze whispered.

"Fuh, fuh, fuh," Tilly said, smiling at her mother.

"Shit," Suze said, louder this time as she looked at her daughter in horror.

Tilly giggled.

I jumped to my feet and clapped my hands so hard they stung. "Shall we go get some tea, Tilly?" I asked, louder than was really necessary.

"Tea, tea, tea," Tilly sang.

Suze let out a breath. "Thanks. See? You're better at this than I am."

I snorted a laugh. "Save that judgment for when you get back and the house is on fire."

Suze paled.

"I'm joking. Sort of. But we'll be fine, and it's only for a few hours." I gave Suze my most reassuring smile, and when she smiled back, I knew I had been convincing—whether or not I felt it myself.

"Right, yes, of course. I'm being stupid. Sorry, Jo, I just haven't left her with someone who isn't family before. And I really like you. I don't want to scare you off."

"What, does she hack up some gremlins if I feed her after midnight?"

Suze frowned. "No."

"Then how am I going to be scared off?"

She shrugged. "Most of my other friends dumped me the minute I found out I was having a baby. The ones that stuck around drifted away once they realized I wasn't just Suze with a baby, I was a *mother*, and Tilly would always come first. No more wine bars after work. No more weekend spa trips. Breast feeding and pooey nappies, that's what my life was about. I just don't want you to think I'm using you, or for you to think we're too much hassle."

I looked at my feet, bare with pink nail polish. "I wouldn't think that, ever. Stop being stupid."

Suze laughed and wrapped her arms around me in the biggest hug I'd had in a long time. "You really have a way with words, Jo."

"Tea. Tea!" Tilly shouted, whacking my leg with a Duplo brick.

Suze bent and hugged her daughter. "Mummy's going now, poppet. You be good for Auntie Jo and I'll be home really soon, okay?"

The two of them were wrapped in their own little universe, giving me a few much needed seconds to stop hyperventilating over Suze's casual use of 'Auntie'.

Tilly puckered her lips at Suze until Suze smothered the girl's face in kisses and Tilly squealed with delight.

With moisture in her eyes, Suze quickly pecked my cheek then darted out of the door.

"Just you and me now, Tilly."

Tilly smiled and nodded.

"You'll take it easy on me, right?"

Tilly laughed and ran out of the room. I tried not to take that as a bad sign.

That evening I was pleasantly surprised to find out toddlers were actually pretty good company. We ate dinner at the island, chicken with carrots and peas that Suze had left to be warmed up. Lucky for me, Tilly was a girl who liked her food and it was demolished in just a few minutes.

We played in the sitting room for a while, me painstakingly building great structures out of Duplo bricks while Tilly charged through the finished products like a child-sized Godzilla. This, apparently, never gets old.

Suze had left some bath toys and a sleepsuit, so Tilly had a great time splashing around in my bath, clapping her hands through the bubbles and making them dance in the air. She almost made my heart stop when she scribbled all over the sides with a crayon, but it proved to easily wash off.

Warm and sleepy, dressed in her sleepsuit after the bath, she cuddled up into me in the comfy sitting room across from my bedroom, and dozed off to the movie Suze assured me she loved. I shifted down on the couch, too engrossed in the film to even think about moving.

* * * *

A hand stroked the hair off my face, a whisper reaching my ears. I lurched up, on my feet before I could even blink.

"Shit," a male voice swore. An arm snaked around my waist as I swayed. "Jo? Are you okay?"

Good voice. It was a good voice. I released the breath I had been holding, and grasped Nate's upper arm for support. "What's going on?"

"I just got in. Sorry, I seem to be frightening you a lot today."

I took another breath, my mind playing catch up, stomach sinking with dread when it did. "Where's Tilly?"

"I took her upstairs, Suze leaves a travel cot here just in case. She's fine, Jo." Nate ushered me back onto the couch and he crouched in front of me.

"What time is it?" I asked, pushing my bird's nest hair away.

"After one. Did Tilly knacker you out? It looks like a toy shop exploded downstairs."

I cringed. "Sorry, I was going to tidy it when Tilly fell asleep. Didn't plan on me dropping off, as well."

"You probably needed it. Don't worry. Mess will keep till the morning."

"Did your meeting go well?"

Nate smiled. "Very well. I need to do a bit more schmoozing though. We're having another dinner next week. Will you come with me?"

I sat back. "What, to a dinner meeting? Are you serious?"

He frowned. "Of course. Why?"

"I'm hardly the sort of woman you're usually seen with, am I?"

"What's that supposed to mean?"

I sighed. "Look at me, Nate. The most expensive thing I own is twenty quid pair of jeans from Next. And I got them in the sale. I cut my hair myself, barely wear makeup and have nothing even close to resembling a dress. Wealthy women fall at your feet, dripping in diamonds."

"And if I wanted to take one of them, I would. Instead I'm asking you. Who gives a shit if you don't have a dress? I'll buy you one. It's you who would be doing me a favor, after all. If you don't want to go, just say. But just so you know, I wouldn't take anyone else in your place."

My head couldn't comprehend his words.

He stood. "Just think about it, okay? I'm going to check on Tilly. You should try and get back to sleep. I'm sorry again for waking you."

I couldn't decide as I watched him leave the room if I was disappointed nothing more had happened. Maybe he knew I needed the breathing room. But surely he must have realized how fragile my willpower was around him?

Chapter Eight

Suze picked Tilly up the next morning, a healthy glow in her cheeks and a smile so wide I was surprised it didn't rip her face in half. Nate was working from home that morning and waved us out of the door with a promise to watch Tilly while we went for a coffee.

Suze linked her arm with mine as we walked to a place in the Quartermile development. The furniture, all large wooden affairs, were at direct odds with the sheer stone walls and both local and foreign artwork.

She returned from the counter with a homemade Jaffa cake each and enormous steaming mugs of coffee. Suze sunk beside me on the couch, resting her head on my shoulder.

"Do I even need to ask if you had sex with Mitch last night?" I asked, blowing on the coffee.

Suze giggled and sat up. "God, am I that transparent?"

"Yes," I said with a smile. "You may as well introduce yourself to people— 'Hello, I'm Suze and last night I got shagged rotten'."

She squealed and whacked my arm. "Jo! You're getting as bad as Nate for being blunt."

At his name my cheeks warmed, but thankfully Suze's head was too full of her new man to notice.

"Am I being a silly girl? I'm sorry. It's just...okay, you know when you haven't had sex for *ages* and then you meet someone who you know you want to get naked with and you just hope and hope and hope it's going to be as good as you imagine it will be and *then* when you do *finally* do it, it just, like...blows your mind and suddenly you can't remember why you ever stopped having sex and what you've been doing all this time *not* having sex and God...just...fucking hell, it was good. That's all."

It took a minute for all that to sink in. I snorted a laugh and pretty soon Suze and I were cackling like a pair of witches in the corner.

"Sorry. I think I just—"

"Wanted to rub your amazing sex in my face?"

She laughed. "No! But I suppose that answers my question on you and Nate."

I huffed. "Christ, Suze, I can't talk about that with you."

Suze raised her eyebrows. "So there's something to talk about?"

"No! Not in the least!"

"That's weird. Because this morning before you got up, all Nate could talk about was how good you were with Tilly."

I frowned. "And how does that mean there's something going on between us?"

Suze shrugged. "Nate's a family man. Yeah, he tarts about, but nothing is more important to him than family. And I think seeing you with Tilly has his sperm all up and excited."

I choked on my mouthful of coffee.

"Sorry," Suze said, not sounding the least bit apologetic. "So, are you going to break his heart and not go to that dinner thing with him?"

"He told you about that?"

Suze nodded and picked a piece of her muffin off. "He asked me to sneakily get you into a dress shop today and see what you liked."

I shook my head, but couldn't contain the smile that pulled at my lips.

"I know I keep saying it, and probably seem way too interested in my brother's sex life to be considered healthy, but I seriously think you could do a lot worse. He seems to really care about you. Way more than he ever did about Kate."

"Suze, seriously, I don't want to talk about this." Sex with Nate was one thing. Actual feelings were something altogether impossible.

She let out a breath. "Fine. Oh, did I tell you about Mitch's car?"

After coffee, Suze did get me in a dress shop. But she didn't pay me the slightest bit of attention. She and the new guy were going to a restaurant opening in a few weeks and she wanted a show-stopping dress.

* * * *

On Thursday evening the next week, a garment bag hung from my door handle. A note was pinned to it in Nate's neat handwriting—

Just in case. I leave at eight-thirty.

It was seven now.

Taking the bag into my room I placed it on the bed and pulled on the zipper. I was terrified I'd find a floor-length thousand pound ball gown. Instead, there was pale green knee-length lace dress with short sleeves and a slight poof to the skirt. At the bottom of the bag were coral hidden platform stilettos that went perfectly with the dress.

Staring at it, I felt like I was at a crossroads. I could take the bag and hang it on the stairs for Nate to see and do what he wanted with. Or I could slip it on and meet him downstairs. One road continued my path of solitude and isolation. The other branched into possibilities.

For once in my life, I was curious what they might be.

At eight-thirty on the dot I checked my appearance in the hall mirror, licking my lips and wrestling with a stray hair that insisted on curling the opposite way from all the others. The dress fitted perfectly and the shoes gave me height I wasn't used to, and also a smidge of confidence.

Nate appeared behind me in the mirror, breathtaking in tailored trousers and shirt. He slid an arm around my waist and pressed his front to my back. "You look spectacular."

My cheeks warmed but I couldn't pull away from his gaze. "Thank you."

He squeezed my waist. "We should go. The car will be here by now."

Nate laced his fingers with mine as he led me outside to where a black glossy town car was parked.

"Why aren't we taking your car?" I asked, sliding into the back seat.

"Because I don't want to worry about losing face in turning down wine. I learned a long time ago that if the client wants to overindulge, it's better to at least pretend to do the same. Plus the town car makes a good impression."

I smiled. "And if he doesn't see you arrive?"

Nate gave me a wicked look. "Then it's just to impress the woman I'm taking."

Shifting my eyes, I looked out of the window at the city lights zooming past. "You don't need to do anything to impress me, Nate."

He brought my hand to his lips and kissed my knuckles. "Can't help trying, though. But thank you."

The town car slowed to a stop outside a restaurant on the Royal Mile. It was one I had passed countless times but had never dreamed of being inside. Nate's arm came around my back as we headed in, the hostess taking one look at him and escorting us to an intimate corner of the room. He asked her for a bottle of wine to be brought to the table when the rest of the party arrived. She nodded, her gaze flickering to me for half a second before lingering on Nate for a moment too long.

Nate pulled my chair out, brushing his fingers across the back of my neck. He took the seat beside mine, smiling as he lowered himself into it. "You look nervous."

"I'm not nervous."

Nate toyed with my fingers, taking my hand in his again. "Your hand is sweating."

I snatched it back.

He smiled, a laugh rumbling low in his throat. "I'm sorry. Can I have it back now?"

"*No*," I said, scowling.

He laughed again but couldn't argue his case further because of the arrival of his potential client. Nate rose to greet the gentleman and his *much* younger wife, shaking his hand and kissing her cheeks. The man came around the table to do the same to me. His wife gave me a cold look.

"Mr Underhill, this is my good friend Josephine. Jo, Mr Underhill and his wife Claudia," Nate introduced.

"It's a pleasure to meet you both," I said, offering them what I hoped was a steady smile.

"Call me Jack," Mr Underhill said, his eyes lingering on me for a moment too long.

Nate cleared his throat and gestured to the waiter that we were ready for the wine. He took our orders once we all had a glass, Nate whispering to me what he thought I might like. I smiled my thanks and from that point on, Nate turned all business.

As the men talked money and ideas, I tried to engage Claudia in polite conversation, but it seemed she was more interested in pushing up her tits to catch Nate's attention than speaking to me.

The food came and Nate was right, his choice was delicious. Roast duck with broccoli. Another few bottles of wine came and went, Jack relaxing and looser in his body language. Claudia took to touching Nate's arm whenever she spoke.

It made me territorial.

Our waiter cleared the table and returned to pour brandy for us all. Jack reclined in his seat, Claudia trailing a finger back and forth above her breasts. The only person who had my attention was Nate.

I had never imagined what it would be like to see the business side of him. It took me by surprise just how aroused it made me. Nate commanded attention and drew everyone's focus. He was sure and confident in his words, charming to a fault and reassuring when he needed to be.

Even though no one really spoke to me, except Jack—but he was soon caught up in another conversation with Nate—I didn't feel like a trophy girl or something pretty on Nate's arm to make him look good.

Claudia launched into a story about a friend who was starting her own business and the hopeless web developer who hadn't a clue what he was doing. Nate nodded politely and placed his hand on my knee under the table.

My heart sped up at the slight touch, even more so when he slid it higher up my leg. When he got to the apex of my thigh, my legs parted, my conscious thought only wanting to know how far he would dare take this.

With one long, teasing finger, Nate stroked my folds through the satin of my now drenched underwear. I ground my teeth together, desperate and burning for more. My face warmed, flushed with pleasure.

Across the table, Jack stared hard at my face. Claudia twittered on in the background, no one hearing a word she said. Nate jerked his hand away and I almost cried out from the loss of contact. Nate cleared his throat and Jack's eyes snapped to him.

Jack smiled and signaled to the waiter. He held out a credit card and told him to take care of the bill.

As we all stood to leave, Nate gripped my hip and held me firm to his side. Jack approached and Nate turned almost imperceptibly, so Jack could only shake his hand. It was only when he glanced at me did Nate's move make sense. Jack could get nowhere near me without appearing over-keen or the lecherous man he was. Claudia pressed her chest into Nate's side as she kissed his cheek and this time it was me who moved us.

The town car was waiting for us as we four exited the restaurant. I slid inside, watching as Nate shook Jack's hand again. He smiled and climbed in beside me, again pressing his thigh along the length of mine.

I couldn't speak. Nate took hold of my hand, teasing my fingers and running my knuckles across his plush mouth. When he parted his lips and bit down ever so gently, I willed the car to hurry the hell up. My rules were officially burned.

Chapter Nine

There was none of the frantic energy that had caught us up the last time we'd returned home together. I waited for Nate to unlock the door and stepped inside after him. He shed his suit jacket and draped it on the cupboard door handle.

I looked at him, wondering, patient.

He took a step closer to me then paused. "Suze?" he called out.

Silence answered him. His smile turned predatory as he stalked toward me again.

"Why did you call her?" I asked, my voice wavering.

"Because if something interrupts us this time, I won't be able to stop. I need to be inside you, now, and I'd prefer it if my sister wasn't present when I am." Nate pulled me to him, his lips pressing into my throat. "Come to bed with me. Please."

His voice was thick with desire. Nate Harding didn't strike me as the kind of man who asked for things. He demanded them. He'd admitted as much to me the night he was drunk — that women begged to be with him. And yet with me, he asked permission.

I slid my hands up his back, the muscles corded with restraint. "Yes," I whispered.

Nate smiled against my skin and nipped at the delicate area before pulling back. He took me by the hand and led me up the stairs.

We passed my floor and up another. The fourth floor opened into a magnificent sprawling room. Full-length windows dominated an entire wall with awe-inspiring views of the city and the river. The lights twinkled off the water and from way up here I felt like a princess in the tower, her prince about to worship her.

His bed, enormous and masculine, faced the windows. He woke every morning to those views and I could imagine the moment humbling. An open door showed a walk-in wardrobe that went on and on, rails upon rails of his clothes.

The fourth floor wasn't overcrowded with things the way it could be. The odd chest here and there, a chaise longue and two wall-mounted flat screens side by side. It bordered on minimal, but really, it was just Nate—practical and useful with a hint of boasting. The room screamed his sexuality and confidence from the royal blue walls to the dark wood of his bed.

The room was lit only by what filtered in from the outside world. I stood in a pool of moonlight, facing out into the city that was becoming more and more like home with each passing day.

I felt him come up behind me and slowly pull the zipper of my dress down. My skin tingled as the fabric brushed over my body as he urged it to the floor. He kissed my shoulder and unclasped my bra, his fingers following the straps down my arms.

I broke out in goosebumps the instant his fingers hooked into the edges of my knickers. I thought Nate would be someone who enjoyed underwear, and maybe he did, but right now it was just a scrap of fabric that was in his way to laying me bare.

My clothes were in a heap on the floor and I stood in front of the windows, exposed and nude and more alive than I'd felt before. Anyone could see us and I not only didn't care, it emboldened me, lit a fire in my veins and a burning in my soul.

Nate turned me and his eyes drank me in. He didn't miss an inch of me and when his gaze met mine, I had the feeling he had me committed to memory.

I loosened his tie and pulled it off, held his eyes as I slipped each button free of its holding. His upper body was bared to me as the shirt fell to the floor. A smile teased my lips as I dragged my fingers down the hard planes of his chest and over the defined ridges of his abdomen.

Nate was a primal male, all man. The strength of his body poured out of him, and once again I was struck with the feeling that his presence took up more space than everyone else.

I traced my finger over the flat disc of his nipple and I leaned into him, pressing my lips to his skin, flicking my tongue out to taste what I had craved all these weeks.

With an impatient groan, Nate grasped my hips and lifted me, my legs going around his waist. His mouth met mine in a clash of desire — tongues mixing and teeth pulling. As though we were competitors rather than lovers, both trying to win the same thing, neither willing to concede.

Nate lowered me and my back hit the cool bedcovers. He crawled above me, the rest of his clothes gone and we were finally bare to each other. Nate kissed a path from my throat, between my breasts to my belly button. He dipped his tongue inside, glancing up at me with a wicked smile. As I reached for him, Nate sat back on his haunches.

He encircled my ankle and raised it up, tracing a finger down the sole of my foot. He held my foot higher to take my big toe in his mouth. Nate sucked and I clenched the bedcovers in my fists. He stroked me once with his tongue before releasing it and moving his mouth to my ankle.

"Do you remember," Nate murmured against my skin as he moved his mouth farther down my leg, "the night you found me drunk?"

God, he was driving me crazy. "Yes," I breathed.

Nate massaged my calf as he kissed my shin. "Do you remember what I said I would do to you?"

My mind was spinning. I knew what he had said, but couldn't articulate it. All I could focus on was his lips.

He nipped my knee with his teeth. Nate released his hold on my ankle and moved his hands to my inner thighs. He spread my legs fully. "I said I would devour you whole." Nate dropped his head and ran his nose along the crease of my thigh. "I'm going to know every inch of you, Jo."

My eyes rolled back as I felt him closer. "Is that a promise?" I asked, panting.

He chuckled and his breath fanned my slit. "No. A promise can be broken. That was a guarantee." He closed the tiny distance between my body and his mouth. Nate speared my cleft with his tongue, working me into a frenzy in a quick few seconds.

My back arched off the bed and I clutched at him as he pulled away. "Fuck, Nate," I cried, at the point of begging him to finish me.

"I'll make you come with just my mouth one day. But tonight you're going to have my cock first." Nate continued his slow exploration of my body, his mouth drifting over my hips and stomach. When he reached my breasts he nuzzled one, and my nipples hardened to taut nubs. Nate dragged his thumb over it as he moved higher still and sucked on the pulse hammering in my throat.

I lifted my hips underneath him. "There's nothing else to know. Christ, Nate, I feel like I'm dying."

Nate held himself above me, his warm-whiskey eyes searing into me. "There are a thousand more things to know." Holding his weight on one forearm, he traced my bottom lip. "I need to know what this sweet little mouth looks like as it's sliding up and down on my dick. I need to know what you look like on top of me. I need to know what it's like to have you come on my tongue. It feels like I've waited a lifetime for you. I want to gorge on your body, but I also want to it last forever."

I moaned and bit down on the thumb he slipped inside my mouth.

Nate pressed his forehead to mine. "I'll know all of it, Jo," he whispered. He flexed his hips and hissed as the tip of his hard-on met the silky wetness of my cunt.

"Nate," I said, unsure whether I was seeking reassurance or demanding to feel the rest of him.

He burrowed his face in the crook of my shoulder. "Fuck, Jo, I need to feel you, need to be inside you."

I arched my hips closer to him, another inch of his rock-hard shaft slipping into me. "Then get inside me, now, Nate."

Instead, infuriatingly, he shifted farther back and I wanted to scream with madness.

"I want feel everything, Jo. Can I?"

It took a moment for his meaning to sink into my lust-fogged brain. I nodded. "There hasn't been anyone in a long time. And I'm on the pill."

His grin was broad. Nate dipped to kiss me quick before gritting his teeth as he resumed his previous closeness. "I'm clean. I get tested regularly but usually use a condom. But fuck, Jo…"

I grasped his face and cut off his words with my mouth. "Just shut up, Nate, I'm dying."

With a groan he sheathed himself in me, filling me to the hilt. Every muscle in his body was corded and strained. I felt the power under his skin, and marveled at the brutal restraint he showed in not fucking me into a different person, some primitive beast that only communicated in feral actions.

I cried out, shocked from the fullness, both needing more and relief all at once. My body stretched for him to the point of pain and I still wanted, needed, more. For a moment he didn't move. We were locked together in the most intimate way two people could be. I touched his hard chest and felt his heart beating as furiously as my own was.

He pulled out to his tip, and I clung to him, desperate to be closer, to feel him back inside. Nate slowly buried deep in my cleft. He found my lips and fucked my mouth with his tongue as he rolled his hips and slammed into me again.

I raised my pelvis to meet his thrusts with beautiful friction, digging my nails into his firm backside and urged him faster, harder. "Please…"

"What, Jo? What do you want?" Nate asked, his voice husky as he growled in my ear.

Our bodies were slick with sweat, the air heavy with the sounds of our purely raw sex.

"Come. Make me come. Hard."

He grasped my leg and flung it over his shoulder. I gasped as he pushed farther inside me. With each thrust he hit that sweet spot and I was a ticking time bomb. Nate gritted his teeth and increased his speed, fucking me harder.

"Fuck, Jo, you feel incredible. So fucking tight," Nate grunted.

"Nate!" I shuddered around him, release perilously close. My core was greedy for everything he could give, and as my orgasm burst forth like an atomic explosion, Nate refused to give even one second of relief. Only when I was fully spent did his strong body go taut and he let himself finish with one final, powerful thrust.

A sob caught in my throat and I panted, unable to catch my breath. My entire body trembled. I'd never had anything like that before. Never.

Nate's breathing was as labored as mine. He kissed my shoulder, still inside me.

As I lay there with his comforting weight on top of me, our scents mingling together, all I could think about was Kate.

How on earth had that woman given up this man?

* * * *

I reclined on the chaise longue, staring out over the city. I wore Nate's discarded shirt, the scent of him wrapping itself around me like a blanket.

Nate appeared at the top of the stairs, nude and without a care in the world. He handed me a glass of water and as I sat up to take it, he slipped in behind me, guiding me back so I rested against his chest.

"Do you spend a lot of nights like this?" I asked, teasing.

His chest moved with his chuckle. "What—with a beautiful woman between my legs, or lying here looking at the view?"

"Either."

"This is the first time I've ever sat on it."

I giggled. "And how are you enjoying it?"

His hand slid inside the shirt and palmed my breast. "A lot."

My smile widened. "So why do you have it if you don't use it? You don't strike me as the kind of man who likes pointless decoration."

"I'm not. It was a gift from Suze. *She* is very fond of pointless decoration."

I shifted against his chest, feeling his impressive cock thicken against me. Nate made a low, tortured sound deep in his throat and I felt the reverberations down my back. He teased my nipple, hardening it to a point until I squirmed.

"I never sent her a thank-you note. She's getting one tomorrow."

I laughed breathily and pressed firmer against him, my head tipping back as he turned me painfully on. "So how did it go tonight? From where I was sitting, it seemed to go well. Though I don't know much about how business is done socially."

Nate's other hand whispered over my skin, heading south. "It went as well as could be expected. With much thanks to you."

I twisted around slightly, looking up at his face. "What do you mean?"

"Underhill. He couldn't take his eyes off you. Didn't you notice?"

"I was more preoccupied looking at you."

Nate didn't smile cockily like I expected him to. His fingers sank into the sensitive flesh of my cleft, making me gasp and involuntarily widen my legs for him. "Fuck, babe, you're so wet for me."

My breath came in little pants and I moved against his hand.

"Why do you think I stopped touching you under the table?" Nate asked, slipping another finger inside.

I bit down on my lip. "Um, because we were in a public place?" I cried out and grasped his thighs.

He pressed down on my clitoris, and I jerked. "Because he didn't have any right to see you like this. See how your face gets this soft glow that makes me want to fuck you even harder next time, just to see if the look gets any better."

I grabbed his arm, nails scratching his skin as he increased the speed and pressure of his fingers.

"He offered me the job." Nate's other hand kept teasing my nipple making my breasts ache for his touch. "And I told him to find someone else."

My mouth fell into an 'o' of surprise and stayed there as my orgasm built. My head fell against his shoulder, my breath coming in pants as he worked me with expert fingers. "Why?" I asked in a rush, the word breaking off into a moan as he used the heel of his hand to circle my clit.

"He would use any excuse to be around you. Invite us to dinner, to the theater…anything. And I would be obligated to keep him happy. And every time he so much as looked at you, I would want to rip his eyes from their sockets." Nate bit down on my shoulder, and I cried out as my release ripped through my body.

Still gasping and with the after-effects of his fingers making my body feel like a thousand raw, exposed nerves, I swiveled around to face him. I moved onto his lap and Nate didn't take his eyes off my face as I sank down onto the long, hard length of his erection.

He swallowed and grasped my hips. A noise lodged in my throat as I rocked, taking a second to get used to the feel of him, so full inside me. Before Nate, no man had penetrated my depths so fiercely.

Nate pushed his hips up to meet me and my throat felt raw from the cries ripping from it. I increased my speed and rode him harder. Nate matched my rhythm. He knotted his fingers in my hair and tugged my face to his. I pulled on his bottom lip with my teeth and he slammed into me in response.

I tipped my head back, knowing it wouldn't be long before I came undone. Nate took my breast in his mouth, teeth grazing over my nipple before he took it into his mouth. I clung to him, pounding faster and faster until my world exploded. Nate held my trembling body, only letting himself come when the last wave of my climax shuddered through me.

"Fuck, Jo," he whispered as I collapsed against him, his rising and falling chest moving me with it.

"What?" I breathed. I tasted the saltiness of his skin and licked up his throat.

His arms tightened around me. "I've no idea. But, fuck."

I smiled into his neck. "I know what you mean."

There had been nothing like this in my past. Nothing like Nate. I had never had such an intense orgasm and even though my body was exhausted and my mind all at once calm and full of racing thoughts, all I wanted to do was get him hard and ride him again. All night. In every way we could.

Nate could become my addiction and I would need my fix. Every day. Every night. Every moment.

* * * *

I felt tiny and delicate in Nate's sprawling bed. He dozed on his side, his hand firm on my hip. But no matter how hard I tried, I couldn't relax enough to fall asleep. After Nate had carried me to his bed and stroked his fingers over every part of my body, whispered filthy words, I was sated—full and confident and calm. Now in the darkness I felt the familiar fear creep in and without Nate's touch or his voice his bed turned into a strange, foreign place.

None of my protective items were up here. If I was found, I would be at the mercy of my instincts.

I couldn't stay here with him. If I stayed, by morning I would be a nervous wreck, twitching and jumping at every move. Easing out from under Nate's hand, I moved as carefully as I could to the edge of the bed. My feet had just met the floor when his hand shot out and encircled my wrist.

"What are you doing?" Nate asked, his voice groggy.

"I can't sleep. I was going downstairs so I didn't disturb you."

"Woman, you have absolutely wrecked me. How are you not tired?" he mumbled into his pillow.

"I am tired. I just can't sleep."

Nate pulled and I fell back into bed with him. He raised himself above me. Even with a sleepy haze clouding his eyes, they were sharp and observing. Nate rubbed at the skin under my eyes and I could only imagine how exhausted I looked.

"I haven't taken care of you properly, have I?" A smile pulled at one corner of his mouth. "I got greedy and enjoyed you taking what you wanted from me."

"You took care of me, Nate. More than you know."

He dipped his head and ran his nose up the length of my throat. "I'm going to fuck you again, Jo. Long, gentle and soft."

Words I would have not have associated with Nate. He wasn't a brutal man by any means, but neither was he gentle or soft. But when he slowly eased inside me again and moved with slow, sure movements, I knew what he meant.

Nate could comfort me with his body far more efficiently than any words could. He kissed me, his tongue giving me long, languorous strokes, and I sighed into his mouth. My release was a slow-burner, not as intense as before. All-consuming passion and pleasure wasn't the point this time.

He rolled us onto our sides and pulled my leg over his hip, still rocking into me. He pulled me close and held me there. I pushed my face into his chest, the beating of his heart soothing and constant.

More often than not, contact with another person made me jittery and uneasy. I couldn't stand to be restrained in anyway, yet here, in the steel fortress of Nate's hold, I had never felt safer. His body locked in and around mine and I happily threw away the key. My body grew limp and languid and a faraway part of me realized that Nate was fucking me to sleep.

Chapter Ten

Soft morning light filled the room, coaxing me awake. Stretching out, I realized I was alone in Nate's bed. My limbs were stiff and the dull ache between my legs made me smile.

The TVs on the wall were both on, tuned into different news channels, subtitles on, no sound. A door opened and Nate appeared, a mist of steam billowing behind him. A navy blue towel hung on his lean hips and he rubbed at his hair with another towel.

"Morning," he said with a smile when he saw I was awake.

"Is that what this is?" I asked through a yawn. "Feels like dawn."

"Little after." He sat on the edge of the bed and twisted around to kiss me. He tasted fresh and minty, the smell of his body wash spicy and delicious. "It's almost six-thirty."

I groaned and made myself sit up. "If I'd known you were an early bird, I may have reconsidered this."

Nate grinned. "Would it make a difference if I made you a coffee?"

"Maybe."

"It's on the nightstand." Sure enough, there was a steaming mug of coffee where he'd said there was. The man had thought of everything.

Nate handed me the mug and I smiled as I inhaled the rich scent. "Good to know you're so easily pleased."

I gave him a look over the mug. "I think you proved that last night."

"I do my best." Nate stood and dropped the towel, a grin spreading across his face when he saw a certain part of him had my full attention. "Keep looking at me like that, and you are going to make me very, *very* late."

Placing the mug back on the nightstand, I raised up on my knees and reached for him. He leaned into me, slowly, teasing. Just before his lips made contact, he gripped the back of my thighs and pulled my legs out from under me.

I let out a startled laugh and he was above me, pushing into me and laughter was the last thing on my mind.

Nate was very, *very* late that morning.

* * * *

Suze called round later in the day, grinning and chattering nonstop. She was distracted enough by her own love life that she didn't notice the goofy smile on my own face or the careful way I sat down.

"Have you introduced Tilly yet?" I asked.

Suze shook her head. "Nope. I don't want to rush it. I mean, we're having fun right now. But I'm not going to shove a new man into Tilly's life until I'm sure he'll stick around. Mitch keeps asking about her, not pushing the issue but showing he's interested. Even offered to set up a playdate with his nephew at the soft play center so there isn't so much pressure."

"That's a good sign then."

"Yeah, I hope so." Suze sighed. "I'm just trying so hard not to get my hopes up. It's been ages since I've really liked someone and this guy...he's pretty bloody perfect. Says all the right things, compliments me, really listens when I tell him stuff. And the sex. Christ, Jo, no one ever told me it could be like that. I had no idea."

My face warmed and I focused on the picture I was coloring with Tilly. "Mmm."

"Sorry, I keep going on about him, don't I? God, I must be boring you."

I smiled. "Not in the least, Suze."

"I'm so glad you moved in here. Nate finally met a girl I get on with."

"You remember I'm his tenant, not his girlfriend?"

"For now, maybe."

My stomach dropped. "That can't ever happen, Suze."

"Don't be daft. Of course it can. He can't keep his bloody eyes off you half the time. And you blush whenever I mention him, so you can't say you don't fancy him back."

"It's not about attraction." I let out a breath. "I just don't want to be involved. With anyone, not just Nate."

Suze sighed. "You're lucky I like you, because you're so bloody weird."

I forced a smile. "I know."

"What are you up to tonight, then? Working?"

"Eight till two."

"How do you do it? I'd be flat out asleep under the bar."

"It's easy when you get your body into it."

"When is your next night off? I want a girls' night out."

"Monday."

"Date?"

I looked at her, trying to remember my reasons for keeping people like Suze at a distance. "Date."

* * * *

Getting ready for a girls' night felt peculiar with an odd sense of déjà vu. Almost like muscle memory, where I could remember when it was part of my normal life but was so far removed from where I was now that it was like watching a movie.

Sitting in front of the dressing table in my bathroom, I brushed on a coat of mascara and some clear gloss. I dressed in a pair of leggings, a long, floaty top and the shoes Nate had given to me.

"And suddenly it all makes sense."

I looked in the mirror and saw Nate leaning against the bathroom doorframe. "What does?"

"My sister begged me to watch Tilly for her tonight. She said it was important and I thought she was off out with her new bloke again."

"Nope. I'm her hot date for the night."

He wandered into the room, holding the back of my chair. "Is it weird that I am completely, insanely jealous of my sister right now?"

I shrugged. "Maybe?"

"Where are you two going?"

"I've no idea. I think we're getting some food, maybe a drink or two." Putting the few makeup products I owned back into their drawer, I stood up and faced Nate.

His eyes trailed leisurely over me. "You look gorgeous."

"I wouldn't go that far."

He grinned. "I would."

I rested against the table. "You sound like you want something."

Nate moved closer. "I always want something when it comes to you."

"You're insatiable."

"You're irresistible."

"You're greedy."

"You're delicious." Nate moved between my legs, hands on either side of my hips. "I've been hard all day thinking about you."

I smiled and he rubbed against me, proving his words true.

"You've no idea how difficult it was to leave you in bed this morning."

"You could have woken me."

He lowered his head, mouth giving me tiny, pulling kisses that left me aching for more. "You looked too peaceful to disturb. And if I had woken you, I doubt I would have ever left."

I licked the seam of his lips, sliding my tongue inside when they parted. Nate lifted me so I sat on the edge of the table, crushing his body hard against mine.

"When will Suze be here?" he whispered.

I moaned and unbuttoned his jeans, his heavy erection falling into my palm. "Soon."

He growled and flexed his hips into my grip. His cock was so hard it must have been painful. Nate was flushed and rigid in my hand, and I stroked down his length, his skin soft, smooth like velvet covered steel. He took control of the kiss, thrusting his tongue into my mouth, taking complete ownership of me. I pumped him harder, faster.

Nate trapped my bottom lip between his teeth as he came, hot, thick semen spurting over my wrist.

"When will you be back tonight?" he asked, his voice gruff and low and achingly intimate.

"I don't know."

"Find me when you are."

Chapter Eleven

Suze took me to a stylish Indian restaurant, ordering us each a cocktail when we sat at our table. She surprised me by whipping her phone out and taking a picture of the drink.

"What are you doing?" I asked.

Suze didn't take her eyes from the small screen. "Tweeting."

I blinked. "What-ing?"

"Tweeting. You've never heard of Twitter?" Suze's eyebrows shot into her hairline.

Crikey, it's not like I'd said I had no idea who Chris Hemsworth was—which would have been really weird. "Oh, the social media site? Yeah, I've heard of it."

"But you're not on it?"

My hand twitched. "I'm not on any. I hate social media."

Suze looked at me as though I'd said I enjoyed dipping babies in molten lava in my spare time. "How can you *hate* social media? It keeps you connected with the rest of the world!"

I shrugged. "I don't want to be connected."

"But—you...*really*?" She spluttered. "God, I love it. Facebook, Twitter, Instagram, Pinterest, Tumblr...you really don't like any of these?"

"Call me old fashioned, but I don't like strangers knowing my business."

"I'd go mad without half of it. After Tilly, most of the people I talked to were online." Her eyes flickered to me, uncertain.

"I'm not judging, Suze. If you like all that stuff, great. It's just not for me, that's all." It's not as though I could tell her why I really hated those sites.

Suze shrugged and lifted her phone, snapping a picture of me.

I glared at her.

"What? You look gorge tonight." She leaned into me and held her phone above us. "Smile for a selfie!"

I didn't smile.

"Tilly loves looking through my photos. She'll love seeing her Auntie Jo."

A waiter appeared and took our order, my heart skipping a beat at Suze's use of the familial word again.

"Guess who I bumped into yesterday," Suze said when our plates were cleared away.

I sat back in my seat, stuffed and happy. "Who?"

"Kate."

My eyebrows lifted. "And?"

Suze smiled. "She was all lovey-dovey with me, waxing poetic about how much she missed me and Tilly. Yeah, right. She was sick on her once, when she was tiny. Kate never went near her again."

I snorted a laugh. Tilly was my kind of girl.

"Anyway, she starts on about how she's *so* worried about Nate because of this new woman he's seeing.

You know, this thin, stunning, dark-haired beauty who works in a bar." Suze gave me a smug look. "What was it you were saying the other day? Something about how you could never go there…?"

I groaned. "God, Suze, really? One night Kate appears at my work, telling me that she's there to find out who her fiancé is sleeping with."

Suze scowled. "She's a fucking nutter, I'm telling you. Go on."

"In a weird coincidence, Nate had happened to be in the area that night and was going to offer to share a taxi home. I pretended to be his girlfriend to do him a favor. Nothing more, nothing less. He'll be pleased to hear we were convincing, though."

She laughed. "You were more than convincing. I thought her head was going to blow off when she was talking about the two of you. She said you were vulgar and a glorified porn star."

"Yeah, well, I hate girls like that. She gives all women a bad name. Wants her cake and eats it, too. Selfish bitch. I laid it on thick and as far as I know, she's backed off Nate."

Suze sat back. "You sound a little territorial there, Jo."

"You're reading too much into things again, Suze."

She laughed again. "Maybe. Can't blame a girl for hoping."

After dinner we walked to the Mile, Suze knowing a few places with good atmosphere. She took me to a trendy club with loud music and pretty young things. As we pushed our way to the bar, she had her phone in her hand again.

"What are you doing now?" I shouted over the pulsing music.

"Checking in!"

"Do I want to know?"

She shrugged and went back to the screen.

I ordered us a couple of a vodka and lemonades then found a recently vacated tall table. Just as I slid onto the stool, Suze's phone lit up.

"It's Mitch, do you mind if I answer it?"

I waved her away and she disappeared into the crowd. Almost the second she was out of sight, someone was in her place. A tall blond with a cocky smile and way too much aftershave.

"Having a good night?" he asked.

I shrugged and sipped my drink.

"Aw, come on, beautiful. You going cold on me?" he asked, moving around the table so he was right beside me.

"Nope. Was never warm to start with," I tossed over my shoulder.

He laughed. "No need to be like that. Can I buy you a drink?"

"No."

"You're a challenge. I like that."

"I'm not a challenge. I'm a fucking impossibility. Go chat up someone who cares." I waved my hand to shoo him away.

Thankfully Suze reappeared and threw an arm around my shoulder. "Bothering my friend?"

"Banging my head off a brick wall, more like," he mumbled before wisely slinking off.

"God, you don't let them down easy, do you?" Suze asked with a laugh.

I shrugged. "What did Mitch want?"

"He's out tonight and wondered if we wanted to meet up with him and his friend. I'm glad I said no, now. Can't have him think my best friend is feral."

The smile fell flat off my face. "I'm your best friend?"

Suze rolled her eyes. "I see you more than anyone else. I tell you everything. You're fab with my daughter and know how to manage my brother. Of course you're my best friend. Yeah you're a bit of a weirdo sometimes, but it only makes you more charming."

I laughed and elbowed her. "Should I be offended or not at that?"

She grinned. "I'll decide later."

We hit four other bars that night. I let Suze buy me a few drinks, stopping when I felt them affecting me. Suze, on the other hand, didn't. By one she was tipsy. By two she was sloppy. I started swapping her drinks for plain lemonade, not feeling like holding anyone's hair back for them.

It took forever to persuade her to leave the last bar. Suze on alcohol was like Suze magnified. She was friendlier, louder and chattier. And no one was safe. A trip to the toilet took twenty minutes since she got a life story each time she went. She chewed the ear off anyone unfortunate enough to be beside us at the bar.

I finally wrangled her into a taxi, giving the driver Nate's address. At the house, she hung off my neck, damn near strangling me. She giggled and whispered that she loved me bestest, and I couldn't help but laugh with her.

As I tried to get my key in the door with Suze pulling me, she suddenly kissed my cheek, sending us into the railing.

"Warn me before you do that next time." I laughed.

Suze giggled and did it again. "I know I'm pissed but I mean it, all right? I do love you bestest. You're fucking awesome, Jo."

I sighed, unable to fight the smile. "At least you're a happy drunk, Suze."

This time I managed to unlock the door and Suze let go of me to stumble in the direction of the kitchen.

"Where are you going?" I whispered as loud as I dared when I heard the contents of the fridge rattle.

"I'm starving!" Suze shouted from the kitchen.

"You do realize what the time is, and your brother *and daughter* will be asleep?"

"Mmm hmm. Did you two eat that lasagna I made the other day?" Suze was crouched in front of the fridge, staring into the sparsity of it and looking for all the world like someone had kicked her puppy. She looked up at me with sad eyes. "I *told* you we should have stopped for a kebab."

"You told me that kebabs were dog food and craving one was a sure sign you were either a student or an alcoholic." I hooked my hands under her armpits and hauled her up. "And if I'm being honest, I can't be arsed listening to you moan at me tomorrow that I let you eat one."

"God, you're fucking mean." Suze pouted before brightening. "Let's phone for a takeaway!"

"Let's have a glass of water and go to bed."

She groaned and pulled away from me. "Do you think Mitch is still awake?"

I scrubbed my hand over my face. I was never getting to bed. "Oh, for fuck sake, Suze. Don't drunk dial."

"I'm fine! Honest!" Suze froze when there was a sound of feet on the stairs. She looked at me in horror. "Shit! You woke up Nate!"

"I did not! You did, you bloody harpy!"

Suze giggled again.

"Are you two pissed?" Nate asked, blinking at the light as he came into the kitchen. He was clad only in tight boxer briefs, his face rumpled with sleep.

"She is," Suze said, pointing at me.

Nate looked between us. "Yeah, looks it. Go to bed, Suze."

"God, you two are so boring." She poked her brother in the chest. "You need a shag. Might put you in a better mood."

"Right," he said, not looking at all amused.

Suze looked at me. "And you, as well. You could have had one tonight, as well. All those poor boys went home with broken hearts."

"What boys?" Nate asked.

Suze waved a finger in my direction. "This one had men all over her, but did she pay them any attention? Nope. Blue Ball Fairy, is our Jo."

Nate snorted a laugh and I glared at him.

Suze gave a heaving sigh. "I'm knackered now."

"Come on, Suze, I'll help you upstairs," I said, linking my arm with her.

She rested her head on my shoulder. "I told you you were lovely."

In the spare room Suze collapsed on the bed and I pulled her shoes off. She was snoring in seconds.

Nate lounged against the bannister, eyeing me as I came out of the room. "Suze had a good night then."

I laughed. "Yeah, I doubt she'll be smiling in the morning, though."

"It's nice you took care of her."

"Anyone else would have done the same," I said as I walked into my room.

"No, they wouldn't." Nate followed me inside.

"Where's Tilly?" I asked, heart picking up speed at his nearness.

"Upstairs." He pulled my top up over my head.

"What about Suze?" I whispered.

"What about her?" He slipped my leggings off.

"She's in the next room."

"Passed out cold." Bra hit the floor.

"She could wake up."

"Do you care?" Knickers followed.

I shook my head.

Nate shed his boxers and ushered me to the bed. Both of us ignoring the door that was wide open.

* * * *

Nate was curled around my body when I wriggled out of his embrace. "Where are you going?" he mumbled.

"I need to shower," I said, leaning over to kiss him.

He raised a sleepy eyebrow. "Do it in the morning. I'll have you again before then."

"I reek of the bar."

"I don't care."

"I do."

Nate groaned and rolled onto his back, freeing me from his arms. "Fine. Hurry up, then. I want that ass back in here in two minutes Use my one upstairs, it has better water pressure."

"God, you're demanding after you come." I smiled, walking around the bed.

He sat up. "I'm demanding when I want to come *again*."

I giggled and closed my bedroom door behind me, hurrying upstairs to Nate's bedroom. And Jesus Christ...I had thought my bathroom was beautiful. Nate's was easily twice the size of mine. Stunning marble walls and counter tops with gleaming chrome accessories and taps. Another freestanding bath and also an enormous shower with marbled seating ledge.

I turned the shower on and the water poured from a large rectangle shower head making it look like a sheet of rain. The temperature was hot, the pressure just the right side of painful.

The glass shower door opened and Nate stepped inside. My stomach quivered as he came closer. He cradled the back of my head and pulled me to him.

"Impatient?" I said into his mouth.

"I don't like to wait for the things I want." Nate lifted me and I wrapped my legs around his waist.

He pressed me into the shower wall, my fevered skin contracting from hitting the cold tiles. I felt his hard-on at my folds a heartbeat before he entered me, quick and hard and I was more than ready for him. Around Nate, my body seemed permanently primed, eager to accept him inside me.

His mouth slammed over mine as though he was claiming it and marking his territory. Nate's tongue plunged inside, massaging mine in a lush, wet kiss. I caught him between my teeth and he growled my name.

"It's such a fucking turn on, how much you like what I give you," Nate said in my ear, his rough, low voice sending vibrations down my spine.

I cried out and squeezed my inner muscles, milking him. "So give me more," I moaned.

He grunted and pounded into me, using my hips to meet his thrusts. The water rained over us as Nate rolled his pelvis and brought me to the brink of ecstasy. I wrapped my arms around his broad shoulders, one hand fisting in his short, dark hair. I screamed his name and it spurred him on. As he threw his head back he gritted his teeth and somehow fucked me harder.

"Give it up for me, Jo. Let me see you come." His eyes locked on mine.

The unrestrained heat in his stare pushed me over the edge. I held his stare as the climax rippled through me. Once he had drunk in every last drop of it, he rocked into me with one last, dominant thrust. Nate held me there, pinned to the wall with his hips.

Then he pressed a breathless kiss to my mouth and set my feet back on the ground and I felt my knees shake.

He reached for his body wash and squeezed some into his palm.

Then Nate started to clean my body. He stroked his hands all over me, planting delicate kisses along the way. His touch wasn't blatantly sexual the way that it more often than not usually was, but it was sensual...caring. I felt worshiped and treasured.

He turned off the shower and wrapped me in a huge, fluffy bath towel, patting me dry. Nate led me back to his bed and slid between the sheets behind me, pulling me into the safety of his body with my back to his chest. His arms locked around me, one hand clamped over my breast the other around my waist.

Nate pushed his face into my hair and just like that, he was asleep. And with a tiny smile I burrowed deeper into his embrace. The scent of him rose up from his pillow. Smothering myself in his essence, I let myself drift off to sleep.

Chapter Twelve

The bacon and sausages spat and crackled in the pan, the kitchen warm and smelling delicious. I tore an extra strip of crispy bacon into small pieces and put them at the bottom of the garden. Sure enough, after a few moments, the skinny ginger cat appeared and ate the lot.

I poured a mug of strong coffee and finished up the last of the fry up. Nate wandered into the kitchen as I was turning the hobs off and wrapped his arms around my waist, kissing my shoulder.

"Fucking hell, a man could get used to this."

"He could. If it was for him."

He groaned. "Is this for Suze?"

"Yep. She'll be hanging today." Pulling out of his hold, I got him a coffee and sat at the island.

"You must have gotten up early. I didn't like waking up to find you gone," Nate said, spinning my stool around so I faced him. He placed his hands either side of me.

I took a breath, getting nothing but Nate. He was everywhere—in my space, my head, seeping out of my pores. Nate leaned into me, pressing his forehead against mine. "You're doing crazy things to me, Jo."

I swallowed. "It's the endorphins."

He chuckled and grazed my mouth. "I doubt."

With a small cry I pulled him into a hard kiss, tired of the distance. He cradled my head and kissed me deeper. I pressed my body into his, feeling him everywhere.

"One day," Nate husked, "I'm going to fuck you on this table. Taste every inch of you."

My head swam. I was dizzy with him, with this wanting that never seemed to fade.

A creak on the stairs had me ducking under Nate's arm and hurrying to get a plate ready. Suze appeared, hair poking up every which way and an unhealthy gray pallor to her cheeks.

"Is there coffee?" she whispered.

"Yeah, sit down. I've got some breakfast here for you."

"Good. Hell. I don't know." Suze sighed, her eyes watery. "So, I thought friends don't let friends drink dial?"

I frowned and started dishing up her food. "You never rang anyone. You tried to ring your man when we got back here but I didn't let you."

"Well, you should know me better, shouldn't you? I must have woke up still pissed in the night and decided to bloody phone Mitch. Can't remember much of what I said, but it went along the lines of telling him to come round and then blowing up when he wouldn't. There was a text from him this morning with my marching orders."

"Oh, Suze, you tit."

She huffed at me, and I couldn't help but laugh. "Your concern is touching, Jo, really."

"What do you want me to say? If someone phoned me at five in the morning demanding I went round to his house and then went mental when I said no, I'd dump them too."

"He was such a good shag as well." Suze slumped over the island, lifting her head when I put a loaded plate of greasy goodness in front of her. She sniffed and rushed from the room. "God. I'll be back in a sec."

When I turned to face Nate and saw the angry clench of his jaw, the air around us turned heavy. He shoved a hand into his hair, his body tense. It was only then I realized what I had done...how I'd unintentionally hurt him.

"You don't want my sister to know about us?"

"She wouldn't understand," I said, looking away from him.

"What the fuck is there to understand, Jo?" Nate asked, his voice not raising but the tone far angrier than I'd ever heard. "We're adults. It's not a crime and we're not doing anything wrong."

"I know. But Suze...she would think it meant something different." My heart sank but I forced myself to keep a neutral expression.

Nate moved to stand in front of me, forcing me to look at him. His eyebrows pinched together. "And what the hell does that mean?"

I sighed. "Come on, Nate. You know what she's like. Everyone has to be happy and riding off into the sunset together."

"I'm sorry, Jo, but I really don't have a clue what you're getting at."

I sighed. "Suze would see a relationship when really we're only—"

"What? *Fucking*?"

Steeling myself, I met his eyes, unflinching. "Yes."

His entire body hardened. "Right. And just so we're clear here, since it seems we've been on two totally different pages, you're quite happy for me to make you come, just so long as Suze doesn't know about it?"

"It's not about keeping it a secret. She just wouldn't understand."

"You're not giving her the opportunity to."

"Why are we arguing about this?" I threw my hands up. "Christ, Nate, what did you think was going on? That one of these days I'd move my stuff upstairs and we'd be a happy little couple? You're my landlord and I enjoy having sex with you. A lot. But I'm not here for the long-term. I never was. You've just come out of an engagement for God's sake! Why would you want anything serious?"

Nate took a step back. "I don't. And quite frankly, this is why I never wanted anything to happen with us. Women can't help but get emotional."

I laughed. "Me get emotional? You're the one pouting because I didn't want Suze to see you mauling me!"

He let out a breath and gave me a tight smile. "Right, well, as lovely as this morning has been, I have a job to be getting too. I'll see you later. You know, if you fancy a shag and my sister isn't around."

The second he was out of sight my body slumped as the adrenaline fled from my veins. Where had that fight come from? And really, what was it about? I could deny all I wanted that I had feelings for Nate. It was impossible to give yourself to someone the way that I did with Nate without feeling *something* for them. It was one thing to start a physical relationship with him, but I couldn't—wouldn't—let it cloud my head.

If I was smart, I would leave now, right this second — pack my bags and never look back. They would all be better off without me in their lives. For a while they would talk, would wonder why I'd left. Maybe once or twice in the future their thoughts would stray to the odd girl who'd once lived in Nate's house for a few months — wonder where she was, why she left.

If I was smart I would leave.

So why wasn't I?

* * * *

I picked up extra evening shifts behind the bar, running myself ragged and exhausted. After that Tuesday morning and the subsequent argument with Nate, I spent as little time in the house as was possible. I tiptoed up to my room and held my breath when I heard him bound down the stairs early in the morning.

Maybe he was avoiding me too. Every time I opened my bedroom door, I expected to see an envelope on the plush carpet holding my eviction notice. But so far, nothing.

Suze, on the other hand, didn't take my absence half as well as her brother. The few times I was at home, I heard her banging on the door and leaning on the doorbell. The house phone rang and rang and rang. Guilt chewed at me but I told myself it was for the best. If I distanced myself now then maybe it wouldn't be so hard when I did leave.

When Suze did eventually catch up with me, two weeks after our date night, the first thing she did was give me a hefty whack on the arm with her handbag.

"Christ, Suze, what was that for?"

"I've been worried sick! Where have you been?" She geared back for another whack and I jumped out of the way. Tilly clapped in her pushchair, watching her mother chase me around.

"Working! Jesus!"

"You couldn't have rung me? I've been round here every bloody day looking for you!"

"Okay, okay, I'm sorry, all right?" I held my hands up.

She looked me over. "Okay. But you have to go for lunch with me and tell me the real reason you dropped off the face of the earth."

I sighed dramatically and looked to the heavens. "Seriously, I've been working. No ulterior motive, nothing sinister."

"Right." Suze took told of the pushchair and walked down the street. "And if that is true, what about Nate?"

My heart stopped. "What about Nate?"

"He spent the night with Kate."

I stopped walking, my stomach dropping. "He what?"

Suze carried on, glancing back at me. "He didn't really. But your reaction was spot on, so thanks for that."

"*What*?" I rushed to catch up with her.

"Why didn't you tell me something was going on with you two? Did you think I'd mind?" Her eyebrows knitted together, her eyes holding a pinch of hurt.

"No, Suze...Christ." I huffed out a breath. "Anyway, I doubt anything is happening now."

"You want to sort that out, because Kate has been sniffing about again and whatever kicked off with you and Nate has him looking like a pissed off, wounded puppy and she's saying all the right things to make him roll over." Her eyes swept over me as though I alone had the power to prevent her brother from falling into the clutches of Medusa.

"You need some better metaphors, because that was seriously creepy."

She sighed. "I'm being serious, Jo. Okay, on one hand I'm really happy that you two got together but on the other I'm pissed off you felt you couldn't tell me. And if it is all over you might want to rethink a few things because I doubt either of us want to see that witch get her hooks into Nate again."

"I didn't tell you because I didn't think you'd want to hear I was only sleeping with him. We aren't having a relationship, Suze. We're having sex. That's it. No ties, no commitment. He's free to do whatever he wants, *whoever* he wants. And if that means Kate, then that's fine."

"Oh you dirty little liar!" Suze exclaimed. "You looked as though I'd kicked you in the stomach when I said he'd spent the night with Kate. You might not be having a relationship but you bloody well care if he's sleeping with someone else."

"This is exactly why I didn't want you to know!" I kicked at the pavement. "I don't need this, Suze. I really don't."

She stopped walking outside a bistro that my manager always said was ripping off her ideas. "Hard as this is for me to say…okay. I'll stop going on about it. I just think you two would make an *amazing* couple. But if right now you want to keep things casual, fine. I can accept that. But just know that I'm here if you need to talk or whatever. And if he goes anywhere near Kate, I'll scalp you, okay?"

I sighed and pushed open the door, holding it for Suze as she clattered the wheels of the pushchair off the doorframe. "He's a free man, Suze."

She gave me a small smile. "No, Jo. He isn't."

* * * *

After lunch we had a little walk around, mooching about Old Town. Suze paused in front of a building. "Oh, I forgot I need to pop in here for a sec. You okay to come in?"

I shrugged. "Sure."

We took the elevator and got out on the third floor. A glossy receptionist smiled at us and got up to hug Suze.

The office was mostly open plan, large desks with complex computer setups to the left of the receptionist's area. A few closed doors were to the right, as well as what looked like a large and bright conference room.

"Is he free?" Suze asked.

"As a bird—for now at least. You know what he's like."

Suze smiled wider at me and turned to the right, knocking once on a closed door at the end of a corridor.

"Oh you sneaky, sneaky, cow," I hissed at her back.

She waved her hand at me and opened the door. Nate's office was a sprawling mass of light and dominance. He sat behind a solid oak desk, a phone to his ear and his feet propped up on the desk. The window behind him showed beautiful views of the city, just like his home. Two walls were lined with bookshelves, the whole thing looking as though one more item and it would buckle under the weight. Suze closed the door and plonked herself on the couch, letting Tilly out of her pushchair.

I hovered like an awkward extra, unsure where to put myself or whether I should flee whilst I still could.

Suze tugged on my hand and I fell onto the couch beside her. Tilly darted to the side and re-emerged with a car in one hand and a book in the other. She crawled up between us, driving the car up and down my leg.

Nate hung up the phone and stood up. "To what do I owe this unexpected visit?"

"We just had lunch and thought we'd bring you some."

His eyes flickered to mine before darting back to Suze. "Did you?"

She reached into the basket of the pushchair and produced a white paper bag. "Chicken, bacon, mozzarella and pesto baguette."

When did she buy that? God, the woman was like a ninja or something.

His face softened and took the bag from her. "Thanks, Suze."

"Don't thank me. It was Jo's idea. She's never seen your office, Nate. Show her about will you? I need to dash off. Tilly has a swimming lesson soon." And as quick as I could blink, Tilly was strapped in and they were both out of the door.

"My sister is a master manipulator and hopeless matchmaker. I apologize." Nate took his place behind his desk once again, creating a firm barrier between us.

"No need. I've known her long enough now I should have really suspected it. Her heart's in the right place." I got up from the couch and walked slowly to his desk. "I feel like I should —"

He held his hand up. "Don't, Jo. There's no need."

"Not one for clearing the air?" Feeling bold, I moved to his side of the desk and perched on the edge.

"Not one for rehashing arguments."

"It should never have been an argument."

"No, it shouldn't have." He let out a breath. "And it was my fault anyway, so you can stop avoiding me at home. We never talked about what we expected from each other. Maybe the lines blurred because we live together. Or maybe you shagged all the sense out of me. Who knows."

I let out a startled laugh.

He smiled and just like that, my heart faltered. I could avoid him all I wanted, not lay eyes on him for days, weeks, months...the instant I was back in his presence I would crave him. I doubted the feeling would ever leave.

"And Suze knows. She tricked it out of me earlier."

Nate's lips twitched. "She's good at that."

"Yeah, she is." I gave him a smile. "Well, I'd best be off. Let you eat your lunch."

He caught my hand. "Wait, why don't you stay for a bit?"

"Aren't you busy?"

Nate stood up, overwhelming me with his body. "Not for you."

I pressed a hand to his firm chest. "Nate, this isn't a good idea."

"What's done is done, Jo. You can't take back what's already happened." Nate cupped my cheek.

I squeezed my eyes shut, ignoring the flutter in my chest from his gesture. "I'm not trying to...but don't you think things are complicated enough?"

"I don't understand you. I really don't. I've never met a woman like you, Jo. The women I meet are desperate to get some kind of claim to me, tie me down, get me to commit. And you..." He chuckled, his breath warming my cheek. "You worry I'm too attached and are terrified I'll try to settle down with you."

"This isn't a joke," I whispered.

"God, believe me. I know that." He moved closer to me. "I'll take you however you'll give yourself. You want casual? I'll be casual. You want me to pretend I'm seeing other women? Done. But I only see *you*."

"I'll leave. One day I'll leave." He had to know that wasn't an idle threat.

"One day I'll let you. Not today." And with that he kissed me.

Chapter Thirteen

Even though I was no longer avoiding Nate, it was still a few days after his office that we saw each other again. I had come back inside from leaving a little food out for the ginger cat that was slowly fattening up when he entered the kitchen, shrugging out of his hoodie.

"Off out?" he asked, taking in my workout clothes.

"Though I'd go for a run then swim."

"Want some company?"

I smiled. "Sure."

Nate kissed my cheek. "Give me a minute to change."

We chatted on the short walk to the leisure center — for once, the atmosphere light. Nate took the running machine next to mine and I stared straight ahead, sure I'd fall if I even glanced at him. He wore loose shorts and a sleeveless workout top, showing those arm muscles that banded around me making me feel protected and hot all at once.

"Do you come here a lot?" Nate asked after we both had worked up a sweat.

I shot him a smile. "Is that a chat-up line?"

He grinned at me. "No. And I didn't think I needed one."

"You know you don't. And yes, I suppose. A few times a week."

"Maybe I should come more often."

"Yeah. Because you look like you need it."

He laughed. "I'm beginning to think building up my stamina is never a bad thing where you're involved. Has anyone ever told you that you have a stunning appetite?"

I nearly fell off the machine. "Is that an insult?"

His smile was wolfish. "You'll never hear me complaining."

My face flushed and I slowed the machine down. "I'm going for a swim. Are you staying up here?"

Nate nodded, and I vanished to the changing room before he could make me burn alive, want to drag him to the nearest secluded area and show him just how starving I was.

* * * *

My arms and legs felt like lead weights when I pulled myself out of the pool. After stopping at my locker for my clothes, I headed for a changing cubicle. As I went to shut the door, a hand shot out and caught it before it could close. Nate slid inside, locking the door behind him.

He crushed my damp body to him, covering my mouth with his before I could utter a sound. Nate's tongue ravaged me and he shoved his hand into my bikini bottoms. His probing, expert fingers sank into the wet heat of my cunt. I was ready for him, aching for him and already felt myself coming.

Nate broke the kiss, breathing heavy. He spun me around, and I pulled the bottoms down, needing him in me *now*. I bent over and grasped the bench in front of me. Nate slammed his dick into me in a single, mind-blowing thrust.

My knuckles turned white from the force of my grip as he fucked me harder than ever before. I dropped my head as I orgasmed and Nate muffled my cries with his arm.

I came hard. Our sex was raw, the culmination of our fight and the length of time since he'd last been inside me. As the orgasm faded, he reached around and teased my clit. Nate increased his pace and he pounded into me, my whole body one giant, exposed nerve ending.

He came ferociously, so much it was enough to prompt a second orgasm. He kept my hips firm against his as the climax overtook my body and every part of me shook.

"I will *definitely* be coming here more often." Nate pulled my upper half back into him, grabbing my chin to turn my head and kiss me thoroughly.

"You'll never hear me complaining," I whispered into his mouth, still trembling.

* * * *

When we returned to the house later that afternoon, Tilly was reaping merry hell in the living room while Suze watched gleefully on.

"Is your daughter ever not going to destroy my house?" Nate asked, dropping down onto the couch.

"Maybe. One day. Don't hold your breath," Suze said with a grin.

"What do you want, anyway? Jo and I have plans. Upstairs. Or down here. Maybe everywhere." Nate winked at me, and I shook my head, unable to keep from smiling.

Suze huffed a sigh. "Lovely as that sounds, it'll have to be put off for a few hours. I'm stealing her."

"Oh really?" I asked, my eyebrows shooting up into my hairline. "Are you not even going to ask nicely?"

"Nope. Go get changed, dressy but casual. Sexy not slutty."

"Just what have you got in mind?" Nate asked, rising from the couch.

Suze shrugged with a coy smile. "I won't keep her out too long. I'm sure you and Tilly will be far too busy to miss us."

Nate laughed. "So not only are you stealing Jo, you're leaving me your demon child?"

"Sounds about right," Suze said before looking at me. "Hurry up, would you? I want to go in half an hour."

There really isn't much point in arguing, is there?

Nate followed me upstairs, watching me shower and get changed into jeans and a floaty green top. He gave me a look so heated that for a heartbeat I thought he would rip the clothes from my body and pin me to the bed, his willing prisoner. Instead, his face softened and he kissed me. Intimate but gentle. A promise of later.

And as Suze said her goodbyes to her daughter, he whispered in my ear all the ways he was going to make up for lost time.

It was a short walk to the coffee place Suze wanted to go to, and as she pulled open the door, she gave me a wide grin, her face more excited and animated than I'd seen it.

Three seconds later, I knew why. She'd dragged me to a bloody singles night. For the next two-and-a-half hours, I politely but firmly rejected all conversation or invitations...some of which were more blatant than others, and watched as Suze soaked up all the attention.

She spent the most time with a tall blond who had a dentist-perfect smile. Suze touched his arm and leaned into him, holding his eyes and laughing at his jokes.

As we walked back to Nate's, she told me all about him, waxing poetic about his eyes. Suze begged me to meet her the next afternoon to go shopping for an outfit to wear on her dinner date with Dan, who had the dentist-perfect smile.

* * * *

If Suze said I liked to bake my feelings, then these cupcakes would be lazy and sated, full and light all at once — dripping with decadence and sensuality. Spending the night with Nate after Suze and Tilly had finally left had my soul lighter than air. Before Nate, I never would have described myself as a sexual person, to the point where my mood reflected whether I was getting it or not. But I felt better when I was with Nate. The feeling followed me into the next day where I could still feel his hands on my body. All bad emotions or tension left me in his company. And I would be a fool not to realize it wasn't just the sex. Nate was good for me.

Once the cakes were iced to the point they should come with a health warning, I left a few under a glass dome for Nate and boxed the rest up. I was working the back shift when it was more bistro than bar and figured the staff room may welcome the desserts.

I was halfway through the shift when Claire, the owner, marched behind the bar, planting her hands on her hips.

"Right, who left those cupcakes in the staff room?"

Paul and I glanced at each other. What the hell had I put in them? Had I mistaken an ingredient and they were inedible? Shit.

"Me," I said, my stomach sinking.

"Made or bought?"

"Made."

"Can you make more for tomorrow? And a tray bake?"

Wait, what? I frowned. "You didn't hate them?"

Claire smiled. "I loved them! I'll pay you, of course. They're a damn sight better than the ones we have delivered from the bakery that cost an arm and a leg. So what do you say, will you be our official baker?"

An excited buzz replaced the dread in my stomach. "I'd love to."

I hit the supermarket on the way home that night to stock up on ingredients. When Nate returned home late that night, he found me putting the finishing touches on the cakes for the next day.

"I'm going to gain fifty stone if you keep this up," he said with a smile before greeting me with a kiss.

"Would it make you feel better if I said none were for you?"

His eyes widened. "What, not even one?"

"Maybe just one," I teased. I picked up a cake. "Will you be my taster?"

He raised an eyebrow. "Thought you'd never ask."

"Cake taster."

Nate sighed. "If I must. What kind is it?"

"White chocolate raspberry."

He took the cake and devoured half in a single bite. "Fuck me."

"Fuck me good or fuck me bad?"

Nate swallowed and pulled me into him, covering my mouth with his. "Fuck me *amazing*." He tasted delicious and I couldn't help but smile against his lips.

"They're serving them in the bistro tomorrow. Claire asked me to be the baker."

"Yeah?" Nate grinned. "Congratulations, Jo. Claire obviously knows a good thing when she sees it."

I shrugged. "It's nothing special, just a batch of cupcakes a few times a week."

"*You* are something special."

Truth be told, I felt it too. It had been a very long time since there had been anything I could feel proud of.

* * * *

A fist hammering on the front door ripped me from sleep. The sound echoed up the stairs and had my heart rate going through the roof. For a terrified moment I lay in bed, sure I'd imagined the sound.

But then it came again and a nauseous feeling crept up my throat. Reaching under my pillow with a shaking hand, I gripped the cool, smooth wood and held on for dear life. There was a lull in the banging and just as I began to breathe easier, it started again.

I jumped out of bed and shoved my feet into the ballet flats, bat in hand. The front door wasn't an escape option. I was too afraid to even go near it, let alone walk right past it to the back door. Rushing to the window, I weighed my options.

Just as I was considering making a leap of faith, footsteps thundered past my door.

Nate.

And suddenly it wasn't just about me anymore.

"Nate!" I shouted. Was that really my voice? Foreign and terrified. "Nate, stop!"

I ran out of my room and halfway down the stairs, grabbing him and nearly sending both of us sprawling to the bottom.

"Fuck, Jo." His voice thick with sleep. "It's okay."

I tried to pull him back up the stairs but he shook me off. "No, don't!"

Nate opened the door, and I nearly fainted with fear. I cowered in the dark, pressing into the wall as though it could absorb me. Any second now he would see me and drag me from Nate's safe and warm haven.

Hands gripped my forearms and I screamed, clawing at them to release me.

"Jo, *Jo!*" Nate gave me a little shake and it was enough to register that it was him. "It was just some pisshead. They're gone now."

I rested my head on my knees and grabbed at my hair.

"What the fuck," Nate whispered, pulling me to my feet. "Jo, what the fuck is wrong with you?"

A sob rose in my throat and he crushed me to him. Nate carried me into my room and lay with me on the bed. He tucked me into him, and I scrambled to get closer. He shushed me and wiped away the tears that refused to stop.

* * * *

It was light when I woke again. I lay in my warm bed and for a tiny moment I convinced myself I'd dreamt what had happened last night. Then I realized the warmth was coming from Nate and his arms were still locked around me.

My cheeks burned. Not only was I mortally embarrassed, but how on earth would I explain my behavior?

Nate stirred and his brown eyes focused on me. "Morning."

I managed a shaky smile.

He rolled me onto my back, nuzzling my throat. "There's something to be said about falling asleep with you." Nate stroked my leg and I hitched it over his hip. The tip of his erection met my wet folds and I arched my hips up to meet him.

Slowly, as though he was savoring the moment, he slid his thick erection inside until my cunt was filled with him, from root to tip. For a moment he didn't move. My body stretched to accommodate him and I whimpered at the sensation. Nate kissed me, his tongue gliding over mine. When he did begin to move inside me, Nate held my eyes through every second of it. He held me captive and by the time he was through with me every last smidge of darkness from the night before had been banished.

Whether it was because he knew I couldn't, or wouldn't, talk about what happened, or because he didn't want to know, Nate used the one thing he knew would comfort me. The only comfort I would tolerate.

* * * *

September had slipped into October and no one had warned me how quick the weather would change. Where once it had been stiflingly hot, now it was dull, overcast, wet and cold. Suze assured me autumn was nothing compared to full-blown winter and I would know what cold really was when it hit. At work I now wore long sleeves and even the crush of bodies on a Saturday night didn't warm the place like it used to.

One particular Saturday night, Suze bopped up and down at the bar. She waved when I spotted her and pushed her way in front of me, ignoring the irate looks she was thrown.

"Hey," she shouted over the music.

I smiled. "All right? Who are you out with?"

"Dan! We had dinner and I felt like coming to see you!" Suze had really hit it off with singles' night Dan—they had been seeing each other for the last few weeks.

Her excitement was infectious, and my smile spread. "Having a good time then?"

"Yeah, it's been brilliant. And Tilly's with my parents all weekend, so I get to have some morning sex!"

The guy beside her was suddenly very interested in the conversation.

"So where is he then?" I asked.

"Keeping our table. God, it's busy tonight, isn't it?"

I nodded. "I'm shattered. Can't wait to get home."

Her eyes glinted. "Is Nate waiting up for you?"

"Have I told you before just how creepy it is how interested you are in our sex life?"

Suze rolled her eyes. "All you two have is a sex life."

I leaned on the bar, my smile wide, and not caring my forearms would be sticky with beer. "And it's fucking amazing, Suze, seriously. He does this thing—"

"All right, all right!" she shouted, clamping her hands over her ears.

A long time ago I learned the only way to beat Suze was to smother her in details. Shooting her a triumphant smile, I mixed her usual drink. When I slid it across the bar to her, she was staring hard at something. I snapped my fingers in front of her nose. Suze jumped and looked at me.

"Have you seen who's here?" Suze asked.

"No, who?"

"Kate. I bet she's still bloody well stalking me on Twitter under a fake account." Suze shook her head. "She's always appearing where I am now, the weirdo. I think she's losing it."

I frowned. "Is she trying to use you to get at Nate?"

He hadn't mentioned Kate in a long time, but that didn't mean he hadn't heard from her.

"Yeah, probably. She should realize I'm the very last person to try that with. Does she seriously think she can win me over after what she did?"

I shrugged and saw Kate pushing her way through the crowd to us.

"Suze! Fancy meeting you here." Kate tried to pull Suze into a hug but would have more luck hugging Edinburgh Castle.

"Yeah, imagine that," she murmured.

Kate turned to me. "I'll have a dry white wine."

"I'm busy. You can ask one of the others."

She laughed. "Excuse me? Who do you think you are, talking me like that? I could have your job for that."

I shrugged. "Do I look like I give a shit?"

Kate looked at Suze. "Nice place this has turned into, isn't it?"

Suze rolled her eyes. "You're only acting like that because of who it is."

Kate looked me over. "And who is this?"

Suze laughed. "You know exactly who this is. Now piss off before I lose my temper."

Rob appeared at my side and took Kate's order. Suze gave me a little wave and disappeared back into the crowd. I thought I had seen the last of Kate for the night but like a bad smell, she lingered for too long.

"You know you won't ever be anything more to him than an easy shag, don't you?" Kate's voice drifted across the bar to me.

I gave her a look. "Kate, let me put this very plainly—I really couldn't care less about *anything* you have to say. Now fuck off away from my bar before I have you chucked out."

She smiled. "Feeling threatened? You should. I see him all the time, you know. Drop in at his office, go out for dinner...make love in his bed."

A laugh bubbled in my throat.

"You can laugh, but it's true. All those long, lonely nights when you're here and he's at home...but not alone."

"Go spread your poison somewhere else."

"I'll get him back. It's only a matter of time."

"Keep telling yourself that, sweetheart."

Kate gave me a smug smile that made me want to punch her in the face then left the bar.

* * * *

It was just after six when I gave up on sleep. My thoughts were swirling and as hard as I tried, I couldn't put Kate's words out of my head. If Nate was sleeping with her, it was really none of my business. But I couldn't ignore the cold, stab of jealousy I felt when I imagined them together...here...in the same bed I spent so much of my time.

Taking some ham from the fridge, I crept outside to leave it for the ginger cat. More often than not, it was lurking somewhere in the garden, growing bolder every time I saw it. But this morning it darted between my legs and ran straight into the kitchen.

"Shit," I whispered, chasing after it. Nate would flip out. He was forever warning me this sort of thing would happen. There was no sign of the cat in the kitchen, or in the sitting room. I crouched down the edge of the couch, peering into the darkness behind. "Here, psss psss."

"What are you doing?"

Nate's voice made me jump up. He stood in the doorway, watching me with a smile. "Oh, um, nothing. Just looking for something."

"What?"

Just then I spotted the ginger cat as it rubbed against Nate's bare legs. He looked down then back at me with an 'I told you so' look. "What the fuck is that thing doing in here?"

I let out a breath. "I didn't mean to let it in! Bloody thing shot past me when I—"

"Went out to feed it?"

I cringed and tried to give him a cute, innocent smile. "Sort of."

"Fuck sake," Nate sighed. "You'll never get rid of it now."

"Sorry."

"Take it to a vet, make sure it's not diseased or anything." Nate tried to nudge the cat away but it only purred louder and wound around and around his legs.

I frowned. "You want to keep it?"

Nate laughed. "No, Jo. I don't *want* to keep it. But it doesn't look as though it's leaving, does it?"

I looked at the cat, cleaning its paws by Nate's feet, no doubt satisfied it wasn't getting the boot. "No, I suppose not."

"Anyway," Nate said, coming closer to me. "I like the idea of you being all happy and grateful."

"I bet you do," I said with a laugh.

He grinned and sat on the couch, patting the cushion beside him. Taking a seat beside him, he grabbed my feet and pulled them onto his lap. "Good night at work?"

I shrugged. "It was work."

Nate pulled my socks off and massaged my feet. "Same old, same old?"

"More or less." I sank deeper into the cushions. "Oh, Suze was in with the new bloke."

He frowned. "I still haven't met him. What's he like?"

"Dunno, I only saw her. He was keeping the table or something." I picked at the lettering on my top. "Kate was in tonight."

Nate snorted a laugh. "And how is Kate?"

I flashed him a smile. "Very well, according to her and all the sex you're having."

His hold on my feet tightened painfully. "Sorry. What the fuck was she saying?"

"You might be home when I'm at work, but not alone, or some shit like that," I said, unable to help smiling when I saw how annoyed he looked.

"She's mad, honestly. I've not clapped eyes on her since that night at the bar."

My mouth stretched into a yawn. "She tried to pretend she didn't know who I was."

Nate laughed. "Like anyone could forget you or your performance that night."

I smiled and rubbed my feet in his lap. He hissed when I ran my foot up the length of his erection, barely contained in his boxer briefs.

"Aren't you exhausted? You look like you should go back to bed for a bit," Nate asked, eyes wide with innocence and moving to settle between my legs with the grace and stealth of a hunter.

I reached between us to free his cock. Nate swallowed. He kicked off his underwear fully and the veins in his neck corded as I trailed a fingertip over the moistened head of his cock. "Only if you come with me."

He smiled and pumped his hips into my hand. "You're like a kid with a bedtime story, only you want my dick instead."

Curling my hand around his thickening erection, I gave him one long, firm stroke. Nate grunted and I moved my hand back up, reaching with my free one to massage his heavy balls. "Oh please, can't you fuck me one more time before bed?"

"And what if *I* want fucked before bed?" Nate asked, grinding his teeth as I picked up my speed. "Can't have you getting greedy."

I gave a short, tight squeeze at his root and released his hard-on.

Nate gasped from the loss of contact.

Sitting up, I forced him onto his back. "Well, heaven forbid you call me greedy."

His eyes widened as I stood up and hooked my fingers into the waistband of the bikini briefs I'd slept in, gliding them to the floor.

There was a coy smile at play on my lips as I straddled his lap. Nate's hands gripped my hips as I settled with his erection nestled flat between my slick folds. Nate hissed and pushed his hips up.

I moaned at the pressure and rocked forward. Nate groaned and tried to move me off him so he could push inside me but I held fast where I was. I splayed my hands over his firm chest. "But then again, maybe I want to be greedy." I moved slowly back and forth, closing my eyes as my clit ground against the hardness of his shaft.

"Christ, Jo, you're going to fucking kill me," Nate growled through his clenched teeth.

I pressed down harder and rocked with a new frenzy, creating dizzying friction and getting myself off with his dick.

He roared. "Fuck it. Do it, babe, make yourself come."

"I'm coming," I panted, throwing my head back. The sound of my racing breath rang in my ears and my heart pounded. "Nate, I'm coming."

Nate's fingers bit into my hips as he barked out a moan. He held me more firmly on his length and the increased pressure on my clit brought my orgasm rushing through my body.

Wrapping his arm around my waist, Nate pulled me under him. He pinned both my wrists above my hand with one strong grip. Nate plunged his cock inside me and I screamed, already so ripened and sensitive. Nate yanked my camisole down to expose one breast and he pulled the nipple into his mouth, grazing the sensitive flesh with his teeth.

Underneath him I bucked and his thrusts became frenzied. I trembled as another orgasm built.

"Come with me, Nate," I moaned in his ear, biting down on the soft curve of his earlobe.

He grunted and pumped twice more before giving one final, earth-shattering thrust, spilling his seed inside me. Nate watched as I rode out my own release, panting for breath and seeing stars. Nate gave me a lazy, satisfied smile before dropping his head on my chest.

"Fuck me," he mumbled into my breasts. "Let me know if you feel greedy again."

A laugh rumbled in my throat and I wrapped my arms around him, pinning him even firmer to me. "Done."

Chapter Fourteen

Nate came with me later in the day to the vet to have the ginger cat checked over. Apart from a bit of malnutrition, it was in fairly good health. He reckoned it was more likely a lost pet or an abandoned one and not feral by its nature but with no microchip, it was impossible to trace where it came from.

Suze and Tilly were playing in the sitting room when we returned home, Tilly's eyes locking on the mewling cardboard box. I placed it on the floor, Tilly glued to my side. The cat, naturally, took one look at Tilly and her grabby hands and bolted in the opposite direction.

She bawled for all of a minute until Nate produced some raisins.

"You two got a cat?" Suze asked with a Cheshire grin.

Nate snorted and sat in the arm chair, giving me a sidelong glance. "No. *She* was adopted."

Suze looked at me with a raised eyebrow.

"It just, you know, sort of decided to live here."

"After Jo fed it every day for months," Nate said in a sardonic voice.

"I think it's sweet you have a pet." Suze couldn't have looked more pleased if she had tried.

"Tat, tat," Tilly sang, stuffing herself with raisins.

"Yes, Tilly, *cat, cat!* Uncle Nate and Auntie Jo got a *cat!*" Suze beamed.

"Tat."

"Cat."

"Tat."

"*C! C! Cat! C*-cat!"

"TAT!"

"Yes, all right," Suze sighed. She looked at Nate. "Have you decided what's happening for Christmas yet?"

He laughed. "It's barely October, Suze."

"And? You know what Mum's like, she needs to know, so she can start planning for everyone."

"Why don't you host it this year? You've gotten out of it so far."

Suze rolled her eyes. "I have a young child, Nate. I can't be expected to cook Christmas dinner for everyone too."

He sighed. "Using the Tilly card again, Suze? I'm disappointed."

She swatted his leg. "Well, *I* think you and Jo should host."

My heart skipped a beat.

Nate glanced at me before scowling at his sister. "Shut up, Suze. We'll be going to Mum's just like we do every year. Now leave it alone, will you?"

Suze tutted. "So grouchy, Nate. Wouldn't kill you to be selfless for once, would it? Don't you think Mum deserves the break?"

He held his hands out. "I offer every year to take everyone out for dinner."

She laughed. "That's not the same and you know it! Jo, don't you think that's a cop out?"

I shrugged. "Not really, if you take his cooking into consideration."

Suze laughed and Nate, mildly offended, threw a pillow at me.

* * * *

Nate and I sat at the island, eating the dinner Suze had cooked and brought for us. Suze and Tilly had already left, Suze exhausted from chasing after Tilly chasing after the cat.

"What's up with you?" I asked, twirling spaghetti around on my fork.

Nate glanced at me. "Nothing, why?"

I shrugged. "You look like you have something on your mind."

"I do." He flashed me a smile. "But it wouldn't be very casual of me to ask."

"Oh. How not casual are we talking?" I asked, trying to keep my face passive while my insides felt anything but.

"I won't know until I ask." Nate shoveled a forkful of spaghetti into his mouth.

"So long as it doesn't involve a jewelry box, I think you should be safe."

"Well, there goes the element of surprise," Nate said with a wink. "Okay. I was just thinking about Christmas."

I laughed. "Invoking Suze, now?"

He rolled his eyes. "I know. I'm a disappointment to my race. I was just curious if you knew what you were doing yet."

Reaching for my water glass, I tried to keep my face as controlled as possible, though my stomach knotted. "Same as most years, I expect."

"Can I ask what that is?" Nate asked.

"You can ask," I said, my voice a pitch quieter.

"Will I get an answer?"

"Probably not one you'll like." I set down my fork and wiped my mouth with the napkin. How could I tell Nate, who had been surrounded with love for his entire life, that Christmas was like any other day, or that I looked forward to it for the simple reason of better tips?

Nate let out a breath.

"I'm not trying to be stubborn," I said, dropping my eyes to my plate.

He snorted a laugh. "What, it just comes naturally?"

My smile was shaky. "Something like that."

Nate looked at me closely. Again, his eyes felt like they saw deeper into me than he'd have me believe. "Okay, let me rephrase. Are you leaving over Christmas to go anywhere?"

This was dangerous territory. I should tease and flirt my way out of the conversation so he would forget he didn't actually get any form of an answer. I couldn't bring myself to lie...but I couldn't let him see the truth, either. "No. More than likely I'll be working."

There was a pause before Nate spoke. "I'm formally, but casually, inviting you to spend it with me. I won't be offended if you decide to work. Just know the offer is there."

"Thank you," I said, my voice soft.

Nate watched me, his eyes not missing a single thing. "Won't your family miss you?"

And for the first time I could give a direct answer. "No."

I went to bed alone that night.

* * * *

Guilt chewed my stomach the next morning and had interrupted most of my sleep the night before. I wasn't sure what was more worrying—how deep my feelings were blooming for Nate, or how close to the tip of my tongue all my secrets had pooled.

Nate didn't deserve someone like me. I couldn't give myself to him the way I wanted to and the way any sane woman would. He knew my time was limited, that one day I'd disappear. But while I was here, I could do things for him, make him feel through my touch that I did care.

Around noon I left the house for his office. When I arrived, the secretary smiled and nodded for me to go through. Nate was on a call when I quietly closed the door behind me. His eyes never left me as I crossed the room to him. His words didn't falter as I dropped to my knees in front of him, grasped his zipper and freed him.

His dick was already rigid and I took him in my mouth. With a few choice words he slammed the phone back into its cradle. Nate's hands knotted in my hair as I worked him—slid up and down on his length, sucked him harder, faster and teased his heavy balls with my hand.

Nate hissed and he gently thrust into my mouth.

I looked up at him through my lashes, painfully turned on by how much I was affecting him. I wrapped my hand around the base of his length, moving my grip with the rhythm of my mouth.

Nate's hold on my hair tightened and I slid my lips over his hard-on faster. I hummed and pumped him harder with my hand.

"Jesus Christ," he grunted, and thrust deeper into my throat. He came, furious and thick and I swallowed every drop. With heavy breaths, Nate fell back against his chair.

I closed his trousers and rose to kiss him. When I made to pull away, he gripped my wrists and forbade my departure.

Nate's hand crept up my thigh but I halted his wandering fingers.

"Later," I whispered against his mouth.

He pulled me closer and kissed me hard, his tongue plunging into my mouth.

"I will return that gesture to you later," Nate whispered throatily. "Completely. Thoroughly. Don't plan on sleeping. I've got to go on another trip in the morning and I intend to spend all night making sure you think about me every moment I'm gone."

My lips curved into a smile, though a strong part of me was disappointed. I knew I would miss Nate a hundred times more this time. "Looking forward to it."

Just as I had straightened, the door to Nate's office burst open. Kate opened her mouth to speak, stopping in her tracks and no sound coming out when she saw me.

His secretary appeared behind Kate, flustered and red-faced. "I'm sorry, Mr Harding, she got past me when I was on a call."

"It's okay, Sarah." His eyes turned steely as he looked to Kate. "What do you think you're doing, bursting in here?"

She smiled, coy and cat-like. "I thought I'd drag you away from your desk for an hour to two."

Nate caught my eye. "I'm rather fond of my desk."

Kate laughed, though it sounded forced. "You need lunch, Nathaniel. Shall we go to our usual place?" Kate glanced at me. "I would invite you, but there are private matters we need to discuss."

I smiled. "I'm sure you do." I headed for the door, stopping when I was level with Kate. "But don't worry about it. I already ate."

My smile widened when Nate's bellowing laughter followed me out of the door.

* * * *

Tilly and I splashed around in the warm pool while Suze swam lengths. Tilly clapped her hands in the water, spraying us both to her delight.

"Having fun with Auntie Jo, sweetheart?" Suze asked as she got in beside us.

"Jojo!" Tilly shouted, her little voice reverberating around the room.

Suze grinned. "I'll take that as a yes."

I splashed Suze.

"So, I'm thinking of throwing Tilly a little birthday party. What do you think?"

"Why are you asking me? I can't remember my second birthday, if you're after ideas."

Suze laughed. "Just when I think you're becoming more normal, you remind me just how stunted you actually are."

"Thanks, Suze. Really."

She nudged me. "You know what I mean. So. Party. Would you come?"

I eyed her carefully. "What would it involve?"

"Eating cake. Then more cake. Then a bit more."

"Will there be loads of screaming children?"

"Just mine, probably."

I smiled. "Sure. Count me in. When is her birthday, anyway?"

"Next weekend. What are you working?"

"Not till eight on Saturday and I'm off Sunday night. Nate's back early Saturday morning." And thank Christ for that. It felt like he had been gone for weeks rather than days.

"Shall we say Sunday afternoon, then? It's the day after her birthday, but I'm sure Tilly won't mind."

"Sunday sounds perfect."

She fluttered her eyelashes. "What would be perfect is if you selflessly offer to make the cake."

* * * *

Nate, surprisingly, seemed even more reluctant to go than I was. Dressed in some warm boots, leggings and a long jumper, I was ready. And Nate was hiding somewhere in the house.

"It'll be worse if you're late," I shouted up the stairs.

Nate's head appeared on the third floor, peering down at me from the landing. "Is it so terrible I want to stay here and watch you try on the rest of the underwear I brought back?"

I smiled and my stomach dipped. I'd rather nothing more, but I doubted we'd survive the wrath of Suze if we didn't turn up. The moment Nate had arrived home the morning before he'd torn into his suitcase and produced a big pinked striped shopping bag from Victoria's Secret.

"You seriously have no idea what you're letting yourself in for, do you?" Nate asked.

I rolled my eyes and folded my arms under my breasts. "Cake and watching Tilly open presents. I'm terrified."

Nate disappeared and few moments later he bounded down the stairs, a wrapped box under his arm. "Suze being driven mad by our mother and enough cake to make you vomit."

I shoved his arm. "Why would my cake make you vomit?"

He grinned. "Because I plan to eat so much of it my stomach simply can't hold it all."

With a sigh, I picked up the heavy cardboard box containing said cake.

Nate plucked it from me and balanced it atop his gift. "Not to mention my dad borderline flirting with you, having the Spanish inquisition into your personal life. And if the new bloke is there, he'll probably be driven off and if he turns out to be a twat, *I'll* drive him off."

Suddenly I wasn't so keen to get him out of the door.

He gave me a smile. "Told you."

My heart thundered. "She didn't tell me your parents would be there."

Nate frowned. "Why would they miss their granddaughter's birthday party?"

They wouldn't. But it had been so long since I'd seen a normal family dynamic in live action that I couldn't remember what was normal anymore.

"You've gone really pale. Are you okay?" Nate asked, holding my arm.

I shook my head. "It's supposed to be about Tilly, no one else."

"Yes, but my family are barking mad. They mean well. They're just proper nosey." Nate tilted my chin up so I would meet his eyes. "You're hating this already, aren't you?"

I bit my lip, knowing any second tears would form in my eyes. God, why couldn't I be *more* for him? The kind of woman who charmed his parents and didn't have a panic attack at the thought of a large gathering of people all asking perfectly normal questions.

Nate guided me backward until I met the wall. He stroked his thumb over my cheek and dipped his head to press a kiss to the corner of my mouth. "I'll protect you, I promise."

I gripped his wrists, wishing more than anything that was true.

"And as a bit of an incentive...if we survive this, when we get home I'll fuck you on the island."

A startled laugh bubbled in my throat.

Nate chuckled and the sound vibrated in his chest. He kissed me again, harder, fuller this time. "Sound like a good deal?"

I nodded and he kissed me harder still.

* * * *

We arrived at Suze's apartment, and when she opened the door, Tilly's screaming rushed out to greet us. Suze herself was not the together woman she usually appeared to be and now more resembled a frazzled lass on the verge of a nervous breakdown. She was covered in crumbs, hair static and poking up every which way and had a Smartie stuck to her cheek.

Nate swallowed his laughter. "Need a hand?"

"She saw the presents in my cupboard and wants them *now*. She won't get dressed and every time I actually manage to clothe her, she rips them off when I leave the room. I burnt the mini-pizzas and haven't finished making the sandwiches. I forgot to buy sausage rolls and there's no more wine left."

Suze's eyes flickered between me and Nate, as though we had brought answers with us, as well as Tilly's presents. Her face turned an unhealthy shade of red, and I rushed to speak, hoping my suggestion would save the day. Ish. "I bought her a party dress, maybe she can open one present now if she promises to be good and get dressed afterward? I'm sure even Nate can make sandwiches and if you put enough cheese on the pizzas, no one will care if they're a bit crispy. And, really, should we be getting pissed at Tilly's party?"

Nate and Suze stared at me.

"What?"

Suze threw her arms around me. "You're a godsend, Jo. Now go see my daughter before she destroys everything in her wardrobe."

Suze disappeared into the kitchen. Nate smiled at me and pulled me in for a kiss.

"You are nothing short of incredible, sometimes."

"Just sometimes?" I murmured against his lips.

He laughed.

"*Nate!*" Suze screamed.

In no time at all, the crisis was averted. After getting Tilly dressed in her pink sparkly party dress—which I feared she would never take off, a fact I didn't tell Suze—and Nate had made a mountain of ham sandwiches, Suze put enough extra cheese on the pizzas to threaten the lot of us with clogged arteries and made a last minute dash to the bakers for sausage rolls. Nothing could be done about the wine.

I was playing with Tilly in her bedroom when Nate and Suze's parents arrived. Tilly sat on my knee, showing me how to brush a purple pony's tail. Maybe I could get away with hiding in there for the whole thing.

But Tilly heard their voices and took off running. Nate's head poked around the door. "Ready?"

He saw my deer in the headlights expression and came into the room, offering me a hand. He pulled me to my feet and patted my bum. "Just think of the island waiting for us at home."

I laughed and swatted his chest. "I'm beginning to think this deal is leaning a little more in your favor than mine."

Nate pretended to look wounded. "So you think you won't enjoy it? You know what? That sounds like a challenge. Just how many times do you think I can get you to come? Pick a number."

My pulse raced.

He pressed closer to me, his hips digging into mine so I could feel just how hard he was.

"Right, you pair of pervs. Care to join the rest of us and stop rubbing against each other in my daughter's bedroom?" Suze asked from the doorway.

Nate grinned and pulled me behind him.

My heart thundered as we entered the living room. An older version of Suze sat beside Tilly on the couch, turning the pages of a book and pointing to the pictures. Nate approached his father, a man just as broad and tall as Nate. They shared the same chocolate hair, though Nate's wasn't yet streaked with gray. Nate slapped him on the shoulder as he perused the snacks Suze had set up on the dining table. "All right, Dad?" Nate asked, his grin broadening.

"I'd be better if there was something other than ham sandwiches."

Nate laughed. "Hey, those are the best ham sandwiches you'll ever have."

He dropped one back onto the platter, his eyes wide with mock horror. "God, did you make them?"

"Christ, Dad, I can make a bloody sandwich."

"I also thought you could make toast. You nearly set the kitchen on fire."

"That was faulty wiring!"

"So you said. Funny how it worked fine for everyone else afterward."

"Yeah, yeah," Nate grumbled.

He peered around Nate. "Who's this then? Not introducing us, Nate?"

Nate flashed me a look. "Jo, this my dad. Dad, this is Jo."

"You can do better than that. I'm Victor Harding." He extended his hand for me to shake, grasping mine just a touch firmer than I'd expected. "How do you know Nate?"

"Jo rents one of the spare rooms. Remember, Dad?"

"*Oh…*" Victor said, a slow smile forming. "Ah, I see. So this is Jo. I thought Jo was a *Joe!*"

"Didn't Nate tell you his Jo was without a penis, Dad?" Suze called from the kitchen. "He's a tricky bugger like that, isn't he?"

Nate swallowed a laugh.

"Suzanne!" her mother admonished, glancing at Tilly to make sure she wasn't about to start calling us all buggers.

My cheeks scalded as Victor continued to study me. *Fucking Suze.*

"I take it the arrangements are suiting everyone then?" He glanced down to where Nate still held my other hand.

Nate rolled his eyes. "Get a grip, would you, Dad? Yes, technically we live together, and yes, technically we are seeing each other. Don't make a fuss."

"Who's fussing?" Victor leaned closer to Nate. "Does your mother know?"

"Does Mother know what?" A voice behind me asked. Nate's mother glanced at me before fixing her son with the same intensity of a look I was so used to from him.

"That Jo would be here today. You remember me telling you about Jo?" Nate let go of my hand to slide his arm around my waist, pulling me closer to him. The affect was as desired. His mother immediately got the message and didn't start the Spanish Inquisition I had been warned about. "Jo, this is my mum, Diane."

"*Jojo!*" Tilly screeched, and having suddenly realized I was in the room, threw herself at my knees.

"My granddaughter certainly seems to like you." Diane smiled down at Tilly, the warmth in her eyes when she looked back at me sincere.

Tilly held her arms up and gave a little jump. I picked her up and she fiddled with the chain of my necklace, trying, not for the first time, to taste the pendant.

"They spend a lot of time together," Nate said.

Suze appeared brandishing a plate full of cookies. "Everyone getting along?"

No one answered her.

"Mum, don't you just love Tilly's dress? Jo bought it for her birthday." At the appearance of the cookies, Tilly made a dive bomb from my arms. I set her down and Suze moved the plate farther back on the heavily loaded table.

Her face softened. "Yes, it's lovely. You have good taste, Jo."

"Only for two year olds, I'm a bit hopeless for myself."

"I don't think so. That jumper is gorgeous. Where did you get it?"

"Oh." I looked down. "Um, Primark. In the sale."

She stuttered a laugh. "Brilliant. Come sit down with me, Jo. Let's grab a chance to get to know each other."

For a brief moment, Nate's hold on me tightened.

It didn't escape his mother's notice. Diane rolled her eyes. "You can survive five minutes without her, Nate. And I promise to be on my best behavior." She turned and headed back to the couch.

Nate pressed a kiss into my hair. "Send smoke signals if you need rescuing."

I laughed, despite my feeling of unease.

Diane smiled, and I slowly made my way over to where she sat, keeping a good distance between us.

"I hear you and Suze are becoming good friends."

I nodded, glancing to where Suze flitted around the room, teasing balloon ribbons and straightening birthday banners. "She's a good person."

"And it's nice to see Nate so happy again. I'm sure you can appreciate how Kate affected him."

"No one should be hurt like that." I looked across the room at Nate, smiling as he laughed at something his dad was saying. Not for the first time, I wondered what was going on in Kate's head when she'd decided to throw away a man like him.

"I think you're a breath of fresh air for both of them. Suze will tell you herself how hard she's found it to regain a social life after her so-called friends ditched her. And you're clearly nothing like Kate."

I shrugged. "It's not difficult being around either of them. They've done more for me than I could ever do for them."

"Suze mentioned you work in a bistro. Do you enjoy it?"

"Most of the time," I said with a smile. "There are good points and bad points, just like any job."

"They just made Jo their official baker, and rightly so. I think I've gained three stone since I met her," Suze said as she passed the couch, giving me an encouraging smile. Bless her. She was like a lighthouse or something else poetic.

"She's exaggerating," I said with a blush.

"Did you make the cake today? It looks amazing! I thought Suze had it made somewhere. Did it take you long?"

"The sugar icing was the trickiest part. There are some right fiddly bits. Other than that, it took no time, really." I had decorated it with different characters from CBeebies that Tilly was particularly fond of. And she had best well appreciate it, as had Suze, the big madam.

"It's my husband's birthday soon. I may call on you for a fabulous creation."

My wide smile was genuine. "I'd be happy to. Are you retired, as well as Mr Harding?"

Diane laughed. "Just Vic, really. And yes, I am. It's nice spending time together again, holidays when we feel like it and not having to plan and wait and such."

At that moment, Suze reappeared with an armful of brightly colored presents. Tilly's eyes lit up and she ran over, attacking the first with gusto. Once the room was covered with shreds of wrapping paper, Suze brought out the cake and helped Tilly blow out her candles. Nate sat close beside me on the couch, his thigh rubbing mine and his fingers drawing lazy patterns on my knee.

The conversations floated around me, and I responded when it was needed and I smiled and hoped to hell it looked more convincing than it felt. Really, Diane and Vic were nice enough people and as much as I did actually like them, I couldn't shake the tiny feeling of panic. This was a whole family, something I hadn't ever really seen up close before. They were clearly close with their children and doted on their granddaughter. I couldn't help but wonder if Kate had charmed them at first—had known what to say to make them smile and make them laugh.

When the food was eaten and Tilly was asleep on the floor on a bed of wrapping paper, Nate cupped my elbow and rose from the couch.

"Off so soon, you two?" Suze asked.

"We have things to do," Nate replied, giving his sister a wolfish smile.

She shuddered and looked away.

Diane stood also and hugged her son, placing a warm hand on my arm. "We'll meet for a coffee sometime, Jo."

I nodded and gave a little wave as Nate guided us out of the apartment. He gently clasped my hand as we walked back to the house, shivering against the cold wind.

"Was that absolutely awful for you?"

A bloom of sadness welled up inside me. "No, Nate, it wasn't. I'm just not used to things like that. You know, family gatherings. People asking questions." People caring to hear the answers.

He snorted a laugh, oblivious to my internal torment. "That was them, muted. It was only because I said I'd leave and never bring you around again if they were badly behaved. Mum is probably cross-examining Suze as we speak."

"God, really? I'm not that interesting."

"You're friends with Suze and you're involved with me. That makes you interesting in their eyes. I don't know what you're worried about. You've already won them over."

"What? How?" I asked, my eyes widening.

"You shop at Primark and you laugh at Dad's jokes. Even when they're *really* not funny. That makes you a keeper in their eyes." Nate smiled.

"What's Primark got to do with anything?"

"Much as I hate mentioning her, it's got everything to do with Kate. She was all labels all the time and it drove Mum mad. It was so obvious she just wanted whatever she could get her grubby little hands on. You don't give a crap about that sort of thing."

"I think there's an insult in there somewhere."

He fixed me with his eyes and warmth pooled in my stomach. "Trust me, Jo. There isn't."

Chapter Fifteen

Nate closed the door behind us and my body jumped to life in anticipation. The energy in the air crackled as he ushered me into the kitchen, his eyes never once leaving mine. At the island, Nate grasped my hips and sat me on the edge of the cool, hard surface. He pulled my jumper over my head and I shivered when the chilly air hit my over-heated skin.

He hooked a hand under my knee and lifted my leg, dragging his fingers down me until he reached the boot and tugged it free. The other boot followed and Nate's eyes drifted to my breasts, heaving in their restraints. He placed one hand near my hip, leaning into me and forcing me back onto my elbows. With his free hand, Nate reached around and unclasped my bra, ripping it free from my body. He dropped his head, his warm breath coming in unsteady pants and pebbling my nipples.

With a groan, Nate drew one into his mouth, his teeth grazing the flesh. I fell back onto the island. He pulled back and slid my leggings and knickers off until I was completely bare to him.

He gripped my legs and threw them over his shoulders, his eyes burning into mine. Nate stroked one long finger between my slick folds, a smile pulling at his lips. There was no humor in the smile. It was a hunter meets its prey gesture and I was willingly at his mercy.

Nate pushed one finger inside then another, slowly, driving me into a frenzy. I cried out when he withdrew them and watched with fascination as he took them in his mouth, his cheeks hollowing as he sucked them clean.

"I've wanted a more thorough taste of you since that first night," Nate said, his voice gravelly and making me even more painfully aroused. "Even more so since you sucked me off at my desk. And you taste beautiful, Jo. Exquisite. Delicious."

My breath caught in my throat as he pushed against my thighs, opening me even more for him. He pressed a kiss onto my inner thigh, then finally, my swollen folds. I felt his tongue flicker out and taste me — softly, slowly — long, deep pulls that brought me to the brink.

A noise rumbled in his chest and Nate devoured me. His mouth worked hungrily against my flesh, his tongue lashing my clit. As my orgasm built Nate held me still with his strong hands as my back arched off the island.

The stubble on his jaw prickled my skin but instead of hurting or irritating, it only turned me on more. Every inch of Nate was masculine and male, the stubble only reminding me of that...of the glorious man between my thighs.

Nate speared me with his tongue. I cried out and fisted my hands in his hair as he fucked me with his mouth. He growled in answer to my obvious pleasure and it sent vibrations through my pussy.

I thought I couldn't take anymore. It was too much. I felt everything and just as I thought I was spent, he sucked on my clit and I came, harder than I ever had before. My heart felt as though it would explode within my chest. I collapsed back against the island, exhausted and shaking as the adrenaline fled my veins, Nate placed featherlight kisses up my body. The kiss on my mouth was soft and brief but with the hint of me still on him, it was more intimate than any other kiss we'd shared.

He gathered me in his arms and pulled me up so I once again sat on the edge of the island, my muscles trembling. I thrust my hands into his hair and claimed his mouth. Nate deepened the kiss and his hold on me tightened as I sucked his tongue into my mouth and tasted myself.

Nate refused to let me dress once he allowed me off the island. Instead he gave me the T-shirt off his back and insisted I wear it. I suspected he was developing caveman tendencies which really, given my history, shouldn't have turned me on half as much as it did.

Cat, who had definitely adopted us and his unimaginative name—I didn't feel at all like Audrey Hepburn—appeared later that evening, prowling around for food. Whilst Nate would insist until he was blue in the face that he had no emotional connection with him, he often stopped to stroke his head and was now the first to offer him a scrap from his plate.

After a late supper of bacon sandwiches and glasses of white wine, Nate led us upstairs to his floor where he fucked me good and thoroughly before falling into a sex induced coma. And as I lay tucked up in his arms, the thud of his heartbeat under my ear, I realized I was more relaxed than I had been in what felt like forever. Not just relaxed, but safe. I felt safe.

And as was often the case, just when I started to feel a change in myself, my subconscious reminded me exactly why I shouldn't.

* * * *

The house was dark and still. Silent, save from the blood roaring in my ears. I pressed tighter against the wall, feeling my way through the pitch black. Inch by inch I moved through the house, biting my lip to keep from making a sound. The floor dropped out from under me and I let out a startled gasp, hands groping around for something to hold onto. My feet found their purchase and a wave of relief washed through me. I'd found the stairs.

I only had to get down them and I'd be at the front door. Then outside.

Then free.

Pale moonlight shone through the crescent window above the wide front door and I hurried toward it.

Just as my hand curled around the cool metal of the door handle, I felt a breath stir my hair. Every nerve in my body stood to attention and before I could even consider fighting my way free his hand stroked my throat in a lover's caress. Pressed a blade to the skin and slit me from ear to ear.

I sucked in air though my lungs but got no relief. Lurching up, I made to get to my feet but couldn't move. Shackles gripped my wrists and in a blind panic I thrashed to gain my freedom. I barely heard the screaming over the pounding in my heart and head.

An unfamiliar shouted name pierced the cacophony of noise seeming to come from inside and outside my body and steel bars locked around my chest and arms, pining me to something hard.

"Fuck, Jo, breathe...*breathe.*"

A mouth pressed against my ear and his voice found its way through the fear. I panted, the screaming stopped. My entire body was racked with violent shaking.

"Jesus Christ," Nate whispered, holding me tighter against him.

My lip trembled and hot tears spilled down my face. I clawed at his arms, at the muscles that were strained and bulging at their effort to keep me from bolting. I clawed at them, now — not for release but for a securer hold.

Nate flopped back against the pillows, managing to turn me, and cradled my head against his chest as I sobbed and sobbed and thought the tears would never end.

I've no idea how long he held me. How long it took for me to calm down. But at some point, the tears stopped, or maybe they just dried up and I had nothing left. Nate rose from the bed then returned with a hefty dose of whiskey. He started the shower whilst I nursed the amber liquid, not caring that it burned my throat.

Nate took the glass and guided me into the shower. He washed the sweat and tears from my body, drying me with an enormous, soft towel when he was done and dressed me in one of his large T-shirts. Once back in bed, he held me just as tight.

I never expected to fall back asleep. I'm not sure that Nate did, either.

* * * *

Nate's alarm bleated a few hours later. At first, neither of us moved and I held onto the last few precious moments of lying in his arms. After last night, would he ever want me in his bed again?

He kissed the top of my head before slowly extracting his arms and getting up. Maybe he thought I was asleep. I heard the shower turn on and I waited a minute before getting up and sneaking downstairs to my room, locked myself in my own bathroom and didn't come out until I was absolutely positive that Nate would have left for work.

I was bone tired as I headed for the kitchen, all my muscles aching and my eyes so weary it hurt to even keep them open. Covering a yawn with the back of my hand, I stopped short as I entered the room.

Nate sat at the island, a steaming cup of coffee in front of him and another one opposite. He rubbed the stubble on his jaw as he watched me hovering in the doorway. "We need to talk."

Of course Nate wouldn't be like most men and prefer not to know what the fuck had gone on last night. All my options raced through my mind. I could lie through my teeth. I could feign brightness and cheer and brush the whole thing off. Or I could tell him the truth.

I smiled and sat across from him, blowing on the hot coffee and taking a sip. "What about? Are you bunking off today?" Option number two it was then.

"Don't, Jo." All at once Nate looked as tired as I felt.

My smile faltered. "Don't what?"

"Feed me fake bullshit. It's a waste of time and it won't work, so don't bother." He sighed. "What was that last night?"

"What was what?" I asked, raising my eyebrows. "Oh, you mean the nightmare? Pathetic, wasn't it? Sometimes I have these stupid dreams if I've been drinking. I told you I don't like alcohol much."

"Are you serious?"

I nodded. "Pathetic. You don't have to say it."

Nate scrubbed his hands over his head. "I don't know what's more insulting—that you think I would actually believe that piss poor excuse or that you don't trust me to be able to handle whatever the truth is."

My heart sank. Despite my hardest efforts, I was hurting this man. Who was I trying to convince? Just by letting myself get involved with him, in any shape way or form, I was going to end up hurting him. "It's nothing, Nate. Just leave it."

He took a steady breath. "I'd never ask you to tell me secrets you didn't feel comfortable sharing. Everyone is entitled to their privacy. But don't ever lie to me."

"So stop asking me questions," I whispered.

"Do you understand that this is me worried about you? I'm not one of those men who run a mile the second their woman shows a hint of emotion or human nature. I'm worried about you, Jo." Nate's eyebrows drew together and irritation as well as concern flashed in his warm brown eyes.

"There's nothing to worry about. Really." I swallowed the lump in my throat, fixed my smile and didn't convince anyone.

Nate drained the last of his coffee and rose to place the cup in the sink. "I wish I could believe you." He turned and bent to kiss my cheek. "I have a few things to do. I'll see you later."

The front door closed behind Nate, and I sat frozen on the stool. My body trembled as a hot wave of rage crashed through me. It wasn't often there was a stronger emotion than fear when I thought of my past, but when there was, I could bet it would be anger. I hated him for how I was. For *who* I was…and how easily I could sabotage myself.

* * * *

It was dark when Nate returned home, many hours later. I heard the front door open and close, the chink of his keys being tossed in the bowl on the sideboard. Cat raised his head from where he lay on my lap when Nate jogged up the stairs and poked his head into the comfy living room.

He sat beside me on the couch and stroked his head. "He's getting friendlier."

I let out a breath and rested my head on his shoulder.

Nate's arm came around me and Cat bolted. "I brought Chinese home. Shall we have something to eat and I'll walk you to work?"

"I'd like that," I said quietly, fighting against the emotion in my throat.

Nate kissed the top of my head and pulled me to my feet.

And so we ate and Nate never once mentioned last night. He held my hand as he walked me to work and was waiting at two in the morning in the freezing cold to see me back home again.

Chapter Sixteen

I wrapped the scarf tighter around me and blew into my hands. Tilly smiled up at me from her cozy pushchair, hat pulled low and mittens flopping around.

"When are you going to buy yourself a proper winter coat?" Suze asked, flicking the sleeve of my military style jacket that did little to stave off the increasingly chilly air.

"When I need one. When are you going to stop harping on at me?" I asked.

Suze gave me her 'mothering' look. "When you realize it's the middle of October and you *do* need one."

I grinned. "So how was the come down after her power nap at the party?"

"Not too bad, actually. She was more hyped up on wrapping paper and shredding it to pieces. Slept like a log that night, I'll tell you." Suze laughed. "You were very popular, by the way."

"Me, why?"

"Mum loved you. She asked me to bring you round sometime." Suze couldn't have grinned wider if she had tried.

Oh, God.

"Don't make that face," Suze said, rolling her eyes. "She's not that bad."

"No, I know," I rushed, not wanting to see the pinch of hurt on Suze's face. "It's just that me and families don't really go well together. Is she like this with all your friends?"

She laughed. "She doesn't want to see you because of *me*. It's because you're Nate's girlfriend."

"I'm not Nate's girlfriend. I'm just the girl he's —"

"Yes, all right, Jo." She huffed out a breath. "You two drive me crazy. Do you know that? I just want to smash your head off a brick wall to get you to see sense."

"I'm not the settling down type." I avoided Suze's eyes as I held the door of the coffee shop open for her.

She clattered the wheels of the pushchair off the doorway and swore under her breath. "Doesn't change how you feel about each other. I think you're being deliberately obtuse."

I nudged her with my elbow. "I think you've just been watching too much Disney where everyone has to have a happy ending."

"Yeah, well, it's all right for some," Suze mumbled, freeing Tilly and handing her a stack of crayons and some craft paper.

"Things not going well with Dan? I thought you two were getting proper loved up."

"I know. He's fine, great even. But he's getting pushy."

"What do you mean?"

The troubled look was strange on Suze's usually optimistic face. "He made a really big deal when I said he couldn't come to Tilly's birthday party. I wanted him there, but my daughter's birthday is about her, not the man I'm seeing. He's making all these noises about having Nate and one of his lady friends over for dinner."

"What lady friends?" I asked, my voice a touch more shrill than I would have liked.

Suze laughed. "Calm down. He doesn't know about you, that's all. I mean, he knows you live with Nate and we're friends, but I haven't told him about you and Nate. Too complicated. I'll wait until you make it official."

I snorted. "You'll be waiting for a while then. So he wants to get the big brother on his side?"

Suze nodded. "He asks me so many questions about him, honestly. I think he's just worried that Nate won't like him or will get all protective or something."

"You are full of contradictions, Suze," I said, shaking my head.

"What do you mean?"

"You want me and Nate to be all serious and betrothed or whatever, and you're losing interest in your boyfriend because he wants to meet your family. Contradictions."

She groaned. "Oh, shut up, you smart arse. Go get me a hot chocolate."

I squeezed her shoulder as I stood up. "With extra whipped cream," I promised.

* * * *

Wednesday night at the bar was utterly dire. I was on back shifts all week and ready to lose the plot. I'd been listening to the banter of a couple of students for the last hour and a half and didn't believe half the stories coming out of their mouths.

Rob was making a pyramid of beer mats when the phone rang. I jumped up to answer it and caused his pyramid to fold and collapse. He shot me a dirty look and I smiled.

"Hello, Red Bar," I answered.

"Jo?"

I knew his voice anywhere and I wasn't surprised by the sudden flutter in my stomach. "Nate? What's wrong?"

"Nothing. Am I right in thinking you're finishing work soon?"

I glanced at my watch. "Yeah, in about half an hour."

"Feel like doing me a massive favor? Bring some food round to the office? I'm fucking starving and probably will be here for another few hours."

"Sure thing. In the mood for anything in particular?"

There was a pause before Nate answered. "Surprise me," he said, with a smile in his voice.

I chose his favorite pizza shop, ordering a large meat feast. It warmed my hands through my fingerless gloves as I walked the cold streets to Nate's office. I called him when I was around the corner and he was waiting for me by the time I made it. He relieved me of the pizza box, groaning when the smell hit him.

He took my hand as he jogged up the stairs and into his office. Nate kissed me briefly before placing the box on the coffee table and sitting on the couch to dig in. I pulled off my oversized jumper I was wearing in lieu of a coat and pushed up the sleeves of the long-sleeved bar shirt, chucking my scarf and gloves on top of the jumper.

"Are you not freezing?" Nate asked around a mouthful of pizza.

"Nah, not really." Lie. I was frozen to the bone but refused to buy a decent coat until the sales.

"How was work?"

"Long and boring. You?"

"Busy. I'm probably going to have to go back out to the States again."

My face fell. "So soon? But you just got back."

Nate nodded. "Tell me about it. But I need this done, get all the details ironed out. It's easier to do it on site."

I didn't like how disappointed I felt that Nate would once again be jetting off for another week or two. It seemed so odd that when I'd first moved in, I'd barely noticed when he wasn't there, only realizing he'd gone anywhere by the suitcase that sat in the hall when he'd returned for a few days. But now, the house echoed with the absence of him.

"You're quiet tonight," Nate said, reaching for another slice.

I dropped my half eaten one back into the pizza box and curled up in the corner of the couch. "Just tired."

Nate took my feet and pulled them onto his lap. He rubbed my calf with his strong, sure fingers. "You could always come, you know."

"Where?" I frowned.

"America."

I scoffed. "Yeah, right."

"Why not?"

"The airfare, for one thing."

"I can expense it."

"I'd have to take time off work."

"You haven't had a holiday, or a weekend off, since I met you. You're bound to be owed some time."

"You'd be working."

"Not in the evenings."

"God, you're serious, aren't you?"

"Very." He smiled. "It's no big deal, Jo. I can expense your flight, you'd share my suite so it's not like it's any more expensive in the hotel. There's loads of museums, shops and touristy things to do during the day. I'd be out of the office by six every night and we could get dinner, see a show, whatever. The offer is there. It's up to you."

It sounded so coupley—a holiday away together. It wasn't a big relationship step, really he was only offering me a free trip to America. It wasn't anything to freak out about.

Nate demolished one more slice before closing the lid. He shifted closer to me, grasped my hips and tugged me down the couch.

"You look exhausted. Chill out here, I'll wake you when I've rung for a taxi." He bent to kiss the corner of my mouth and I wanted nothing more than to pull him on top of me. Nate smiled as though he could read my mind and got up to remove himself from my temptation.

I closed my eyes and listened to the clack of his fingers hitting the keys, the sound soothing and very Nate. After a few minutes, I didn't hear anything at all.

* * * *

Pale gray morning light filtered through the window blinds when I woke after sleeping more fitfully than I had since the night Nate had witnessed one of the nightmares. I was cozy, wrapped in a pair of arms with a heartbeat beneath my head. I shifted, realizing my body was wedged between the back of the couch and Nate's long form. Burrowing deeper in his arms, I breathed him in. That smell, that purely masculine scent, made me dizzy.

Nate moved and his grip on me tightened. I smiled into his soft T-shirt and a low laugh rumbled in his chest. "Morning."

I pushed up to kiss the bristles on his jaw. "Morning."

He caught my face and kissed me soft, routine. Like we had woken up beside each other for a thousand mornings. "Has there been any noise out there?"

"None that I've heard."

"Must be early." Nate sat up and groaned, the muscles in his back contracting. "Fuck, this is going to be a long day."

"When did you crash last night?"

"I'm not sure. You were out for the count. Decided that couch looked way more tempting than going out in the pissing rain to get home."

"Good thing it's a very comfy couch," I said, standing up with a smile. My things were still flung over the arm of the couch and I began to pull them on.

"Are you heading straight home? Stay for breakfast, if you want. There should be stuff in the kitchen."

I shook my head. "I might drop in on Suze. She'll feed me."

Nate wrapped my scarf around my neck, using it to pull me closer to him. "Thanks for dinner last night."

"No bother. Thanks for letting me sleep over."

Nate laughed. "You're always invited for that. How about another one tonight? Don't bother with pajamas."

I smiled and pressed my lips to his. "It's a date."

* * * *

Suze took forever to answer her door. I bounced on the balls of my feet until at last the key turned in the lock and the door opened a crack. Suze had one eye squeezed shut, her normal glossy mane poking up in all different directions and dressing gown not knotted properly.

"Morning. Can you put your boobs away, please?" I asked.

She let out a colorful word and opened the door wider to let me in. "What the hell are you doing awake? It's not even eight yet."

"Isn't it? I wasn't sure. Figured you'd be up with Tilly."

"She's at Mum and Dad's. This was supposed to be my first long lie in bloody ages. Cheers, Jo."

"Shit, sorry." I paused. "Wait. Are you alone? Want me to go?" I asked, cringing that I may have interrupted some grown-up time.

"You're here now, and yes, I'm alone," Suze said, padding into the kitchen and flicking on the kettle.

"Oh. Is that why you're crabby?"

Suze shrugged. "I told Dan I wasn't interested in taking the relationship further. I'm not ready for what he clearly wants."

I patted her shoulder. "Sorry, Suze."

"It is what it is. I'll meet someone sometime. And when I do, I'm taking things snail slow." Suze let out a breath. "What brings you round at this godforsaken hour?"

That was all we were talking about that, then. "I fell asleep at Nate's office last night. Decided to pop in and see you before heading home."

She frowned. "Why were you sleeping at the office?"

"I took him dinner since he was working late. We both fell asleep."

Suze sighed. "He works too hard."

"Mmm." I agreed. "And he's off to Washington again shortly."

She leaned her hip against the counter and pouted. "Aww, you going to miss him?"

"Not one little bit," I said, as I sat at her tiny breakfast table.

"Heartless cow." Suze pulled out two mugs and added an extra teaspoon of coffee for each of us.

"I'm going with him."

Suze gasped and dropped the spoon with a clatter in the mug. "*Lucky* cow. How'd you swindle that one? No, wait—I don't want to know."

I grinned. "Jealous?"

"Completely."

"I'll bring you Lucky Charms home."

She smiled. "You're forgiven then. Breakfast?"

"Mmm, yes please."

Suze and I spent a large chunk of that day curled up on her couch with a blanket over our knees, watching rubbish TV and munching on the fairy cakes she insisted I bake for her.

Chapter Seventeen

Perhaps I was only being thoughtful and conscientious by bringing in extra baked goods but really, they were more a cleverly disguised bribe. I tapped on Claire's office door and pushed it open when I heard her welcome.

"Been busy have you, Jo?" Claire asked, lifting open one of the box lids to peer inside. "Ooh, red velvet. My favorite!"

"I thought I'd get a big batch done. There are extras if you want to take some home with you."

Claire sighed and closed the lid. "How can I say no to that? The husband would pinch all of these though. I'd better think of a good hiding place. Like my stomach."

I laughed and hesitated to speak.

"Something on your mind?"

"Well, yes." I took a breath. "I wondered if I could possibly take some time off?"

Claire sat back in her chair, a frown pinching her forehead. "How much time are you talking?"

"Um, a week? Ten days would be ideal." My palms were sweaty and I resisted from wiping them on my jeans.

Claire let out a laugh. "Jo! You had me worried you wanted an extended leave of absence or something! Call it two weeks, okay? When do you want to take it?"

"Is next week too short notice?"

"Strictly speaking, yes. But don't worry. You've pulled more hours than anyone else covering the holidays." She reached into the box and withdrew a cupcake. "So where's he taking you?"

"Who?" I asked, scanning her face. If Nate thought I was reserved about my life at home, then it was nothing compared to what I shared at work, which was virtually nothing.

Claire's face softened. "The tall dark and handsome I hear the other girls swooning over that likes to visit you here from time to time. Is he whisking you away?"

A blush warmed my cheeks. Of course I'd noticed the looks Nate received from my colleagues. He and his ego did not need to know. "America. He has to work but..."

"Fantastic! You get a well-deserved holiday and you aren't obliged to spend every waking second with him!"

I smiled, relief filling my blood. "Thank you, Claire. I'll make some plain cakes to freeze here, so all that needs doing is the icing. Do you think one of the others could do it?"

"If they can't, I'd be worried. You're a very considerate girl, Jo." Claire waved a hand at the cake boxes. "I'll sort the rota for next week so don't worry about a thing. Take these away, would you? Before I fill my face."

With a nod I scooped them up and practically skipped out of her office.

* * * *

After leaving the house at an ungodly hour for the journey to the airport, a thirteen hour delay once we arrived and a canceled connection flight on the other side meant it was a full twenty-four hours before my head met anything closely resembling a pillow.

Exhaustion fought the battle effortlessly over excitement and I was unconscious before I could even blink. When I woke, my watch and my body said it was two in the afternoon, but Nate's phone insisted it was only nine in the morning.

The bathroom door opened and Nate emerged, a gust of steam behind of him.

"How in the hell are you so fresh looking? I feel like I died. And was brought back to life. And died again."

He grinned. "You're best just to get up. Don't try and sleep it off."

I groaned and hid my face in the pillow.

"Seriously. Go shower, then I'm taking you for breakfast."

So, he may have been right. The shower was heavenly and the diner around the corner from the hotel smelled like bacon grease, pancake syrup and coffee. I could totally do America.

After breakfast—or late lunch, whatever the hell it was—Nate took me on a mini tour of the area. Bethesda was one of those cities that seemed at total odds with itself. Downtown the architecture was incredible, with large glass structures in shapes so foreign from the buildings back home. Trees lined the streets, lush and colorful with reds and golds streaking the leaves. Canopies hung above the shop fronts for cute little coffee places or independent shops.

Nate loosely clasped my hand in his and pointed out things—interesting buildings and scenery, shops I might like—a bagel place that was to die for. As we walked the streets of Bethesda, it felt like I was living someone else's life—that I was watching this strange girl I didn't recognize. I saw with fascination as she pressed closer to the man by her side, her eyes lighting up when he smiled at her and the tender return of hers.

"What do you think so far?" Nate asked, swirling the wine around his glass.

After walking around town for hours we'd gone straight to dinner, Nate steadfastly ignoring my pleas for a quick nap.

He sat back in his chair and smiled his thanks as the waiter cleared our dinner plates.

I rubbed my eyes. "I still can't take it in. It's the same but different. So pretty, though."

He nodded. "You'll experience it better tomorrow when your body has had time to adjust."

"Yeah. I still think it's unfair how bright eyed and bushy tailed you are. I feel like the walking dead."

"I have done this once or twice. I'm used to it." Nate reached across the table for my hand and pressed a kiss to my knuckle. "Come on then. You look as though you're going to fall asleep at this table."

Nate's hand found my lower back as we walked out of the hotel restaurant and toward the bank of elevators. Inside, his hand crept around to my hip and tugged me closer to him. I let out a sigh and melted against him, my tired eyes closing as my head met his chest.

A chime sounded and the doors slid apart. Nate kissed my temple and fished the key card out of his pocket.

"Would it be terrible if I went to bed now?"

He smiled. "No, but you should try to stay up for a while."

I kicked off my shoes and collapsed on the enormous bed. Nate turned on the TV and tossed me the remote. A yawn split my face in half as I settled back against the plump pillows, watching, but not really seeing, what was on the TV.

Nate bent and kissed me briefly. "I have some things to check before I go into the office tomorrow. Do you mind?"

Slipping my hand behind his neck I pulled him close for a longer kiss. "No, I don't mind. It's not a holiday for you."

His lips twitched as though he was going to make a joke, but his features smoothed over and he stroked a finger over my bottom lip. The intensity in his eyes seared through me, his voice low and gravelly when he spoke. "I'm glad you're here."

I tried to smile but it felt wobbly. "So am I."

Nate kissed me again, soft and lingering. "I won't be long."

"Good."

He smiled and rose to the desk on the opposite wall. He pulled his jumper over his head, the muscles in his back rippling under the thin fabric of his T-shirt. He sat back in the chair, his fingers gliding over the track pad, a tiny frown creasing the space between his eyebrows.

I never did really watch the TV. My eyes never left Nate until I couldn't keep them open for a second longer.

* * * *

The room was dark and silent when I woke. Beside me, Nate lay on his back, the sheet bunched around his waist, exposing his bare chest. I stretched and yawned, feeling refreshed and energized. My mind flitted over the sights we'd seen yesterday, shops I was excited to explore when I was left to my own devices whilst Nate worked.

I hovered over Nate, reaching for his phone. The screen lit up and said it was only four in the morning. With a groan I flopped back against the pillows. By the time my body got used to the stupid time difference, we'd be back home and I'd be struggling all over again.

As carefully as I could, I crept from the bed and silently closed the bathroom door behind me. I stayed in the shower for a long time, enjoying the hot water and scrubbing the last of the travel grime away. Nate was still sound asleep when I finished, even after blow-drying my hair. Lucky bugger. He slept through just about everything, where the slightest thing had me wide awake and on my feet.

I shed the towel and climbed back into bed. Nate still didn't stir, even when I slid my hands through his hair. Inching closer, my breasts brushed his arm and my nipples hardened to a point. I kissed his lips, his jaw, his throat. Flicked my tongue over the flat disc of his nipple.

The sheet tented above his groin and I smiled when I pulled it back to see his glorious erection. I traced a line down him and back up again. Nate shifted in his sleep, his hips rising ever so slightly into my touch.

With a wicked smile, I kissed the tip of his hard length, keeping my eyes on his face. I teased it with my tongue, lapping up the bead of moisture. Nate made a noise low in his throat as I took all of him in my mouth. His hands fisted in the sheets, hips arching up. I worked him hard and fast and knew he was moments away from release.

Nate's eyes flew open and he gritted his teeth as he spilled into my mouth, hot and furiously thick. I swallowed everything he gave me and Nate relaxed into the bed, his breathing quick. I kissed a path up his abdomen, sucking on his nipple for a moment. His arms banded around me as I laid my body flush against his.

"Jesus Christ, woman."

"I couldn't remember if you had requested a wake-up call. Thought I'd better give you one, just in case." I kissed his throat.

A laugh rumbled in his chest. "I was having a fucking amazing dream. And then I woke up and the reality was even better." Nate rolled me over so he pressed my back into the mattress, covering me with his warm body. He ran his nose up the length of my neck, planting a kiss just under my ear.

I hitched my leg over his waist, gasping when I felt his hard-on.

"You know that I'm more than ready, but are you?" Nate asked, sucking on my earlobe.

"Feel me and find out," I breathed, my chest rising and falling faster as my arousal grew.

He dragged his hands down my body, kneading my breast and with the other he teased the small manicured thatch of curls on my mound. Nate groaned as he stroked between my folds and felt just how primed I was for him.

I grasped his cheeks and slanted my lips over his as he fucked me slowly with his fingers.

Nate moved his thumb in lazy circles over my clit and I squirmed beneath his touch.

"Nate," I breathed. "I want you to come inside me."

"I will," he rumbled. Nate withdrew his fingers and raised them to his mouth and licked my lust from him. "I fucking love how you taste, so hot for me."

I moaned at the sight and wrapped my legs over his lower back to urge his hips closer.

Nate grinned as he hovered with just his tip in my cleft. He covered my mouth with his own and I arched my hips to meet his erection.

My back bowed off the bed as he filled me, inch by delicious inch. I knotted my hands in his hair as he rocked into me, fueling my climax. Nate clutched me, held me close as my body shuddered and roared to life under him.

I panted his name as the orgasm hit and his thrusts pounded harder. Nate tensed and he came, burrowing himself even more fully into me. He pressed his face into the crook of my neck, his hard breaths warming my skin.

"Every morning should start like this. Every single morning," he said.

My heart skipped a beat. "I think you would get sick of me after a while."

"That's what's so great about role play, gorgeous. The possibilities are endless."

I laughed and poked his ribs. Nate caught my hand and kissed my fingertips.

"So. Can I expect this kind of wakeup call for the rest of the trip?"

I grinned. "Depends on the tip."

Nate rose onto his elbows. "I'm sure we can work something out."

* * * *

Later, after we did indeed work something out in the shower, Nate took me for breakfast again at the diner then I walked with him to the office building where he would work for the week. People passed us where we stood, dressed to impress in their power suits, clutching their coffee flasks.

Nate pulled me against him, kissing me briefly. "You sure you're going to be okay?"

I nodded and kissed him back. "I'll be fine. There's loads I want to see. Plus Barnes & Noble has three floors. I'll probably be in there till dark."

He smiled. "You'd better not be. You promised to meet me for lunch."

"I'll try my best."

Nate kissed me one last time, gave me a wink then headed inside the building. I stood to the side, watching him pass through the entryway and wait at the bank of elevators. When the doors slid open he turned and saw me looking. I couldn't see his face clearly enough to read his expression, but I thought I caught the ghost of a smile before the elevator doors closed and took him from my sight.

I waited another moment, ignoring the fluttering in my chest. With a breath, I turned to face Bethesda.

Chapter Eighteen

Oh yeah, I could do America. After a brief moment of panic at being left on my own in a foreign country, I reminded myself it was no different from when I first arrived in the dozens of new cities I used to start over. And unlike those times, I could enjoy the new surroundings instead of pinning down the basics—studying street maps, finding cheap accommodation and looking for easy work where I could earn tips to build up a nest of cash.

I retraced the steps Nate and I had just taken to a coffee place. After ordering, I sat at a table outside and skimmed through the guidebook I'd bought at the airport. All around me people moved to and fro. Fast and slow. Shop owners setting up for the day, office workers quickening their step. I felt like Alice down the rabbit hole and couldn't stop the smile from spreading across my face.

As it turned out, I didn't stray far from the immediate area, though not on purpose. I got caught up in the atmosphere and enjoyed spending huge chunks of time browsing through the shops. When it neared lunch, I once again found an outside table at a restaurant across the road from Nate's office. My stomach fluttered when he stepped out of the building and into the pale afternoon sun. He scanned the street for me and pulled his phone out of his front pocket. Mine vibrated on the table and I answered with a smile on my face.

"Afternoon. Nice morning at the office?"

"It was fine. I take it you must be enjoying yourself."

"Immensely."

Nate chuckled and leaned against a railing, folding an arm across his chest. "Glad to hear it. I'm disappointed that I've been deserted for lunch, though."

"Sorry about that. Why don't you try the place across the road?"

His gaze swung around to meet mine and his grin widened. "Hello, beautiful."

"Get your ass over here. I'm starving."

"Yes, ma'am."

* * * *

The next day I ventured farther afield and lost myself in a comic book shop. I met Nate again for lunch then spent my afternoon trolling the floors of Barnes & Noble before retiring to the hotel to read for a while until Nate finished work. We ate at a grill restaurant that night, both of us taking down steaks and beers.

I hit the Smithsonian on the third day and only made it to the hotel moments before Nate did. I chewed his ear off all that night about the exhibits and couldn't believe that he'd been to Washington so many times and never gotten around to going. After I started again on how amazing it was, he held a hand up and said he would see for himself on Saturday when I gave him the guided tour.

Nate told me to dress up the next night. We had dinner at a tiny out-of-the-way place, sitting close to each other and talking in low murmurs and whispers. Afterwards, he slipped an arm around my waist and held me close to his side and I shivered, hiding my face in his arm from the cold of the night. A few streets away, Nate guided me inside a doorway and up a brightly lit flight of stairs. He nodded to a man in a suit who checked in our coats and Nate slid the ticket into his breast pocket. Nate clasped my hand as he led us into the main room and accepted a glass of champagne for us from a passing waiter.

"I thought you would enjoy this exhibition. I've heard a lot about the artist."

I scanned the walls bearing the paintings, all abstract. They were lit from above by bright spotlights, about twenty paintings in total. I had never been to an actual art gallery before. Museums, yes. But this was something different. It felt intimate, perusing the paintings. The artist had laid themselves bare for us all to see and I felt humbled.

The other people enjoying the art were more cultured than me. There was no doubt in my mind. They talked about brush technique, speculated on the meaning and compared it to other works.

"I'm not sure what any of it means," I admitted in a low voice to Nate.

He found my hip with his hand and we moved on to the next piece. "It doesn't matter what it means. How does it make you feel?"

I didn't answer him right away. Instead I turned to scan the room as a whole and that's when I saw it. In the far corner on a stark white canvas with slashes of color, was the painting that made me feel something. Nate caught my look and led us over, stopping a foot away. I broke from his hold and got as close as I dared, hoping I didn't even breathe too hard on it.

To a novice like me, there didn't appear to be any rhyme or reason to the piece, but something about the dramatic splash of colors, as though the artist had just squeezed the paint tube and aimed at the canvas. It was chaotic and beautiful. And I could picture it in Nate's entrance hall. Above the table he dropped his keys on every day, so it was the first thing we saw when we got home.

"You like this one?" Nate asked, his arm coming around my waist and his chest pressing against my back.

I smiled. "*Love* this one."

We lingered in the gallery a while longer and as we left, I couldn't help but twist around for one last look.

* * * *

Every day I lost myself in the city. I played tourist to my heart's content, seeing all the hot spots but also took the roads less traveled and found the places locals knew and loved. And in the evenings, I got Nate all to myself. We went to DC one night to see all the monuments lit up and Nate bought me a souvenir of Lincoln in his chair to remember the experience. Before I knew it, the days had bled away and the trip was almost over.

And as promised, on Saturday, we went to the Smithsonian together. I showed him my favorite exhibits and explored new areas with him. That entire day, Nate always touched me. Whether he held my hand or cupped my elbow when he was eager to see something or his arm draped over my shoulders, to keep me tucked into that spot in his side I seemed to fit into as though it had been carved just for me. The day was damn near perfect, though, as we went back to the hotel to get ready for dinner, Nate swore the best was yet to come.

The whole evening with him was foreplay. From the satin feel of the dress he'd bought for me to the quiet, tucked away restaurant. Every brush, every smile, every look stoked the fire building inside me. I wasn't an idiot. I knew Nate knew exactly what to do to please a woman. He understood the fine art of subtlety—that less was more, and privacy and low lighting went a hell of a lot further than a flashy, trendy restaurant where they didn't print the prices on the menu.

No, I wasn't an idiot. Nate knew full well how to seduce a woman. But it didn't stop me from feeling every single second of that night with him—of trying to imprint the taste of the wine, the smell of his aftershave or the way his eyes glinted in the light into my mind. A mental video to look back on in my later years when I would think of the single most perfect date of my life.

In our hotel room, a bottle of champagne rested in a bucket of ice on the sideboard with two gleaming glasses. Nate slid my coat from my shoulders, planting a kiss on my neck.

"When did you arrange this?" I asked with a smile.

"Before we left."

I turned in his arms, looping mine around his neck and teasing the ends of his hair with my fingers. "You get that I'm a sure thing, right?"

Nate laughed and bent his head to kiss me. "Of course. But this isn't about that. It's a thank you."

My eyebrows pinched together. "What? Why?"

He stroked his thumb across my bottom lip. "For making this trip a thousand times better than any other."

"Oh," I said quietly. "Well, you're welcome."

He chuckled again and pulled my arms from him, kissing the back of my hand before dropping them. I watched as he moved across the room, rolling up his shirt sleeves as he went. Nate reached for the tap on the enormous free standing bath which had been teasing me all week. The only thing that had stopped me was the idea of just how much water it would take to fill a bath that size, and I couldn't justify that much wasted water just for me.

"Take a bath with me." He didn't pose it as a question, but I heard it nonetheless. From anyone else it would have sounded corny as hell but in that second, it only added to the perfection of the evening.

To hell with wasted water…sharing didn't make it half as wasteful. Environmental, even.

Nate poured us a glass of champagne as we waited for the monster to be filled. When it was finally ready, we climbed in. I lay between Nate's legs and against his chest, the hot water lapping around us. He stroked his hands everywhere, over my breasts, neck, legs. His heartbeat was steady beneath my ear, its constant thump my anchor to the moment.

"I meant it, you know," Nate said, threading his fingers with mine and bringing them to his lips. "It's been amazing having you here for this."

I smiled. "I can't believe you're short of company anywhere in the world, Nate."

His chest rumbled with a laugh. "Incomparable to your company, Jo. You're like having a piece of home with me."

"Is it hard leaving Tilly and Suze so often?"

"Yes and no. Depending on Suze's mood it's a welcome break."

I laughed and nudged him. "Charming. She dotes on you."

"I know, and truthfully, I'd be lost without her. But sometimes I wish she would stop worrying about me and concentrate on her own happiness."

"She seems happy with the new bloke."

"For now. We'll see in time, I suppose."

"Do you think she and Cat are getting on all right?"

Nate snorted. "She's probably fattened him right up. Don't be surprised if he's moved in with her by the time we get back."

"Huh! Ingrate."

He laughed again. "Last day tomorrow. What's your plan of action?"

"I'm not sure. There's still so much, isn't there?"

"Yeah. I'm sorry if it's not been so enjoyable for you. It's not ideal, me working all the time."

I turned to face him. "Nate, this has been an amazing trip. Okay, I'd be lying if I said I didn't wish I'd had more time with you, but it's been really exciting, exploring on my own. And the evenings with you have been brilliant. And you know tonight was perfect."

He smiled and stroked my cheek. "I'm glad."

Inching closer to him, I straddled him, my legs looping around his waist. I planted a soft, lingering kiss on his lips. "You may feel thankful for me being here, but I am beyond gloriously happy that you brought me."

"We should do a proper trip. Just the two of us. No work, just us."

My chest tightened as it always did when possible future plans were made. I knew my smile wouldn't convince him of anything, so I did the only thing that would—kissed him. My breasts brushed his chest and he tugged me closer. Nate deepened the kiss and I reached between our bodies to take his pulsing hard-on in my hand.

Nate groaned as he swelled, his skilled fingers probing my pussy. I cried out and rocked against his hand, tightening my grip on his cock. He grunted and pumped faster.

"I need you now," I demanded, catching his mouth in a hard kiss and releasing my hold on him. I raised myself up to guide him between my folds and impaled myself on his hard length. I gasped as my body accommodated the thick magnitude of him. "I feel every bit of you," I breathed, easing myself back up to slide down his dick.

Nate teased my nipple, making the flesh sensitive and achy. "You feel incredible to be inside. Hot, silky…so fucking tight that when you come, it ripples down my cock."

I moaned, the sound loud and agonizing, as my speed increased, the desire taking over all conscious thought. Nate grasped my hips and burrowed his face in my throat as he helped to quicken my movements as though my fever had spread to him. My nails sank into his hair as I rode him, hard and fast. Too impatient, too desperate to even think about taking things slow.

My body trembled as it approached release. Nate held me tighter, his fingers giving a soft bite of pain, and when I came, Nate roared and slammed into me with such force the sensation of his own orgasm fueled my own into something more intense than I'd ever felt.

His breath was hot against my skin and I could feel his heart racing. "Fuck, Jo. You take my breath away."

I chuckled. "I aim to please."

Nate laughed and gently pushed me back so I could see his face. "I mean it. You're constantly surprising me, doing things when I least suspect them. You're like a firework, Jo."

"Explosive and colorful?"

He laughed and kissed me. "Beautifully so. Explosive and colorful. God, I fucking —"

I got caught up in his excitement and kissed him. "You fucking what?"

All humor had drained from his face. "Nothing."

It was then my heart sank and the seriousness of the moment caught up with me. "Okay."

"Jo —" he started.

"No, Nate. Don't. Really." I smiled and kissed him again. "We should have more champagne before it goes flat."

He caught my wrist as I made to leave. "You're fucking killing me right now. Do you get that?"

I laughed. "You're not usually so moody after I fuck your brains out."

"Goddamn it, Jo, this isn't funny!" I'd never seen Nate so angry.

His eyes narrowed, his whole body tensed and I had no idea how to get us back to a few moments ago where we'd both been so happy.

"I know you aren't ready to hear it, but I've been ready to say it for a long fucking time. And I can deal with that. It's one of the many things I don't get, but accept about you. What I can't bloody take is you *knowing* I was about to say it and trying your hardest to get away from it." Nate dropped his head. "Fuck, Jo."

"Don't you dare say it." My voice wobbled and I barely recognized it.

His head jerked up. "No? Well I do. I love you. I'm in love with you. You're everything to me. My soul is shredded and *you* are the one responsible. I was broken and you fixed me just to pick apart the pieces."

He threw his words at me as though they were weapons, each one sinking deeper than the previous. A single tear slid down my cheek as I shot to my feet. I scrambled from the bath, wrapping a towel around me.

"I am a wretched, wreck of a man and I love you so completely, despite all the ways you refuse to love me."

"Stop it."

"Stop what? *Loving* you?"

"You don't love me! You don't, so just stop saying it for chrissakes! God, Nate, it's the sex! When it's this good, of course you're going to get confused and mistake affection for all it really is!"

"The sex, as fond of it as I am, has nothing to do with my feelings for you. I love you, Jo."

"No, you don't!" I screamed, turning from him.

Nate was out after me in a heartbeat. He caught my elbow when I refused to look at him and spun me around. "Yes, I fucking do!"

"How, when you don't even know my name?" The venom in my voice surprised me. My most powerful weapon in my arsenal was out in the open with no hope for retrieval.

Nate dropped his hold, eyes narrowing and breath coming hard and fast. "What did you just say?"

I turned again, not knowing what to do. All I knew and everything I held close had bubbled dangerously close to the surface.

"What did you mean by that? For God's sake, Jo, answer me!"

I let out a breath. "I didn't mean anything. I was being dramatic. We barely know each other, not really, Nate."

"Bullshit. I don't believe you."

My body was as taut as a bowstring but I forced my shoulders to shrug as though I couldn't care less. "Then don't."

For a moment Nate was silent. "This is it, Jo. I've never pushed you to let me in or— Christ, just tell me something about you and whatever the hell you're running from."

I didn't have to look to know his body would be trembling with impatience and adrenaline.

When I didn't answer him, Nate let out a frustrated groan and grabbed my arm to once again force me to look at him. "You have to tell me. I can't ignore it anymore."

"Get your hands off me!" I shrilled, startling him into dropping his hand. "You have no idea what you've done."

"What have I done, Jo?" His voice was softer now, melted chocolate over sandpaper.

I knew every tone of his voice and I adored them all. The desperate passion may have fled from him, but I think he knew I was as skittish as I appeared.

"You've ruined everything! Why did you have to tell me?" The tears soaked my face. He had backed me into a corner and now there was no escape, no excuse and no other option. Fight or flight. I only knew how to do one.

"You already knew."

"You shouldn't have said it out loud. I could pretend, but now you've said it and I can't pretend anymore."

He tried to brush some of the tears away but more kept replacing them. "Well, neither could I."

My whole body felt exhausted. "I have to go."

Nate let out an exasperated laugh. "And go where? It's late and you're in a different fucking country! Jesus, Jo. Do you want another room? Are you serious?"

"No, I have to *go*." My voice broke and I pulled away from him. I slumped on the edge of the bed, my wasted head in my hands.

If I were honest with myself, I should have left a long time ago. But I'd tricked myself into feeling safe and fooling my head and heart with useless fantasies that maybe this time I could stay.

"No."

The simplicity of his word broke my heart. As though it was really that easy.

"Did you hear me? You're not going anywhere." Nate sighed and he crouched in front of me. "Jo, I'm fucking begging you here. You have to tell me what you're running from."

"I have to keep you safe," I whispered.

"*Safe*? What the hell does that mean?"

"Nothing, nothing. It means nothing. Nate, please just give me space."

"You know, even if you'd asked me that an hour ago, I would have done it. Not now." Nate stood and I heard him pacing the floor. "I've done as you've asked for too long. I've given you space, I've stood back when everything in me told me to push. Now it's time to remember you have a pretty big pair of balls and tell me what you're so afraid of."

I hitched in a breath. I had no idea if he was right or not. The last thing I wanted to do was drag Nate further into my twisted world. I could only hope the need to protect his family would be greater than the need to keep me in his life.

So I would tell him my story. And hope to hell once he'd heard it he'd let me flee.

Fight or flight.

I didn't know how to fight.

Chapter Nineteen

I wiped the last of the tears from my cheeks and dragged my eyes up to meet his. Nate sat back, no doubt surprised by the steeliness in my stare. Because that was all I felt in that moment, as though a witch had cursed me and turned me into stone.

"How many times have you fallen in love, Nate?"

His eyebrows rose but he humored my question, settling back into the chair and folding his arms. "Not many. Fairly grateful right now."

"And how many people do you love?" A lump formed in my throat and I forced it down. "I have loved exactly one person in my entire life."

"You mean you've fallen in love once?"

My story wouldn't be easy for Nate to hear, but to understand some of it, he had to know all of it. "No. I mean exactly what I said—I have loved *one* person in my life. My childhood...it wasn't like yours and Suze's. When I was four I was taken in by social work after my mother overdosed and they had no idea who my father was. Nobody wanted me. I was never in one place for too long. Temporary placement for the most part, never bothered making friends because I got sick of saying goodbye to them and the disappointment when none stayed in touch.

"But I worked hard in school, kept to myself and for the most part, kept out of trouble. At university I qualified for financial help and for the first time ever, I had a somewhat structured life. I made an effort and found some decent friends. And then one night, I met Scott."

The dark stab of fear hit me as it always did when I thought of him. My hands clenched instinctively to hide the trembling. Nate sat forward with his elbows on his knees, his own hands in tight fists. Men like Nate always knew, could always read the signs. But mine didn't show what he thought they did.

"I'd had experiences with guys before. Meaningless encounters where I didn't care that I was being used. And then this guy comes into my life and makes me feel things totally foreign to me. I came to life around him. I was happy...bubbly, even. Scott was older than me, just by a few years, but enough to seem worldly and mature to my naïve nineteen years. He had everything going for him—good looks, charm, intelligent. And he chose *me*. It never made any sense, not when he could have had any girl he wanted. But Scott adored me. Gave me the attention I'd always craved.

"It was flattering. *I* was flattered. That kind of adoration is damn hard not to let it go to your head. It made me dizzy, knowing he was so addicted to me." I laughed, bitter and humorlessly and looked at the floor. "I thought it gave me power. Thought that because his feelings were so intense I had control over him.

"I had nothing. No power, no control. By the time I realized he had been taking mine...there was so much gone that when he took the rest, I barely felt it. He was all I thought about and I couldn't get enough. We moved in together and all my spare time was his. I didn't realize at first what was happening. It was like one day I looked up and the life I had worked so hard for had disappeared. My friends gave up, sick and tired of hearing my pathetic reasons for ditching them. I was one more failed course away from getting kicked out of university." I forced myself to raise my eyes to Nate's.

His expression was neutral but I knew better than to believe it. It was sure to falter when he knew my ugly truth that I had been every bit as addicted to Scott as he was to me.

"Sometimes I remember the good times I had with him and I miss them. I remember them and I miss *him* and the way he made me feel about myself. He was my lover, my future, my best friend. He was my whole world. It wasn't until the bad times started outweighing the good...until the hurt was more prominent than the love that I realized the relationship was so unhealthy — that it was hurting us both. Scott had turned paranoid. I couldn't wear makeup, skirts, dresses — anything with shape to it — because he said other men were looking at me.

"I tried a few times to leave him. But he would beg me to stay and I could see how much I was hurting him and I could hardly stand it. The first time I went back to him he started getting violent. A few slaps here and there until the night he beat me unconscious because I smiled at a waiter. The relationship was destroying both of us and I barely recognized not only myself, but the man I had fallen in love with. When I finally got the courage to throw in the towel, Scott tried to kill us both. Came very close to succeeding. Sometimes I wish he had. Maybe then all this would be over. Maybe then he would have some peace and I wouldn't be hurting anyone anymore."

Nate scrubbed a hand over his face. "What did he do?"

"Swerved us into oncoming traffic. I was released from hospital first, a mercy I'm still not sure I deserved. Scott was in a medically induced coma to try and ease the swelling in his brain. It would only be a matter of time until he came round, so I did the only thing I could think of—I ran. Blazed a fake trail across Europe using Facebook and Instagram, paid a computer person to set me up with different IP addresses that would make it look like I was actually there. I knew the few friendships I'd destroyed would see I was where I was if Scott asked any of them. And if he looked for himself, he'd think that I was getting over the accident and the relationship, when really I was erasing my life."

"So, what you said about your name. You really meant that, didn't you?" Nate asked.

I nodded. "I legally changed my name, applied for a new passport and disappeared. It was easier than I thought it would be. I move around a lot, rent rooms so there's no lease and take easy jobs where no one cares if you stop showing up. Be friendly, but forgettable."

"And you've lived like this for years? How do you know he's even looking for you?"

"Because I know him. He once told me that he would always know where to find me. And he would always look. I thought it was his way of reassuring me, not the promise it really was." I sighed. "Believe me, I know how crazy all this sounds. But it's reality for me. Scott will never give up. Never. The only thing that could is one of us being dead."

Nate stood up so abruptly the chair toppled over on its side. He paced back and forth, that carefully disguised agitation finally rising to the surface. "How long do you spend in one place?"

I picked at a nail. "Usually? Six months at the very longest."

He stopped, his eyes raking over me. "You told me you got to Edinburgh in February."

"Yes."

"So you've been there almost ten?"

"Yes."

"Why?"

"I would have thought that was obvious." I stood up and wrapped my arms around myself. "I've made so many excuses, given myself so many reasons to stay. If I was honest with myself, they should all have been reasons to leave."

Nate laughed. "Suze and I really fucked things up for you, didn't we?"

My eyes narrowed at his tone. "Yes, Nate, you did really fuck things up. Is that what you want to hear? Does it make it easier? If I'd had half a lick of sense, I never would have moved in."

He let out a rush of breath. "Do you even hear yourself? Jesus, it's no way to live. How can you expect to go through life making no connections, forming no bonds?"

"In case you weren't listening, it's what I'm used to. People caring—*that* is what's unusual for me."

"So how would you do it? How would you leave us?" Nate asked. "I wake up and there's a letter on my pillow? Or would I merit an actual goodbye?"

I couldn't answer him. But my silence was all he needed to hear.

"Fuck me, *nothing*? Just, one day you're here and the next you're not? Christ."

"It's better that way."

"Better for who? Because it wouldn't be fucking better for me! Wouldn't you care that I would spend the rest of life wondering if you were even safe?"

"Not knowing keeps you safer."

For a moment, I thought Nate was going to pull me into his arms as the full weight of understanding finally dawned on him. But instead, he dragged his hands through his hair. "I don't know what to do with all of this."

It felt like I was breaking. That one by one my cells were breaking down until there was nothing keeping me together anymore. "There isn't anything to do. Suze knows I'm a drifter. Tell her we had a big argument while we were here and I decided it was time to move on."

Nate's arms dropped to his side. "What are you talking about?"

"My leaving. What else?"

"Are you joking? You tell me all this and then expect to just disappear?"

My heart gave a little flutter of both hope and dread. "Have you not been listening? Why on earth would you want me around after hearing all of that?"

"Do you think so little of me? I'm having a hard time processing all of this, but Jesus, you only told me five minutes ago."

"I told you I'd leave one day."

"And I told *you* that one day I would let you. It's not that day."

I hardened my stare. "You can't stop me."

"No, I can't. I'm hoping you'll stay on your own." Nate righted the fallen chair and gestured for me to sit.

Once I was, he crouched in front of me, his height keeping us at almost the same eye level. "There is no way for me to understand what you went through, but I do understand that you're scared. The one thing I really don't get, is how you think he'll find you. From the sounds of it, you've done a bloody good job at hiding all these years."

"Exactly," I whispered. "But I'm hardly hiding anymore, am I? Shit, Nate, I'm practically building a life with you."

"What's so wrong with that? You're entitled to happiness—more importantly, to freedom. Because the way you have been living…you're still his prisoner."

A tear slid down my cheek. I had never thought of it like that before, but of course, he was right. All this time I had congratulated myself with staying off Scott's radar, but he'd had just as much control over me as he always had.

Nate brushed the tear away. "I can keep you safe."

I shook my head, eyes widening. "No, no, I couldn't bear it if something happened to you."

He dropped his eyes for a moment. There was a determined resolve to them when he raised them again. "I would leave with you."

"What?" I breathed.

"If you truly believed he had found you, there was proof he was going to do something to hurt you, then I would leave with you."

With shaking hands I cupped his jaw, the rough stubble prickling my skin but only showing me how much of a man he was. "You've no idea what you're saying."

He frowned. "Yes, I fucking do."

I bit my lip, and gave my head a tiny shake. "No, you don't. How could you leave with me, Nate? Could you leave behind your business? Suze? Tilly? Your parents? Could you live knowing that if Scott had found me, he had surely found out you were my lover and therefore know exactly where your family lived? Could you make love to me knowing I was the reason he would hurt them?"

Nate gripped my wrists but didn't speak.

"I told you."

He groaned. "Fine, then we wouldn't leave. There is such a thing as the police, you know. Have him arrested. Get the psycho locked up."

"With what proof? By the time he does something that warrants an arrest then someone, more than likely me, will be dead, so what's the point?"

Nate shoved to his feet. "Fuck! How am I supposed to just sit back and do nothing? Tell me what to do!"

I slowly rose and placed my hands ever so gently on his chest. "When the time comes, don't look for me."

Chapter Twenty

Nate cracked open the mini bar and poured a miniature bottle of whiskey into a tumbler. I watched his back, the muscles tense, and I felt a deep ache in the center of my chest. This should never have been his burden. I pulled on a thick, fluffy dressing gown and curled up in a chair facing the window. Guilt and fear was a swirling dervish inside me and I wrapped my arms around my middle, as though to hold myself together.

The room plunged into darkness and Nate's silhouette appeared by the window. He held out his hand and I took it, letting his firm grip ground me to the present and not the past.

"Let's go to bed," he said, his voice tired and spent.

I nodded, though I doubted he could see me. I dropped the robe to the floor and climbed into bed behind him. Nate didn't wait before pulling me into the warmth of his body. His legs intertwined with mine and his arms banded around my body and I let him be my shield. And with Nate protecting me, I actually managed sleep.

* * * *

Soft morning light filtered into the room. Nate's sleep heavy body was pressed against mine, warm and intimate. I tried to get closer. Nate stirred in his sleep and pressed a kiss to my shoulder. His hand slid from my waist to my knee where he gripped it and pulled it over his hip. I looked up at him and whatever he saw in my eyes must have told him that I both wanted and needed him.

When he sank inside my cleft, Nate held me close, making love to me slowly. I felt him everywhere — in my body and my mind. His eyes never left mine and they devoured me when I came. Afterwards he just kissed me, almost as a reassurance. I wasn't sure if it was because of the night before, or if now there was finally nothing between us, but things felt different.

"Get dressed, we're going out today."

I frowned. "Don't you have to go into the office?"

He shook his head and kissed me again. "Not today."

We had breakfast at the diner again, the waitress smiling and waving a hand at the table that had become our usual. Later we walked to the metro to get a train to DC and spent the day being tourists. Nate held my hand and kissed me, soft, like routine. And to anyone looking in with no idea what was going on beneath the surface, we were just an average couple.

* * * *

We traveled through the night. The excitement I'd felt on the previous journey had been replaced with a dull sense of dread. No longer was the world full of possibilities. For a time, I had been able to pretend I was the kind of girl who deserved a man like Nate. But my eyes were open now and I remembered my fate.

Nate was quiet in the taxi. He kept my hand encased in his but didn't stray his gaze from the window. When we arrived home, Nate jogged upstairs with the bags, asking over his shoulder if I would stick a couple of slices of toast on.

As I moved through the house, I couldn't help but think back to the first time I'd set foot in this place. I had been awed by its gentle, subtle elegance. Contemporary meets traditional, designer meets homey. I hadn't known where to look, what to gobble up with my eyes. Now I knew every inch of this house. I knew its nooks and crannies, its quirks and defects. But I felt every bit as alien as I had that very first day.

The smell of toast filled the kitchen when Nate appeared, having changed into his usual garb of jeans, T-shirt and Converse, with his hair still damp from the shower. He retrieved his travel mug from the cupboard and filled it with the coffee I had started.

"I need to give an update to the team on what the American's want. They're breathing down my neck to see some progress." He huffed out a breath. "They'd see a damn sight more if they'd stop changing their bloody minds."

I forced a smile. "Okay, but won't you be exhausted?"

Nate shrugged. "I should be okay. Be fine as long as I keep going. I'll be back around the usual sort of time." He kissed me briefly, reaching around to snag a piece of toast, winking at me as he took a bite.

My heart lurched and I couldn't look away as he left the room and shortly after opened and closed the front door.

"Goodbye," I whispered.

It was as though I was separate from my body, looking down at this girl who moved with purpose. I was numb from my fingers to my toes as I walked upstairs and into the room I had called home for all these months. The holdall I was used to living out of was still shoved under the bed and I pulled it free and laid it open on the bed.

I moved slowly, almost methodically as I neatly folded my clothes into the bag. It didn't take long. Despite straying so far from what was normal to me during my time here, I hadn't gone completely native. For a moment I hesitated, but decided to leave the two dresses Nate had bought for me hanging in the armoire. Not only did I not deserve them, but when would I ever have the occasion again to wear them? And even if I did, I didn't want such a strong reminder of Nate.

The sound of the zip echoed around the room. Fifteen minutes and my life was packed. I should never have forgotten. How could I have been so stupid to think I could have something different, even if just for a little while?

I left my backpack on top of the holdall outside my bedroom door. I told myself just to leave, to get it over with—I couldn't stay away. I climbed the stairs to Nate's floor and paused for a second in the doorway.

Even though he hadn't been in there for a week, the room exuded Nate. It smelled like him and I could *feel* him everywhere. My body shook as I trailed my fingertips over the solid bed frame, a lump lodging itself in my throat when I pictured us sprawled in that big bed of his, every inch of ourselves touching.

Releasing a shaky breath, I sat on the chaise longue and pulled my knees up to my chest. The city was laid out in front of me, all sprawling rooftops, eccentric, almost random twists and turns of the streets. Views of the Water of Leith and the Gardens broke up this ancient city that had worked itself under my skin...not unlike Nate.

He had given me the perfect opportunity. The moment I told him the story of my past was the moment my fate was sealed, and the first chance I got I would leave his world behind. And now here I was, poised above departure but unable to move.

When had it happened? I couldn't pinpoint the moment everything had changed. When it had become an impossibility for me to leave.

I watched the light change. The pale sun sank over the buildings, casting shadows into the room before twilight began and the sky turned a dusky purple. It was fully dark when I heard him behind me. My heart didn't thump. I didn't panic. It was almost as though I was resigned.

He crouched in front of me. "You're still here."

"I've been trying not to be."

Nate dropped his head. "I'm not sure if I should be relieved by that or not." He pulled my arms free from my knees, stroked his long fingers over mine. "What's going on, Jo?"

"I—" I choked on my words, sudden emotion swelling in my throat. "I don't know when this happened."

"When what happened?"

"When it became too late for me to leave." A tear escaped and trailed down my cheek. "I need to leave, but I don't know how."

Nate kissed my knuckles. "Maybe you're right where you need to be."

"Nate, we talked about this. It isn't safe for me to be here. If he finds me—"

"He won't."

"He has before," I whispered.

He rocked back on his heels. "What?"

My stomach rolled. "A few years ago. He found me, I don't know how. I was working in a bar and I saw him."

"Jo," Nate said slowly, "can you even be sure? We've all got people who look like us...couldn't it have been your mind playing tricks on you?"

"You know, I thought that too. But my manager at the bar was attacked. He beat him within an inch of his life with a crowbar. His name was Doug and he was a friendly guy, always quick with a cuddle or a kiss on the cheek, but he never felt inappropriate. I think he saw us and decided it meant something else." I dragged my eyes up to Nate's. "And it's not the first time something like that has happened. Once when we were together, a guy hit on me. He was mugged and got his jaw broken. Another night when he was drunk he accused me of having an affair with my tutor. The guy was involved in a hit and run. I have no proof Scott did any of those things, but I know it was him."

Nate was silent and I couldn't read his expression.

"I couldn't bear it if something happened to you," I whispered.

He rose to his feet, gently pulling me to mine. "I can't make this decision for you. I left today to give you the chance to leave, if that's what you wanted. So why are you still here, Jo?"

"I know I should leave. I *know* it."

Nate cupped my cheeks. "I won't stop you. If it's what you need, then I won't stop you. I'll give you money and you'll take it because I won't take any other answer. I need to know that you'll be okay. But if you want to stay, then *stay*. And be with me. No more hiding."

No more hiding…

Somehow that thought was almost more terrifying than disappearing again. It had only been *me* for as long as I could remember. Did I even know how to be a part of something? One half of a whole? Nate had no idea what he was asking me. He wasn't just asking me to stay but to shake off everything I had been carrying.

"What does your heart tell you?" he asked.

With every beat of my heart it had told me to be alert, always careful. Now, it simply said *him, him, him.* "It isn't that simple."

Nate smiled. "Yes, it is."

My breath left me in a rush. "No, it isn't. I don't know how to be in a healthy relationship or, God, how to be *normal!*"

"Jo, you'll never be normal. Chrissakes, you're almost as mental as Suze, and that's saying something. I'm not going to influence this decision but I will say this—I think you owe it to yourself to try. To give us a try."

I grasped his wrists and squeezed my eyes shut. "I'm broken."

"You're healing. And I would do anything you want to help you feel safe."

"I'm not enough for you."

"You're everything to me."

He'd said it so simply that a laugh bubbled in my throat. How easy it was for him to say how he felt. Over these last few months I had wanted to tell him what was in my heart a thousand times but I'd kept it inside because I knew it would make leaving a thousand times harder. But here we were and I still wasn't leaving, and I still hadn't told him how I felt.

Nate deserved so much more than I could give him, yet he believed in me. He believed this was something I could get over. "How can you want me?"

"Because I love you. You're it for me."

I pressed my forehead to his and let out a shaky breath. "I don't know what I'm doing."

"I can teach you."

Chapter Twenty-One

The hot water of the shower went some way to rinse away the stress of the last few days. My eyes were gritty and tired, a sign of both emotion and jet lag. And despite the turmoil still circling in my mind, I couldn't help but notice the tiny flutter in my belly.

Me and Nate.

No more running.

When I emerged, dressed in one of Nate's old T-shirts, soft and smelling like him, he was lounging on the bed with a pizza box beside him.

Nate smiled and opened the lid. "Hurry up, the smell of this thing has been driving me crazy."

A movie played on one of the flat screens and I curled up beside Nate on the bed and reached for a slice of pizza. I could do this. I could do this. I *would* do this.

* * * *

When I woke the next morning with Nate's body curled around mine, there was a sleepy smile on my face. He stroked a hand up my bare leg, making the flesh breakout in goosebumps.

"I know you're awake," he whispered in my ear.

My smile widened and I rolled over to face him.

He kissed me. "Good morning."

"Hi," I said, kissing him back.

"I think you should move your things upstairs today."

Okay, I was awake. I sat up in bed and shoved the mass of hair out of my face. "What?"

Nate tucked both arms behind his head and gave me one of his cocky smiles. "You heard. Move up here."

"Not one to do anything by half, are you?" I took a breath, my heart thundering.

He grinned. "Nope."

"Nate," I sighed. "I don't want us to rush things."

"We're not rushing. We've been together for ages now. You spend most nights up here anyway. Really, I'm just saving you the constant trips downstairs for changes of clothing for me to rip off you."

A laugh bubbled in my throat. "Well, when you put it like that…"

He winked. "Told you."

I rested my hand on his stomach. "I want to say yes. I really do."

"So say it, it's easy." He caught my hand and sat up. "Come on, Jo, this is what we talked about last night. We're all in now. Let's do this right."

I studied his warm brown eyes and yet again couldn't believe it was me he was seeing.

He tugged me closer. "Say yes."

"Make me," I said with a smile.

Nate's eyebrows rose into his hairline. "Oh, I will."

I had a split second of anticipation before he grabbed me and flipped me onto my back.

When I emerged from the en suite after a relaxing bath, my backpack and holdall of clothes was in the middle of the bed, the two dresses I had left in the wardrobe spread out beside it. He winked and strode into the wardrobe. I heard the chime from his phone and a moment later, Nate poked his head out from his walk-in wardrobe. "Hurry up and get that stuff put away. Suze texted. She's cracking up with the cat."

I snorted a laugh and picked up the bag and dresses, following Nate back inside the wardrobe. "Why? I thought for sure she'd love doting on him."

"Yeah, well, it seems as though he only has love for his mistress. He's spent all week hissing at Suze and biting her ankles when she doesn't feed him fast enough."

I smothered a laugh with my hand.

Nate smiled. "You can laugh, but it'll be you moping when next time we go away we have to put him in a cattery."

My cheeks warmed and I turned from him, busying myself with emptying the bag onto one of the shelves.

"What?" Nate asked questioning my blush, his arms coming around my middle.

I let out a breath. "I'm looking forward to it."

"Locking the poor boy in a kennel?"

"No," I laughed, turning in his arms. "Going away again. Yesterday I would have dreaded you saying something like that. I don't have to now."

He smiled. "You're still allowed minor panics every so often. I won't judge you for them."

"I know. But I've decided I'm just going to be happy."

Nate kissed me. "I like that idea."

So did I. It would take some getting used to...but so did I.

* * * *

Suze flung open her front door and shot us both scathing looks before turning and marching down the hall. Nate and I exchanged looks and headed after her.

"So...everything go okay?" I asked.

Suze stood with her hands on her hips, glaring at me. From somewhere in the flat, Cat meowed so loud I'm surprised the pictures didn't wobble on their hooks. She shoved her arm in my face and only when I pulled back a bit did I see the long, livid scratches.

"Oh, sorry. Did you two not get along?" I asked.

"Not get along?" she squawked. "Jo, that fleabag is like the devil incarnate!"

I cringed. "He's always been fine with me."

"Well, clearly he likes you better."

"Mmm. I brought you doughnuts. To say thank you."

Suze's jaw ticked. "Did you make them?"

I nodded.

"Custard?"

"And jam."

She groaned and let her arms flop by her side. "Using baked goods as bribery should be illegal, you know."

"Where's Tilly?" Nate asked, shoving the cake tin at Suze and placing his hand on my shoulder, pulling me into him.

"At Mum and Dad's. They want to know if you're coming to dinner tomorrow night," Suze said as she walked toward the kitchen.

Nate raised his eyebrow at me in questioning. A brief flare of discomfort, before I smiled and gave him a short nod. "Yeah, we'll be there."

There was a pause before Suze poked her head back into the room. "We? Did you just say we? Seriously? We? As in, you two? Seriously?"

Nate rolled his eyes. "Yes, Suze. Seriously. Seriously, seriously."

"What the fuck?" She came fully into the room and took stock of us for the first time. "What's going on here? Don't tell me you're actually over the bullshit and doing this properly?"

"Fuck off, Suze," Nate said in a tired voice, though the corner of his lip twitched.

She gave a squeal of delight and rushed forward to hug me. "About bloody time!"

"Am I forgiven for my hell cat now then?"

Suze snorted in my ear. "I'm not that happy for you. When are you taking that beast?"

"Right now. I need to get back home so your brother and I can continue to fuck each other senseless."

Nate let out a barking laugh whilst Suze shot me a filthy look. "I'm never going to win now, am I?"

I grinned. "Nope."

"Then let's get that bloody cat."

When I opened the door to Suze's spare room, Cat rushed out and wound himself around my legs. He went into his travel kennel fine but when Suze put her face up to the bars, he hissed and swiped a paw at her.

"Ingrate," she mumbled.

I hugged her, and kissed her cheek. "Thanks, Suze."

She looked past me to Nate, who was opening her front door. "No, thank *you*, Jo."

* * * *

Claire took one look at the pile of cake boxes on the bar and swore very colorfully. "You're timing could *not* be better, seriously."

I paused from transferring the cakes to glass stands. "Um, you're welcome?"

Claire let out a tired sigh as she peered inside one box. "You've no idea the trouble you've caused around here, have you?"

My stomach sank. "No."

"Well, it turns out freezing batches of your cupcakes and leaving the should-be simple task of having one of the other motley crew ice them was a good idea in theory, not so much in practice."

"What do you mean?"

"Let's just say there's no substituting you, Jo. And it seems you've picked up more than a few regulars who have been on at me every blooming day since you left, asking when you'll be back." Claire gave me a smile. "You've become indispensable, love."

"Is that a good thing?"

She squeezed my arm. "It's a great thing. Now, tell me all about America."

My cakes sold out before three p.m. that day. If things kept up like this, I could become the main cause for diabetes.

* * * *

Nate and Suze's parents lived in a modest family home on a quiet street near The Meadows. A couple of boys were kicking a football back and forth across the road as Nate pulled up. One of the boys whistled to Nate to kick their ball back. He flicked it into the air and did a couple of tricks before kicking it back to the boys. He winked at me and gave me his arrogant smile before opening the door to his parent's house.

Suze and Tilly sat on the living room floor, CBeebies blaring in the background. Vic appeared and slapped Nate on the shoulder. "The prodigal son returns."

"So he does, Father. How's it going?"

Vic shrugged. "Can't complain. Jo, lovely to see you again."

"You too," I said.

"Where's Mum?"

"Kitchen."

"Cooking?"

Vic scoffed. "Ordering."

Nate laughed. "Nice. Where from this time?"

"Whichever one she fishes out from the back of the drawer."

I smiled at their banter and moved around them. Tilly noticed me and stood up, squeezing her chubby little fists at me. I swung her up and kissed her cheek in a loud raspberry.

Tilly giggled and smooched my face. "More kisses."

"I would, but I think Uncle Nate would get jealous."

She shook her head. "More kisses!"

"No idea where she gets her temperament from, Suze," I said, sitting beside her on the floor and passing Tilly a handful of wooden bricks.

"No, me neither," she said, shooting a glance at her brother. "I swear your kisses are made from crack or something. No one can be *that* appealing."

"I'm going to take that as a compliment."

Suze grinned. "Brave of you."

Diane appeared in the doorway from the hall and smiled at her son. "Ah good, you're both here. I'm about to order. Chinese all right with everyone?"

We all nodded our assent.

"Jo? Anything in particular you're fond of? Or despise with a fiery temper?"

I laughed but it was Nate who answered before I could, "Lemon chicken, Mum. She'll eat it by the truck load."

Diane winked at me. "Done."

"And for after's, Jo made one of her revolting cakes. Make sure you fill up beforehand so you don't need to force down too much."

Vic laughed and slapped his son's flat stomach. "Doesn't look like you've been avoiding any, Nate. She's softening you up."

Diane took the box from him. "About time someone is. Thanks, Jo, I bet it's lovely."

I shrugged. "Just a simple sponge. I knew Tilly would be here, and she seems to like it."

Suze snorted a laugh. "Understatement. You're turning us all into cake whores, Jo. I hope you know it's you I'll be asking to replace my wardrobe when I don't fit into my clothes anymore."

"There is such a thing as moderation, Suze," Diane said, smiling. She held up the cake box. "Jo? Could you help me with this?"

I followed her into the kitchen and watched as she transferred the cake onto a stand and covered it with the lid. She seemed to have things under control.

"Sorry, daft diversion tactic I think," Diane apologized. "I just wanted to ask you something and didn't want to put you on the spot with everyone in there. Nate mentioned you hadn't decided on your Christmas plans yet, and I wanted to formally — but with no pressure — invite you here. With totally ulterior motives, of course. If you decide you would like to come, would you sort out the desert? We usually buy something, but it would be lovely to have something homemade. And as I'm sure you've gathered, they all seem to be mad on what you make."

A tickle of nerves fluttered in my belly. My default settings weren't stuck on flight anymore, but they still hovered somewhere close to that region. It wouldn't be an overnight thing, this whole me giving life a chance, and more often than not I'd prefer to avoid something rather than take the less traveled road and make the effort. But anything worth having was worth fighting for. Even if it was my own nature I was fighting against.

I touched her arm. "Thank you, Diane. I'd love to."

She smiled and I thought for sure she'd gush or hug me, or, I don't know, do something. Instead she simply said, "Good."

When I turned around to go back into the living room, Nate was leaning against the wall in the hall. He gave me a lopsided smile and kissed my temple, and like his mother, didn't make a big fuss out of something that was definitely huge for me. Maybe this was a learning curve we were all adjusting to.

Chapter Twenty-Two

Over the next few weeks we slid into an easy, new routine. The more baking I was doing for the bistro, the more they wanted me to do. It got to the point where I would work my shift, come home and spend hours baking for the next day. Claire slowly reduced the amount of nights I worked, which Nate whole heartedly supported. We went to bed together almost every night until it no longer felt new and different but more like something we had been doing for years. Intimacy took on new meaning for me and it stopped being something to fear. And once I'd stopped trying to shut him out, I learned more about Nate in those three or four weeks than I had in the months we'd been sleeping together.

I learned that after a bad day or if something hadn't worked out as he had hoped at work, he needed time to put it out of his head before he went back to deal with it. He would grab a beer from the fridge and sit in front of the telly for an hour or so until he would seek me out and tell me what had happened. He liked homemade soup and liked it even more when I surprised him at work with some for lunch, along with homemade crusty bread.

In the mornings, he knew exactly the right spot on the back of my neck to kiss to wake me up and turn me on simultaneously. And in return, all it took to let him know what I wanted was to slip my foot over his. While he never once pressured me to spend time with his family, the happiness he exuded at now being able to flaunt our new found relationship status made me proud, and somewhat humbled, to be with him. Nate's family meant everything to him, and the fact he wanted to show me off to them? I still couldn't get my head around that.

I walked into the bistro feeling lighter than air. I was finally in a place in my life where not only was I happy, but I was also letting myself be happy. My demons hadn't been fully excised but they were definitely getting their ass kicked.

Paul was behind the bar and glanced at me as I struggled through the door with all my goodies.

"Claire wants to see you as soon as you're here. Best hurry up. She's in a spectacular mood today."

Shit. What does she want? My stomach churned and I left the boxes in the kitchen. My mind careened to wild and improbable reasons for her requesting my presence. I made my way slowly, but not slowly enough, to her office. I tapped gently and almost immediately she barked for me to enter.

Claire sat behind her desk, shuffling through a mountain of papers. She looked at me and gestured to the seat in front of her desk. "Be with you in a sec, Jo. Can't find this fucking application— *Ah ha*! About time."

"Application?" *Wow. So not nonchalant.*

"Mmm. We're going to need a couple of other members of staff, especially for behind the bar in the evenings and weekends." Claire cleared the papers into a more organized pile and leaned back in her chair. "To put it frankly, things just aren't going as I'd hoped."

Oh, God. This is it. My marching orders. *Jesus, why does something* always *have to go to shit?* Was this just how it was supposed to be, a few other areas of my life was swimming along nicely so the balance had to be restored?

Claire let out a breath. "Jo, get that look off your face would you? I'm not sacking you!"

I slumped in my chair. "You're not?"

Her smile was kind. "No. I'm promoting you."

"Pardon?"

"It's true that things can't keep going as they have been. You're burning yourself out, Jo. I think it's admirable you want to work as many shifts as before and do the baking on the side, but really, it's a little naïve."

Truth be told, I was knackered. But I'd once overheard one of the weekend girls bitching about me and how she bet I'd try to use the baking as a way to get out of shifts. I was already doing less nights. Okay, more day shifts, but still. I didn't want to give anyone any ammo if I didn't have to.

"So would you like to hear my plan of action?"

I sat up straighter. "As long as it doesn't involve me getting the boot then yes, I would."

Claire laughed. "I take on three new members of staff, mostly for evenings and weekends. Despite what some people may think, it doesn't take twenty minutes to throw one of your cakes together and so your hours spent baking will be like a shift in itself. And when you're here, you'll be my new manager."

There was a pause after she spoke, where I knew I heard the words but somehow they weren't making any sense. Claire blinked and I realized she hadn't misspoken. "I'm sorry...manager?"

"You've outgrown your role here, Jo. And it's not because of the cakes, which are, quite frankly, making us more popular in the daylight hours than we have been in years. This place...it's like a little family. Dysfunctional, but workable. And whether you've realized it or not, you're a big, big part of that now. Yes, I will admit in the beginning you were so...separate from the rest of the team but in the last few months, you have blossomed before all of us. I have no doubt you will thrive in this role."

My stomach fluttered as though a thousand butterflies simultaneously took flight and my heart gave a little pinch as I wondered how peculiar I must have seemed to Claire when I'd first come to work for her. "What would it mean?"

"You would take over some of my responsibilities that are becoming a little time consuming and tedious. My husband is getting sick of waiting on me to slow down, and it's about time I met him halfway. You'll sort out staff rotas, compile orders, open up and manage the cash. Tony and June will still be my night supervisors. They've handled the cashing up and closing down of the place for years, but neither wants to move into a more daylight, or official, role."

"Christ, have you thought about this?"

"Yes. And ask anyone—I'm never wrong."

I leaned forward. "Okay...okay. When do we do this?"

Claire grinned. "Right now."

* * * *

I hit the supermarket after work, smiling like a nutter as I threw things into the trolley. Claire and I had spent hours that day going over in minute detail what my new responsibilities would be. She'd talked me through the opening up procedures and the banking. My mind was swirling with all the new information and all I could think about was how I couldn't wait to tell Nate. I practically ran home.

I couldn't keep the goofy smile off my face as I prepared dinner. He was home around the usual sort of time, whistling as he shed his coat, satchel and keys. When he appeared in the kitchen, his smile turned wolfish, flashing strong white teeth. "What's all this?"

I was dishing up the steaks, along with potatoes and coleslaw. Two beers dripped condensation onto the coasters and a cake made just for Nate was on the stand on the counter. I smiled at him. "I had a good day."

"Must have been pretty spectacular." Nate popped a potato in his mouth and bent his head to kiss me briefly. "This smells fantastic."

"Well dig in."

Nate squeezed my waist but did as he'd been told and sat before his dinner. "I want to hear about this good day."

"Later. Eat first then we'll talk."

He took the answer well and he talked about his day throughout the meal, but I could see the curiosity behind his eyes.

I served us another beer each and cut a slice of cake.

"God, this looks sinful. What is it?"

"Chocolate Guinness cheesecake."

Nate groaned and gave me a look as if I'd just told him he was in for hourly blow jobs for the next three weeks. He looped his arm around my waist and pulled me into his body. "Stay here. I hate eating on the other side of the table from you."

"Yes, two feet is such an intolerable distance."

He tugged me so I fell onto his lap and he kissed my throat. "It is when it comes to you. Now tell me about this day of yours before I lose my mind."

"Claire made me manager today."

"What? Fucking hell, Jo! That's amazing!" Nate kissed me full on the mouth, laughing. "I'm proud of you."

My heart skipped a beat.

"What?" Nate asked, his eyes searching my face.

I shrugged. "I don't remember anyone saying that to me before."

"Well, get used to it from me. And a shitload of other compliments so outrageous you'll never get your ginormous head out of the front door again."

I laughed and fell against him, happier, and more content, than a Disney fucking princess.

* * * *

When I returned home after work on Saturday, the first thing I saw as I stepped inside the house was a garment bag hanging from the coat stand. Through the translucent plastic, I saw a sparkly blue dress, one shouldered and mid-thigh length.

Nate appeared and arched an eyebrow in question.

I couldn't help my smile. "You buying me dresses is becoming a habit, Mr Harding."

He came closer and kissed me, lifting the bag from the coat stand and motioning for me to follow him upstairs. "You'd better get used to it then."

"Is this your way of telling me we're going out tonight?"

Nate threw me a smile over his shoulder. "Something like that."

Our bedroom smelled heavenly, a sweet, intoxicating smell emanating from the open door. Nate tossed the bag on the bed and took me by the hand, leading me into the bathroom. Every surface was covered with candles and the soft light flickered, sending dancing shadows on the walls. Steam rose from the filled bath tub, the smell coming from the oils we used in Bethesda.

"God, where did you find that?" I asked, breathing in the scent.

"I ordered it online. It finally arrived today. Couldn't have timed it better myself." Nate grinned and hit a button on a remote control he'd produced from his pocket and José Gonzalez sang from some unseen speaker. "Have a good soak then get ready. I'll be downstairs. Take your time."

Before I could even respond, Nate had left, closing the door behind him with a gentle click.

I stayed in that bath so long my skin shriveled and the water dropped significantly in temperature. But eventually my curiosity got the better of me and I emerged, refreshed, pampered and ready for whatever Nate had in store.

And he wasn't the only one who had been shopping recently. The black silk strapless basque and matching thong I'd purchased the other day made Nate's dress slide effortlessly onto my body, giving me fantastic curves and enough anticipation that I couldn't wait to strip for him later in the night. And I knew the seamed stockings and suspender belt would have him ripping it off me with his teeth.

On top of the garment bag was now a pair of black leather Alexander McQueen peep toe stilettos with missing front panel, giving the outfit and edgier look and a sway in my step that simply oozed sensuality.

I slid my hand up the doorframe and leaned my hip against it, arching my back. When Nate turned, the look in his eye turned feral. He stalked toward me, slowly rubbing his thumb over his jaw.

He gripped my hips and pulled me into his body, his thick erection pressing against my belly. "I'm a fucking idiot."

"How so?" I asked, running my fingers over the collar of his shirt.

"I've made plans to take you out like this tonight." Nate lifted me, turning us and placing me on the edge of the island. With his hands on either side of my thighs, he inched the dress up my legs. Nate hissed in a breath when he got to the top of the stockings. "And fuck me, Jo. The way I need to have you right now? I'd make it last all night."

My heart was pounding and it took all my self-possession not to beg him to get me off right that very second. Instead I wrapped my legs around his waist and pulled him closer. I took his earlobe between my teeth, biting hard enough that he gripped me tighter. "It wouldn't happen, Nate."

A laugh rumbled in his chest. "Oh no?"

I kissed his jaw, loving the rough scratch of his stubble then hovered just a fraction above his lips. "No. Because tonight, *I'm* going to have *you*. Any and every way I want."

Nate gave a tortured groan and took my mouth hard. His tongue stroked mine and I scraped my teeth along it. His hands slid farther up my leg, curving to my inner thigh until his fingers grazed the satin of my soaking knickers. "I can't start this, Jo. If I do I won't be able to stop."

My lips curled into a smile. "It certainly feels as though you're talking yourself out of it. Do me a favor? Move those fingers a little higher whilst you try and tell yourself this isn't you starting anything."

"I'm going to have blue balls from hell tonight," Nate groaned, dropping his forehead to mine.

"It'll be worth it. I promise."

"I believe you."

* * * *

A taxi arrived to pick us up and Nate gave a nod to the driver with no need to give a destination. We arrived outside Castle Terrace, a restaurant I had been dying to go to for months. It was fresh and ultra-modern and, so I'd heard, had food to die for. Nate helped me from the taxi and slid an arm around my waist. He introduced us to the hostess, who smiled and led us through the busy dining room to a half-filled table.

It was Suze I recognized first. Our eyes met and her grin was huge. She rose from the table and threw her arms around me, hugging me close as if to suppress my central nervous system and, hopefully, prevent me from running in terror.

"What is all this?" I asked when she loosened her hold enough for me to breath.

Paul and his girlfriend, Mel, from the bar also rose from their seats, as did Claire and her husband, Mike.

Claire kissed me on both cheeks and rubbed my arm. "Well, darling girl, when that exquisite man of yours called me and said he wanted to take you out for the evening and spoil you rotten, not to mention have all of us here to witness...how could we say no?"

A lump grew in my throat. "Wow, that's um, that's really nice." *That's really nice?* Dazzle the crowd with your conversational skills, Jo.

Nate's squeezed my shoulder with his large, warm hand. "Yes, very nice, Jo. Now, let's eat, shall we? Because I'm fucking starving."

I laughed and the nervous energy that had swamped my mood dissipated. Suze clutched my hand and pulled me to the empty seat beside hers. She chatted non-stop, pulling people into her conversation at total random and totally charming the socks off pretty much everyone.

Claire marveled at her tales of mischief she and Nate had gotten into as children. Paul and Mel swapped Rose Street drinking stories and even Mike fell for her around the time she told the story of her short-lived gymnast career at aged seven and three quarters.

I looked at this remarkable woman who had slowly slipped into the role of my best friend and as my eyes stung with tears, I realized just how much she meant to me. I adored her, almost as much as I did Nate, and I wanted to hug her and tell her of all the thousands of ways she has helped to piece me back together.

Nate leaned into me and his rough cheek pressed against mine. "Should I be jealous of the way you've barely taken your eyes off of my sister?"

My lips twitched into a smile and I turned, resting my forehead against his and releasing a breath. "I was caught up in my thoughts. I'm sorry."

"Don't be. What were they?"

"You'd laugh."

"I wouldn't."

I kissed him briefly. "I was just thinking about how much I love her. I've never really had a friend like her before and, well, I suppose I'm really proud that she's adopted me."

Nate's face was solemn as he stroked a finger across my lips. "You should tell her."

I laughed. "She'd think I was hitting on her."

He didn't make a lewd joke like I expected him to. "You should always tell the people you care about the things that are in your heart."

My response died in my throat. Was he talking about himself? My heart sank as I imagined him hurt that I hadn't admitted to feeling for him what I just had for Suze? But before I could overthink it he kissed me again, firmer, and said, "I hope those shoes are up for a few bars, because this night is far from over."

Suze, overhearing her brother, turned to us and grinned with child-like glee. "Ooh can we do Grassmarket? I've been itching to get Jo to Under The Stairs."

"Sure thing," I said, smiling when Suze literally squealed with excitement then asked the table who else was joining us — which was everyone.

* * * *

By the fourth bar, our numbers had dwindled. Mel had been the first, saying she had an early shift the next day, followed by Claire and Mike who insisted they were too old for cocktail bars. Suze and Paul were enjoying harmless flirty banter and seeing who could out-move who on the dance floor. Nate and I watched from a safe distance, cracking up when one of them brought out the old school robot or clubland big fish little fish.

Nate and I sat huddled together on a low sofa in a dark corner of the bar, the music pulsing and the air dark and heavy. Every touch between us was intoxicating and as much as I couldn't wait to get home and ravish him senseless, I was having an incredible night.

"I'm having the best time," I said in his ear.

Nate's arm around my waist tightened and he tugged me closer. "I'm glad. You deserve it."

When he spoke, I felt the rumbling of his deep voice in his chest and his breath on my ear sent shivers down my spine.

"Get your tongue out of her ear and get one of these down you!" Paul exclaimed.

We looked up to see him carrying a tray of drinks with Suze following close behind, clutching a handful of straws.

So far I'd managed to avoid drinking much. I'd had a small glass of wine with dinner and no one had noticed that I'd actually only had one cocktail since leaving the restaurant, making timely trips to the loo or suggesting a dance when rounds were mentioned.

"You know you're safe, don't you?" Nate asked, his tone more serious than before.

My heart picked up speed. "Yes, I know."

Nate kissed me. "I just mean you can have a drink. I stopped after the second bar. Nothing will happen to you, not while I'm here."

I managed a weak smile. "And here I was thinking you wouldn't enjoy sloppy drunk sex."

He grinned. "I'm quite looking forward to seeing what you're like with lower inhibitions."

My laugh was full and sudden. "I think my inhibitions were shattered with you a long time ago."

Nate kissed me again. "Never say never."

Three cocktails later and I was enjoying the first semi-drunken buzz I'd had in years. Suze was still having the time of her life on the dance floor and ignoring the looks she was getting from the pretty young things who, she claimed when she sat down to catch her breath, were mad with jealousy at her moves.

Nate had tugged me so close we were bordering on an inappropriate seating arrangement and I was enjoying just being there with him. We talked and laughed and kissed and as I rested my head against his shoulder I couldn't imagine being any happier than I was in that moment.

A flash startled us, and Nate laughed. "Suze, put the fucking camera down, would you?"

"Hey, my best friend and my brother look fucking happy, okay? Excuse me for wanting to immortalize the moment."

Nate sighed and stood up, holding out his hand for me to take. "I'm officially ending this evening."

Suze and I both pouted. "Why?" we asked.

"Because I've had enough of watching you shake your ass at poor student boys," Nate pointed at Suze then swung it around to me, "and I've got ball ache because of you, so yes, I'm ending the bloody evening."

Suze made a gagging noise but I couldn't stop the grin as I jumped to my feet. I threw my arms around his shoulders and kissed him so hard he stumbled back.

"God, I am so *not* sharing a taxi with you two," Suze said as she marched past us toward the exit.

"Good," Nate and I said.

* * * *

The night was cold but my blood was on fire. And Nate was taking entirely too long in opening the door. I pressed against his back and slid my hands into his front pockets. Nate jerked and let out a breath between his clenched teeth.

"You know, for someone who is doing her best to rush me, you're failing miserably by doing that."

I grinned and hid my face between his shoulder blades.

At last he shoved the door open and I stumbled behind Nate. I dropped my clutch, shed my coat and turned on my heel. Nate took the time to hang his coat on the hook and dropped his keys in the dish. When he glanced at me over his shoulder with a taunting smile I groaned and flung my arms out to the side.

"You're doing this on purpose, aren't you?"

"Doing what?" he asked, flashing me an innocent smile so fake I doubted anyone would have fallen for it.

"Whatever game you're playing, you have no way of winning."

"I always win."

I smiled. "You won't this time." I took a step closer to him, swaying my hips and getting a surge of confidence when his eyes followed the movement. I brushed past him, smiling with my eyes as I traced a fingertip around the key dish before perching my ass on the edge of the table.

Nate visibly swallowed. "I don't know... Right now it doesn't seem like I can lose either way."

He hadn't moved but I could see the tension in his body. The vein in his throat jumped as I slowly slid the bottom of my short dress up, showing the suspender straps. "Aren't you curious what I have on under here?"

"Right now I don't give a fuck," Nate said, his voice hoarse.

Finally he moved and in a heartbeat he was between my legs, sliding his hands up my inner thighs and shoving aside my knickers. His thumb grazed my folds and my whole body quivered.

I arched my back but he was teasing me, driving me crazy, and wouldn't push those fingers inside. I was dizzy with need and he was holding back. But like he'd said, this wasn't a situation where anyone could lose, and I could torture him just as efficiently. I reached for his slacks and unzipped them, his erection straining to be set free. Nate smiled as I stroked him through his boxer briefs but he soon gritted his teeth as I applied a little more pressure. He fell into my palm, hot and pulsing, as I pushed his briefs down.

Nate thrust into my hand as I pumped his length with slow, agonizing strokes. Finally he pushed his fingers inside my throbbing pussy that was desperate for his touch. I grasped his heavy balls and gave them a gentle squeeze.

It pushed him over the edge. Nate swore, and with one hand he grasped my hip, and with the other he guided himself to my cunt. I wrapped my legs around his waist and he slammed inside me, filling me to the brink of pain. He pressed his face into my neck, his breath hot and fast. I bit down on his earlobe, and with a grunt Nate fucked me harder.

I grasped his firm ass, my nails digging into the skin. He fucked me quick and rough. My throat was raw from the cries that ripped free from every powerful thrust, and I came hard. I felt his cum spill inside me, adding to the aftershock pulses of my orgasm.

My body trembled when he withdrew from me. Nate kissed me and laughed against my lips. "I don't care if I never win again...as long as that happens when I lose."

I kissed him back. "Deal."

Upstairs, Nate undressed slowly, never taking his eyes off me. When clad in only his boxer briefs, he folded his arms and crooked an eyebrow at me, a little smirk playing on his lips. He knew I wasn't done with him, but must have wondered why I was still fully dressed.

"Am I fucking you again in that dress? Not that I mind, but since you mentioned it downstairs, I am curious as to what's underneath it."

I slinked closer to him, placed my hands on his chest and kissed him. "Just building up the suspense."

"I have a feeling it's going to be worth it."

"Oh, it is," I said, my hands drifting to the side zipper.

Nate's hand fisted as I slowly pulled the dress over my head and let the fabric drop to the floor. Resting my hands on my hips, I cocked my head.

Nate's smirk fell right off his face and he picked me up and flung me on the bed. "When did you get this?" he asked, hovering above me and trailing his hand down the satin of the basque.

"Yesterday. You could say I saw it and thought of you."

He let out a heavy breath and sat up on his knees between my legs. He stroked one finger across the crotch of my knickers. "I'm going to have to insist you *always* have me in mind when you're shopping."

I touched his cheek. "I do anyway, Nate."

A fierce look flashed in his eyes and he ripped the knickers clean off me.

"Though if you carry on like this, *I'm* going to have to insist you do the shopping next time."

Nate flashed me a wolfish smile. "We'll go tomorrow, sweetheart." He held my eyes the entire time it took him to slowly lower his head and press his lips to my cleft. His tongue plunged inside me and I cried out, already sensitive from our rough sex in the hall but more than ready for him. Nate worked me with his mouth and when he sucked hard on my clit I came undone.

Nate pulled away and dropped his boxers to the floor. I rose to my knees and beckoned him closer for a kiss, stroking his hard dick. He tried to nudge me onto my back but I turned and crawled farther up the bed on my hands and knees, peeking at him over my shoulder.

He was after me in a heartbeat. I pushed my ass against his hips and he groaned, pulling back just enough to guide himself into me.

I gasped at the new sensation of him from this position. He filled me deeper than ever and I felt every single movement he made tenfold. Nate hissed through his teeth and pounded into me. I gripped the duvet in my hands, perilously close to orgasm already. He increased his speed and I cried out, pushing back to meet his thrusts.

Nate reached around and fingered my clit and I was thrown over the edge. I collapsed onto my elbows and Nate gave one last hard thrust and followed me into ecstasy. We stayed like that, panting and connected for a few moments, and I shivered when he pulled out of me. He gave my ass a gentle slap and I laughed, still breathless.

"I have a feeling," Nate said, his voice hoarse, "that I am going to spend a fucking fortune tomorrow."

I sat up to face him. "And I have a feeling I'll never get another full night's sleep again."

* * * *

Nate and I collapsed into bed, freshly showered and perfectly sated. I laid my head on his chest, my leg thrown over his as he drew lazy patterns on my back. My body was aching and spent but it was the best feeling in the world. Nate kissed the top of my head and I felt his breathing even out. I was moments from sleep myself, but words spoken earlier in the evening kept playing in my head.

'You should always tell the people you care about the things that are in your heart.'

I swallowed the sudden rise of fear in my throat and wriggled further into his embrace. His arm tightened briefly and just like that the fear was gone. Because it occurred to me that when it came to Nate, there was absolutely nothing to be afraid of. Even the things I'd trained myself to over so many years.

"I love you," I whispered, squeezing my eyes shut and vowing it would be the first thing he heard me say when we awoke in the morning.

Nate shifted in his sleep and brushed his lips across my forehead. "I know."

Chapter Twenty-Three

A low rumble stirred me out of sleep. It came again, then again, more defined now as I surfaced into the morning. Nate curled around me, his hand tightening on my hip and I sank back into the mattress.

The fourth sound of his phone skittering around on the bedside table had me sitting bolt upright. "Who the fuck is that?" I shoved my hair out of my face and Nate rolled onto his back, groaning and rubbing his eyes. "It's Sunday, for chrissakes."

"A fiver says it's—"

"Nope. I'm not setting myself up to lose that bet." His phone vibrated yet again and I shot him a look. "Shouldn't she be hanging her head down the toilet all morning?"

Nate yawned and sat up. "You'd think, wouldn't you? Ah, fuck..."

"What?" I asked.

"The only thing that would distract Suze from her hangover would be the immortalizing of the night before."

I blinked. "I'm not sure I want to know what that means."

He reached for his phone and slid his index finger over the screen. A few moments later he tossed it onto my lap, a picture of me and Nate from last night taking up the screen.

"Who took that?"

"Suze, who do you think?"

It was actually a great picture of us. Nate was whispering in my ear, probably something filthy as my smile and whole body language was practically purring. Every part of our bodies was turned into the other and to us, we were the only two people on the planet, let alone the room.

"So she's sending you all the photos she took last night? Wouldn't like to be her phone bill."

Nate snorted a laugh. "God, I wish. No, she's posting them all to Facebook and tagging me in the photos, hence all the fucking notifications."

My stomach clenched, a knee-jerk reaction. And, being Nate, he caught the immediate shift in my temper.

"You don't like it, do you? Facebook?"

I shrugged, more to try to ease out from the suffocating blanket the fear used to keep my under permanently. "No, not anymore."

He powered off his phone and dropped it off the bed. Nate reached for me and tugged me back down. "I don't know about you, but I'm not done sleeping yet. And I need all my rest for this shopping trip later."

I laughed quietly and burrowed deeper in his arms, closing my eyes and refusing to let the dark thoughts in. Nate let out a heavy breath and squeezed me closer before the mattress dipped and he swore.

Cat's faced pushed into mine, and I giggled as he rubbed me with his cheeks, purring like a revved up tractor.

"Fuck sake," Nate muttered into the back of my neck. "Between that thing and my sister, I'm doomed to forgo a Sunday lie-in."

I scratched under Cat's chin, and, in his typical fashion, he leaped off the bed as quickly as he'd appeared and clattered down the stairs with all the grace of a tap-dancing elephant. "I think you hurt his feelings."

"I don't give a shit," Nate said as he kissed my shoulder. "And don't try giving me the look. I'm not getting up to feed the wee rat."

As if on cue, Cat yodeled from somewhere in the house—loud, with no sign of stopping.

"Oh, fucking hell, I give up!" Nate threw back the covers and swung his long legs out of bed before throwing me a smile over his shoulder. "What's it worth if I bring you a coffee?"

I kicked the rest of the duvet away and stretched languidly. "I don't know…what do you want?"

His lips twitched and suddenly Nate lunged and grabbed my ankle, jerking me to him so quickly I shrieked. His grin was infectious and I couldn't stop the laugh. Nate bent to kiss me, soft and routine. "That'll do for now."

I smiled and watched him leave, admiring the view of his beautiful backside.

* * * *

We enjoyed an idyllic lazy Sunday. Nate made us breakfast and we ate at the island, browsing the newspapers and sipping coffee before taking a walk down the Waters of Leith and hitting up Princes Street so Nate could replenish my ruined underwear. Later, we watched a corny family movie and fooled around on the couch, and I felt as though I could burst with happiness.

Early the next day instead of heading to work, I was baking up a storm in the kitchen. Nate's iPod that he'd loaned me was plugged into the speakers and Pink filled the air as I created new and old recipes. My baking buddy in the form of Cat was nowhere to be seen, which was unusual for him, as, like Nate, he took whatever chance he got to lick the spoon. Before lunch, I took the baking to the bistro and sat for the rest of the day with Claire in her office as she went over my new responsibilities in more detail. She was easing me in slowly and I couldn't have thanked her enough.

When I left the bistro just after six, I was surprised to see Nate leaning against the building wall waiting for me.

A smile spread across my face at the sight of him. To the casual observer, he was a scruffy hunk, probably a mature student as he slouched against the wall in jeans that hung off his lean hips, aged Converse and tan military style jacket. He pushed off the wall and scratched the stubble on his jaw and I shivered at the sound.

"Keep looking at me like that," Nate said, hooking his fingers into the collar of my jacket and pulling me into him, "and I'm going to drag you down a close."

I grinned. "Is that supposed to discourage me?"

Nate laughed and kissed me, looping his arm around my waist as we headed toward home. "Filthy woman. How was work?"

I groaned and leaned into him. "My head is full."

"How long has it been since a job has challenged you?"

For a second I wondered if he was being cruel, or maybe insensitive. But glancing at his face I realized he was simply curious.

"Too long. But it's muscle memory. I'll get there."

"Of course you will," Nate said, kissing the side of my head. "But if you decide you don't want to, my offer still stands."

I elbowed him, laughing. "The offer where I come to work with you every day, sit on your desk in a short skirt with no knickers and feed you cake, you mean? Let's call that plan B, shall we?"

Nate huffed. "Fine, fine."

A giggle bubbled in my throat. "How was your day anyway?"

"Utter shite. You weren't sitting on my desk with no knickers feeding me cake."

"Tough life, eh, Nate?" I asked with a grin.

He smirked at me. "Yeah. It's okay, though. You'll make it up to me later."

"Oh will I?"

"Yes," he assured. "You're good like that."

"Thanks for letting me know."

He flashed me a boyish smile. "I'll keep you right."

I smiled back. "Good to know someone will."

We stopped at the traffic lights at a busy crossroads and that's when I saw him. My stomach bottomed out as our eyes locked and his mouth twisted into a cruel smile. It barely last a second before he was swallowed by the crowd but it felt like an eternity to drag a breath into my lungs. Pressing a hand to my forehead, I thought I was going to be sick as pure, unadulterated fear raced through my body. I stood on my tiptoes and strained my eyes to see across the road, trying to get another look but there was no sight of him.

All I could hear was the blood rushing behind my ears. It wasn't until Nate gave me a little shake that I snapped to attention and the present came rushing back in a flood of color and sound.

"Jo!" His brown eyes were full of concern as they swept over me. "What's wrong?"

I shook my head to try to clear it. "I saw — I think I saw…"

"Saw what?" Nate asked, pressing closer.

I took a breath but the fear didn't dissipate. It clawed at my throat and all I wanted to do was run. Could I be one hundred percent, absolutely certain it was him? If I told Nate, he would worry. And Scott would have ruined this perfect night. Whether it was really him or not.

"Jo?" Nate asked again.

My mind could have playing tricks on me. How many times over the years did I think I'd seen him? Dozens? Hundreds? I forced a smile. "Robert Downey Jr."

Nate barked a laugh. "Robert Downey Jr? You thought Iron Man was here?"

I shrugged. "A girl can hope."

He dipped his head to growl in my ear, "*This* girl can hope to experience all the things I'm going to do to her when I get her home."

His words went someway to expel the unease in my stomach. "Promise?"

Nate pulled back and gave me a quizzical look. "Always."

I pulled him down to press my lips to his. Nate wrapped his strong arms around me and I sighed into his mouth. How on earth had I denied I was in love with him for so long?

Nate squeezed my waist. "So…any leftovers from today at home?"

"You'll have to wait and see."

Nate threw his head back and groaned. "If there are, I sincerely hope you put a brick on top of the cake box this time. That flea bag of yours licked all the icing off last time."

Ah yes, my icing loving fiend, Cat. The vet had warned us that his eating habits would be sporadic for a while and he would more than likely eat anything and everything he came across, after God knows how long of not knowing when he would next eat.

We walked the rest of the way in silence and turned onto our road. The house rose up, tall and proud, illuminated only by the old-fashioned lamp over the front door, spilling light over the steps.

"I seem to remember it was you who first offered him some off your finger and that gave him the taste for it."

Nate sighed. "That's the trouble these days—you offer someone a little treat and they just take the piss. Ah look, the fat thing is there waiting on us."

I squinted and sure enough, saw that Nate was right and Cat was lay sprawled out in front of the door. Nate clicked his tongue but Cat didn't move and it was then, as we drew closer, that I realized something was wrong.

As the dread settled in my stomach, Nate seemed to realize also that something wasn't right. He slowed and withdrew his arm from my waist, pressing a hand to my midsection probably to keep me back. But I pushed past him and ran the last few feet home. I bounded up the steps and dropped to my knees in front of Cat's body.

His eyes were open and glassy, pale tongue hanging out one side of his mouth. His thick fur was mottled and streaked with mud. But must disturbing was how concave his little belly was, how his ribs were clearly broken and the wrongness of the position of his back legs.

Nate hauled me to my feet and pulled my back, and I didn't even realize I was sobbing until he shook me so hard my teeth rattled. "Jo, fucking breathe!"

I gasped in a breath and held onto his forearms.

He crushed me to his chest and somehow maneuvered me into the house. Nate took me into the sitting room and sat me on the couch. He sat opposite me on the coffee table and rubbed my hands between his.

"I need you to stay in here for a while. Can you do that?"

I nodded and Nate turned on the TV, not changing the channel from it what it was already on then left the room, closing the door behind him. Sometime later, though I've no idea how much later, the door opened again but it was Suze who stuck her head into the room. She took one look at my tear stained face and rushed to me. She dropped down beside me on the couch and threw her arms around my shoulders.

"Oh, Jo, I'm so sorry, babe."

I turned my face into her, neither of us caring that I was covering her in snot. "What the fuck, Suze?"

Beneath my ear Suze's heart pounded. "I don't know. I don't know." And she just held me, stroked a hand over my hair whilst crooning that it would be okay.

I clung to her and drank in all the comfort she could give me.

When Nate eventually came back, he looked between me and Suze and for a moment seemed loathe to come any closer.

"Where is he?" I asked, my voice hoarse and broken.

Nate let out a breath and took his seat again on the coffee table. "I wrapped him in your purple blanket and buried him beside the bird table."

I frowned. "It's all stone out there."

"I prised up some of the uneven stones from the patio and dug a hole for him, put the stones back on top so nothing—"

My breath hitched and I dropped my eyes to his hands. His knuckles were red and angry, faint crusts of dirt in his nail beds as though he had scrubbed and scrubbed his hands and still couldn't get them clean.

Suze kissed my temple and rose from the couch with a promise to call round tomorrow.

For a few moments neither Nate nor I spoke. But when a fresh tear spilled down my cheek he reached forward to cup my elbow and pulled me to my feet. He guided me into the kitchen where I stood at the island with my back to the French doors and watched as Nate poured me a healthy glass of red wine.

"What do you think happened?" I asked, stroking the rim of my glass.

Nate sat on the stool behind me and tugged me back between his legs. He wrapped an arm around me and kissed my shoulder. "Looks like he was hit by a car. Somehow managed to get up the steps. Wanted to come home, I suppose."

I blew out a shaky breath. "Poor Cat."

"Poor Cat," Nate agreed.

My heart hurt and I hated that I wasn't here for Cat when he'd needed us. "Thank you for giving him my blanket — and for taking care of him."

"I think he used that blanket more than you in the end."

I smiled, thinking about how many times I'd found him curled up in a little nest he'd made for himself out of my blanket.

"Get that drink down you and then we'll eat. What do you feel like?"

"Nothing."

"Jo…"

"I know, I know. But nothing sounds appealing." I sighed. "What about you?"

Nate thought for a moment. "Chips and cheese. With lashings of salt and vinegar."

A laugh rose up my throat. "How do you make that sound like heaven?"

"Because chips and cheese *is* heaven." Nate released his hold on me. "Go put on your comfiest clothes and I'll ring for a takeaway."

Usually, Nate never passed up an opportunity to watch me dress. Or undress. Or anything that came with the possibility of nudity, partial or otherwise. But I knew this was his way of giving me a breathing moment, to process this evening in private, if that was what I needed.

Instead, the second I was clad in comfy leggings, thick socks and one of his T-shirts, I headed straight back downstairs to be with Nate again. He was back in the sitting room, crouched in front of the large fireplace, setting it up. A few minutes later it crackled to life and he turned the overhead lights off then went around the room lighting the candles. When he finally joined me on the couch, I crawled onto his lap, aching for him.

"How are you feeling?"

I curled up, resting my head on his chest and letting the thrum of his heart ground me. I answered as honestly as I could, "Grateful. You're incredible, Nate."

"Whatever I am...it's only what you bring out in me."

I splayed my hand on his pec. "I'm so glad I have you."

Nate stroked my arm. "You always will."

Despite my bleak mood a ghost of a smile hinted on my lips. "I'd better. I'm going to hold you to that."

Nate pressed a kiss onto my hair, a gesture that made me feel more protected than a suit of armor, more comforted than a favorite pair of pajamas and more loved than a Shakespeare sonnet. "It's soon, too soon, but I want you to know that if you want to get another animal of some sort, I'm with you."

"Cat was the first pet I'd ever had." I chuckled. "Pet seems too tame a word for what he was. I liked that he sort of chose us, you know?"

"Chose you, you mean. And your buttery toast."

I smiled. "You're right. He definitely chose the toast."

Nate shook his head. "It was you and you know it. But whenever you're ready — tomorrow, next year, just let me know and we'll sort something out, okay?"

I nodded and turned over on his lap to watch the fire. Nate stretched out behind me, his arm draping over my waist bringing peace to my wounded heart.

* * * *

I baked the hell out of my feelings the next morning. Nate caught me standing at the French doors, staring at the patio and wishing for the millionth time we'd been home sooner. He squeezed my shoulder and made some coffee but didn't comment, simply watched and waited and took his cue from me.

At work Claire knew the second I walked through the door that something was wrong with me. She brewed us some coffee and instead of sitting at her desk, she sat on the ancient couch against the wall and patted the cushion beside her. I took a sip of my coffee and the words just blurted from my mouth.

"My cat died last night." My throat tightened and no amount of swallowing could dislodge the hard lump.

Claire put her coffee down on the table and pulled me into a hug. "Oh, Jo, I'm so sorry. How are you doing?"

I shrugged. "Pretty crap. Nate thinks he was hit by a car. I can't stop picturing him lying there so broken."

"You can take today off if you need to. Go home, be sad. Console yourself with that man of yours." Claire winked but her face soon reformed into the sad smile she'd worn a moment ago.

"I'll stay, if that's all right? Nate has to work anyway, so it would just be me rattling around by myself. Here I can be busy."

Claire patted my knee. "Whatever you need. I've more than enough work to keep your mind from wandering. The mid-morning rush is about to start. Why don't you work out the front for now, then after lunch come back here?"

"Sounds perfect. Thanks, Claire," I said, swallowing the lump that had formed in my throat because of her kindness.

The morning hours passed by in a rush of orders and coffee, and around lunch time a familiar voice bellowed from the door as I was making another batch of coffee behind the counter. "Jojo!"

I looked around to see Suze negotiate the pushchair into a free area near the window. Tilly clapped her hands and grinned at me. Suze unbuckled her and she toddled straight for me. I whisked her up into my arms and she smooshed her snotty, dribbly little face into my cheek.

"Tilly, you've no idea how much I needed that," I said as I set her back down and she took off for the sofa by the window.

Suze pulled me into one of her trademark bear hugs and rubbed my back.

"This is a nice surprise."

Suze shrugged. "Tilly wanted to see you and I wanted to make sure you were okay, even though you won't be."

"I'm better for seeing you two. Coffee? And tell me something that will make those big Disney eyes of yours a little less 'devastation before the big happy ending'."

"God, yes, coffee! I'm knackered. Tilly woke up pre-dawn this morning the little bugger." As if on cue, Suze yawned so wide it nearly split her face in half. "Plus I was texting most of the night."

"Is that a euphemism?" I asked with a grin. I popped into the office to ask Claire if I could take my lunch then brewed Suze and I a coffee each and gave our food orders to the kitchen.

Tilly busied herself with some obnoxious, noisy book that giggled when you pressed a button. Which she did. A lot.

"So. Texting." I slid Suze her coffee.

"I sort of met someone. A nice someone. Someone who doesn't mind slow."

I reached across the table and squeezed her hand. "I'm happy for you. But how slow is slow? You have actually had face-to-face contact, yet?"

She laughed. "Yes! I met Greg, the guy, the other night when we all went out. Early, so he didn't see me smashed off my face. Totally forgot we'd swapped numbers until he texted me the next day asking to meet up. Mum and Dad still had Tilly, so we met for a coffee and I told him about her, and how I wasn't ready for a super sexual relationship."

"How did he take that?" I asked.

"Seemed to take it well enough. His girlfriend died a few years ago, and he's only just getting back into dating, so he's looking for slow and casual too for now."

"Sounds like a perfect match."

"Yeah, just have to wait and see, I suppose. I'm just trying not to get my hopes up," Suze said, wincing when Tilly slammed the book on the table when it refused to make a noise but stroked it with a smile when it finally cooperated.

Suze's eye twitched every time Tilly pressed the button but she always gave her daughter a praising smile when she would look up to make sure Suze had caught the action.

Yeah. My heart just melted.

"Suze, why don't I have Tilly one night this week? It'll give you a chance to rest and relax, see that man of yours. What do you think?"

For a moment Suze didn't move. I don't even think she breathed. But then a single tear leaked from her eye, and I, horrified, covered my mouth with my hands.

"Shit, sorry, have I overstepped a mark? God, I'm sorry, Suze—"

She held a hand up. "Shut up, you bloody nutter!" Suze laughed and carefully wiped under her eye before reaching across the table to squeeze my hand. "I'm so glad I found you."

"Even if I am a twisted little freak?"

She laughed again. "Especially because you're a twisted little freak."

"Is that a yes then?"

Suze snorted. "Too bloody right. Are you sure you and Nate have nothing on?"

"He has another trip in a few days. It's no trouble at all, Suze," I said, squeezing her hand back.

"Brilliant. In that case, do you mind if you come over to ours on Friday? The little demon has decided to stop sleeping, so I'm doing a routine every night and I don't want to disturb it if I can help it."

I smiled. "Of course."

When Suze left, I went into Claire's office and we camped out, munching on cookies and sipping freshly brewed coffee, going over the rotas for the next few weeks.

After the schedules, we worked out what cakes to make permanent that I would make every day and what baked goods to make specials. Claire was scanning the bar receipts on her computer, trying to figure out what sold out quickest when the phone on her desk rang.

"Red Bar," she answered, not taking her eyes off the screen. "Sorry, we don't have a Holly who works here. Okay, yeah, bye."

I froze.

"Right, by the looks of things, the chocolate fudge is a clear best seller, and so are the lemon cupcakes. Anything you can think of?" Claire asked.

Clearing my throat, I flipped through the notes I had on what I had made for the bistro in the past. The page in my head fluttered, and that's when I noticed how badly my hands were shaking. I dropped the notes and rubbed my eyes.

Christ, Jo, it's a coincidence. Relax. It's your mind playing tricks because you're upset about Cat.

"Jo? Jo, anyone in there?" Claire laughed, snapping her fingers under my nose.

I started. "Sorry, sorry."

"You were somewhere else," she said.

Not somewhere, someone. The girl I used to be.

Holly.

Chapter Twenty-Four

For the next few days I was jittery and paranoid. I took taxis home instead of walking, checked and double checked all the doors and windows and never answered the phone. Nate was so busy with work he never noticed I only left the house to go to work and Suze was preoccupied with her love life. By the end of the week, I rationalized that I was just stressed and upset over Cat. Nothing had happened. No one had come for me. No one had called the bistro.

I felt stupid for overreacting and thankful I hadn't said anything to Nate. I was sure he would look at me as though I was a paranoid crazy person. By the time Nate's trip to the States came around, the incident was almost forgotten and the fear had drastically subsided.

He had tried to coax me into going with him again, but there were already two people on holiday at work and Claire and I had too much to do. So he had to go alone, and I had to rattle around the house by myself.

The morning he was flying, I made him an omelet for breakfast and watched him eating it across the island. I loved his strong jaw and watching it clench as he chewed.

"Are you enjoying yourself?" Nate asked, with a smirk, shoveling in another mouthful.

"Immensely," I said, going around the island to kiss that jaw.

His arm came around my waist and he shoved the empty plate away. "You can always change your mind and come with me. There's still time."

I laughed. "You fly in four hours."

Nate grinned. "See? Plenty of time."

With a sigh I stepped between his legs. "You'll just have to miss me."

"And I will. What about you?"

I shrugged. "I'm sure I'll find something to occupy my time."

Nate laughed and grasped my hips, lifting me onto the island as he rose from the bar stool. "Flippant as ever. Shall I give you something to remember me by?"

"If you insist," I said, my heart racing.

"I do." He grinned. Nate tugged on the waist of my pajama shorts he'd gotten for me the last time he'd gone shopping—red satin with matching lacy camisole.

I lifted my hips and he pulled them off, dropping them on the floor. Nate pressed his lips to my throat, his grip on my hips tightening. "How do you want it?"

"Any way you'll give it to me," I panted, letting my head drop back.

His tongue flicked against my pulse. He moved one hand to cup my aching pussy, slipping one long finger slowly between the folds. "Tell me."

"Fuck, Nate."

"Tell me," he repeated, his voice thick and low. Nate nipped at the flesh of my throat with his teeth.

"Hard."

"How hard?"

"So hard when I make myself come tonight, I'm still tender from you." I bit my lip as the need for his touch rose up in me like a tidal wave.

"Fuck," he said, "I want to see that."

"Not now. I need *you*," I moaned, as he slipped that finger inside me and my muscles clenched around him.

Nate pressed the heel of his hand to the small bundle of nerves as he added another finger inside me. I cried out as he worked me, on the brink of release. With no warning he ripped his hand back, and I sat up with a gasp. Nate shoved his jeans and boxers down, his beautiful hard cock springing free. He buried his cock inside me, and I gripped his shoulders as his mouth came down on mine, fucking my mouth as he pounded into me.

He gave it to me exactly as I'd asked. Nate held nothing back and he thrust into me so hard if it hadn't felt so good it would have hurt. I sucked on his tongue as my orgasm took hold, and as I shuddered around him Nate groaned and somehow took me harder.

He dropped his head to my chest, pulling one nipple into his mouth through the camisole. I gripped his hair as my heart felt as if it would burst free of my body. He came as I did, both of us panting as the feelings coursed through us.

"Hard enough for you?" Nate asked, kissing me.

I laughed breathily. "I should be recovered by the time you get back."

"This is how I'll think of you when I'm away. Spread out on this island, waiting for me to eat you whole."

"I like this island."

He laughed. "Yeah, me, too."

* * * *

Later, when it was time for him to leave, I watched as he double checked his messenger bag for the essentials—wallet, passport, and so forth.

"Any plans while I'm away?"

"Work, mostly. I'm babysitting Tilly tomorrow night for Suze. She's off, out with the boyfriend."

Nate closed his bag and pulled it over his shoulder. "It's only five days, short trip this time."

"Good," I said, clasping the edges of his jacket and kissing the stubble on his jaw.

"Doesn't mean you can't still miss me," he said with a wink.

The smile fell from my face. "I'll miss you every second."

Nate's eyes lost their playfulness. He stroked my cheek. "So will I. I'll call you when I can, okay?"

I nodded, trying to shove the lump that suddenly rose in my throat. "Let me know you get there, all right?"

"Yeah." Nate kissed me and gathered me into his arms. "I love you, Jo."

I laid my head against his heart, listening to the strong thump. "I love you."

"I'll bring you some Victoria's Secret if you're good."

"Just bring me you."

"Done." He released me from his arms and picked up his travel bag. "I'll see you soon."

I nodded and wiped away the single tear that slid down my face when he closed the door behind him.

* * * *

Tilly and I sat on Suze's bed watching her get ready for her date. Tilly was battering her little xylophone and singing some indiscernible tune.

"Where is he taking you tonight?" I asked.

"Some restaurant in Old Town. He had a meeting that side of the city, so I'm meeting him there."

"He's not picking you up?" I tsked. "Better not let big brother find out he isn't a gentleman."

Suze tossed a pillow at me. "He's a perfect gentleman."

"That's what they all say, but when the sun goes down the man comes out."

A faint blush tainted her cheeks.

I sat up straighter. "Suze, just how slow are you two taking things?"

"*Slow* slow. I learned my lesson after the last one, so I'm taking my time." Suze sighed. "I'm worried he'll lose interest, though. He's been patient, hasn't even pushed for a kiss, always being respectable."

"That's what counts, then," I said, getting off the bed to sit beside her on the little stool in front of her dressing table.

"I hope so." Suze picked up a perfume bottle and sprayed her throat.

Unease prickled the back of my neck, old memories surfacing. "Is that Eternal Love?"

"Mmm," Suze said, dabbing her wrists with the scent. "He gave it to me last week. Bit sweet for me, but I'd better wear it tonight for him."

"Yeah," I said quietly. "He's lucky to have you, Suze."

"Damn right," she agreed, laughing. Suze stood up and went to the bed, kissing Tilly's hair. "Be a good girl for Auntie Jo."

"Jojo," Tilly said with a smile. "Good Jojo."

"Yes, make sure she's good too. No drinking all Mummy's wine."

I rolled my eyes and stood to hug her. "All right, out you get. Can't have Mr Dreamboat thinking you've stood him up."

Suze laughed again and picked up her bag and coat. "Bye then! I shouldn't be later than midnight."

"Any time is fine," I said, waving her out of the door.

The front door clicked behind her and I looked at Tilly. She was watching me with large eyes. "Good Jojo."

I sighed. "Yes, Tilly, I'll be good."

She beamed and started again with her xylophone.

Once Tilly was in bed, I settled on the couch to watch a movie. I cuddled under the tartan blanket that Suze kept draped across the back of the couch and tucked my feet under me. About three quarters of the way through the film, my phone vibrated on the coffee table. It lit up with my favorite picture of Nate. He looked over his shoulder at me, a smirk at play on his lips and eyes hidden behind dark aviator sunglasses.

"Hey you," I answered with a smile.

"Hey yourself. How's it going?" Nate asked.

"Good. I'm babysitting Tilly but she's abandoned me for bed."

"What are you doing?"

"Watching a movie with Channing Tatum in. He's wearing a dirty white vest and shooting people. Yum."

"Perv," Nate said, laughing.

"Yup," I agreed. "How was work?"

"Good, we're making progress. I'm just about to head out for dinner."

"Where are you going?"

"That pasta bar we went to."

I groaned. "God, that place was amazing. Fill your boots."

Nate chuckled. "I intend to."

The sound of a key in the lock came from the front door. "That sounds like Suze getting in."

"Okay, I'll let you get on then. Talk to you tomorrow?"

"Definitely."

"Night, gorgeous." Nate hung up, and I shoved the phone in my pocket as I stood up. I took my mug into the kitchen and placed it in the sink as Suze came into the flat.

"Jo?" she called.

"Here," I said, walking into the hall.

Suze flipped on the hall light and I saw she wasn't alone.

He stood with his hands shoved in his pockets, a cocky smile on his face. He lifted his eyebrows as I stared at him. My vision sharpened, the colors crisp and bright to the point of pain. A whine rang in my ears and I thought I was going to faint.

"Jo, this is Greg Scott, Greg, Jo. She's a bit weird but you get used to her." Suze laughed.

He stepped forward and placed a hand on Suze's shoulder.

My stomach churned, vomit rising in my throat.

"Tilly okay?" Suze asked.

"What?" I asked, blinking. "She's fine."

"Are you? You look a bit off."

"I'm, um, not feeling well. I'd better go," I said. Before I could change my mind, I bolted past them with my jaw clenching, almost screaming when I felt him reach out and brush my hand.

"Jo, wait! Don't go rushing home if you're ill, stay here!" Suze called after me.

I hurriedly pulled the door closed and rushed down the stairs of Suze's building, almost tripping twice. The nausea came back and I clamped a hand over my mouth as I ran all the way home.

I slammed the front door behind me and struggled to pull the chain across with my shaking hands. Rushing into the kitchen, I dragged a bar stool to the French windows and wedged it under the handle. I checked the downstairs windows were locked and charged upstairs, going from room to room and drawing all the curtains closed and ensuring all the windows were locked.

With the house locked down I turned off all the lights, plunging me into darkness. I found my old baseball bat in the deep recesses of the wardrobe I now shared with Nate and tiptoed downstairs.

I took quiet, measured steps to the front door and looked out of the peephole, holding my breath in case he could even hear that. There was no sign of anyone outside. And I turned on the camera on the intercom system by the door.

He wasn't here. I let out a slow breath, trying to reassure myself that I was safe in this fortress. He wasn't here.

He was where I'd left him...with Suze and Tilly. My stomach twisted and I ran into the kitchen, the vomit that had been threatening spilling out of me. With frantic hands I yanked my phone out of my pocket and dialed Suze.

"Jo? Are you okay?" Suze asked, her voice groggy.

"Are you alone?" I asked, my voice hoarse.

"What?"

"Is he *there*?" I asked, clutching at my hair.

"Who, Greg? He left shortly after you," Suze said, and I almost cried out with relief. "Jo, what's wrong? You looked seriously ill—"

"Can you meet me tomorrow? I need to talk to you." I scrubbed at the silent tears falling down my face.

"Of course, what's wrong?" Suze asked, her voice full of concern that doubled my guilt.

"Nothing, nothing. I just need to talk to you. I'm sorry I woke you."

"It's fine. Say three o'clock at that cafe in Stockbridge?"

"I'll see you there," I said, biting my lip so she wouldn't hear me cry.

"Night, Jo," Suze said, her voice soft.

"Night, Suze," I whispered.

Tomorrow afternoon I would lose the best friend I'd ever had, because it was time for her to learn the truth. To save her, I had to break her heart. Because Greg Scott was really Scott Hudson. And he had found me.

* * * *

All night I sat vigil at the front door, clutching my bat as though it was a life raft. Every time a car drove past or I heard someone on the street, I was sure he was coming for me. Around five in the morning I thought I saw a flicker of movement in the shadows by the intercom camera, but I strained to see out of the peephole so I reasoned it was my overtired, over stressed imagination.

All I wanted was to hear the soothing familiarity of Nate's voice. But he would know in a second something was seriously wrong and I couldn't risk him coming home early or calling his family for help.

It took me an hour to work up the courage to leave the house.

I didn't even change out of the clothes I'd worn last night or wash my face. I scraped my hair back into a short ponytail and after triple checking the coast was clear, rushed out to meet Suze.

She was already there, of course, and alone. Good. That would make this easier.

"Hi," I said, out of breath from walking so quickly, feeling vulnerable to be out in the open.

"Hey," Suze said, getting up to hug me. "Are you sure you're not ill, because you look like shit. No offense."

"I'm not ill. Where's Tilly?"

"At Mum and Dad's. They're taking her to some puppet show at the library then giving her tea. We could crash, have a nice free meal?"

Pain squeezed my heart. "I'd love to, I really would, but in a few minutes you won't want me anywhere near your family."

Suze sat down, a frown on her face. "Why, what's going on?"

I sat beside her and as I studied her beautiful, innocent face I couldn't find the words. How could I tell her I'd put not only her life, but her daughter's, in danger? She would never forgive me and I didn't deserve her forgiveness.

In an instant I thought of another way to keep her safe. And maybe spare her a little pain.

"I know Greg," I said.

Suze sat back. "What do you mean? How?"

"A few weeks ago he came into the bistro when I was working. He asked me out and I said yes. I met him that night for a drink and he asked me back to his place."

Suze forced a laugh. "This is a joke, right?"

A lump the size of a football lodged in my throat. I knew exactly what to say for her to believe me. "He has a tattoo of a Chinese dragon on his right shoulder." I had been with Scott the day he'd got that tattoo. For weeks he'd flashed it at anyone who would look and his narcissistic side would have wanted to show Suze.

She reared away from me as though I had struck her. Tears welled in her eyes.

"Suze, I am so sorry," I said, looking at my hands.

"How could you?"

"I never wanted to hurt you—"

"Hurt *me*? What about Nate?" Suze stood up. "He fucking trusted you!"

*God…*Nate. I hadn't even thought about how my lie would affect him, but I couldn't take it back. Not that Suze would believe me, anyway. This was how it had to be, for me to keep them all safe.

"I'm leaving. You don't have to worry about seeing me again."

Suze's face was stony as I stood up.

"I want you to know how much I loved our friendship." My eyes spilled over. "I won't forget the kindness you showed me. No one's ever done that before."

"Don't be so dramatic, Jo, I'm bound to see you at some point." She chuckled with no humor. "And I find it difficult to believe Nate won't forgive you."

I started. "No, I mean, I'm leaving the city."

Her lips curled in disgust. "You coward."

"Yes, I am. It's all I've ever been." I moved around her. "Goodbye, Suze."

I left her standing there and half expected her to come charging after me in typical Suze fashion. When she didn't, I knew I had been successful in breaking her.

* * * *

He was nowhere in sight when I arrived home and I hurried inside, locking up just as tight as last night. With a heavy heart, I started to climb the stairs. If I had been thinking clearly I would have packed my emergency exit bag and taken it with me to meet Suze. Coming back here was an unnecessary risk, but one I was willing to take. This house was so full of Nate I needed it to at least say goodbye to some part of him.

I would never get over Nate. Never. He had proven how completely I could give myself to a person when it was healthy. I loved Nate with every breath I took and my heart was breaking to leave him. He would know why I left. Or maybe he wouldn't. Who knew? Maybe he would believe Suze and the lie I'd told her. But if he did figure out the truth, I just hoped he wouldn't tell her. I'd rather she hated me for sleeping with her boyfriend than despise me for endangering her family.

On the last staircase I dropped onto one stair and hugged my knees, my body racked with sobs. Years ago Scott had almost killed me, but I was certain that leaving Nate would destroy me in a way I would never recover.

Pulling myself together, I forced myself to get up and pack my stuff. The essentials. Only what I'd come with. Get in, get out and get away. That was the plan.

Climbing the last of the stairs, I stepped into the bedroom. It took me a few moments to see him. The light of the day was fading and his silhouette was swallowed by the shadow from the curtains as he stood by the large windows.

His back was to me but when I gasped he turned, a smile on his lips. "About time, Holly. I've been waiting."

Chapter Twenty-Five

I couldn't move. Terror had paralyzed me and I was rooted to the spot. Scott walked toward me, his movements slow and confident. My throat tightened when he was right in front of me. All at once I was nineteen again and that same crippling fear took hold of me.

Scott raised his hand as though to caress my cheek but at the last second, his face twisted into a scowl and he backhanded me so hard I fell to the ground. "Do you have any idea how long I looked for you, bitch? And here you are, acting like a little whore!"

He reached down and hauled me up, but I flinched away from him. He shook me and my teeth knocked together as he hit me again. My vision swam and he shoved me into the dresser. I hit into it with full force, crying out when my back connected with the solid wood.

Scott crouched in front of me and I shrank back.

"How could you do that to me?" he asked, his voice broken. When I didn't answer, he struck me again. "I said, how could you do that?"

I held my arms up trying to shield myself. "I'm sorry. I'm sorry."

His face softened. "I know, Hol." He rubbed my tear stained cheeks, and I winced when he caught the spot he'd hit. "Were you going to leave again?"

My breath caught in my throat. I knew Scott was unstable—even more so now than he was before. There was every chance he would kill me unless I played my only advantage, and convinced him I loved him. It could be the only way to give myself an opportunity to escape. "I was coming to find you."

Scott pulled back a fraction, his eyes studying mine. If he found the slightest hint of the lie he would be enraged. "You were?"

I nodded, holding my breath.

"Why did you hide all these years?"

"I— I was afraid."

His eyebrows knitted together. "Of what? You were afraid of me? Why the fuck should you be afraid of me? I love you!"

"I know, I know," I rushed. "I was afraid of my feelings, because they were so strong. I didn't know if you felt the same. I had to—to see if you really loved me enough to find me."

Scott rubbed his mouth as he considered my words. "You were testing me?"

There was a dangerous edge to his question. My hand shook as I reached out to touch his. "I'm so glad you finally found me. How...how did you do it?"

Scott's face twisted into a smile as he stroked his fingers across my face. "You would be surprised how far technology has come, and how accessible it is at the right price. Really, you have Suze to thank for everything."

My stomach lurched. "Suze?"

"She posted all those pictures of you on social media. You were gone for years, Holly, and then...you were everywhere. She told me where you were, what you'd been doing, where you would be...she put it all out there...and I found it. She was even kind enough to leave her keys unattended and didn't notice when I borrowed her one for here to copy and then replace." Scott grinned. "Did you know she has the security code on her phone, in case she forgets it?"

Oh, Suze... I squeezed my eyes shut and tried not to let the tidal wave of grief drown me.

He took my hand and laced our fingers. "I gave you clues that I was here."

"The perfume." My mind raced. "The phone calls."

"I knew you would think it was me." Scott's smile widened before his face darkened. "You made me angry, though, and that stupid fucking cat was here."

He had been in our home. He'd murdered Cat... I swallowed my revulsion and tried to smile. "That's okay, Scott. I've missed you so much."

His smile was sudden and full. He lurched forward and planted his lips on mine. I remembered the sensation of Scott's kiss. I remembered there was a time I'd needed them like I'd needed air. But all I could think about was how Nate would never kiss me again. It felt like Scott was erasing every part of him, sucking him out of my system.

My tears came harder and Scott pulled back, his eyes suspicious, so I grabbed his face and kissed him with all my might. He gripped my hair so he pulled on the roots and assaulted my mouth. With his free hand Scott wrenched on my jeans button.

A fierce wave of nausea swept through me. God, I couldn't do it. Not here. I'd rather he killed me. Scott broke the kiss and dragged me to my feet. He yanked at my clothing like a man possessed and ripped my T-shirt. He stripped me bare and I forced myself to stand, to not crumple like I wanted to. I waited for his touch but it never came.

Instead Scott circled me, his eyes scanning every inch of my body. It struck me that he was trying to see any physical evidence of Nate—or maybe any emotional trace of him. I've no idea how long I stood there. Hours, maybe. All I knew was I was exhausted and full dark had drawn in outside.

"I don't like your short hair," Scott said.

I swallowed, my throat dry and scorching with thirst. "My long hair was for you. No one else had the right to see it."

He liked that. His smile was cocky and arrogant. "Grow it back."

"I will." I smiled at him, shyly, peeking through my lashes. "We have forever."

Scott stood up straighter. "Yes, we do. I might have to lock you up so you can't run away again."

My knees shook. "Only if you're locked up with me."

Scott sneered. "I'll be there every day. Every night. Making sure you've forgotten every man you whored yourself out to."

"I only did it to make you jealous." I winced. "I loved how possessive you were."

"*Love* how possessive I *am*!" Scott growled.

I nodded quickly.

Scott seemed pacified for the moment and leaned in to kiss me, soft and lingering. His idea of intimate. "You must be hungry. Why don't we make dinner?"

"Yes." *Compliant. Agreeable. Keep him happy until I see an opportunity.*

Scott retrieved a bag I hadn't noticed on the bed and pulled out clothing. He looked over his shoulder at me. "I brought some of your things."

Some of my things... Jesus, he had kept my clothes after I'd disappeared. Scott brought over a short denim skirt he'd only ever let me wear at home for him and a T-shirt of his I used to sleep in. No underwear. I smiled to hide my disgust and let him dress me.

Scott held my hand as we walked downstairs, his distaste curling his lips as we made it into the kitchen. "How much fucking money does the dickhead need? Snobby prick."

"What would you like for dinner?" I smiled up at him. "Macaroni cheese?"

"Mmm," Scott replied, looking around the kitchen.

I followed his gaze and it was then I noticed many missing items.

The knife block. The cordless phone. Any sharp or heavy utensils.

I felt his eyes on me and I forced a neutral look to hide my blatant fear. He must have been nearby the house and found a way inside when I'd been out breaking Suze's heart. I was betting my bat was also gone, and my phone that I hadn't taken with me.

Scott sat at the island as I prepared his dinner and my insides churned with anger at his invasion of Nate's home. This was *his* island. This was *his* home. But that was Scott's intention, to show he could come anywhere he wanted and take what was his. Because in his eyes, I would never be anyone else's.

He insisted we sit at the dining table which Nate and I rarely used. Scott watched me like a hawk, barely taking his eyes off me. The macaroni sat in my stomach like lead but I forced myself to try to eat normally. When we were both finished, I looked across the table at him. *What game is he playing?* I had thought the minute he found me he would throttle the life right out of me. *Is he taking the time to break me psychologically then kill me? Or...does he think we would ride off into the sunset together?*

Can he really be that mentally broken that he believes I'd been waiting for him all this time?

"What are we going to do, Scott?" I asked.

He frowned. "What do you mean?"

"Well, we're not going to stay here forever, are we?" I smiled and tilted my head to the side.

"I haven't decided what to do with you yet." Scott folded his arms, his eyes shooting holes straight through me.

I rose from my chair and picked up the dishes. "Why don't I wash these while you have a think?"

As expected, Scott followed me into the kitchen. I placed the dishes in the sink, my eyes landing on the framed photo of me and Suze, both of us pouting, our faces pressed together. I wasn't Holly anymore. I was Jo. Jo was a baker and she had the love of a man named Nate. She was best friends with Suze, Auntie to Tilly. She had a job and a social life, and she thrived in this world.

Holly was dead. Scott had already killed her. He couldn't do it again. Holly had died, but Jo knew how to live.

Turning around, I gave Scott my best smile and sauntered over to him. "I have an idea what you could do with me."

"What?" Scott asked, eyeing me with caution.

I laid my hands on his chest and peered up at him with wide, hopeful eyes. "You could give me my ring and marry me."

Scott closed his eyes and stepped back. For a second I thought I had gone too far, too big and he hadn't believed me. But he dropped to his knees and shoved his face into my stomach. His arms banded around me and a moment later his body shuddered with sobs. "Holly, Holly."

Emotion welled up in my throat and I touched the top of his head.

"I missed you so much," he cried.

"I missed you too," I whispered.

Scott stayed like that for a long time. But eventually he quietened and released his death grip on me. He rose to his feet and kissed me fiercely, not allowing me a second to catch my breath. When he broke the kiss, Scott reached under the collar of his polo shirt and pulled free a silver chain. And on it dangled the tiny diamond ring he had bought for me. I had left it on his bedside cabinet in the hospital before I'd run, never expecting to see it again.

He freed it from the chain and held my hand, slipping the thin band onto my finger. He raised my hand to his lips and kissed the ring. My hand shook.

"Forever," Scott murmured. "For this life and the next."

My smile was wobbly as I finished the promise we used to make each other, "And whatever comes after that."

Scott grinned, wide and manic. "You and me, Hol."

The base unit for the cordless phone rang and hope soared. If it was for me then someone was looking for me and after long enough, they would realize I was missing and come looking for me. It rang and rang and irritation ticked in Scott's jaw.

After a minute the answering machine kicked in. And Nate's voice flooded the house.

"Hey, gorgeous, just me. I've tried your phone a few times but can't get you. Left it at work again, have you? Anyway, just checking in. I'm going to bed now. I'm bloody knackered, think the jet lag is kicking in. And I didn't get much in the way of rest last night. I kept imagining us on the island the other morning and my fucking balls are aching. Right, I'm going before I leave a very detailed message on all the ways I'll have you when I get home. Talk later, beautiful."

Was it that late? How long had I been here with Scott? The hope deflated when I realized that Nate wouldn't try to call me again until tomorrow afternoon, morning his time.

The machine beeped to signal the end of the message and Scott was shaking.

I opened my mouth to soothe him, maybe try to make a joke but no words came out. I had seen that look before and it didn't matter what I said, nothing would break through that red haze.

"You fucking whore," he said quietly.

"Scott," I whimpered.

With a snarl he made a fist and hit me. My eye felt like it exploded. I stumbled, my feet sliding out from under me and I landed awkwardly on the floor. Scott dropped on top of me, his knee connecting with my back and winding me, and I heard an ominous snap.

Pain lanced up my arm but I couldn't scream, could barely gasp in a breath. Scott flipped me over then wrapped his fingers around my throat. My eyes bulged and I clawed at his hands, feeling the skin rake off but it did nothing to loosen his hold. I kicked and kicked until my vision went spotty and I had no more fight left.

Just as everything started to go black, Scott released my throat. He jumped to his feet, and I sucked in painful breaths. When my lungs finally filled, I screamed in pain and terror and at the utter hopelessness of the situation.

"Just kill me," I pleaded. "Just fucking kill me, Scott."

He was in my face in a heartbeat, eyes narrowed and his words hissed. "You make me want to watch the life bleed out of you. I love you that much. I want to see myself reflected in your eyes as I strangle you. I want to be the last thing you ever see, ever smell, ever *feel*. I want to kill you so no one can ever have you but me."

"That isn't love!" I screeched. "You're fucking insane! You don't kill the people you love!"

Scott's face twisted in pain as tears filled his eyes. "I don't know how else to show you! I love you so much I want to die and for you to die, so we can be together forever."

I cried louder, my bruised throat making the sound shrill.

"Please don't cry, Hol," he pleaded.

"Then let me go! Let me go or kill me, please. Please," I begged.

"I can never let you go." Scott grabbed my arms and lifted me to my feet.

I screamed again and when he let me go, I cradled my arm to my chest. "I think my arm is broken."

"You see what you make me do?" Scott's voice softened. He took my other hand and pulled me out of the room and up the stairs.

"What are you doing?" I moaned.

"Getting you cleaned up. You look a mess," he answered. In the bedroom I shared with Nate, he looked around the room. "I can feel him in here."

So could I, but I didn't think telling him would help me any. Scott dropped my hand and stalked over to the bed, a look of disgust curling his lips. With his bare hands he picked up a pillow and ripped the case to pieces, stuffing falling onto the floor and bed. He started on the duvet and the sheets until his hands were red. He panted with exertion as he shredded our bed.

Scott marched into the wardrobe and came back with my bat. He held it in both hands and swung it against the bed frame. Over and over he swung it, chunks of wood splintering from the frame. Scott glared at me as he went back into the wardrobe and came back out minus the bat. His body shook with adrenaline and he started pulling off his clothes.

"Scott," I whispered.

When he was naked, he moved to where I stood and yanked the T-shirt over my head, doing nothing to take care with my arm. I bit my lip to keep from crying out and my mouth filled with blood. Scott pushed the skirt down my legs. "Get in the bathroom."

Chapter Twenty-Six

Scott ushered me into the shower, turning the temperature to a notch below scalding. He stepped in behind me and reached for a loofah. His eyes roamed over every inch of my body, his lip curling into a sneer. "I can see him all over you. Did you like whoring yourself to him? You fucking bitch, I can see him. He's everywhere."

I didn't say a word. Scott scrubbed my body with loofah until my skin was red raw and bleeding in some places. I knew he was trying to destroy every trace of Nate and I didn't have the fight left in me to stop him.

Closing my eyes, I conjured up the image of Nate when I'd first seen him. Tall, gorgeous and taking up more space than any other person I'd ever met. Scott could kill me, set fire to this house with my body inside it and he still wouldn't have cleansed the place of Nate.

Afterwards he dried me, dressed me in the same T-shirt then guided me to the ruined bed. Nausea rose in my throat and my heart pounded. He pressed his front to my back and wrapped an arm around my waist. His other hand came around to rest on my arm and while his touch wasn't threatening I knew the message.

And that was how we lay all night. He didn't try to force anything…perhaps it was his idea of intimacy.

I don't know if Scott slept, but I didn't. I lay staring at the wall and watched as the light changed, the dull, pulsing ache in my arm that flared with every breath was the only reminder I was still alive. My mind was blank. No escape plans, no consoling thoughts, no fears…not even any memories flitted across my mind.

Scott withdrew his arms and sat up in bed. He didn't need to check to see if I was awake. "We should get up and ready. It's time we left. There will be plenty of trains leaving soon."

Once again, Scott picked out a selection of my old clothes and I dressed with no complaints. He made us toast and jam for breakfast, something that used to be a staple for us, morning, noon or night.

I didn't touch it.

After he'd eaten, Scott disappeared for a few minutes and only when he returned with the bag that he had my clothes in did it occur to me that I didn't even try to run. I left my bad arm out of the hoodie sleeve and held it to my chest. Scott smiled as he pulled a beanie down low on my forehead and placed a pair of large hipster glasses on my face as though it would hide the marks he'd left.

Scott kept a tight grip on my hand as we walked outside. We ended up on Princes Street and as we passed by a dark store front, I stumbled. Seeing my reflection was like seeing a ghost. Holly often dressed down, too afraid of receiving attention and upsetting

Scott. Holly also wore fake glasses and beanies a lot to hide the few times he hit her.

Seeing her was the wakeup call I needed.

I had to find a way to get away from him. Even if it killed me.

"Jo?"

Turning away from my reflection, I saw Claire a few yards away from us. Scott's grip tightened on me.

"I'm sorry. Do I know you?" I asked, tilting my head and feigning confusion.

Claire's eyes swept over me and landed on Scott. Her body stiffened as she looked back at me and focused on my bruised cheek.

"I think you have me confused with someone else. Excuse us."

"Of course, of course. Sorry, stupid old brain. Have a nice day. It's looking like a good one!" Claire said with a smile.

"We will. My fiancé and I are taking a trip." I smiled at Scott. "We'd better go, darling, our train will be here soon." I tugged him past Claire and prayed she understood the message.

"Yes, we'd better go. Because if that nosey bitch lets anyone know where we're going and they find us, I'll cut out your fucking tongue." Scott grinned down at me.

Waverley Station was confusing at the best of times with all the works they had going on all the time, let alone when my brain was firing in a million directions with all stress. Hundreds of people surrounded us. I could kick and scream and make such a scene Scott would have no choice but to let me go. I was running out of options, but that would only be a quick fix and I needed a permanent one. One where he couldn't come back.

He scanned the departures board and when I followed his stare, I saw a train leaving in ten minutes for Carlisle. Scott rushed us to the platform and I tried to slow him down.

"Will you stop fucking around!" Scott bit out.

I tried to tug my arm free, panic rising in my throat when I couldn't think of a way out of this mess. "Scott, please don't make me leave. Just go and live your life and let me live mine! I'll only torture you and I wish we could both be free."

"We'll be free when we're dead. Until then we will live our lives *together*."

"Scott, stop, *please!*" I tugged harder, and he slapped me.

Several people looked as he pulled me past them, a few tittering that they saw him hit me.

I caught the eye of a man traveling with his family. "Help me, please!" In my head I screamed the words, but they came out as a breathy whisper as though I was trapped in a nightmare and unable to make a sound.

His wife tugged on his arm, speaking in a foreign language and turned away from me.

"Please!"

We arrived on the platform and it was relatively quiet. I tried to grab a high vis vest, making the worker wearing it stumble and drop his polystyrene cup.

"Help!" *What was wrong with these people? Why would no one help me?*

Scott yanked me with so much force I thought my shoulder would dislocate. I tried again and again to pull my hand free. I could see the train arriving and it was like a physical embodiment of the end of me.

Once I got on that train, I wouldn't be Jo anymore and Scott would have taken another life.

"No!" I shouted and gave one last almighty pull. Finally my hand was free. Scott lunged for me and I stumbled to the ground. His feet tangled on my leg and he lost his balance.

It was as though the world stopped spinning and I could see what was happening in ultra-slow motion. I scrambled to my feet and reached for him but Scott's momentum pulled him in the direction of the tracks.

Scott's eyes locked with mine and for a second, everything was still and quiet. I reached for him and our fingertips grazed for the briefest of moments.

He fell in front of the oncoming train and the sound came rushing back in a loud, desperate scream.

* * * *

I opened my eyes and it took a couple of blinks to clear my vision. I was flat on my back and it felt as though I was moving. An unfamiliar face came into my line of sight and even though I could hear the words and see their mouth moving, I didn't understand what they said. The stranger's voice drifted over me, muffled, like my ears were stuffed with cotton wool.

There had been an accident. I was being taken to hospital. I had fainted and hit my head. Did I feel nauseous? Dizzy? Could I remember my name? My arm was broken. Was I in much pain? Did I have someone they wanted to ring for me?

Do I have someone?

That thought swirled in my mind as my eyelids fluttered closed and the questions stopped.

At the hospital I was taken for an X-ray which confirmed my broken arm and it was a surprise that it was clean break and only needed a cast with no re-setting, despite having broken it yesterday I had no more harm to it. I was given pain medication and after an exam of my other injuries, I was told I had—though they felt like anything but—minor bruises. My face was simply cosmetics, and arnica would help speed the bruises to heal.

I wanted to scream that they had to fix what couldn't be seen. That thing that Scott had broken somewhere inside me was now a dead, rotting thing, and I wanted more than anything for them to fix it…fix *me*.

I was interviewed by the police. I told them everything—my past with Scott and his sudden reappearance into my life. Eyewitness accounts told them it was an unfortunate accident that morning, that I didn't push him. Scott was confirmed dead at the hospital minutes after arriving.

Then I was alone.

No more people.

No more questions.

This room with fabric walls was my safe haven.

"You fucking bitch." I gasped at the venom in Nate's voice.

"How could you let that monster near my daughter?" Suze's soft, lyrical tone was twisted in fury.

"You fucking freak, what's wrong with you? You let this happen! You did this, this is your fault!"

"I wish I had never met you."

"Fuckinghateyouhowcouldyou Itrustedyouhecouldhavehur themyoubitchthisisyourfaultthisisyourfaultthisisyourfaultth isisyourfaultthisisyourfaultthisisyourfaultthisisyourfault…"

I rolled onto my side and pulled my knees up to my chest. I wrapped my arms around them and rocked myself back and forth. Their voices shrieked louder and louder in my head, all the things I knew they would think...knew they would say. I clamped my hands over my ears but it did nothing to drown them out.

* * * *

Someone came back.

Did I have someone they could ring for me?

While I could physically hear what they were saying, Nate and Suze were all I could focus on.

I was taken to the nurse's station where I was allowed to make a phone call. I'd had to ask...I couldn't trust a stranger to convey the message.

The phone rang and rang. I squeezed my eyes shut and shrank back into the chair, the people walking back and forth paying no attention to the broken girl in the corner. I'd been in this hospital for hours. The doctors were done. The police were done. *I* was almost done.

Finally the answering machine picked up, the familiar voice making a lump form in my throat. When the beep came I started to speak, though not much came out. I cleared my throat and started again.

"Claire, it's Jo. I'm really sorry but I need a favor — "

"Jo? Jo?" Claire's frantic voice suddenly burst across the line as she interrupted the message.

"Claire?"

"Oh, Jo, thank *God*! I was worried sick about you! Who on earth was that this morning? I've tried calling Nate but there's no answer! I don't have his parent's number and I can't find them in the phone book. Where are you? Are you all right?"

Am I all right? Am I all right? "I'm at the hospital."

"You're *what*?" she shrieked.

I winced and clutched the phone receiver tighter. "I'm fine, I just…I need a favor, can you do that for me?"

"Darling, I can do anything for you, what do you need?"

"In my locker there's a spare key for Nate's house. I can't remember if I set the alarm, but if I did the code is star, seven-six-zero-two, star. Go to the fourth floor and into the walk-in wardrobe. You'll see my clothes. Above the cardigans is a shelf. On that shelf is a holdall and inside the holdall is a black backpack. I need you to bring the backpack to the accident and emergency department at the hospital."

There was a heavy pause once I'd finished. Claire let out a breath and I could almost picture her, sitting at her desk with her head in her hands as she tried to work out this puzzle. "Jo, what's going on?"

"Please, Claire," I whispered.

"All right. All right. I'll be there as soon as I can."

"Thank you and, Claire?" My throat seized up and the tears in my eyes finally spilled over. "Remember, it's star, number, star, okay?"

* * * *

My mind was like a black hole. No thoughts. No emotions. I watched the clock on the wall tick for an hour and fourteen minutes until a nurse pulled back the curtains. Claire stepped inside, her eyes welling up when she saw me.

"I knew that bastard had hurt you," she whispered fiercely.

"I'm fine," I said, swinging my legs off the bed and standing up.

"No offense, Jo, but you look anything but." Claire touched my arm and ushered me back to the bed.

I sat on the edge and accepted the backpack that she held out.

"Do I even want to know what happened in the bedroom?"

I shook my head and unzipped the backpack. My breath left me in a rush. It was all still there. Everything. Thank God.

"I still haven't been able to get in touch with Nate. Do you have your mobile? Can you get a message to him?" Claire asked.

"No, he's in America. He's back in a few days." I zipped it back up.

"Do you want to come home with me?" Claire asked. She sat beside me on the bed. "It's no trouble. I can't imagine you want to be alone."

I gave her a wobbly smile. "I really appreciate that, Claire. Suze and Tilly are on their way to pick me up. I just needed a few things before they got here. Thanks for bringing the backpack."

Her eyebrows pinched together. For a moment she quietly observed me before patting my hand. "I'll keep you company until they get here. Traffic at this time of day is a nightmare. How about a coffee while we wait?"

I sagged with relief. "I'd love a hot chocolate."

Claire's smile widened. "Chocolate cures all ails, doesn't it?"

"Of course," I said.

Claire picked up her handbag and gave me a wink before disappearing behind the curtain.

"Who do you think you are, lying to me? Using me? You absolute coward." Claire's unspoken words whispered in my head.

I gave it forty-five seconds before I picked up the backpack with my good hand, shoved back the curtain then walked out of the door—across the car park, down the street and into the city. With the cash which was stuffed in various pockets of the backpack I bought a bus ticket at the terminal for the one leaving imminently.

Relief mixed with guilt when the bus was on its way to Glasgow. I had successfully evaded Claire. I was out of the city that ironically I had fought so desperately mere hours before to stay in. No one had to see me again.

* * * *

It was full dark when I dragged my weary body off the bus and the city was still alive. I made my way to the budget hotel recommended by the person at the information kiosk in the bus terminal. It felt like every step I took, I was shedding parts of myself.

Thankfully there was a single room available so I didn't have to share with anyone. They took cash and the door locked, though I wedged a wobbly chair under the handle just in case. I lay down on top of the scratchy covers and hugged myself.

I drew my knees up to my chest and felt my body tremble.

I widened my eyes in the dark, straining to see something that wasn't there.

He's dead. He's dead. He's dead.

"He's dead," I made myself say out loud. "He's dead, he's dead, he's dead."

Chapter Twenty-Seven

I jerked awake as someone ran past my door laughing. I winced when moving my broken arm and used my good one to rub the grit from my eyes. Sleep must have claimed me at some point, though I didn't remember falling asleep. My body was stiff and sore from the uncomfortable bed and the beating.

Standing in front of the grimy bathroom mirror, I tentatively took off my clothes. The bruises were turning a deep purplish blue. My ribs were the worst, with my arms and face coming a close second and third. I remembered each strike from Scott's fists. I felt the pain as if it were happening now.

This was my penance.

I deserved this.

It was my fault he'd got anywhere near Nate's family.

'Youfuckingbitchhowcouldyoulethimnearmyfamilyhecouldhavehurtthemthisisyourfault.'

I should have died.

* * * *

For three days I stayed in that room. The countless stale granola bars in my backpack sustained me, though I didn't even feel like eating them. It was only common sense that told me to. I paced around the room, desperately craving something. Not pain relief, though my arm hurt like a bitch. I wasn't afraid and I was terrified all at once.

It took an hour for me to psych myself up to go for a quick walk around the block, thinking maybe fresh air would clear my head and make me feel better. But the second I was back inside my dingy little hotel room, the feeling was back.

Maybe it was time to move on. I pulled the basic mobile phone out of my backpack and powered it on. I left it on the bed while I went into the bathroom to wash my face, and as I splashed myself with the cold water, I heard a chime.

With a frown I picked up the phone and saw the voicemail symbol. No one had this number. I dialed the voicemail, fully expecting it to be a message from the network or a wrong number.

"Jo?"

Nate.

I dropped to the floor, my breath coming in panicked pants and my heart beating ferociously. With both hands I pressed the phone harder against my ear, scared to death of missing even one sound.

Nate let out a weary breath. "Jo, I hope to God this is you. I found this number stored in your mobile. I rang every fucking person you had in your contacts and this *has* to be you...it *has* to be. You're the only person I know who would have their own phone number in their bloody phone."

He was right, of course. Wasn't he always? I'd stored the number for my escape phone in my everyday phone in case I ever needed it for whatever reason.

"If you get this...please, Jo...please just fucking ring me. I need to know you're okay."

The message cut off and I didn't move for at least ten minutes.

'You fucking bitch.'

My knuckles turned white from clutching the phone in a death grip. I forced myself to lower the phone. Hold down the power button and replace it back in the backpack.

There was a soft knock on the door. My heart soared, he had found me! God, that man was incredible! I kicked off the threadbare blankets and pulled the door open, a smile so wide on my face. "How did you find me?"

He turned and my blood turned to ice. "Because I'll always find you, Holly."

Screams ripped from my throat until it was raw and hoarse. I was vaguely aware of pounding on the wall and someone yelling for me to shut up. I lurched to my feet and stumbled into the bathroom, only just making it to the toilet before my stomach emptied its meager contents.

* * * *

With my stale sandwich bought from the express supermarket on the corner, I sat cross-legged on the bed and picked at the crust. After three mice-like nibbles, I shoved the rest back in the container and dumped it on the floor. Everything tasted like ash in my mouth.

I felt like I had been disconnected not only from my life but also from my body. I was numb and I was a raw, screaming nerve. I was dead and I was in so much pain I had to be alive.

The mobile peeked out from the pocket in the backpack. It had been three days since Nate's message and I didn't have the guts to turn it back on.

He couldn't have known the whole story. Was Suze sparing his feelings? She *couldn't* have told him the lie I concocted about me and Scott. Once he knew, though…I would be as good as dead to that entire family. To everyone who thought they knew Jo Carpenter.

Nate.

Suze.

Tilly.

Vic, Diane, Claire, Paul, Carly, Mel…

Nate.

In the end, I only wanted to prove to myself that there would be at least one vicious and angry, heartbroken message waiting for me. I powered on the phone and sure enough after a few minutes it beeped with a new message.

You have seven new messages.

My stomach twisted. I'd heard Nate angry, but was I ready for all of it to be aimed at me? To hear the words my mind had haunted me with since the hospital? Before I could change my mind I pressed *one* and waited for his voice.

"Jo, please, just ring me. Send me a text, *anything*. Just let me know you're safe."

"I'm going to keep leaving messages until you get in touch with me."

"This is getting ridiculous! I don't know how the fuck I'll do it, but if I don't hear from you by tomorrow morning I'm coming to look for you."

"Jo, I'm begging you now, babe. *Please* tell me where you are."

"I mean it. I won't stop ringing."

"Jo, for fuck sake, stop being so fucking stubborn!"

"Please come home."

His tones ranged from pleading, furious and broken. His last message was spoken in a whisper, a useless wish in the dark.

I deleted the messages and dropped the phone on the bed. Pulling my knees to my chest I wrapped my arms around my legs and dropped my head onto my knees.

Maybe it was time I wasn't Jo anymore.

Maybe I should be someone new.

The phone let out a shrill ring and I jumped a mile out of my skin. A number flashed across the lit up screen with an incoming call.

Nate.

Oh, God, I hadn't turned it off.

My heart pounded so hard I was almost sick and I couldn't tear my eyes from the phone. It finally stopped ringing but I still couldn't move. Then the voicemail symbol appeared on the screen.

With a shaking hand, I reached for the phone. My eyes stung with tears and I once again dialed the voicemail.

"Jo? Jo? Fuck me, are you there? It's always gone straight to voicemail before. Jo, call me *as soon as you get this*! I need to talk to you, I need *you*, Jo. Please, I am on my knees begging you to call me back. I just need to hear your voice. Fuck, Jo…"

There was a beep in my ear and I yelped and fumbled with the phone.

He was calling again.

And maybe it was masochistic or just plain stupidity, but in that second I needed to hear him speak to *me*, even if he would scream and yell and curse the day he'd ever met me. I answered the call and raised the phone to my ear again.

For a few seconds there was nothing. Just a faint crackle of static across the line. And —

"I know you're there."

Nate sounded exhausted. Like he hadn't slept for weeks and everything had been drained from him.

"I can hear you breathing."

My breath hiccupped and the tears started to stream down my face.

"Please don't cry." Nate's voice was thick, as though he fought back his own emotion. "Jo, please talk to me."

"I—" I started.

Nate's breath left him in a rush. "Jo?"

"I am so sorry," I said, barely recognizing my own voice. "Just know that I'm sorry—for everything."

"Don't you dare hang up!" Nate bellowed and I froze, my finger poised over the disconnect button. "I need to see you. Where are you? If you don't want me to come to you, meet me somewhere. Anywhere. The park? That bridge in Stockbridge?"

"I'm not in Edinburgh," I whispered.

"You—you really left." Something in the way he'd spoke those words broke me in a way Scott had never been able to. Was he resigned that I had kept my word? Disappointed? Relieved?

I nodded.

"I don't care. Either get to Edinburgh *now*, or tell me where you are." Now he sounded determined and I was reminded yet again what a force of nature Nate was.

"Glasgow."

He let out a breath that definitely sounded relieved. Maybe he'd thought I'd gone so far as to leave the country. Through the line, I heard a door slam and the opening and closing of his car door. "I'll be there in less than an hour. Meet me at Glasgow Central."

My heart picked up speed again. Could I do this? See how much I had hurt him in person?

When Nate spoke again his voice sounded further away, and I realized he had switched to his hands-free device. "Jo? Don't hang up, okay?"

"Okay," I breathed.

We didn't say another word, but the line was open the entire journey. It took twenty minutes to work up the courage to leave the room, and it was only Nate's constant and reassuring presence on the other end of the phone that made me open the door and step through it.

This last week I could count on one hand how many times I had been outdoors, and how many minutes I'd been out there. Glasgow Central was a two minute walk from my hotel and teeming with life. Busy commuters rushed past with their travel mugs, travelers clipped the ankles of unsuspecting people with their overstuffed suitcases.

I sat on one of the cold metal seats in front of the departure and arrival boards and crossed my legs, my foot drumming against the seat leg. Something brushed my hair and I bolted to my feet, eyes scanning the area for someone I knew couldn't be there. I felt dizzy as I sat back down, my head telling me it was impossible, that he wasn't, would never again, be there, but something in my gut insisting it was possible.

My eyes flitted to the train tracks and Scott's face as he fell flashed in my head. I dug the heel of my hand into my eyes as though I could rub the image away.

"Jo?"

The voice came from behind me, not in my ear. I lowered the phone, my arm complaining. I stood up but couldn't bring myself to turn around. His battered Chuck Taylors came into my line of sight as I stared hard at the floor.

He touched my chin and gently lifted my face. And as I took in the sight of him, I felt myself crumble. Nate's eyes roamed over every inch of me, his face falling at the sight of the bruises that had turned a greenish yellow but hadn't had time to heal properly yet. I wondered if he was disgusted by them, by my unwashed hair and clothes I'd worn almost exclusively for the last week and a half. Maybe he thought I should look worse. Deserved worse.

Nate dropped his hand from my chin and scrubbed it down his face, and I heard the scratch of his stubble against his palm that was longer than I had ever seen it. He had dark circles under his eyes and his clothes were crumpled and unkempt, as though he had slept in them. It was my fault he looked so tortured. It must have torn him up inside that it was because of me that the monster had gotten close to his sister and beautiful niece.

"Can—" Nate cleared his throat and jammed his hands in his front pockets. "Can we go somewhere to talk? Preferably somewhere private. I feel like I'll do a lot of swearing."

I nodded. Nate was likely to do a lot more than swear, and I doubted that he wanted an audience when he did. We walked in silence to the discount hotel and I felt his eyes on the peeling wallpaper and flickering hallway lights, but he never said a word. He would be glad I wasn't anywhere nice or comfortable.

Nate moved to stand by the window in my room while I hovered near the door. I gripped my fingers to stop fidgeting and try to stop shaking.

"I've spent all this time desperately trying to reach you. I never thought about what I would say if I ever found you," Nate said, not turning around.

"I'm sure it will come to you."

He turned and his eyes were so sad it made my insides hurt. The warm whiskey-brown of his irises held a lifetimes worth of hurt, and I wished that Scott had hurt me more. There was no punishment good enough for what I had done to Nate.

"It's not, though. I haven't got a fucking clue what to say to you." Nate took a step toward me before stopping. "I will never forgive myself, Jo."

I shook my head. "You have to. You didn't know what you were getting into. I should never have let myself get involved with you."

Nate let out a heavy breath and sat down on the edge of the bed. It creaked and dipped under his weight. "How can you say that? Jo, you fucking *left!*"

"Of course I did." *What else could I have done?* There was no point staying in the city where I could bump into any of them and remind them once again of what I had done.

"Well, if that wasn't a clear indication of my blame, I don't know what is," Nate muttered, twisting his hands. "I should have known. Somehow, I should have known you were in trouble. Fuck, you were all alone, Jo. I will *never* forgive myself."

My spine straightened. "What?"

Nate raised his head to look at me, his face tortured. "The one time you needed me I wasn't there. He could have fucking killed you…and I was on the other side of the world."

I stepped back, needing distance and shaking my head. Nothing he said made any sense.

"I don't expect you to forgive me. But I'm going to spend the rest of my life trying to make it up to you," Nate said.

"Stop it," I whispered.

His head snapped up. "Jo—"

"No, please, Nate. I deserve everything you want to throw at me, but please not that." My voice broke and I rubbed my eyes, trying to keep the tears inside. "I deserve it, but please don't."

Nate stood up. "Don't what? What the fuck are you talking about?" He took a step closer, his features flattening out. "Do you not believe me?"

"What is there to believe?" I cried. "I did this! I brought that monster into your family, into your *home*! I don't know how you can stand to look at me!"

He held his hands out. "Jo, why did you leave?"

I bit my lip, trying to keep from completely breaking down. "Because I'm a coward."

"Why?" he asked quietly.

"I couldn't face any of you. Couldn't see your anger. I didn't want to be a constant remind to you all of what I did."

Nate came one more step closer. "And what did you do, Jo?"

"Put you all in danger. Suze, *Tilly*…" A sob broke out of my throat. "My God, he was around Tilly! What if he hurt them? He could have. He *would* have if he got impatient or angry. He would have killed you. I'm so glad you were gone. It's the one thing I'm thankful for."

"Jo," Nate said, his voice thick. "I do not blame you. I am not angry with you."

My eyes filled and I shook my head.

And he was right in front of me, wiping my cheeks and overpowering my senses with the nearness of him. "I am not angry with you. I do not blame you. I'll say it a hundred, a thousand, a million times until it sinks in. *I do not blame you.*"

"No, no, you don't make any sense!" I cried.

"I thought you left because you were disappointed in me, that you blamed me for not being there when you needed me." Nate dipped his head to touch our foreheads together. "I swear to you, I thought you left because of me."

My head swam. I desperately wanted to believe him, but that nagging doubt in the back of my mind told me it would only be a matter of time before he saw things clearly.

Chapter Twenty-Eight

The light was fading from the day. Nate moved away from me to switch on the overhead light. There was no lamp. "Jo, we can't stay here."

I frowned. "Why?"

"Are you serious? Jo, it's disgusting. I'm not letting you spend another night in here. You've probably already got fleas." Nate glanced around the room. "We can stay in Glasgow or drive back to Edinburgh. It's up to you."

My heart skipped a beat. "What's the point in going back for me to leave again?"

Nate looked as though he was holding back a slew of comments. "Let me make something clear. I want you back. Forever. I never want to let you go. But I will, if it's what you want. Not because you think you deserve it as punishment or because you think I'm playing some twisted joke. If you don't want me, I can accept that. Just know I will always want and love you."

How can he? Is that even possible?

Nate reached for my hand. "Will you come back with me? We have lots to talk about. No pressure about us."

I nodded.

We barely spoke on the drive back to Edinburgh. Nate kept the radio at a low murmur, and I snuck glances at him, at his handsome face illuminated with the dashboard lights. He sat low in his seat, his long body somehow both tense and relaxed as he maneuvered the car with skills I had always admired about him.

Without needing to ask, Nate didn't take me to his house. He parked at a hotel in Grassmarket and walked close beside me as we went inside. Nate procured us a room and when we were inside the luxurious and beautifully comfortable space, he immediately went into the bathroom and turned on the shower.

He found a bin bag and gestured for my broken arm. Nate managed to fashion me a waterproof cover for the cast and followed me into the bathroom.

"You'll feel more like yourself after a long hot shower and some food. I'm ordering some right now. Chinese okay?"

I nodded and Nate gave me a small, tight smile before leaving the bathroom and softly closing the door behind him. Letting out a shaky breath, I peeled off my clothes and tentatively stepped into the shower cubicle. Thankfully it was big, enough so there was plenty room for me to move my body around whilst keeping my broken arm away from the direct spray of water.

There was a quiet knock on the door sometime later, with Nate's voice floating into the room. "Are you managing okay?"

"Yeah, sort of," I said.

There was a pause. "Can I come in?"

I swallowed. "Yes."

The shower had steamed the glass door but I made out the dark outline of Nate's body. "Do you want me to help you?"

"Okay."

Nate opened the shower door and I braced myself for his look of disgust. Each bruise was a physical reminder that Scott's hands had touched me. Even if he could forgive me for endangering his family, how would he get past my broken body?

He stepped inside, fully clothed, apart from his socks and shoes. His eyes were hesitant. It had been sixteen days since we had last been last intimate—that erotically memorable farewell at the island. I knew every single inch of Nate's body, and he was more than familiar with my own. But we faced each other almost as strangers, with neither of us sure how to proceed.

"Turn around," Nate said, the deep timbre of his voice curling my toes.

I complied, and Nate reached around to tilt my chin up. He massaged shampoo into my hair, his fingers strong and gentle. When rinsing it, he took care to shield my eyes and made sure every bit of soap had washed out. Nate turned off the shower and stepped out, waiting to wrap my body in the gigantic and fluffy-soft bath towel.

He patted down my body, taking extra care when he knew he was on a bruise. Nate towel dried my hair then added some leave-in conditioner and combed it until it was completely knot free. He dropped the towel and held out a huge bathrobe and I slid my arms in. Nate scooped my hair free and I shivered as he stepped closer to knot the robe closed. "You almost look like you."

"Your jeans are wet," I said quietly.

Nate touched my cheek, his fingers gliding over the mark Scott had left. "I don't care."

More than anything, I wanted to sink into his body. I'd thought I'd never see him again and all I wanted were his arms to band around me and never let go. He had taken care of me and I didn't deserve his kindness but I couldn't help but crave it.

"I don't have any clothes. Do you mind if I wear a bathrobe too?" Nate asked, his eyes searching my face.

"No," I said, frowning in confusion.

"I just don't want you to think—" Nate paused, unsure. "I don't want to frighten you or have you think I'm trying anything."

I jolted when I realized what he meant. "Nate, I'm not afraid of you. Scott...he didn't— I thought he was going to, but he didn't. Even if he did, I wouldn't be afraid of you. I could never be afraid of you."

A small smile touched Nate's lips and he closed his eyes as if in relief. "Good."

I left the bathroom while he peeled off his wet clothes and sat on the edge of the bed. There was a knock on the door and I jumped to my feet. Nate emerged from the bathroom and eyed me warily. "It's okay, it's just the food."

I nodded and took a deep breath, trying to slow my racing heart.

Nate took the bags of food and paid the delivery man, closing the door quickly. He put the food on the coffee table and found some plates in the kitchenette area. I sat on the couch and watched as Nate turned on the TV, settling on an *Iron Man* movie, winking at me when Robert Downey Jr came on screen.

He had ordered all my favorites—lemon chicken, ribs, spicy chips, curry sauce, won tons, prawn crackers, garlic mushrooms. He scooped a tiny amount of each onto a plate and sat a bottle of full fat Coke in front of me.

"You haven't eaten since the hospital, have you?" Nate asked, dishing up a heaped plate for himself.

"Yes."

He glanced at me. "I could practically see every bone in the shower. You've always been slim, but Christ, Jo. I wasn't prepared for that."

I looked at my plate, my stomach twisting. "I'm sorry."

Nate sighed and sat beside me. "No, don't be. I didn't say that to make you feel bad. I'm worried about you. That's all. I'm trying to take care of you. Will you let me?"

A lump formed in my throat and I nodded, trying to smile.

"Tonight we're going to eat and watch TV. That's it. Tonight is about relaxing. We can talk tomorrow." Nate opened his own bottle of Coke and took a swig. "But don't think I'm watching this arrogant dick all night."

My smile was genuine and I picked up my fork, slowly eating the food. My stomach filled quickly, but Nate told me to nibble often to stretch my stomach to how it used to be. I didn't know what time it was when Nate ushered me into bed. He tucked me and looked at me in questioning as he lay down on top of the duvet, the biggest distance there had ever been between us in a bed before.

I fell asleep quickly, full and more relaxed than I'd been all week.

I felt him behind me, stroking a line up my thigh. I smiled sleepily and pressed into his body. His hand came around my middle and moved me onto my back. As my eyes opened I saw his face in the moonlight, his maniacal grin and cold, dead eyes.

Scott straddled me, his hands locked around my throat as he leaned down to whisper in my ear. "How do you know I'm really dead? Did you see my body?"

I woke up with Nate brushing the hair off my face and trying to calm me. I gulped in deep breaths, trying to fill my lungs. When I realized where I was and that Scott wasn't here, my cries slowed to a stop. Nate rubbed my cheeks with his big hands, drying my tears.

I still couldn't catch my breath. The blood roared in my ears and it felt as though my heart would burst right out of my chest. Nate swore and lifted me easily. He leaned against the pillows and moved me onto his lap, his arms coming around me. My ear rested over his heartbeat, which thundered just as fast as my own. He stroked a hand over my hair and kept the other locked on me.

His comfort eventually penetrated my fear. My breath came in little hiccups and once his heartbeat had slowed to a constant and reassuring beat, my own followed.

"I'm glad he's dead, because I would *end* that fucker's miserable life," Nate spat, the venom in his voice surprising me.

I was back at Waverley Station. Scott's hand was outstretched, his eyes pleading for me to save him.

Nate swore again and dropped his head to rest his cheek on my head. "I'm sorry. I can't imagine how hard it must have been to see that."

"I will remember the look on his face right before he fell for the rest of my life."

Nate's hold on me tightened as though he could protect me from my own memories.

I leaned into his touch. "He looked so betrayed. So, so, *hurt*, that I would do that to him. All he wanted was for me to save him—and I couldn't."

"You couldn't have done anything," Nate said softly. "It was an accident."

I let out a shaky breath. "If it wasn't for me, none of this would have happened. He would never have gotten near Tilly or Suze. Your house is a wreck. Scott would be alive."

"Maybe. It was Scott, not you, who had the problem. If it wasn't you he fixated on, it would have been someone else. What if he killed that girl? And another?" Nate shook his head. "You can take yourself out of the equation but you can't say that things would be better. Nothing happened to Suze or Tilly. The stuff in the house is replaceable. But you aren't."

I sniffed and closed my eyes.

"You're probably still in shock. I know the things I say won't really sink in yet, not while everything is still so fresh." Nate kissed my forehead. "I'm not going anywhere, *ever*, okay?"

"Okay," I whispered. Maybe I was starting to believe him.

Chapter Twenty-Nine

With Nate holding me I fell back asleep for two blissful nightmare-free hours. He made coffee with two heaped teaspoons of sugar and toast for breakfast, dripping with butter. We sat on the couch to eat again, Nate considerably closer than he had been last night. When breakfast was finished he cleared our plates away and came back to sit beside me.

"Are you ready to talk?" Nate asked.

I felt anything but. I nodded.

"Do you mind if I go first?"

"No, go ahead," I said, the toast now cold and heavy in my stomach. Was this it? Was this when Nate flipped and—

"That look on your face is exactly why I wanted to go first." Nate looked at his feet and shook his head. "Jo, I want you to talk to someone. I think you have PTSD. Not just from what happened, maybe even from when Scott almost killed you in the car."

PTSD? What? No, that's ridiculous.

"Your reaction after Scott died wasn't normal." Nate continued, "I think you were in shock—

understandably so—and I think you might still be. What happened... Jo, I would never blame you for that. You were, are, a victim. I can see it all over your face that you're waiting for me to finally tell you to go to hell. That it's all your fault. You'll be waiting forever, because I'll never say it."

My throat tightened. "It doesn't make sense to me that you don't blame me for what happened."

Nate's face softened. "And that's exactly why I want you to talk to someone. Mum knows a doctor in private healthcare who deals with psychotherapy, specializing in PTSD patients. Whenever you're ready, she's waiting to help you."

*Psychotherapy...*the word rattled around in my head. "Do you think I'm crazy?" I whispered.

Nate smiled, the corner of one lip pulling up. "No, I don't think you're crazy. There's no shame in therapy, Jo. If it makes you whole again, then I'm all for it. Call me greedy, but I want as much of you as I can get."

A single tear escaped my eye. Nate brushed it away and stood up. He held his hand out for me, and I slid my own into his warm, strong hand. Nate pulled me to my feet and slid his arms around my middle, holding me to his chest.

Instinctively my arms went around his broad shoulders. He buried his face in my neck, and I closed my eyes at the familiarity of it. If what he'd said was true, that he really wanted me in his life, then I had to have it. There was something broken inside me and to be with him properly then I had to fix it. For Nate, for myself, I had to fix it.

"When can I go?"

* * * *

Nate called the psychotherapist, Dr Alison Hugo, and managed to get me an appointment for the very next morning. I hadn't expected it to be quite so soon, but Nate told me his mother was good friends with the doctor and had gotten me in as a favor. I felt a little better when the appointment had been made. Things were moving forward, for better or worse.

"I called Suze to bring some clothes over for us," Nate said when he came back into the hotel room after leaving to pick us up some lunch.

"Oh," I said, quietly.

Nate crossed the room to where I stood by the window. He stopped behind me and wrapped his arms around my middle, resting his chin on my shoulder. I touched my head against him.

"Are you okay with that?"

I let out a breath, trying to choose my words so he would understand the torment in my mind. "You know family is the most important thing, don't you?"

"Yes," he agreed.

"Suze won't forgive me, Nate." *And I won't ever make you choose between me and them.*

Nate sighed and turned me in his arms so I was facing him. "Please stop thinking about that. We both need clothes but if I'm being honest, I wouldn't have asked Suze over until you'd had a few sessions of therapy. That said, I really do think seeing Suze will go some way to getting through to you."

"I do need to see her. She deserves some answers."

Nate kissed my forehead. "I think you both do."

I paced the hotel room, anxious, nervous and nauseous all at once as we waited for Suze to arrive. When she did, Nate let her in and took the holdall from her. He sat it on the bed and kissed my cheek then grabbed his wallet and phone. "I'll be downstairs. I think you two need space to talk."

My stomach sank. I wouldn't even have him as a buffer. Not that I deserved it. I should face the full wrath of Suze.

The door clicked behind Nate and we were alone.

"I don't even know where to begin apologizing to you," I said after a minute that nobody had spoken.

"I thought about all the things I would say to you on my way over here." Suze crossed the room to look out of the window. "But right now all I've got is you have to be the most infuriatingly stubborn, headstrong and masochistic person I have ever met!"

Not what I was expecting. "What?"

"Why couldn't you have trusted me with the truth?" Suze turned around to face me, her face hard and closed off.

"I'm so sorry, Suze. I know. I swear to you if I knew all this would happen, I'd do everything differently." My voice cracked. "I can't even imagine how much you hate me."

"For God's sake I don't hate you, Jo. But I'm so *mad* at you!" Suze's face turned red. "If you had told me the truth then all of this could have been avoided!"

Tears spilled down my cheeks. "I know. I know. I feel sick to my stomach imagining him there with you. I picture him near Tilly and I hate myself so fiercely I think I'll combust."

Suze's shoulders slumped. "God, Jo, he was never near Tilly."

My head snapped up to look at her and I took a step toward her before stopping. "What? He never... Oh thank God."

She frowned. "Is this what you think you need to apologize for? That he might have been around my daughter?"

I nodded furiously. "Not just that—so many other things. He was in your life because of me. He could have done any number of things to you. And he may not have ever met Tilly but who's to say it would always be that way? If I hadn't been at your flat the other night, God alone only knows how long he'd have been around you."

"Do you even remember what else happened the night you saw him?" Suze asked, wrapping her arms around her body. "I knew there was something wrong with you and I had no idea, couldn't even fathom, what the real reason was. Now that I know all the facts, I'm guessing you ran home and barricaded yourself inside the house. And once it hit you where you had left him, what did you do?"

"I phoned you," I said quietly.

"You phoned me and made sure he wasn't there. And then you made me agree to see you the next day where you told me the one thing that would ensure I never saw him again. Even if it made me hate you." Suze blew out a shaky breath. "I can't imagine how terrified you were, and all you could focus on was keeping him away from me and my daughter."

The tears streamed down my face freely. I couldn't have spoken if I wanted to.

"I'm standing here looking at my best friend in the whole world and how broken she is. And all I can think is I wish she had told me so I could have protected her, when all she was doing was protecting us." Suze scrubbed a hand over her face. "I'm mad that he used me to get to you, and I'm furious with myself for believing that bullshit story you concocted. Don't ever think that I blame you."

"I don't understand," I croaked. "Do you mean...Suze, do you forgive me?"

She laughed and crossed the room to wipe the tears from my face. "Of course I do, you idiot."

"Why?"

"Well, for one thing, you haven't actually done anything that warrants forgiving. And the other? This is what families do. They forgive each other. You're my family, Jo." Suze smiled.

If anything, I cried harder at her words. Even more so when she threw her arms around me and hugged me with all her tiny might.

Nate found us like that, hugging the life out of one another and sobbing into each other's hair.

I would never tell Suze that she was the real reason Scott had found me. She was too kind, too soft to carry that kind of burden. Suze had to stay optimistic and pure, or else her light wouldn't shine as bright...and Scott would claim another victim.

* * * *

Bright and early the next morning Nate walked me to Dr Hugo's office. He loosely held my hand and held it tighter when the sound of a distant train had me fighting for breath. Nate made himself comfortable in the waiting room, flipping through a trashy magazine.

When the closed door opened, a tall blonde woman peeked her head out. "Jo?" she asked with a kind smile. "Come on in."

Nate gave me a wink then went to back to his gossip rag. With a deep breath, I got up and followed Dr

Hugo into her room. It was nothing like I'd expected. She had a large corner couch and several other arm chairs. Potted plants were everywhere and the entire room was bright and airy. Several photo frames littered the small desk with her computer, and of course the obligatory credentials were framed on the wall.

Dr Hugo sat on the couch and tucked her legs underneath her. She smiled and waited patiently as I scanned the room and tried to decide where to sit. I had the horrible feeling this was some sort of test and after debating back and forth I let out a breath and joined her on the couch, pulling a bright pink pillow onto my lap.

"So, Jo, tell me why you're here."

Part of me wanted to hold it all in. But I glanced at the closed door and pictured Nate reading his magazine, deciding who wore the dress best, then looked back at Dr Hugo. If I was going to do this, I was going to do it right.

And for the next hour and a half, I told her everything.

At the end of my life story, I took a deep breath and hugged the pillow tighter. "Well? Am I unfixable?"

Dr Hugo smiled. "Nothing is unfixable, Jo. But we do have a lot of work to do." She stood up and moved to her desk.

"How much work?" I asked, following her and stopped on the other side of her desk.

"It's hard to say," she said, her voice soft. "You want to be here, which is extremely encouraging. I want to start cognitive behavioral therapy, have you ever heard of this?"

I shook my head.

"Basically it's a form of psychotherapy. We'll use it to retrain your behavior and thoughts. We'll give you the tools to help you deal with stress. Because of what has happened in your past, you are hardwired to run when you think you are at fault for something, and also to absorb all the guilt when it doesn't belong." Dr Hugo gave me a reassuring smile. "I have lots of tricks to help you, Jo. You did the right thing in coming to see me."

Nate jumped to his feet the moment I opened the door. He tossed the magazine away and marched across to me. "Well? How did it go?"

"Better than expected," I said, accepting my coat from him. "She wants to see me every morning at the same time for two weeks. Is that weird?"

Nate shook his head. "She must think it's the best thing for you."

* * * *

That night we curled up in bed together watching a movie, Nate seeming a little more confident in touching me than the previous nights. I was tucked under his arm and I was as close to him as I could possibly get.

Nate slid down the bed and after a moment I felt his eyes on me.

"What's wrong?" I whispered.

A half smile pulled at his lips and he stroked my face. "Nothing. I'm just happy."

"Really?"

Nate pressed his forehead to mine. "Really. Being here with you... I'm happy, Jo."

My smile was wobbly with emotion, but genuine and I touched his chest.

"Can—? Jo, can I kiss you?"

I sat up and hugged my knees. "I wish you didn't have to ask," I said, my throat croaky.

Nate pushed up onto his elbow. "I just don't want to rush you. That's why I'm asking."

With a shake of my head, I hugged my knees tighter. "I told you that Scott didn't rape me."

Nate sat up properly. "Are you saying he did?"

"No, no, he didn't." My breath caught in my throat. "But he did kiss me. And I kissed him— I was trying to convince him I loved him. I hoped that...fuck, I don't know, if he thought I loved him then he would trust me and I could somehow escape. I was such an idiot."

Nate rubbed my shoulders. "I don't care if you kissed him, Jo. I'm all for anything you could have done to get away from him and back to me. What's worrying you about it?"

"It's like he's still there," I croaked. "What if it doesn't ever feel like before with you? What if he's ruined us?"

He gently pulled me around to face him, placing me between his legs. Nate caught my ankles and pulled my legs behind him. He stroked my collarbone. "Nothing can ruin us, I promise you. I still want you, Jo. In that, crazy, borderline nymphomaniac kind of way—will never get my fill of you, stop wanting you."

I let out a breath and our faces came an inch closer.

"Do you want to kiss me?" Nate whispered, and I felt his breath on my lips.

"Nate," I said, bringing my hands to his face.

He held my hips but he didn't move. It was me who closed the tiny distance, and I think he knew I needed to make that choice to move forward. Our lips brushed and heat scorched through me.

I knew this man. And he knew me.

I deepened the kiss, Nate letting me take control of it. His dick hardened, pressing against the softness of me but he didn't make a move to take things any further.

We kissed like teenagers, for hours, and I loved it.

* * * *

At first it felt odd, spilling my guts to a stranger, but I came to realize it was actually easier rather than trying to explain my inner workings to someone I knew. We arranged an appointment every morning at eight for two weeks, during which we stayed in the hotel. Nate would walk me to Dr Hugo's office and wait for me, sometimes in the waiting room, sometimes he would disappear off somewhere but would always be there waiting for me when I came out.

Dr Hugo said I made excellent progress in those weeks and I was now on a twelve week program. My visits were cut to once a week and at the end of each session, she would give me tasks to complete for the next week. The first one was to go home.

"You're quiet today," Nate observed as we walked back to the hotel.

"Sorry," I said.

He nudged me with his elbow. "Did you get your first task? What is it? Streak naked down the Mile?"

I snorted a laugh. "I wish."

"That bad?"

I shrugged. Nate had never mentioned going home. Could I even still call it home? Was I welcome there? Nate was so proud of that house and because of me—

No, because of *Scott*, there was negativity and bad vibes hanging over it.

"Can I ask what it is?" Nate asked, his eyebrows pinched together.

"I'm not sure you'll like it," I said, looking at him and darting my eyes away again.

"Try me."

I blew out a breath. "Dr Hugo wants me to go back to the house."

Nate laughed quickly. "Christ, Jo, you had me worried then!" He shook his head and squeezed my hand. "I know it's a big deal for you, but I am totally behind Dr Hugo. This is a step I want to make, but I want you to both want and be able to make it. You've got a week, but if you don't feel up to it, then there's no rush, okay?"

I stopped walking. "You mean, you're okay with this?"

Nate frowned again. "With what?"

"Me. Going back there."

"Going home, you mean?"

"Is it still my home?" I asked, chewing on the inside of my lip.

Nate's face softened and he bent to plant a chaste kiss on my lips. "For as long as you want it to be."

Something heavy lifted from my heart at his words. The last two weeks with Dr Hugo had gone a huge way in helping me to believe the things that Nate said.

"I'm scared," I admitted.

"Of course you are. But you won't get over that fear unless you go back." Nate wrapped an arm around my waist as we started walking again. "I think it's a great idea to go back to face what happened there, but if you decide you don't want to live there, we can get somewhere new."

"What?" I asked, my head swiveling around to look at him.

"Whatever you need, Jo," he said simply.

"But you love that house."

Nate shrugged. "I love you more."

Chapter Thirty

Three days later Nate and I stood across the road from the house. My heart was pounding and my head felt faint but Nate was an anchor at my side, grounding me to both the present and to him.

"Do you want me to go in with you?"

I let out a breath. "I think I need to go in alone first."

He kissed the top of my head. "Just shout if you need me."

It was now or never. I took Nate's house keys since mine were still in there somewhere. Once inside, I remembered with a faint smile it was star, number, star.

The house was quiet. There was an emptiness in the air that came with the absence of life. Dust motes filtered in the pale winter light streaming in from the window above the front door. I carefully placed Nate's keys in the bowl, hung my coat on the stand.

I heard my breath in my ears as I tiptoed into the kitchen. The surfaces gleamed, all the stools were pushed neatly under the island. My eyes landed on the spot where Scott had thrown me and broken my arm. It itched under my cast and I saw Scott standing before me, on top of me as he choked me.

Walking backwards out of the room, I swallowed the thick knot of fear. I closed my eyes and forced myself to remember the hundreds of happy interactions that had taken place in there. Nate guiding the wooden spoon into his mouth, his eyes hungry and wild on mine. Tilly in her high chair throwing Cheerios at me shouting, *"Eat, Jojo. Eat!"*

I gathered my nerves and padded softly upstairs, the thick carpet familiar beneath my feet. Up and up I went. Past the floor I used to sleep, past the sprawling office Nate had built for himself until I was in the bedroom.

Scott stood in front of the window, the city spread out behind him. I blinked and he vanished.

The bed was gone, all traces of the carnage disappeared. The space was empty, a massive cavity in the room. I thought I would be overcome with horrific memories of discovering Scott in this room, of him beating me, of thinking I would never survive. Yes, they were there. But the first thing I focused on was the chaise longue. That beautiful piece of furniture that I'd straddled Nate on the night we'd first spent together.

I saw us there, Nate behind me with his hand inside his shirt that I wore, fondling my breast. The memories of Nate were more potent than the ones of Scott, and like he had been since the day I'd met him, Nate dominated the space. There wasn't room for both of them, and Nate cast out the darkness. I would never forget what had happened in here. But I would never forget all the good either.

With my hand on the doorknob, ready to rejoin Nate, I turned, looking toward the kitchen. There was something else I needed to do.

I opened the French doors and stepped out into the cold December air. I crouched beside the bird table, my hand on the stone that protected Cat.

"I'm sorry. I miss you," I whispered.

Nate was exactly where I'd left him, leaning against the railing with his hands tucked under his armpits to protect them from the cold.

"I was expecting you to be longer."

I frowned. "How long was I?"

"About half an hour."

It felt a hundred times longer.

"How do you feel?" Nate asked, pulling me into his body.

I blew out a breath. "A thousand times lighter."

"I'm glad."

"Nate, can we go home?"

He kissed the top of my head. "I thought you'd never ask.

* * * *

We didn't move back into the top bedroom, instead moving into my old one. Nate dropped our bags on the sleigh bed and ran upstairs to get more of our things. When he did, I quickly unzipped the backpack and tipped the contents onto the bed. I was jumpy, jittery and nervous, breathing heavily when Nate came back into the room.

"What's wrong?" Nate asked, squeezing my waist.

"For seven years this backpack was my lifejacket. It was never out of reach and it held everything I would need if I needed to run at a moment's notice." I let out a shaky breath. "I don't need it anymore. I don't need it. I don't want it, but it still feels… It's hard."

He kissed my shoulder. "Of course it is. Christ, how much money is in here?"

I shrugged. "Few thousand?"

"Shit, Jo, you've got a bloody fortune in here. First thing tomorrow you're putting that in the bank." Nate sifted through the large notes, shaking his head.

I shoved the mobile phone back in, along with the few clothes that fell out of it. My passport and the cash were all I really needed. "Can you throw this out, please?"

"Consider it done," Nate said, planting a soft kiss on my lips.

Nate barely left my side that first night. He ordered us pizza and we ate it in the comfy living room across from my bedroom while watching a Will Ferrell movie. Later he drew me a bath with relaxing oils and left the en suite door open so I could see him sprawled shirtless across the bed. I dressed in a green satin nightdress and slid into bed beside him. His body was heavy with sleep, though he moved his arm so I could snuggle into his warm embrace.

He sighed in his sleep and I tried to get closer, wishing I could climb inside him but doubted even that would be close enough.

"What's wrong?" Nate mumbled, turning his head toward me.

"I'm not sure. I'm on edge."

"What can I do?" Nate asked, rolling onto his side and rubbing the sleep from his eyes.

I searched his face, running through my mind all the places our bodies were touching. I adored Nate's body and the way it could make me feel. For the first time since he'd come to get me from Glasgow, I felt the stirring of lust.

"Kiss me."

Nate grinned wolfishly before claiming my mouth. I sighed and he nudged me onto my back. I threw my leg over his hip and Nate rubbed his erection against me.

I cried out and Nate reared back.

"Fuck, Jo, I'm sorry," Nate rushed. "I didn't mean... Are you okay?"

Reaching between us I stroked his thick erection through his boxers. "Make love to me, Nate."

He exhaled. "Are you sure? Are you ready?"

"I'm more than ready. I want you, Nate," I breathed.

Nate squeezed his eyes shut. They were tortured when they fixed back on me. "I fucking hate myself for asking, but is this about forgetting him? Forgetting he was in our home?"

I shook my head and leaned up to kiss him. "This is about remembering us."

Nate traced his fingers over my face, an intimate smile on his full lips. "I love you, Jo." He bent his head to kiss me again, long and sweet with his tongue massaging mine.

His cock twitched as I peeled down his boxers and guided him toward me. Nate sank inside me achingly slow, his eyes never once leaving me. My body greedily welcomed him, and as he started to move, I arched my hips up to meet him.

Nate didn't stop kissing me. He made love to me completely, beautifully. I sank my nails into his firm ass and he moaned into my mouth as the slow-burning orgasm swept through my body. When Nate reached his own climax, he didn't pull out of me. He rolled us over so I lay on his chest.

His semen seeped out of me, coating our bodies and making us sticky but I didn't care, and I doubted he did either. Nate traced lines up and down my back. It had been a long time since I had felt so relaxed and well loved.

I ran my fingers over his nipple and smiled when Nate started to tense under me, trying not to move his hips. I raised myself up a little and felt Nate's cock stiffen inside me. Dipping to kiss him I sat up properly, crying out from the way he filled me as my body stretched to accommodate his size. Nate gripped my hips, throwing his head back as I rocked back and forth on his dick.

Heat flared through my veins and I held nothing back, moaning his name.

"Fuck, Jo, just like that," he growled through clenched teeth.

I moved faster and he yelled.

"Just like this?"

Nate slammed his hips up and I screamed. I palmed my breasts and he groaned.

"I'm coming, Nate," I moaned.

Nate thrust up once more and came inside me as I shuddered with the force of my own orgasm. Nate panted and pushed his body upright, kissing me fiercely. "That was a fucking awesome welcome home."

I giggled. "I'll say."

* * * *

The night before my next therapy session, the doorbell rang and Nate got up from the couch to answer it. The cacophony of noise that always seemed to accompany Suze and Tilly floated into the living room. I stood up and headed for the hallway, watching as Suze unfastened Tilly from her pushchair. The second her little eyes saw me they lit up.

"Jojo! Jojo, Jojo! Tilly up! Now, Jojo!" Tilly screamed, making a beeline straight for me. She hugged my legs and jumped up and down, pulling a face when I didn't immediately swing her into my arms.

I looked at Suze, uncertain. She rolled her eyes and marched toward us. "Why is Auntie Jo being weird, Tilly?"

Tilly laughed. "Jojo weird!"

Suze gave me a look and elbowed me on her way past. "Cuddle my daughter, you twisted little weirdo."

I dropped to my knees, and Tilly squeezed the life out of my neck, her chubby arms surprisingly strong for a toddler. She burbled a little song and twirled my hair around her fingers.

Tilly eyed my cast. "Sore bit?"

"Sore bit," I said with a nod.

She blew a kiss in the vague direction of my cast.

I picked her up with one arm and my eyes welled up as I held her little body tighter. Nate caught my eye and he smiled, leaning over Tilly to kiss me. Tilly squealed and pushed her uncle's face away.

"My Jojo! Jojo, kiss, now." Tilly smothered my face in noisy piggy kisses, and Nate laughed and tickled her.

"I'll share for now, but Jojo is mine, all right, little demon?" Nate said, tweaking her nose.

Tilly smiled. "Jojo mine."

"Yes, yes, we all love Jojo!" Suze called from the kitchen. "Now can everyone please get in here so I can make us dinner?"

My heart almost burst with fullness.

* * * *

Dr Hugo was thrilled with my progress. She was over the moon Nate and I had moved back home and had been intimate, and also that I had spent time with Tilly. My next task was to start a scrapbook filled with things I loved. It could have absolutely anything in it, so long as it had positive feelings attached.

I went straight to a cute little independent stationary shop and bought an A3 colored scrap book and an assortment of pens. I was sprawled out on the living room floor that evening armed with sticky tape, pictures, recipe cards and my new pens.

Suze and Tilly came over again, Tilly dropping down beside me on the carpet with the grace of an elephant.

"What doing?" Tilly asked, stuffing chocolate buttons in her mouth.

"I'm making a book that makes me happy," I said, stealing a button.

Tilly grinned and leaned over to plant a chocolatey kiss on a blank page. She then placed her empty sweet bag beside it. "Happy?"

I kissed her cheek. "Happy." I flipped back a few pages and pointed to a picture of Suze and Tilly blowing kisses to the camera. "Happy."

"Jo?" Suze said, standing beside us.

"Hmm?" I asked, scribbling Tilly's name and the date beside her kiss.

"Would you babysit Tilly this weekend?"

I sat bolt upright. Scanning Suze's face, I saw no evidence of joking, but my first reaction was that it had to be. Shaking my head, I tried to invoke Dr Hugo. "Are you serious?"

Suze crouched down so we were at eye level. "Yes. I'm desperate for a weekend away, and Mum mentioned she'd love to go to Newcastle for Christmas shopping. We could have a night away together." My eyes scrunched up, and Suze's face turned horrified. "Oh, fuck, how inconsiderate does that sound? Nate can babysit! You come too!"

Tilly clapped her hands. "Fuh—"

"Oh, Suze, you idiot. I'm so *happy*!" I said, laughing through the sudden tears that appeared.

"You are? You don't really look it, to be honest."

I picked at a hole in my jeans. "I'm over the moon. I honestly never thought I would ever see Tilly again, and now you trust me with her?"

Suze huffed. "I've always trusted her with you, you numpty."

"You know what I mean," I said quietly.

"Yeah, I do. I've always trusted her with you. So is that a yes then? I can have a grown-up weekend away, even if it is with Mum?"

I laughed and threw my arms around her neck, causing her to fall over.

Tilly patted Suze's cheek. "Tilly cuddle?"

"Tilly cuddle," Suze and I said in unison and opened our arms for her.

* * * *

That week I started baking again. Just a few basic recipes to get the motors running. Nate had gone back to work and after reassuring him a hundred times that I would be fine, he eventually took my word for it and left me alone. It was an adjustment, there were a few hairy moments but thanks to my therapy, I knew how to cope.

The kitchen counter resembled an assembly line for cupcakes and I boxed most of them up and picked up the phone. Taking a deep breath, I dialed a number.

"Hello, Red Bar," Claire answered.

"Hi, Claire. It's um... It's Jo."

There was silence.

"I'm sorry, I shouldn't have—" I stopped myself and squeezed my eyes shut. "Claire, I'm really sorry for lying to you. Can I come and see you?"

"How soon can you get here?"

I smiled, relieved, and said I was leaving right away.

It felt odd to be out alone after having Nate stuck to my side for so long, and I walked quicker than usual, but all in all I survived my first outing. There was a new girl behind the bar when I got there, and she smiled and told me to go on through to Claire.

I knocked on her office door and went in, smiling at the familiar sight of Claire behind her desk, lost in a mountain of paperwork.

She smiled and stood up. "I hoped you'd bring baked goods."

Placing the box on her desk, I threw my arms around her neck. "I'm really sorry, Claire."

Claire let out a shaky breath and pulled out of my embrace. She ushered me to the couch and sat beside me. "I understand. I'm not thrilled you lied to me, but I do understand. Nate's been keeping me up to date on how you're doing. You look well, Jo."

My eyebrows shot up into my hairline. I shouldn't be surprised, not really.

"So you've started baking again?" Claire asked.

I nodded. "Nate's gone back to work. I needed something to do."

Claire patted my knee. "Why don't you start baking for me again? I'm not asking you to come back as manager, strictly as my baker."

My breath left me in a rush. "Really? Claire, that would be amazing, really."

"Great, it's official!" Claire clapped her hands and stood up. "Why don't we seal the deal with tea and cake?"

I giggled. "Done."

* * * *

When I arrived home after that afternoon to prepare for the Tilly invasion, I wasn't surprised to find I had beaten Nate, even though he swore blind he would finish sharpish. Just as I reached for my phone to ring him, I heard the front door open and close.

I walked into the hall, stopping abruptly when I couldn't see Nate's face because a ginormous bunch of flowers, bright, leafy and full, obstructed the view.

He moved them aside, raising his eyebrows and grinning.

With a laugh, I skipped toward him and took the flowers he offered. There was something so special about that man. I placed them on the sideboard and Nate was in the process of taking off his coat when I threw my arms around his shoulders and kissed him hard.

He laughed against my lips. "I'm sure this is all kinds of unfair that I'm basically in a straitjacket."

I shoved the coat off the rest of the way and kissed him again. "Better?"

"Much. I like the way you greet me now."

"Get used to it."

"I intend to."

I chuckled and pressed firmer against him, and Nate cupped my face in my hands. A tap on the door broke us apart and I smiled at the annoyed look on Nate's face.

He swung the door open and glared at his sister. "You always did have impeccable timing."

Suze kissed his cheek on her way past him. "One of my perks. Hope you two are ready for this. She's been on top form all day." And her words were proved when she released Tilly from the restraints of the pushchair and she ran screaming into the living room.

Nate and I exchanged looks whilst Suze smiled gleefully at us.

She shoved a weekend bag at me. "Everything is in here that you'll need. I'll see you Sunday night."

Tilly raced toward us and Suze snatched her into the air to kiss her whilst she squirmed like a worm on a hook before setting her free once again. Suze waggled her fingers and was gone. *Lord have mercy on us.*

Nate occupied Tilly in the living room whilst I started making dinner and prayed to the heavens that Tilly was still a girl who loved her food, and my spaghetti bolognese would go down well. I smiled to myself at the happy squealing and giggling from Tilly and the answering deep rumbling from Nate.

I dished up dinner then pulled Tilly's high chair up to the island and served Nate and I a hefty glass of red wine each. And it did indeed go down well with Tilly. She devoured her plateful so fast it was gone within minutes and had coated half her face. Nate volunteered for clean-up duty so I took Tilly for her bath, giving her the bath crayons again and letting her go nuts. She drew Mummy, Jojo and Nay. Even though they weren't much more than squiggly lines and circles, it brought a lump to my throat.

We sat on the bed to get her cozy pajamas on and once she was dressed, she clambered onto my lap for a story. As I read to her, she patted the book and pointed to pictures, babbling away. But before long her body grew heavy and she slumped against me, popping her thumb in her mouth.

Nate found us like that a short time later. He sat beside us on the bed and brushed Tilly's thick dark hair off her face. I closed the book and he dropped it on the floor for me, kissing my shoulder as he leaned back into me.

"She's out for the count," Nate whispered. He maneuvered an arm under her little body and lifted her from my lap before successfully transferring her to the travel cot set up, without disturbing the sleeping babe.

I stretched my arms up and felt my back crack.

"Do you want a bath?" Nate asked, sitting behind me to rub my shoulders.

With a smile I relaxed against him. "You read my mind."

Nate wrapped an arm around my waist, his long fingers stroking the underside of my breast. "You're really good with her."

"I think it's more the other way around. She makes it easy." I laughed. "Knackering, but easy."

"Did you ever want any of your own?" Nate asked, kissing my throat.

"It wasn't something I really thought about. To be honest, I suppose I dismissed the idea because it just wouldn't be in the cards for me." I twisted around to look at him. "What about you?"

He blew out a breath. "Much the same as you, really. I was with Kate and she never wanted kids. Ever. So I didn't give it another thought."

"And now?" I prodded with a smile.

Nate smiled back and pressed a brief, dry kiss to my lips. "Who knows. Maybe. *One* day. Right now I'm extremely happy doing lots of practicing with you."

I laughed. "Such a typical male answer."

"Can't go disappointing my race, can I?"

"Heaven forbid, Nate," I said rolling my eyes.

Nate laughed and kissed me again. He got up from the bed and sauntered into the bathroom. Once I was in the bath he brought me another glass of wine and had a movie playing quietly when I emerged, wrinkled beyond belief and so relaxed I was practically boneless. We both wore pajamas and fell asleep early, intertwined with each other. Like a little old, totally innocent with no hanky-panky, married couple.

* * * *

The next morning Tilly was up before the birds, standing up in her travel cot and calling for Jojo and Nay. Nate groaned and burrowed deeper under the duvet, pressing his face into my neck, apparently under the assumption if he ignored her long enough she would decide to go back to sleep. But no, in typical Tilly fashion, she only shouted louder.

I rolled over and kissed his jaw before slipping from the bed and retrieving Tilly, raising a finger to my lips and shooshing. Tilly giggled and held her arms out to me. Being up early gave me a good head start to the baking I needed to, and Tilly was more than happy to putter about on the floor with an empty mixing bowl and a wooden spoon whilst she made her own cakes.

Nate eventually appeared later in the morning, bleary eyed and groping for the coffee pot. He kissed me good morning and Tilly made kissing noises from the floor, squeezing her fists at Nate until he swung her up into his arms and smothered her little face with loud smooches.

Later, after we'd dropped the cakes off at the bistro, we took Tilly to a soft play center and spent two hours chasing her around as she tried to sneak into the over-fives' area and pelted us with plastic balls from the ball pit.

Sunday was spent at the swimming pool then the park then building and rebuilding magnificent towers made out of stacking cups. By the time Suze rang the doorbell at six–thirty, Nate and I were ready to cry with relief.

Her eyes flickered between us and the ruins of the living room then she cracked the biggest smile I'd ever seen on her face. "Three of you have a good weekend?"

Nate forced a smile and reached for me, throwing his arm around my shoulders and holding on so tight the joint popped. "We had a brilliant time, didn't we, Jo?"

"Yep," I squeaked before clearing my throat. "A brilliant time. We should have her more often."

Nate laughed, loud. "She's missed her mum. I bet she's really clingy and won't want to leave her for ages."

"Of course, of course," I rushed. "Well, Suze, did you have a nice trip away?"

"Yeah, it was nice to have some grown up girl time with Mum." Suze touched my arm. "Next time you're coming too, okay? We'll do a spa weekend or something."

My chest tightened and I took a moment to let her words sink in. This wasn't something to avoid anymore. This was a good thing. I smiled, a little wobbly with emotion. "Definitely."

"I'm meeting Mum for a coffee in the morning. She wants to know if you're coming?" Suze asked.

"I'd love to," I answered, almost immediately.

Nate's hand squeezed my shoulder. "Well then, she'll see you tomorrow, Suze?"

"Trying to get rid of me? You pair of pervs having withdrawals after your weekend as an old married couple?"

"Exactly." Nate looked at his watch then flashed his sister a grin. "Isn't it time you were off?"

"Don't be daft! I brought dinner," Suze said, holding up the cotton shopping bag she carried before turning to head into the kitchen.

"She is evil. Evil, evil, evil. What the hell did I ever do to her?" Nate mumbled, pulling me into his chest.

I wrapped my arms around his middle and he rested his chin on my head. "At least we don't have to cook."

"Hmm."

Suze cooked us up spaghetti with spinach, garlic and baby tomatoes and I was so grateful for the carbs. I needed the energy like I needed air.

"Okay, seriously, was everything okay?" Suze asked as she helped me clear the empty plates.

"Seriously, everything was fine. Knackering, but fine." I rubbed her arm. "Was it hard leaving her?"

Suze nodded and gave me a small smile. "And before you ask, it had nothing to do with leaving her with *you*. I knew she'd have a ball with her Auntie Jojo. I know I joke about the little cretin but that was the longest we've ever been apart."

"Hasn't Nate ever had her for the weekend before?" I asked.

"He's had her for the odd night, but first there was Kate—she hated anything to do with babies—and he's usually so busy, you know." Suze shrugged. "I just… I'm so glad we have you. I've always wanted a friend like you, and it's plain to see how much Nate cares about you… My own daughter would probably sell me for one of you in a heartbeat."

I ducked my head and laughed quietly. "You're mad."

She nudged me. "I'm telling the truth. So, thanks, Jo. For you."

"I'm the lucky one, Suze. You've no idea." I gave her a rueful smile. "Well, actually, you sort of do now, don't you? You know how much of a twisted little weirdo I really am."

"You'll always be my twisted little weirdo." When she looked at me her eyes were misted over. "I'm so glad you came back to us." Suze wrapped her arm around my shoulders and squeezed me tight. She laughed and bumped me with her hip then gathered the last of the dishes. "God, listen to us getting all chick-flick emotional! Speaking of, do you fancy a girls' night next week? I'll cook us something yummy, you bring us something yummier for pudding and we'll gorge on trashy movies?"

"I'm there," I said with a laugh.

"Let me know when's good for you," Suze said as she went into the living room and gathered up Tilly's things. "All right, little miss, you ready?"

Tilly looked up from her spot between Nate's legs and smiled. She whacked her stacking cups, sending them scattering across the floor and stood up, heading for her mother. Suze picked her up and kissed her cheek, taking just a moment to breathe in the smell of her.

Nate picked up Suze's bags whilst she wrangled Tilly into the pushchair. He crossed the room and pressed a kiss to my cheek. "I'm going to walk her home. I'll be back in a few."

I tidied up while he was gone, straightening everything away and regaining order. Folding the travel cot was harder than I'd anticipated, and Nate found me wrestling with the thing and swearing like a sailor. He nudged me aside. With a few twists and pulls, the thing was flat, compact and disappeared somewhere in Nate's cupboard.

When he returned, Nate flopped face down on the bed. "Is this how parents feel, but all the time?"

Smothering a laugh I sat beside him and rubbed his back. "Maybe. I think after a while you build up some kind of tolerance."

"I'm too tired to take my shoes off," he mumbled into the pillow. "I think Suze feeds that girl speed or something."

"You might be onto something there," I said, getting off the bed and pulling his shoes off.

"Are you trying to seduce me? I think I might be too tired for that." Nate rolled onto his back and I tugged his jeans down with his underwear. His erection sprang free. "Okay, so maybe it would work."

I laughed and hovered over his body, kissing his lips. "You're incorrigible."

He sat up enough to let me pull his T-shirt over his head before flopping back down and giving me a boyish smile.

"You're cute," I said, tapping his chest.

Nate caught my hand and kissed my palm. "I know."

"I'll be back, I'm going to brush my teeth," I said, tugging my hand back and walking into the bathroom for bedtime prep. After washing my face I stripped, leaving on my underwear—a navy blue lace set that Nate had picked out. When I returned, Nate was propped up against the headboard, covered to the waist with the sheet.

He laced his fingers behind his head when he saw me coming, eyeing me from head to toe as though he was planning on devouring me but couldn't decide where to start. Nate pushed down the sheet and I climbed onto the bed, swinging a leg over him so I straddled his lap.

"How tired are you?" I asked, peering into his warm whiskey eyes and rubbing my finger over the puffy skin underneath.

"I'm fucking shattered," Nate said, running his hands up my back. "But never too tired for you."

I smiled at that and leaned to kiss him, running my tongue over the seam of his lips until he granted me access. Nate's lips parted and he let me take control of the kiss. I ground against him as I deepened the kiss, teasing his tongue with mine. He unhooked my bra and slid the straps down my arms, tossing the material away. Cool air brushed over my naked breasts and hardened my nipples to points. Nate held me closer, keeping me pinned against his chest.

I maneuvered off him quickly to get rid of my knickers, the only remaining barrier between us. Straddling him again, I gently guided him inside me. Nate groaned and tightened his hold on my hips. I kissed him, slow and deep as I rode him. We made love like we had all the time in the world. There was no rush and we were borderline lazy. Our bodies were soft and languid by the time we finished, content and sated.

Nate tucked my into his arms as we fell asleep, early, like a little old married couple.

Chapter Thirty-One

I met Suze and Diane at the Starbucks on Princes Street at ten the next morning, coming straight from my session with Dr Hugo. Tilly wasn't there and the women already had their drinks.

Suze saw me and waved me over to their table. "I got you an eggnog latte. That okay?"

I grinned. "Perfect, thank you. Where's Tilly?"

"With her darling papa," Diane said, rising from her chair to hug me, holding on extra tight. "They're doing story time at the library, giving us a nice break."

I scoffed. "Didn't you just get a nice break at the weekend?"

Suze scowled at me. "I don't turn down babysitting. *Ever.* They might never offer again."

A laugh bubbled in my throat. "How wise, Suze."

"Are you all set for Christmas, Jo?" Diane asked, sipping her drink.

"Oh." I looked down at the table for a moment. "Um, not really."

"Well done, Mum," Suze muttered.

"No, Suze, it's fine," I said, my eyebrows drawn together. "If I'm being honest, I sort of forgot about it. I spent so long never doing Christmas that it kind of became habit to not give it much thought. And then everything with Scott happened and I never expected to be here."

Suze and Diane blinked at me. Given my history, I shouldn't have been shocked at *their* shock. I wasn't exactly known for sharing, after all.

Diane cleared her throat, her eyes red. "You know the invitation still stands, don't you? I'm expecting both you Nate bright and early Christmas morning."

I gave her a smile and nodded.

"Mostly because I can't wait to try your Christmas cake."

Suze barked a laugh and swatted her mother's hand.

"I'd better get shopping today then, hadn't I? Gift vouchers okay for everyone?" I asked with a smile.

"Make mine Zara and you've got a deal," Suze said, winking over her coffee mug.

"Done."

"So what was your task this week?" Suze asked.

"Go to the Christmas market."

She snorted. "I think I should go to therapy if you get homework like that."

Diane tutted her daughter. "I'm sure there's more to it than that. Jo?"

I sipped my coffee, considering the question. "I'm not sure, really. The other things have been pretty obvious—face my past, make a scrapbook with things that make me happy so I'm thinking positively...but I'm a bit stuck on this one. I mean, I'm not over the moon in crowds right now. But I'm getting past it." I shrugged. "Maybe it's a stepping stone to Christmas. I've never spent Christmas as part of a family."

"How about we all go this weekend, then?" Diane suggested. "Tilly will love it and Nate and Suze have *always* adored the city at Christmas."

"That sounds great," I said, meaning it.

Suze laughed. "It'll be the last weekend before Christmas. It'll be pandemonium."

* * * *

She was right. The Harding clan and I descended on the Mound for the Christmas market and it was full to bursting with bodies. Nate kept a tight grip on my hand and Suze cleared a path for us all by clipping unsuspecting pedestrians with the pushchair. Tilly clapped her hands and giggled when people jumped out of the path of destruction and agony. We took Tilly to the children's market so she could see all the toys and meet Santa, with whom Suze flirted shamelessly. Nate took great pleasure in showing me around, dragging me onto the big wheel and sampling loads of different foods from the stalls. We sipped our mulled wines and soaked in the atmosphere and despite the crushing crowds, I fell head over heels in love with the magic.

* * * *

I couldn't help but gush with excitement when I told Dr Hugo all about the weekend that Monday in our session. She smiled along with me and seemed to take great pleasure in my happiness.

At the end of the session, she asked me a question. "Jo, have you ever heard of animal therapy?"

I frowned. "No. Why?"

"Because, if you're willing, I think it would work incredibly well for you." Dr Hugo placed her notepad on the couch beside her. "Animal therapy is being used as a legitimate therapy tool. It's incredibly successful in PTSD patients. A lot of veterans recover with the aid of animal therapy."

"What would I do, like, take a dog a walk once a week or something?" I asked, picking at my cuticles.

"No, you would have a think about what animal you're drawn to and think about adopting one. Jo, don't get me wrong, I think you are making astounding progress with our sessions, and I really admire how you've handled each and every task I've set for you. But animal therapy would take you that step forward in your sense of responsibility and nurture." Dr Hugo sighed. "I know how much Scott hurt you by what he did to Cat."

"That wasn't my fault. I can't control someone else's actions," I said, sitting up straighter.

She smiled. "I know. And I am thrilled that *you* know that. You don't have to get another cat. You could get a dog, a fish, a snake...anything that you will form a bond with. I personally think you would have the best success with a dog. In training it, you would get used to praise and encouragement and you would feel that pride when it pays off. But most importantly, that bond would be there."

"But, I am bonded. Nate and I...we're closer than ever, really we are, and Suze is the best friend I've ever had. Diane and Vic, I love them all, and I *tell* them." Panic started to rise in my throat and I clamped a hand over my throat before it burst from me.

"Good. That's good. Jo, do you love yourself?"

I reared back as though she had hit me. "What?"

"Do you love yourself?" she repeated.

"Isn't that narcissistic?"

Dr Hugo didn't say anything. She picked up her notebook and wrote something down.

"How can I love myself? Look at what I did to that family." I closed my eyes. "It wasn't my fault, I *know* that, but it still happened to them because of me."

"They love you unconditionally, Jo, and that is exactly why I want you to try animal therapy. An animal is loyal to a loving master wholly and unconditionally. It doesn't care where you've been or what you've done. It loves you, and until you can understand that kind of devotion, you will never believe how much those people love you."

A tear trickled down my cheek. She was right, as always. I had no idea how they could love me.

"I'm terrified one day they won't anymore," I whispered.

"Relationships carry that risk," Dr Hugo said gently. "But I think finding a way to really love yourself will help you be more accepting—whether it's accepting their love or anyone else's. Once *you* love you, it will be easier to see how much other people do too."

That night I held Nate extra tight. I tried to pass through the weight of my feelings for him from my body to his. He held me back just as tight, and I think he was doing the same.

"How was Dr Hugo today?" he asked when I didn't let him go after ten solid minutes.

"She had an interesting theory. I think she might be right." I let out a breath. "Nate, can we get a dog?"

"Yes," he answered instantly.

We spent the evening researching breeders in the area.

* * * *

On Christmas, the plan was for everyone to sleep at their respective houses and make their way over to Vic and Diane's for mid-morning. Nate and I spent Christmas Eve with a takeaway and a bottle of wine, watching Christmas specials on TV. In the morning I snuck down to start breakfast and put his parcels under the tree.

Considering it was my first Christmas in an extremely long time, I didn't do too badly. A bottle of prosecco for Diane, whiskey for Vic. Designer scarf and perfume for Suze, a proper set of play baking equipment for Tilly. For Claire, I got a make-at-home mojito kit and a massive box of chocolates. For Dr Hugo, I got a 'Keep Calm, I'm a Therapist' novelty mug.

For Nate I had been collecting things here and there—book, DVD, iTunes gift card, but for his main present I got an experience day of flying and a sexy number for him to unwrap me on Christmas night.

I was pouring us a mug of coffee each when he appeared in the kitchen, wrapping his arms around me and kissing my neck.

"Merry Christmas," he whispered throatily.

"Merry Christmas," I replied, turning in his arms to kiss him on the mouth. "Breakfast is almost ready."

Nate inhaled deep before a grin spread across his face. "Pancakes?"

"With warm maple syrup."

He groaned and swiped one of the mugs of coffee. "I am so ready to start this day of food."

"Sit," I said with a laugh and retrieved the plate of pancakes I'd been keeping warm in the oven.

We ate quickly and the moment my plate was empty Nate grabbed my hand and pulled me into the living room. He sat in front of the tree and laughed at the shocked expression on my face.

Where Nate had maybe six parcels, I had dozens. Never in my life had I seen so many gifts for one person. I knew Nate was generous but this went beyond anything I'd expected. He tossed me a small parcel and reached for one of his. Dropping beside him, I tentatively unhooked the sticky tape and peeled back the paper.

"Christ, Jo, are you afraid it's going to bite your fingers off?" Nate asked with a laugh.

I rolled my eyes. "No. I just didn't expect this."

Nate put his arm around my waist and brought my closer to him. He kissed me and stroked my cheek. "Christmas is all about spoiling the people you love. This is you being spoiled. Deal with it."

"Just like that?"

He nodded and proceeded to rip open his parcel with all the gusto of a six year old.

With a laugh, I followed his lead. In no time at all we were surrounded by a mound of ripped wrapping paper and piles of gifts. Nate had seriously gone to town and with each parcel I opened, the more my heart swelled with love. Each gift showed how well he knew me. From the intimate—my exact size in the clothing and shoes he bought, to personal—bath bombs and gorgeous smelly stuff from my favorite handmade cosmetics shop.

When Nate opened his experience day voucher he pulled me onto his lap and kissed me hard and fast. He flipped through the voucher and kissed me again, his excitement contagious.

I flopped back against the couch when everything was open, staring in disbelief at the amount of stuff in the room. Nate clasped the necklace, a rock cluster pendant on a snake chain, he'd given me around my neck, and jumped to his feet.

"Where are you going?" I asked.

"Just sit tight," he said, flashing me a grin over his shoulder.

He returned a few minutes later carrying a heavy looking big box wrapped in paper decorated with cupcakes wearing Santa hats. Nate placed the box in front of me.

"Nate, you've really done enough," I said.

"I know. But you won't be arguing when you open it."

Rising onto my knees, I shot him a reproachful look before ripping into the paper. After shoving it away, I paused and slowly looking up at Nate. Then back at the box. Then back at Nate. Box. Nate. Box. Nate.

"Surprise?" he asked with a laugh.

"Oh my God!" I yelled, pouncing on him and knocking him back onto his ass. I laughed and hugged him tighter.

"I take it this means you like it?"

"I *love* it!" I said, kissing him quick and turning back around to open the box. He'd only gone and bloody got me the mixer we'd seen months ago. The black cast iron five hundred pound mixer. It was like baking porn. "I can't believe you remembered."

Nate kissed my shoulder. "Hard to forget. You left such a big puddle of drool, they had to get their mops out."

"*Why* did I make the Christmas cake yesterday?" I moaned.

He chuckled. "Sorry. Should I have made this an early gift?"

"No." I twisted around to give him a smile. "But you can ring your parents and tell them we'll be a little late."

"They wouldn't expect any less, Jo," Nate said, pulling me to my feet and retrieving the box from the floor.

In the end, we arrived just after twelve. Diane looked between us and gave us a very 'mum' look. I thrust the cake box at her. "I was baking. Red velvet cupcakes."

Her eyes lit up. "With cream cheese icing?"

I shook my head. "Cinnamon cream cheese icing."

Diane laughed and with her free hand ushered me into the house. "All is forgiven then."

"I helped with the mince pies!" Nate called behind us.

"Very good, darling," Diane said, not even turning around.

Suze was in the kitchen, peeling a load of spuds. She gave me a dirty look and slid her gaze to the clock on the wall.

"Sorry, sorry," I said, kissing her on the cheek and taking off my coat. I rolled up the sleeves of my jumper dress and washed my hands.

"Just do me a favor and spare me the details of why you're late."

I nudged her with my hip and grabbed a potato and the spare peeler. "Nothing sordid or kinky, I promise. Had to break in my new mixer."

Suze laughed. "I should have known. Nice surprise then?"

"The best surprise."

Diane kept us busy in the kitchen over the next few hours as we got the dinner ready, shooing Vic and Nate when they came sniffing around to steal scraps. By three we were setting the table and just in time as the collective rumblings of our stomachs sounded like a low flying plane.

Diane poured us all wine in copious amounts and each person refilled their plates. We pulled crackers and wore the party hats, groaned at the cheesy jokes. The atmosphere in the house was light and joyous, everyone in good spirits.

After dinner we all collapsed in the living room and Diane handed out gifts for everyone, Suze and Nate sitting beside the Christmas tree, and for a moment I could picture them exactly like that as children. Tilly adored her baking set and toddled around giving us all the imaginary cakes she made.

Vic and Diane gave me a large Sanctuary gift set, and from Suze and Tilly there was a gorgeous vintage style apron with red and white gingham material, sweetheart neckline and full skirt with black tulle petticoat.

Suze and Nate both tore into their parcels with such speed I could barely keep track of them past the shredded wrapping paper. When they both opened novelty woolen Christmas jumpers, I laughed so hard my stomach cramped.

"I don't know what you're laughing at," Nate said, before he tossed me another wrapped parcel.

I glanced at Diane who smiled. "Couldn't have you feeling left out, Jo."

Unwrapping the parcel revealed a similarly horrifying jumper, so bad it was almost good. *If you can't beat them, join them.* I pulled it over the top of my dress. I was going to own this jumper.

Later, when Tilly and Vic were passed out cold on the couch, the rest of us sipped Disaronno and watched a classic movie on TV. Suze and Diane bickered about which was the best Christmas movie ever. Suze insisted it was *Love Actually* whilst Diane went with *A Muppet's Christmas Carol*. Nate and I watched them with amusement, laughing when their arguments grew ridiculous.

Around midnight, when my face was splitting in half from yawning, Nate took my hand and tugged me to my feet.

"I think this is our cue to leave," he said.

I nodded and Nate held up the coat, which Suze had pestered me to buy, so I could slide my arms inside. At the door Diane kissed my cheek and hugged me.

"Thank you for today."

"It was a pleasure having you," she said with a smile.

Outside the night air was bitter cold and Nate hurried me into the waiting taxi he had ordered. "On a scale from one to ten, how painful was that?"

I looked at him in surprise and chuckled. Somewhere along the line, I had lost the last piece of fear that came with getting close to people. "It wasn't painful, Nate. In fact, it couldn't have been more perfect."

Nate's smile was broad and infectious. He cupped my face and kissed me thoroughly, and I felt every ounce of love that he poured into it.

Chapter Thirty-Two

That week we visited a few puppy breeders and ended up going back for three visits to one in Pennycuick. They had absolutely gorgeous eight-week-old German Shepherd pups and after checking their pedigree, seeing the parents and deciding they definitely weren't a puppy farm, we adopted the most adorable little boy pup I'd ever seen.

We called him Ace and the moment we had him home, I knew exactly why Dr Hugo had recommended animal therapy. It wasn't because puppies were cute, but because seeing him in our house pulled at my heartstrings and almost immediately I felt protective, responsible, and full out adoration for him.

Ace gave me something positive to focus on. The breeders told us German Shepherds are extremely intelligent and Ace proved this straight off the bat. After a few days of routine, he was house broken. He knew where his food bowl and bed were and started to recognize his name.

Dr Hugo grinned when I showed her photos and scolded me for not bringing him.

My task that week was to go to celebrate New Year's Eve. The reason behind that one was easy. New Year was the time for new beginnings. What was past was past and I should welcome the birth of the new year with open arms.

I smiled and told her Nate and I already had street party tickets.

On the night itself, I was literally hopping with excitement. Everyone knew Edinburgh was legendary for Hogmanay, second only to Times Square for throwing the bash. The whole city was alive and electric as thousands of people arrived to celebrate.

Nate looked absolutely delicious in dark jeans and a slim fitting shirt that showed off his broad shoulders and narrow hips. I was rocking a green and black dress with thick woolly tights and black boots.

We walked to Princes Street, the crowd growing thicker the closer we got until it was a sea of bodies. Everywhere I looked, people were smiling, singing and raising their plastic cups full of Tennent's. My body thrummed with energy and in no time I was smiling, singing and raising my plastic cup full of Tennent's.

The music was incredible and it set fire to the air. We watched a few of the bands playing the street party, dancing in the small space we had. It was a night I knew I would remember forever.

Nate had spun me in a circle and tugged me back to him. I threw my head back and laughed then pulled him down to press my lips to his. Nate wrapped his strong arms around me and I sighed into his mouth. How on earth had I denied I was in love with him for so long? And, had I really tried to walk away from this?

The countdown for midnight began and at one the night exploded. Fireworks from the castle shot here and there, lighting up the sky with their colors and bangs. The crowd started singing Auld Lang Syne, and Nate bent his head again to croon in my ear. I laid my head against his chest and closed my eyes.

"Happy New Year," he whispered.

"Happy New Year, Nate."

"I love you."

My heart skipped a beat. This was what was important. This moment. Nate and me, happy, together, safe.

I would remember it forever.

"I love you, too."

* * * *

The dawn was breaking but I was nowhere close to tired. After the party, I was ravenous for Nate. He was only happy to sate my appetite.

We lay in bed, my leg between his and I ran my fingers over his chest. Nate's arm was around my shoulders and he tickled the back of my leg with his other hand.

"Nate, why did you really want a roommate?" I asked.

His lips twitched. "Because I hoped she would be a gorgeous young thing that would fall for my rakish good looks."

I swatted his chest with a smile. "Seriously."

Nate blew out a breath. "I was tired of the silence. It's a big house, and you can hear the lack of life."

"Did you care if your roommate was male or female?"

He shook his head. "I didn't care either way, though if I'm perfectly honest, I would have preferred a male."

I pulled back and he laughed, pressing a finger to my lips before I could splutter a sound.

"Calm down. I wanted a bloke roommate because I know how some women are. They see wealth and looks and little else and that's how infatuation happens. I couldn't be arsed with the grief."

"Yeah, look how well that turned out," I mumbled.

He chuckled and kissed me. "Exactly. It's no secret how I liked my women before you."

"Available and at a distance." My stomach curdled at the memory of Nate and the woman in the living room.

"Yes. Life has a way of giving you the opposite of what you thought you wanted—and giving you exactly what you need."

"How very spiritual of you, Nate," I said, rolling my eyes. "At the risk of sounding like a typical girl, why did you choose me?"

Nate seemed to think about his answer. "You seemed to need it as much as I did. That morning, you were this quiet little mouse of a thing. When I looked at that newspaper with about three thousand shitty housing ads circled, I just wanted to take care of you, I suppose. I've lived in this city my whole life. I know exactly what some of those areas were like. That, and you seemed the exact opposite of trouble."

And yet look at how much I caused.

"I bought this place at auction on the cheap. It was nothing like it is now. It was pretty much falling apart. This little old woman owned it and lived out of one room." Nate blew out a breath and jerked his head toward the ceiling. "Those two floors were uninhabitable and the roof was about to cave in. Kate hated this house. She called me a fucking idiot for buying it when it needed so much work. She had wanted one of those pretentious half a million pound luxury penthouses at Quartermile. We lived here whilst doing it up, and for years, we only had the first two floors.

"When we split up I threw all my energy into doing up the top floors. This used to be the bedroom I shared with her. I knew you could breathe new life into this place and get rid of Kate forever."

All those months before I had been sleeping in Nate and Kate's old bedroom. And now we were again. How was that for irony? I remembered the smell of fresh paint when Nate had showed me around that day, all those months ago.

"Does it bother you?"

I shook my head. "I knew she lived here. I assumed she was upstairs, so it's no different."

"It still makes me smile, thinking that all this happened because of a mistake Suze made. Did I ever tell you it was her who placed the ads for me?" Nate grinned. "One of her better cock ups, giving the wrong price for that newspaper."

"Really?" I laughed. "I'd say so."

"Just don't ever tell her. We'll never hear the end of it if she knew she was responsible." His eyes scanned my face. "Have you had a good night?"

"I've had the *best* night." I smiled.

A laugh rumbled in his chest. "Good. Are you tired yet?"

"Not in the slightest," I purred.

"Even better," Nate grinned as he rolled over and pinned me to the mattress.

* * * *

January passed in a blur. After talking it over with Nate, I decided to tell Claire officially that I wasn't coming back as her manager. She understood, and swore colorfully in relief when I said I would still be her baker, though. I just wasn't up to the responsibility yet.

Ace became my new baking buddy. He would sit patiently at my feet, never taking his eyes from me as I worked. He barked when I tried to sing along to the radio and curled up in front of the oven when the cakes were in. Afterwards we would have our afternoon walk around the Dean Gardens and do some training. Time and time again he surprised me by being quick as a whip and recognizing commands.

Nate never said he wanted to keep Ace out of our bedroom, but at first I tried to keep that barrier up. While he never howled or whined at being left in the kitchen at bedtime, I started to feel more and more guilty at leaving him alone down there. And so one night I sighed and patted my leg for him to come and he followed me up the stairs, his chubby little legs struggling to get up them. Nate gave me a small smile as I lifted him onto the bed. Ace curled up on my side, his ears alert and his eyes on my face, even when he was desperately needing to fall asleep.

For a week straight I didn't have a nightmare. When I woke with a start in the night, he was right there, totally in tune with me. Ace would lick my hand and shuffle closer to me, his growing weight a reassurance. His loyalty and protectiveness took my breath away.

Each week when I told Dr Hugo the progress Ace and I were making and the progress I was making all on my own, she seemed more and more thrilled.

"I am really proud of how far you've come, Jo." Dr Hugo tucked her legs underneath her. "Today I want to talk about something a little harder."

I laughed. "What could be harder than what we've already talked about?"

"I want to talk about your birth name."

My smile fell. "Why?"

"Have you thought about going back to it?"

I crossed my arms over my chest. "No. Holly's dead. Scott killed her. I can't undo that."

Dr Hugo tilted her head to the side. "You talk as though Holly is a different person, but she's who you are, Jo."

"No, she's who I used to be," I said coldly.

"And who did you used to be?"

My sigh was dramatic and I threw my hands out to the sides and let them smack off my thighs. "You know who I used to be. I told you what happened with Scott in the beginning."

"It wasn't always about Scott, though. You had nineteen years before you met him." Dr Hugo wrote something on her notepad. "You *are* Holly."

"I'm not. Holly was a girl who thought she fell in love and he killed her. Holly was a victim."

"And what happened to Jo doesn't make her a victim?"

"Jo fought back."

"Then how did Holly become Jo if she didn't fight back?"

I rubbed my eyes. "You're making me sound crazy, like I'm schizophrenic. I'm *not*!"

"I'm not saying that, Jo. I'm trying to understand why you don't accept Holly as part of you."

Pulling my knees up to my chest I hugged them. "After the accident with Scott when Ho—when *I* was nineteen, I was broken. He had killed part of me. Whatever part that was, it couldn't ever be fixed. I knew I had to hide, that one day Scott would wake up and come looking for me. Changing my name, moving from place to place, I shed every bit of Holly and became Jo. Jo knew how to survive."

"Don't you miss her?"

"No, I don't." I sighed. "Holly's life was miserable long before Scott ever came into it. Yes, he took away the semblance of normality she built, and I think I hate him for that the most. He took way the potential for her to have a happy life."

"You could give it back to her. If you went back to your birth name, then Holly is a survivor too, just like Jo. Holly is also free of Scott."

I shook my head. "I'm okay with Holly being dead. You know, Nate asked me once if I wanted to go back to my birth name."

"What did you tell him?"

"What I just told you—that Holly is dead. I think he understood as best he can."

"Have you grieved for her?"

"Holly?"

Dr Hugo smiled kindly. "Yes, for Holly. You keep saying that she's dead, that Scott killed her, and maybe he did. But did you ever grieve for her?"

I shook my head and hugged my knees tighter.

"That's your task for this week, Jo."

* * * *

I told Nate, like I told him everything now. But I turned down his offer for him to come with me. Saying goodbye was something I had to do alone. I bought a white rose from a florist and walked to that bridge in Stockbridge. Standing at the edge, I let myself think about Holly, properly, for the first time in years. She—*I* was a fighter. I hadn't realized it before, but looking back at how I'd gotten through all the foster homes and got myself into university, I was a fighter. But I was also desperate for love, and when Scott had shown up and made me feel like the most special person in the world, I hadn't stood a chance.

Looking back, the beginning months of my relationship with Scott were the hardest. Hindsight was a bitch and I could easily recognize the signs of Scott's unbalanced mind but then I had been a love-struck girl.

But...but.

I was here now.

The paths I chose, including Scott, had led me here.

I had a man who loved me waiting at our home. Dr Hugo said I could still give Holly a chance to survive, like Jo. I had the power to give her, her happy ending. Really, Holly had given me mine.

I kissed the cool, soft petals of the rose and with tears streaming down my face, I dropped it into the river below. "Goodbye, Holly."

It landed on the surface of the water and disappeared under the bridge.

As I walked home, my emotions were a swirling dervish. I didn't feel pity anymore for Holly. I felt gratitude but mostly I felt acceptance about my past. Nate swept me into his arms the second I stepped inside. He held me as my heart broke with love for that silly nineteen-year-old girl. She had given me the man holding me now.

* * * *

In my last session with Dr Hugo, she asked that I bring my scrapbook. It was full to bursting now, with photographs, movie stubs, our street party tickets, recipe cards and stories of memories.

She flipped through the pages, smiling and giggling. When she reached a terrible picture of a cupcake and *Jo's Bakery* scrawled above it, she looked at me. "What's this?"

I blushed. "Oh, nothing. Just a doodle."

"Jo," she pressed.

"Fine. It's— I don't know. Right now it's just a daydream."

"Of?"

I shrugged. "The future?"

Dr Hugo tapped the page. "This is good, Jo. Very good. I'm proud of you."

"Is that the Dr Hugo stamp of approval slash discharge?"

She laughed. "You know, I think it might be. I want you to keep my number. Call me anytime, set up a session if you feel like you need it. But I really doubt you will."

I stood up from the couch and accepted the scrapbook from her. "Thank you just doesn't seem strong enough."

Dr Hugo pulled me into a hug. "Thank you is plenty strong enough."

Nate tossed the magazine onto the coffee table when I emerged from Dr Hugo's office. Ace, triple the size now, didn't move from where he sat perfectly behaved, but his tail started a fast tempo on the floor.

Nate stood up and I threw my arms around his neck. "You done?" he asked.

"I'm done."

"Good girl," he growled in my ear.

I pulled back and searched his face, trying to think of something stronger than 'thank you'. "I love you."

He grinned. "I love you too."

With a laugh, I pulled him down for a kiss, my stomach tightening as he deepened it. Nate's hands drifted from my hips, over my ribs until his thumbs stroked the underside of my breasts.

"Home?" I breathed into his mouth.

Nate kissed me again. "I wouldn't have you anywhere else."

Epilogue

Two years have slipped by since my past collided with my present. I never did need to see Dr Hugo again, but Nate and I send her a huge bunch of flowers and a ridiculously expensive box of chocolates every Christmas.

In the end, we decided to sell the town house. But it was on our terms and because of that, it didn't feel like defeat. We bought a quirky coach house in Morningside that was a good size smaller than the town house on Ainslie Place. Sometimes I missed it, but the coach house belonged solely to us. The memories belonged to us alone and the people we loved.

"Did you bring them?" Suze asked, popping up at my elbow.

I had no idea how she managed to surprise me when she was the size of a bus.

I grinned and hugged her, made difficult by the child she was growing. She cracked her knuckles, the one she'd broken still giving her grief a year and a half after chipping a tiny piece off it, thanks to Kate's face.

Kate, still having not learnt she'd be better off keeping clear of the lot of us, had appeared in the bar we were all in one night and made a catastrophically bad comment about hot Steve was.

It was one of the best moments of my life. Ding dong the Wicked Bitch needs a nose job.

Nate rolled his eyes. "Yes, Suze, we brought the novelty scissors."

Suze rubbed her inflated belly and leaned into Steve, who kissed his wife's cheek. "Stop making fun of me. I caught you playing with them last week, remember?"

Nate coughed. "I was testing them out."

"Yeah, yeah."

He nudged me. "Look, Claire's here."

"Nice deflection," Suze mumbled.

Ignoring her I accepted Claire's hug. "I'm so glad you could make it!"

Even though I never did go back to Red Bar except in a baking capacity, Claire stayed an incredible friend to me. For eighteen months things ran smoothly for me as her baker and when she eventually pried it out of me what was wrong, she was the first to tell me to get my ass in gear and make it happen.

"Of course I made it! Do you think I'd miss this?" Claire laughed. "When are you doing it?"

"As soon as Diane gets back with Tilly. She needed the loo," I said.

"They'd better hurry up because I'm bloody starving," Nate said.

As he spoke, Tilly barreled into my legs. "Are you going to cut now, Jojo?"

I tapped her nose. "I'd better, or Uncle Nate might eat you."

Tilly squealed and ran to hide behind Steve's legs. Ace barked and ran after her, pushing his nose into her hand until she petted him. She giggled and threw her arms around his neck.

I laughed and took the giant scissors Nate handed me. With a deep breath, I moved to stand in front of the double glass doors and faced the small crowd that had gathered on the narrow Stockbridge street.

"Hi everyone," I started. I cleared my throat and forced myself to look around the smiling faces of the people I loved, the familiar customers I'd gotten to know at the bistro and a few unfamiliar strangers. "I'm not used to doing things like this, so I'll keep this short. And no, Suze, it's not because I'm a twisted little weirdo."

The crowd laughed, Suze and Nate the loudest.

"I want to thank everyone for coming down here today. It really means a lot to me. More than any of you will ever know." I smiled and swallowed the emotion that rose. "This was a dream I never knew I had, let alone one that could come true. It just goes to show that with determination, and seriously good mixer, your future is what you make it. So come in, eat, eat more, and then some more. Because now I have a mortgage."

I lifted the scissors and cut the fat red ribbon Suze and Diane had tied to the door. "I now declare *Jo's Bakery* open for business!"

Tilly was the first to rush through the doors, having been made to wait all morning with the promise of as much cake as she could handle and being the first to try out the kid's corner. Everyone else shuffled in in a more appropriate manor, smiling and giving me kind words on their way past. Suze looked as though she could wee with excitement, or maybe that was just the baby, as she hugged me.

I paused at the door, Nate at my side as my little bakery filled with people and noise.

"Is it everything you hoped it would be?" Nate asked.

"It's so much better," I said breathily.

He grinned. "You'd better get in there and feed them before Tilly riots."

"I'm on my way."

Nate lowered his head to kiss me and patted my bottom as he entered the bakery.

I touched the lettering of my name on the door, unable to help the smile on my face.

I am Jo. I am here. I am alive with life.

About the Author

Pamela has adored books since she can remember. There was no greater pleasure than discovering a new world to venture into, a new character to fall in love with…until she created her own and realised there was something even more magical.

When she isn't locked away at her computer, or scribbling in a notebook, Pamela can be found as her alter ego—namely wife to Matthew and mother to Todd. They also share their home with a schizophrenic cat and two greedy goldfish.

Pamela L. Todd loves to hear from readers. You can find her contact information, website details and author profile page at http://www.totallybound.com.

Totally Bound Publishing

Home of Erotic Romance